THE CELESTIAL COUPLES SHOW

A GAME OF LOST SOULS

BOOK TEN

LISA SILVERTHORNE

LISA SILVERTHORNE

THE CELESTIAL COUPLES SHOW

A GAME OF 10 LOST SOULS

When dark, overwhelming forces kidnap an angel of death and carry her off to Hell, Jack must confront his deepest fears as Lucifer taunts him to come save her.

Meanwhile, Talia struggles to keep her new husband from falling back into his old life as rumors circulate among the cast and crew of the new show.

Together, Jack and Talia must confront temptations and sabotage on the new show's set as they prepare to storm Hell.

As Lucifer's dark vengeance takes shape, Jack and Talia go to war alongside Archangel Aural and the death angel guard to assault the Gates of Hell. Before a redeemed angel falls and Lucifer launches his nefarious plan.

The Celestial Couples Show is the tenth book in *A Game of Lost Souls*. Dark, irreverent, and always romantic, this action-packed 13-book fantasy romance stars two lovers entangled in a mythic battle between good and evil that begins with a simple wager with the King of Hell.

THE CELESTIAL COUPLES SHOW

ACKNOWLEDGEMENTS

A heartfelt thank you to these wonderful people who supported me and my writing. Without your support and encouragement, this book might not have been written.

Jerry Ackerman
Ember Blackthorn
Alexandra Brandt
Jessica C.
Ron Collins
T. Thorn Coyle
Joe Cron
Dayle Dermatis
Erin
Christy Fifield
Deborah A. Flores
Karen Fonville
Susan Franzblau
Barb G.
Dara Girard
David H Hendrickson
Tony Hernandez
Kari & Jason
R.S. Kellogg
Sana Khan
Michael Warren Lucas
maileguy

Georgiana Mann
Robert J. McCarter
Debbie Mumford
Vera Nazarian
Patricia Duffy Novak
James Novak
Beth Paul
Mark Posey
Mary Jo Rabe
Annie Reed
Johanna Rothman
Carolyn Rowland
Anthea Sharp
Dean Wesley Smith
Kat Tipton
Rob Vagle
Leslie Claire Walker
Laura Ware
Kelly Washington
Ryan M. Williams
Lyn Worthen
Melissa Yuan-Innes (aka Melissa Yi)

Novels by Lisa Silverthorne

Standalones:

ISABEL'S TEARS

LANDFALL

PACIFIC BLUE TATTOO

A Game of Lost Souls series:

THE CINDERELLA HOUR

THE PRINCE CHARMING HOUR

THE EVER AFTER HOUR

THE FALLEN HEARTS SEASON

THE RISING SPIRITS SEASON

THE ETERNAL SOULS SEASON

THE ROYAL WEDDING HOUR

THE HEAVENLY HONEYMOON HOUR

THE DIVINE NEWLYWEDS SHOW

THE CELESTIAL COUPLES SHOW

THE ENOCHIAN APOCALYPSE SHOW

Curse and Crown series:

THORN & BLADE

FORTHCOMING!

A Game of Lost Souls series:

The Angelic Anniversary Hour, Book Twelve

The Perdition Picture Show, Book Thirteen

Curse and Crown series:

Storm & Steel, Book Two

Dagger & Flame, Book Three

The Spiral series:

Ruin, Book 4

Descent, Book 5

The Resurrectionist Papers:

Corpses Delicti

Stiffed Again

Cease and Deceased

SCIENCE FICTION WRITING AS **L.S. SILVERTHORNE**

Experiencing True Purple series:

Cipher, Book 4

Renascence, Book 5

1

JACK CASEY KNEW IT WAS A DREAM. BUT BEHIND THE HORRIFYING torrent of Hell images, Berith was warning him not to try and rescue her from Hell. And to stay far away.

Either way, it made him recoil.

Tossing and turning in the dark, unfamiliar set trailer bedroom, wearing only green boxer briefs, he tried to shove away the sweltering visceral heat, the stink of brimstone, and the constant roaring wail of damned souls that echoed above the ubiquitous snap of whips.

He was drowning in a sea of red-eyed demons leering back at him.

Flinching with every biting crack of the whip, he remembered the lash endlessly cutting into his flesh, shredding his clothes. Felt the deep, burning ache that never left his skin—or his heart—down there in Hell.

"Talia!" he shouted, unsure if his call was out loud or just in the nightmare.

Seas of those glowing red demon eyes surrounding him were seared into his memory, haunting him. Even now. They burned like embers through the shadows. In the dark, rocky crevices. Along the dim, ruddy gleam of steaming lava rivers that gave Hell's cavernous depths a lurid neon glow, deepening the shadows—and his despair.

Dense, suffocating heat pressed against his body, weighing him down, his clothes heavy and wet with sweat. Hanging in tatters. With every heated breath, his lungs ached, every inhale and exhale singeing his insides, and his heart broke at being so far away from Talia.

"Talia!" His voice echoed through the caverns, lost again in the wail of souls.

He shifted again in the bed, trying to escape the heat and the pain and the images. And that constant feeling of being watched, of being hunted and cornered, had persisted long after he'd escaped Lucifer's domain. In Hell, his every movement had been on display, like the cage fights he'd endured.

Sweat slicked his body as he struggled against the covers, breath huffing as he fought against the barrage of images that rushed at him like a bad acid trip. Like those flaked-out parties at Lare's beach house. Dredging up out-of-focus, hazy memories of distorted figures tangling around him until he couldn't breathe. Couldn't focus. Couldn't move.

Everything tilted. Like when a bad trip spiraled into an overdose. Everything hurt. Slowing. Fading. Blacking out.

He tried to shout again. Couldn't.

But in that nothingness, those crystal-clear memories flooded over him in waves of torture, pain, and anguish. The ones that he'd blocked out since escaping Hell. Stored and kept out of focus deep inside his head, right beside those distorted—and missing—beach house party memories. Those unnerving flashes of demons and horns after he'd woken up beside Rachel. Without his clothes.

Sparks of things that he didn't want to remember. Couldn't face even then. All this time, he'd hoped that all of the memories would somehow disappear and he wouldn't have to deal with them.

Ever.

Things he couldn't give voice to, things he'd never even told Talia. Things he couldn't tell her. Or himself. Much less face.

Jack!

The lyrical alto voice was sharp. Crystalline. Angelic. It was Berith! Desperate. Despairing. Determined.

Jack!

She shouted in his ear and her voice filled his entire being.

Do NOT try and rescue me. It's you that Lucifer wants—and I don't know why. Stay away or he'll consume you! Stay. Away. You can't save me this time...it's too late. Tell Azrael—that I love him. For eternity.

Abruptly, Berith's warm and kind mothering presence melted into a blistering wave of hatred and vengeance as he felt Lucifer wrest control from her.

And takeover his dream.

Sympathy for the Devil screeched through his head, electric guitars wild and distorted against the staccato beat of drums that pulsed through his bloodstream.

His heart raced, breaths coming in gasps. His skin burned, temples pounding. Chills roiled across his body that shook in time to the drums and guitar riffs. And he thought his heart might explode.

Hello, Jack! Welcome home. I've set up a brand-new rack in your honor. Can't wait to beat the life out of you. And drench the ground with your blood. Every last drop. Until I consume your soul.

You will be mine again, Jack. Soon. So very soon. Can't wait for your arrival.

Lucifer's dark laughter spiraled around him, stirring up all of Hell's memories that Jack had suppressed.

Gut-wrenching images flooded his brain, blazing through him all at once like a California wildfire. Lucifer's laughter intensified as everything went up in flames around Jack. Blistering. Searing. Suffocating.

Oh, and Jack...those memories at the beach house...the horns—the bedroom...that was me.

Lucifer's malevolent laughter was caustic.

Horrified, Jack recoiled. It was the realization he'd felt deep in his soul, but couldn't bring himself to say out loud. Or ask.

Those fleeting pictures of waking up naked in bed with Rachel and —he shuddered—those shadowy flashes of horns and demons... He felt the grim dread deep in his soul that it had been Lucifer.

God, he felt sick all over.

Smothering heat mixed with the cloying stink of sulfur and ozone. He was drowning in lava and demons. And screaming as he jerked up from the bed, queasy, drenched in sweat, and hurting all over.

He grabbed the small grey trashcan near the bed and threw up in it, his stomach heaving only air. When the dry heaves subsided, he set down the trashcan and stared around the dark room, shades still down. He stared into the abyssal darkness until the room began to look almost familiar again.

He was still at the studio. In his and Talia's set trailer beside Studio 22 at Four Acre Studios in Burbank.

In the pre-dawn greyness, the trailer's modern bedroom took shape around him. Taupe, grey, and white with lacquered cabinets. His sweat-slicked skin was chilled, his mouth dry, his gut hurting.

Disoriented, he searched through the darkness for something he recognized. For Talia's comfort that he needed more than ever at this moment. But he was alone in the queen-sized bed, wearing only boxer briefs, his blond hair drenched, and his face a mask of sweat.

The grey and white comforter lay crumpled on the floor. Crisp white sheets smelling of sunlight were tangled around him as the world buzzed with a cacophony of noises that had become one dull roar he couldn't separate into things. Until, at last, he realized that the buzzing rumble was his cell phone lying on the nightstand beside the bed.

Vibrating. Screeching out *Sympathy for the Devil*.

His blood turned to ice.

"Jack!"

Talia's musical soprano voice cut through his turmoil. He realized that he was finally awake. His phone was really ringing.

And it was Lucifer.

The soft gold light of Talia's halo warmed the room as she moved toward the bed.

"Jack, don't answer it," she whispered.

But he'd already grabbed the phone off the nightstand. With shaking hands, he answered the video call.

Lucifer's blond hair was a tangle of sunlit golden curls, blue eyes hypnotic against a white hoodie over a grey *SanFran Confidential* T-shirt, and faded jeans.

"You bastard," Jack growled, glaring at the screen, his voice scratchy and thin.

Talia was beside him now, sitting on the side of the bed, hands kneading his bare shoulders. His skin had turned to gooseflesh and he had to fight to keep his teeth from chattering.

"And it's good to hear from you, too, Jack," said Lucifer, smiling through his steepled fingers, sounding so smug. "Sleep well?"

Lucifer's laughter was thick. Dark. Mocking. Like his tone of voice, so precise and enthusiastic. Cheerful. British. But so damned arrogant with dark, dark undercurrents.

"What do you want?" Jack demanded, his gaze steely as he tried to control his shaking and the panic rising inside him.

At the revelation that his nightmares—and Berith's warnings—had been real. Every. Single. Moment.

"You really are grumpy in the mornings, Jack," said Lucifer, his smile broadening into a grin as he leaned back in a white leather chair, hands behind his head. "Even grumpier than you were here—if that's possible." Lucifer clicked his tongue and abruptly leaned back toward the screen again, letting his arms fall into his lap. "What's the matter, Jack? Have a bad dream? Show not going well? Run out of those horrid toaster pastries again? You really should stock up on those if it makes you that irritable."

"I said!" Jack shouted, "what do you want?"

Jack felt Talia's arms slide around him protectively. She had no idea how her touch was holding him together right now. He fought down his rising panic, trying to take deep, measured breaths and not show Lucifer how unnerved he felt at this moment.

He stared down the King of Hell, challenge white-hot in his game face as he struggled to hold it in place.

"No jokes, Jack?"

The light-hearted glow in Lucifer's tranquil blue eyes began to fade into a stormy, piercing stare as the smile slid from his face.

"You know what I want. Jack." Lucifer didn't blink. "Tick tock.

Tick. Tock. Berith's time is fleeting. I didn't think you were man enough to actually return to Hell. Afraid of my restored powers?"

Jack glared at him. "I'll match my seraphim powers with yours any day, Lucifer. Try me."

"Jack, don't," Talia whispered.

That deadly twinkle lit Lucifer's dangerous gaze.

"Berith doesn't have time to waste, Jack. Hoping that a coward like you will muster enough false courage to come save her. Perhaps a line or two of cocaine—that is your poison, isn't it—will bolster your courage? Like it used to, Jack. Remember?" That vicious, charming smile returned. "At those beach house parties. I remember." He chuckled. "And so do you now. Don't you?"

Jack swallowed the panicked gasp that tried to escape through his gritted teeth. He did his best to hold onto his game face that was already slipping, the horror of those memories sizzling through his brain now.

"Don't you worry, Luci," he said, forcing a smile. "Party's just getting started. And I wouldn't miss it for all the flake in the world. Neither would Azrael and Talia. And hey—I'll bring the tunes. Got an awesome demon-splattering playlist I can't wait to play for you. Along with a shit-ton of murder marbles. Enough for everyone, I promise. So, dust off your dance floor, dude. I've got some new moves that are gonna rock your world, you colossal douchebag."

He reached down and cleared the connection. Hanging up on Lucifer for a change. Felt good.

"Jack!" Talia cried. "What did you just do?"

He collapsed onto the bed, shaking, the chills shuddering through him as his breaths came in gulping gasps.

"About time I hung up on him for once."

His stomach lurched. He scrambled up from the bed and grabbed the trashcan again. Heaving into it. But only air came up.

"Jack, what is it? What's wrong?" Talia blinked in front of him, dropping down on her knees and putting her arms around his waist.

His game face fled and he couldn't stop his face from scrunching into an anguished frown. What would she think of him when she found out what really happened at Winter's Revenge in Malibu? After he'd been blacked out on flake.

The awakened memories made him sick all over and he gagged.

Gently, she took the trashcan that he'd been white-knuckling and set it beside the nightstand. She held his hands, her luminous grey eyes lit with fear and worry.

"Talia, I...I..."

His mouth bobbed open, but he couldn't pull it all into a coherent sentence. Or even twelve.

Talia's wings curved around him as she held him in her arms.

"You're shaking," she said. "Tell me what's wrong. It's more than that phone call from Lucifer. You were having terrible dreams. What is it, Jack?"

Every word hurt. "The beach house, Tal—" He stuttered through more gulping breaths, the shakes coming in tremors now.

She held him closer, wings cradling him.

"What about the beach house?" she asked in a soft voice.

God, he didn't want to say it out loud. Didn't want to make it real instead of a shadowy figment of a flake-fueled hallucination. A what if. Just a distant but unlikely possibility. But if he was remembering those moments now, wouldn't they already be appearing in his damned Book of Life and Death? Penned there by Pravuil. Affirming that they were real.

He shuddered. And they were about Lucifer.

"The memories," he hissed, sucking in another quick breath. "They're all coming back."

"The blacked-out things you couldn't remember?" she asked in a patient voice.

He nodded and her arms tightened around him.

"Oh, God, Talia," he moaned.

She stroked his hair, the gold light of her halo merging with his. "Jack...what happened to you in that room?"

"In the bed, Talia," he said through gritted teeth, his voice so small and raw. "It was him."

For several long, aching moments, she didn't say anything.

"Lucifer!" he spat.

She forced him to look at her, holding him steady. "Lucifer put that memory in your head just now."

He shook his head. "No, he was at the beach house. In that bedroom—"

"Jack, it was the dream," she said, her voice rising. "He planted those images in your head through the dream. Using your hazy memories against you. It's what he does."

Jack winced. "But how can I ever be sure?"

The silence was deafening.

"Rachel," Talia said finally as she enfolded him in her arms again until he felt the beat of her angel heart against his chest, felt the warmth of her human soul enveloping him. Calming him. "Jack, Rachel knows what happened to you at those parties. She'll tell you the truth."

He didn't fully trust Rachel, even now, but maybe because he'd saved her, she'd tell him the truth.

"What about my book?" he asked in a hoarse voice. "Is it in Pravuil's book about me now? For every angel of death to read?"

"Your Book of Life and Death?" she asked.

He nodded against her midnight curls that smelled like roses and rainwater.

"I'll find out," she said. "After you've had some more sleep."

He pulled away, shaking his head. "After those nightmares and Face-timing Lucifer, I'm not gonna sleep for a long time."

Talia picked up the comforter off the floor and draped it across the bed again. After untangling the sheets, she sat him down on the bed and crawled in beside him.

"Let's go back to bed, Mr. Casey," she said, fingers tracing across his shoulders and down his chest.

He let her pull him under the covers. Still shaking, he snuggled against her, his wings and body feeling weary. Heavy. Broken. And not knowing whether Lucifer had planted that memory in his head gnawed at him.

Along with Berith's warning.

"Talia, Berith told me not to try and rescue her."

"When?" Talia asked.

"She spoke to me in my dream, but Lucifer hijacked it."

Again, Talia was quiet for several moments.

"You're sure it was Berith?" Talia asked finally.

He nodded against the silky black waves of her hair. "She told me that Lucifer was after me not her. And…" He sighed. "To tell Azrael she loved him. For eternity."

Talia pulled in a heavy breath. "Then it was a warning from her. To keep you away. To say goodbye to Azrael."

"Like it's a big secret that Lucifer's after me?" he replied. "Doesn't matter. I'm going after her, Talia."

"We're going after her, Mr. Casey," Talia corrected him.

He couldn't hold back his grin. "Marrying you was the best decision I ever made, Mrs. Casey."

He kissed her, stroking her face as he laid his head against her shoulder.

"Loving you was the best decision of my existence, Jack Casey," she said, snuggling against him. "Now, sleep. We have to be on set early today."

Nodding, he tried to let go of the horrors that had sprung out of his nightmares and the dread and worry knotting his gut. He had to get to Berith fast. Before Lucifer extinguished her life force and returned his attention to hunting Jack again. But first, Jack needed to ask Rachel what really happened in the Breckinridge Suite.

He had to know if Lucifer was lying. He had to.

NOT LONG AFTER the alarm rang and Jack climbed into the shower, the entire trailer filled with light. Not someone had turned on every light in the place kind of light. More like someone had poured light into every corner and crevice and painted the trailer, floor to ceiling, in warm, radiant light.

That only an archangel gave off.

Jack wrapped a grey towel around his waist and with damp hair, he padded barefoot into the bedroom in the wake of Archangel Azrael's angelic light. He had his back to Jack, Talia standing in front of him. His wings were unfolded to their full wingspan, halo spinning with red-gold light. But Jack couldn't hear what they were saying. Damned angel notes.

Talia's gaze abruptly shifted to him, causing Azrael to turn around.

"Jack!" Azrael cried and grabbed him by the shoulders. "I came as soon as I heard!"

"Heard what, archangel?" he asked, shaking his head.

Azrael cast a forlorn look at Talia and then fixed Jack with his tough, unaffected archangel stare. But his massive, soot-colored wings drooped against his shoulders, silvery black hair unusually disheveled.

The archangel couldn't hide that he was hurting. Or how much he loved Berith.

After enduring millennia without her, expecting it to be forever, she came back to him. Only to have that douche-canoe, Lucifer snatch her away from him again.

Despite his marble exterior, pain radiated from every feature of the archangel's face. Even the dude's red-gold halo looked pale and washed out.

"Berith contacted you," said the archangel, her name aching on his lips.

Jack smashed his eyes closed. Of course. The archangel hadn't dropped in for a visit. Azrael wanted to know what he saw.

"The dream—sorry."

"Jack, what did she say to you?" Azrael's grip on his shoulders tightened. "Tell me…please."

"She was adamant, archangel," he said, trying to make her message clear. "She said not to try and rescue her."

Even as he ramped up to tell his account, he felt his words stabbing the archangel in the heart. Azrael's face pinched, mouth pressing into a tight line.

"Why?" he asked.

Jack bowed his head, hands on the towel around his waist.

"She said it was me that Lucifer was really after." Each word was an apology. "She said he'd consume me." His heart twisted into a knot. "Azrael, she said I couldn't save her this time. That it's too late now."

Azrael's shoulders slumped, his charcoal grey eyes losing their radiance.

"She said to tell you that she loved you, Azrael. For eternity."

That was the final blow that made the archangel's knees buckle. He grabbed hold of the lacquered taupe dresser and eased himself onto a wooden chair beside it. He stared past Talia now, the pain etched into his face.

"Then it's over," Azrael lamented and laid his hand against his forehead. "I've lost her again—this time for eternity. I'm too late to save her."

Jack understood that pain. He'd felt it when Erica Thomlin fired that gun and Talia stepped in front of him. He'd felt it again at the beach house when Lucifer dragged him off to Hell. And he'd felt it a third time when he had to wipe Talia's memories to save her from Vassago, knowing she wouldn't remember him—or that she loved him. Worst pain he'd ever felt and he hoped he never felt it again.

He moved over to the wilted archangel and gripped Azrael's forearm.

"And that's why we're gonna ignore that warning and storm Hell's Gates anyway."

Talia was beside him now, an arm around his waist, holding him close.

Confused, Azrael frowned, shaking his head as he glanced from Talia to Jack. "What? But Berith said Lucifer planned to capture you, Jack."

Jack scoffed. "Like that's a big revelation? It's old news and I'm still going after Berith."

Azrael looked alarmed now. "Jack, no! I won't risk your life and immortal soul by delivering you to Lucifer in Hell."

"It's my risk, dude," he said, a hand against his bare chest. "And I'm taking it no matter what you say. Berith deserved that chance at redemption. At love. I'm not gonna let Luci stomp all over it because he's jelly that dad let Berith move back home and not him."

Azrael was smiling now.

"Besides," said Jack, moving out of the way as Azrael stood up, those huge soot-grey wings expanding again. "Berith's the mom I never had. I'd do anything for her." His voice got all tight and quiet. "And you, archangel."

Those charcoal eyes went from steely to watery. Azrael looked moved by his statement, but it was true. Azrael had done a lot for him. It was time he returned the favor.

Talia pulled Jack into an embrace and he wrapped her in his arms.

"So, we're agreed?" Jack asked, glancing from Talia to Azrael. "We're still gonna crash Luci's party? With every uninvited guest we can muster."

Azrael nodded. "When you put it like that, Jack," he said, holding out his arms. "How can I disagree?"

"But Lucifer's up to something, archangel," he said, his tone darkening. "I don't know what he's after, but it's more than petty vengeance against me."

Azrael's brow furrowed and he cast an unsettled look at Talia.

"Explain, Jack," said the archangel.

Jack shrugged. "We all know the dude relishes his petty vengeance, but this is much, much more than that. And I can't figure out what he's after. Or why he's so focused on dragging my ass back to Hell. He says it's because he wants to murder me personally, but I'm not buying it. Why have me, Berith, and the Book of Secrets? Doesn't make sense. Besides, those three things don't exactly go together."

"Jack's right," said Talia, slipping her arms across his bare chest, turning his skin to gooseflesh. "What's the connection between Berith, Jack, and the Book of Secrets? We still need to figure that out."

Azrael shook his head, hands on his hips. "It doesn't make much sense, does it? Especially when you toss in the rare transference power. Why all of those things? Why now? He's locked in Hell even if his tether breaks because Abaddon still holds the key. The Book of

Creation is out of his reach and he can't awaken any of those powers in the Book of Secrets."

"I thought only the Maker could break the first seal on the Book of Creation," said Talia.

Azrael nodded. "That's correct, Talia. If Lucifer had stayed the Light Bringer, God's left hand, he may have had the power to destroy the Book of Creation and break the first seal. According to Pravuil anyway. But Lucifer lost that standing when he fell from Heaven."

A knock thrummed through the studio trailer.

Startled, Jack glanced at the clock. It was after seven. First reminder that they had a set call in thirty minutes. He glanced down at the towel he was wearing. He hadn't even dried his hair yet.

"Dude, we've gotta go," said Jack. "Herb's expecting us on set at seven-thirty. First day of filming today."

"Go ahead and get dressed, Jack," said Azrael, motioning him toward the bathroom. "And thank you."

Jack gave him a sharp nod and headed back into the bathroom.

"Talia," said Azrael, his attention returning to his right hand angel of death. "Pravuil needs you to return to Heaven right away. He said it was about the transference power. And if you see Kesien, tell him to return to Eolowen immediately. On my order."

"Kesien?" Talia replied in surprise. "He's not training with the guard?"

"He disappeared while on patrol. Muriel's fuming and Deemah's furious. I can't protect him from Muriel's wrath for long."

With a rush of air, Azrael blinked through the ceiling, wings whispering as the trailer went dark again.

2

AZRAEL WOULD BE FURIOUS AT HIM FOR SLIPPING AWAY FROM HIS PATROL duties. But right now, the archangel of death was down on Earth, shaken and preoccupied with Lucifer throwing down a challenge to Jack Casey. After taking Berith right off the steps of Eolowen and dragging her back to Hell alongside the Book of Secrets. Challenging Jack to come and get her.

In Hell.

With Azrael down on Earth, the archangel couldn't deny him this *unexpected* mission. Besides, he couldn't let this chance slip through his fingers, permission or not. He'd take this one on alone, without his squad—or Deemah—backing him up. It was too dangerous and he didn't want to be responsible for extinguishing the light of one more angel of death.

Muriel, acting commander of the guard in Azrael's—and Talia's—absence, probably knew that he had vanished from his patrol by now. Muriel would be furious at him for risking his life and abandoning his post.

As would Deemah. She wanted to bring them all to justice. After all, they were her former guard, too. But it was too dangerous. This way, he could atone for his lapse in judgment that had led to dozens and dozens of death angels' lights being extinguished by Samael and his guard.

She would get her chance when he went after Samael, but Asmodeus was a dangerous, more immediate threat.

He hadn't planned to slip away from his patrol or defy the archangel. But when he saw Asmodeus, masked in shadows at the crossroads, Kesien knew that he had to follow the Hell prince. Find out what he was doing. Where he was going. And what he was after.

Somehow, Kesien had to protect the other angels from this monster.

No one would come looking for him yet, so he still had a little time. Muriel was too busy preparing the guard for the descent into Hell. And the assault on the Gates. No one, including the Maker's Scribe, knew where Lucifer's gauntlet would lead yet. Including his target: Jack Casey.

And that made this whole situation terrifying. One thing was certain though: Asmodeus was handling Lucifer's dark agenda. And Kesien had a chance to discover where the Hell prince was going.

And who he was targeting.

This might be Heaven's only chance to discover Asmodeus' mission. There was no time to report back and ask permission. Besides, his honor demanded that he follow Asmodeus—before he disappeared to wreak havoc in Lucifer's name. He had to risk Azrael's wrath and leave his patrol.

And Asmodeus might lead him to that traitor, Samael and Kesien's former squad mates: Lix, Pharzus, and Reptev.

Once, Kesien would have given up his existence to protect Archangel Samael and his former squad.

Now, he only wanted to bring them to justice. Angels that had trusted their new squad mates from Baladon, treated these rival angels of death as colleagues, as equals after Samael attacked Eolowen again and again. And then those death angels betrayed Azrael's entire guard at Samael's request. Joining Lucifer.

Kesien felt the fury rise within him, sending his gold halo spinning faster as his anger flared. He balled his hands into fists, wings twitching, wanting to rage at Lucifer and Hell and Archangel Samael —every celestial being that had been part of this duplicitous act.

Kesien's upper lip curled into a snarl. And now Archangel Samael had released this banished demon monster from Purgatory and set him loose to do horrible things to humanity. A demon so vicious that Lucifer banished him.

Asmodeus' second favorite thing was the hunt and he wasn't particular about his prey either—although he preferred humans. And weaker celestial beings—like Watchers. But the Hell prince had extinguished the lights of dozens and dozens of angels, too. He'd probably hunted too many demons, maybe some archdemons, or killed targets that Lucifer wanted alive.

Because Asmodeus' favorite thing was killing.

Now, this monster was back doing Lucifer's dirty work while indulging in hunting and killing along the way. Kesien feared what Asmodeus might do on Earth—especially to human, Jack Casey.

Or to the redeemed angel of death, Berith.

He knew how much Archangel Azrael loved Berith—the whole guard did—and how Jack Casey saw her as a mother figure. Kesien knew that both Azrael and Jack would stop at nothing to rescue her. Lucifer was counting on that.

And so was Asmodeus.

Kesien felt guilty for leaving his patrol without a word, but this couldn't wait. Asmodeus was too dangerous. And Kesien vowed to bring down this heinous Hell prince, one of Lucifer's seven princes of Hell. Before he did irreparable damage. As Lucifer's destroyer. Or as one of the Seven Travelers that would devastate the Earth when the seven seals were broken. But then, the Hell princes became Abaddon's to battle. When he became the Maker's Destroyer.

At least only the Maker could break the first seal, according to the seraphim. Maybe that failsafe would keep this horrible darkness in Hell where it belonged?

Flying low over the crossroads, Kesien blinked down the road to Hell, soot-grey wings spread wide. The skies darkened, scent of brimstone sharp as the air grew warmer despite the passing clouds that had massed into tall thunderheads. He soared across the storm grey skies. Toward the black abyss that was the entrance to Hell. Following Asmodeus.

Kesien dimmed his halo and flew low over the thinning foliage and dying trees that dropped dry brown leaves. The dead leaves clattered across the road when the wind rose.

Ahead, in the growing stormy darkness, Asmodeus, stocky and forbidding, stepped out of the shadows and boldly traveled the road to Hell now. Like he owned it. His shiny black bat wings were in furious motion, thump of wings like thunder. The seven-foot-tall Hell prince looked formidable with pale, dusty red skin and curled horns the color of flames that crowned his head. He craned his neck, looking around in every direction, his long, pointy face scrunched in annoyance.

Was Asmodeus meeting someone here? Kesien gritted his teeth. Archangel Samael perhaps? To commit more treason against Heaven? Hunt humans—starting with Jack Casey?

As Kesien edged closer, he saw the anger ignite in Asmodeus' large dragon-like eyes that were the color of fire. His long, wavy hair the color of mustard seeds whipped against his face as the Hell prince kept glancing over his shoulder and to both sides.

Kesien froze. Did Asmodeus sense his presence?

Why would a Hell prince, one of the seven travelers, be looking over his shoulder? The Hell prince's pace was brisk and his attention kept shifting behind him. Like something pursued him. Or he was afraid of something?

What did this monster have to fear besides Lucifer?

When Asmodeus turned away, looking toward the craggy rocks, Kesien landed behind a thick stand of dry brush. He blinked his way along the edge of the hazy road to Hell, keeping distance between him and Asmodeus.

The wide path snaked down a rolling hillside toward craggy black rocks that broke through the supple earth like charred bones and gouged the blue-grey skies ahead. Thunder rumbled. Lightning flashed in bursts of electric purple as the brimstone scent sharpened, smell of ozone rising as the vegetation thinned out, the air already tainted with dust and ash.

Asmodeus paused near the rocks, ducking underneath a shadowy outcrop. Just steps before the uneven, rocky trail led downward into a cavern. And deep into a pitch-black abyss that was pure darkness. Leading to the Gates of Hell.

Kesien blinked closer, behind some scraggly yellow brush about forty feet from Asmodeus, shielding his presence from the Hell prince in the flashes of lightning.

The Hell prince cast one last look over his shoulder and then held out his hand. Something began to shimmer in his meaty palm, turning into a ruddy sphere of images.

Kesien crouched low behind the brush, wings flat against his back. Listening. Waiting. Not quite sure what Asmodeus was doing. And he desperately needed to know. For Berith and Jack. He sighed. For Azrael and Talia—Deemah and the guard.

"Your lackey did his job," Asmodeus said to the glowing sphere in his big hand. "I'm out, but I think one of those damned angels heard that idiot spouting off to you inside Purgatory. Why don't you end that sorry excuse for a soldier now? Before he ruins anything else."

"Patience, Asmodeus," said a familiar voice that made Kesien's wingtips burn. "Everything to its season. Samael is loyal to a fault. He knows who is his master. And how slowly he'll be taken apart if he betrays me. Unlike you, Asmodeus, who considers betrayal a sport like hunting and killing."

Lucifer!

"For now, Samael still has his uses," said Lucifer. "As slight as they may be."

"Like what? A footstool?"

"Oh, no—that role is reserved for Jack Casey. Amongst others—if he's lucky. After I get hold of him, there won't be much left...even for a footstool."

Asmodeus grinned, a mouthful of pointy white teeth looking so unnatural in the dusky mist settling across the road. This Hell prince looked hungry. Ready to eviscerate poor Jack Casey. He feared for the tenacious young human that Talia loved so fervently. He'd done so much for the guard, the world, and Heaven. It made his heart ache.

And Jack had no idea that this monstrosity was on the way to ambush him. Somehow, he had to warn Jack.

"Well, I intend to slow him down and confuse the hell out of him," said Asmodeus, his voice deep and a little raspy. "To get me past those damned seraphim powers. Long enough to immobilize him and drag him back to Hell—after a little fun."

"You're not going down there for fun!" Lucifer's voice was sharp, his anger rising. "I want you to put pressure on him. Lots of pressure! To return to Hell to save dear, precious Berith."

Lucifer glanced sideways and reached out toward something just beyond the image in Asmodeus' hand. Kesien cringed. No, it was a someone.

A muffled female voice rang out, but Kesien couldn't hear her words. But it chilled him to his wingtips. Within those muted sounds, he heard the clear, anxious angel notes. Urging all angels of death to stay away. To keep Jack and Azrael away, too. Warning that when Lucifer set his deadly plan in motion, it could be the end of the Creation. Of Earth.

Abruptly, the sounds went silent.

"That's right, you traitorous harlot," said Lucifer in a precise and pleasant but lethal tone. Bright. Cheery. Deadly. "After what you've done…your existence is forfeit. When I get what I want, I will erase you from existence. Soon." He laughed, the darkness pouring out. "Very, very soon. And I always get what I want."

Asmodeus grinned like he was enjoying Lucifer's threats, feeding off them, but Kesien was surprised that Lucifer and Asmodeus had missed the surge of crystalline notes that Berith intoned in her highest soprano ranges. And held them, their intensity thrumming through the air like a warning siren.

Had she disguised them somehow? Or had Lucifer's fall and tenure in Hell shrank the range of angel notes he could hear?

Regardless, Kesien worried about how Azrael would react when he heard Berith's warning. Sound carried, much slower than light, but it was only a matter of time before the notes reached Eolowen.

And Azrael.

The archangel would be murderous. And desperate to rescue the angel of death that he had loved for millennia.

"Asmodeus!" Lucifer shouted, glaring at him through the image that wavered in the demon prince's heavy hand. "Lean on Jack Casey —as hard as you can. As long as you can. Kidnap him or his angel of death wife. Lure him down here any way you can. I don't care how… just—get him down here!"

"Relax, my king," said Asmodeus with a sharp exhale. "Jack Casey won't know what hit him. I can handle that little shit, even with seraphim powers. My cherubim shapeshifting skills are the best you've ever witnessed. Casey will show up in Hell. I'll make sure of it."

Lucifer's laughter was piercing as it echoed above the crash of thunder. "Can't wait for that moment, Asmodeus. Or the one where I kill him again. A pleasure I've been denied all these months."

Asmodeus glanced around the road, looking behind him and ahead as the road curved sharply to the left. The burly demon laid a hand against his bare, scaly chest.

"Maybe this will finally prove to you that I'm still fighting for Hell? And finally put me back on your good side again, my king."

"Instead of fighting for yourself—or against the other six princes?" Lucifer quipped in a playful tone, but Kesien felt the promise of retaliation beneath it. "Narcissism becomes you, Asmodeus—but only to the point that it doesn't interfere with my plans. We shall soon see where your loyalties lie, won't we? And whether this task will earn back your princely crown." Lucifer paused a moment. "By the way, did you encounter my archdemoness lieutenant along the roads? Zanth?"

"No, my king," said Asmodeus, shaking his head. "She hasn't been seen or felt outside of Purgatory."

"Dammit!" Lucifer shouted. "Jack Casey's going to burn for destroying my new first lieutenant. I'll make certain he regrets that move every single day when I get him back down here." He laughed again, the deep, cruel laugh making Kesien's skin crawl. "Which shall be soon. Very, very soon."

Asmodeus sighed and glanced at the road to Hell's sharp curve and the downward slope into the the subterranean tunnel's inky blackness.

"I've got cherubim-level powers and I can shapeshift. I will outmatch his seraphim powers, Lucifer—or outlast them. He won't know what hit him, I promise."

"One way or another," Lucifer said with a growl, "I will have that smart-mouthed, betraying, winged rat back in my hands. Alive. You'd best make sure it's sooner rather than later, Asmodeus. And that he's alive. Or you will pay a price, too. A very heavy one. That's the only reason I've agreed to release you from your banishment."

Asmodeus glared at the images writhing in his hand. "Me? Why me? I just joined this fight."

Lucifer nodded. "Yes. Just like Samael and his guard. After they've outlived their usefulness. Like that stupid squad of death angels that he brought with him. They will all wind up on the rack or in the cage —sooner or later. Fail me and you will join them, Hell prince no longer. Now, get down to Earth and handle this, Asmodeus—or I'll return you to Purgatory to rot amongst the idiot human souls."

"Relax, I'm on my way. With one of Samael's squads helping me. Reptev, Pharzus, and Lix."

Reptev? Pharzus and Lix?

Kesien ignited in rage, his eyes guttering with white flames. His former squad mates were helping this monster hunt down Jack!

Kesien clenched his hands into fists, the fury trembling through him, wing feathers shaking. It would be the last betrayal they'd ever enact in Lucifer's name. Or Samael's.

He'd see to that.

A smile curved across Asmodeus' dusty red, sandpapery face. "Can't wait to kill Jack Casey."

"You'll do nothing of the sort!" Lucifer's voice was sharp and feral, surprising Kesien. "That kill is mine! Besides...I need him here and you know it. In Hell. Alive, like we discussed. Kill him and I extinguish you from all existence. Don't fuck with me, Asmodeus. I am not in the mood."

Asmodeus swallowed a breath, as he dropped his arms against his sides. He stared at the shimmery image floating in his palm in silence for a moment as if trying to compose himself. Lucifer's threats had finally sunk into his thick demon skull. He pulled in a bath and lifted the sphere again.

"I'll bring him to Hell like you asked, Lucifer," he said in a quiet voice. "You have my word."

"Excellent," said Lucifer who pointed at Asmodeus. "Your existence depends on it, Asmodeus."

The image floating in the Hell prince's fleshy palm disappeared in a puff of smoke. Grumbling, the demon prince turned away from the path leading to Hell. He growled, bat wings stretching wide, and took to the air, flying across the jagged, black rocks.

Kesien groaned. Toward Earth.

Was his former squad really down there waiting for Asmodeus, so they could go after Jack?

Kesien wasn't strong enough to attack a Hell prince alone, as much as he longed to plunge his Eternean sword into this demon's chest and watch him turn to vapor, his essence disintegrated by Holy force. Only the seraphim and Abaddon were powerful enough to take this monster down.

And hopefully, that short list included Talia and Jack Casey. He would gladly help end this monster's existence for all time.

Somehow, he had to get to Earth and warn Jack and Talia before Asmodeus arrived. He needed to warn Azrael and the guard. And Talia needed to know that Asmodeus was on his way to drag the love of her life back to Hell.

With the remnants of his traitorous former guard safely in Hell, Kesien couldn't pursue them yet. But apparently, his former squad was a different story. He would hunt Archangel Samael another day.

But it looked like he would finally get his chance at Lix, Reptev, and Pharzus.

3

"Cut!" Herb, the show's director, stood up from his chair behind the cameras and the dude's face was as red as the stripes in his dress shirt. "Rachel! I said unscripted. Not whatever you feel like doing! Stick to the script or we'll be here all night."

Set coordinators, Steve Kosinski and Jennifer Collins shrank back, shielding the new script supervisor as Herb stormed onto the set of *The Divine Newlyweds Show,* shouting, arms flailing. His blue dress pants were as wrinkled as his forehead, black dress shoes ticking across the concrete terrace.

The set was a sunny summer terrace just past the studio buildings that stood on the edge of a pond and some woods owned by Four Acre Studios. The terrace set had been arranged with two oversized, yellow outdoor couches. Two white wicker end tables sat on either side of each couch and a cobalt blue and butter yellow rug covered most of the pocked concrete.

Between the couches stood an oversized teak coffee table arranged with appetizers and drinks. A big pitcher of frozen strawberry margaritas sat in the table's center and eight frosted margarita glasses were scattered around it. The script called for each of them to pick up and hold a glass throughout most of the scene. And then toast each other at the end.

In charcoal grey dress pants, Doc Martens, a silky blue-grey dress shirt, and no tie, Jack sat with Talia and the show's other three couples on one of the two couches, the one facing the pond. And he tried to hold in his frustration. Rachel was unhinged, forcing take after take. They'd been out in the July sun for hours and he was totally over this scene—even before the first take. It was the worst script (if he could even call it a script) he'd ever read. Full stop.

The poor crew had replaced the frosty glasses a dozen times or more now. Jennifer looked frazzled, white-knuckling her clipboard after the latest replacement and looking overheated in black leggings and a black tunic. Steve Kosinski's dark brown hair was half out of its ponytail as he glanced from script to set to Rachel. Dude probably had whiplash by now.

Everyone held a newly frosted glass in their fist, the script calling for them to look tense as they awaited phone calls about dream houses.

That was the scene setup anyway. And the script blocking. Jack hated it. It felt contrived and felt about as tense as ordering a pizza.

Besides, fans of the show wouldn't give a damn about this scene unless the couples interacted somehow. Competing. Not sitting around, waiting for phone calls.

Talia, dressed in an ice blue minidress and grey flats, sat with Jack beside Armand and Izzy Gianni on one couch. Gianni wore black pants, a tan shirt, and a black tie, and Izzy had on a short coral dress and green heels. Talia's short dress showed off her long legs and beautiful body, but she was stuck sitting on a couch, her gorgeous figure hidden.

On the other couch facing the camera, Mark Banks and his wife, Morgan, sat beside Eric Saunders and Rachel Daniels. Banks wore tan pants and a chambray shirt and Morgan wore a bright blue dress. Rachel wore one of those tight-fitting pink lace dresses that hugged her body and tall pink heels with those damned red soles. Eric wore an ivory suit, grey shirt, and pink tie.

Everyone looked primed and ready to brawl. And Rachel looked like a wind-up toy about to launch into orbit.

There was some drama primed and waiting to happen.

Jack knew that Rachel was about to cause another scene. Like she had all day. It had already been fifteen minutes since her last drama, so she was overdue. At least it would give him a reason to break some glass and let off some steam. Lucifer's call and the remnants of those nightmares were still fresh in his head.

Herb called for them to hold places as the oversized teak coffee table was restaged—again—with another pitcher of frozen strawberry margaritas. A new charcuterie board replaced the previous one, one that would have even impressed Chef Alain Ducasse.

One of the production assistants set down a fresh stack of black and white China plates rimmed with gold and removed the used ones.

Okay, mixing margaritas with charcuterie felt a little weird, but he didn't judge. He was more of a nacho's kind of dude anyway. Regardless, he wanted to guzzle that whole pitcher, but it was just a prop. Probably slushies from the 7-Eleven and leftover cold cuts from craft services.

This whole train wreck had been staged beside the manmade pond framed with trucked-in willow trees that stood on the edge of the studio's back lots. Giant fans created a gentle breeze through the willow trees to create a lazy summer feel. But it was late afternoon of a long, tense day of painful script reads followed by filming the first couple's interviews. Completely made up. Describing their non-existent struggles to find their dream homes. Now, they were filming a supposedly tension-filled scene during the golden hour to capture that fragile, ethereal light that made everything look…well, divine. Celestial. Four couples waiting to hear whether they'd gotten their dream houses or not.

The reality was nobody had bought anything. Their dream houses would be staged like everything else about this season. And Jack hated it. This season was already feeling like the tired old reality shows that he despised. And had never wanted to be part of—kind of like right now.

And it really made him miss *SanFran Confidential*. He was an actor, not a prop and that's what this season (and Lucifer) made him feel like —a prop.

The July air smelled like eucalyptus and Rachel's too many damned flowers and too much freakin' spice perfume. Things were looking up though. The scene was becoming tense...he sighed... because no one knew what Rachel would do next.

And that list was quickly expanding to anything and everything.

Herb bellowed again across the outdoor scene, Phil and Rhonda shifting camera angles, but Jack couldn't hear him over the latest fights that had broken out on set. They'd all been friends before this season started filming. What happened? But he knew the answer to that.

Rachel Daniels.

"Roll it again," Herb said, sounding annoyed.

"Queue it up and roll, Phil," said Steve, standing behind the cameras as Rhonda shifted around the terrace, camera balanced on her right shoulder.

"Rolling another take," Phil replied. "Sound's rolling."

"Marking scene one, take 31," Steve said to the camera, clapping the slate.

"Action, people," Herb announced.

For the thirty-first time, the prop phone in Jack's hand rang. He pressed it to his ear, struggling to muster excitement over his and Talia's make-believe dream house after thirty-one takes, Rachel's antics, no breaks—and hours in the July sun.

Rachel rushed at him, smiling like a kid that had robbed an ice cream truck as she threw her arms around his neck, her mouth an inch from his. She smelled like spearmint and pain. Drenched in that hideous, over-the-top *L'Ange* perfume.

"Congratulations, Jack!" she cried and then kissed him in the mouth.

Eric Saunders rushed at him, outdoor furniture squeaking across the rug and concrete. The bodybuilding financial planner shoved his way past Gianni and Talia who were on their feet now. To hell with the blocking. And the script.

Eric tried to take a poke at him, swinging for the fences. All because Rachel kissed him. *She* kissed him.

Jack didn't want ANY part of her despite her alleged change of heart. If she still had one. He just wanted her to answer one question for him and then he'd keep his distance for the rest of time.

"Cut!" Herb shouted again. "CUT!"

A collective groan rose from the crew as Steve's ponytail completely fell out of its holder and Jennifer threw down her clipboard in exasperation.

Talia was on Jack's right, putting herself between him and Eric. Ready to smite this dude—or maybe someone else? Jack couldn't tell by the fury flaming in those grey angel of death eyes that scowled past Eric at Rachel. She stood on Jack's left. With her arms locked around his neck.

"Dude, what's with you?" Jack shouted at Eric, still standing on his mark beside the outdoor sofa, prop cell phone clutched in his hand. "I didn't start this."

Jealousy blazed in Eric's eyes.

"Back off, Casey!" Eric shouted, pointing at him. "That's my fiancée! You had your chance and she dumped you like rotten fruit."

Jack quickly untangled Rachel's arms from his neck and extracted himself from her *unscripted* embrace. Rachel was grinning, looking unconcerned about the huge fight she'd started. After thirty-one takes. Thirty-one!

By kissing him. Right in the mouth.

During another *unscripted* moment between the four couples supposedly enjoying drinks and deepening their friendships. With more spontaneity and sunshine that the network wanted Herb to push at viewers. But there was nothing spontaneous about this season and anything unscripted came from Rachel's increasingly erratic behavior. Besides, there were only three friendships. And right now, Jack was even questioning that.

Except for Gianni and Izzy. That one was unquestionable.

Unlike this lousy scene that was about as tense and captivating as a public service announcement for STIs.

But like a pro, Rachel took her cue and ran it into the ground as she tried to steal the whole scene. Again. The moment Jack's prop phone rang, she flung herself at him, kissing him, congratulating him. Setting Eric off—at him not her. The four of them had been seated on these two damned sofas for hours. Until Rachel finally turned the scene into a bar brawl, blocking marks forgotten, tempers flaring.

He really wished those margaritas staging the table were real. Because a trip to Margaritaville was the only thing that would save this first episode of *The Divine Newlyweds Show*. Which was looking more mundane than divine right now.

"Let him go!" Talia shouted, shouldering Eric backward and pushing Rachel away from Jack. "Now! That's my husband you're messing with." Her grey eyes sparked with fury, arms crossed, and Jack worried that white Holy fire would appear in her eyes at any moment. "He chose me not you. Now, back off!"

Jack smiled. He loved it when Talia's angel of death side surfaced. She was throwing Eric Saunders' words right back at him.

But the arguing and shouting continued. Standing beside the table dressed with prop drinks, Gianni and Banks argued about neighborhoods alongside Izzy and Morgan.

"Mark! It's Brentwood or nothing!" Morgan demanded with a firm nod, brown hair in motion. "I'm not living in any of those overcrowded neighborhoods or commuting an hour and a half each way."

Morgan and Banks should spend the night at his place and she wouldn't be so picky afterward.

"I said cut already!" Herb yelled from somewhere behind the sofa, out of camera range, but none of his actors was listening anymore.

Izzy's mouth fell open. Looking shocked, she stared at Gianni who was trying to diffuse the situation, but anger sparked in Izzy's warm brown eyes as she pointed at Morgan.

"I had no idea that you were such a snob, Morgan," Izzy replied. "There are plenty of wonderful neighborhoods across Los Angeles. But they're spendy, too. If you'd get off your high horse and give them a chance."

"Yeah," Jack replied with a smirk. "Like the Fashion District or South Park. Great amenities—including all the weed and demons you can handle. And no need to call the cops because they're always there. It's your chance to star in your very own crime drama."

No one was listening to him though.

"I'm a snob?" Morgan shouted, hands on her hips as she scowled at Izzy. "I'm a snob! Says Mr. and Mrs. Paradise Cove Bluffs! Unlike you and Armand, Mark and I don't have millions to throw at a mansion."

"Come on, Izzy, that's unfair," Banks replied, brushing his spiky brown hair out of his eyes. "Morgan's no snob."

Izzy crossed her arms, scowling at Morgan. "She is if she says it's Brentwood or nothing! And for the record, we're *looking* at Pacific Palisades, not Paradise Cove Bluff. And it's most likely out of our price range."

"Relax your tabloid reporter reflexes, Izzy," Banks replied, an edge in his voice. "None of this is decided yet."

"Tabloid reporter?" Gianni replied, bristling, Cary Grant-brown eyes narrowing as he glared at Banks. "Insults? At my wife? This needs to stop, Mark. Now."

"Morgan just wants a little more room and we can get that in Brentwood," Banks replied. "That's all."

Izzy rolled her eyes at Banks. "In Brentwood? Without millions to throw at a mansion? Good luck with that, Morgan. All you'll get is a room for that price. A small one."

The whole set devolved into heated arguments as Eric came at Jack again, swinging for the bleachers.

The muscled financial planner shoved the yellow outdoor sofa farther across the concrete as he swung his fist, almost clocking Jack in the mouth. But Jack caught his arm and held it in mid-swing.

His wings twitched at his back and he fought down the urge to fly out of this chaos. With one of those strawberry margaritas melting in the summer heat. Dammit, a real one! With enough tequila to knock him out—so he wouldn't have to listen to any more of this fighting.

"Dude, seriously?" Jack replied, holding Eric's fist back. "*She* kissed me, remember? I was answering my phone. According to the script."

"You were flirting with her!" Eric bellowed, coming at him again, fist swinging for the lights. "I saw it!"

Jack ducked and pushed him backward. "Then you'd better get your eyes checked, dude," he replied and held out his left hand, letting the sun glint off his wedding ring. "Happily married to the love of my life. No other woman's been on my radar since I met Talia, so chill already."

Why did Eric think he was flirting with Rachel? He hadn't so much as blinked at her, much less spoken to her. They didn't even have any lines together during this scene. What was with Eric all of a sudden? And the others? All of this arguing and fighting was so out of character and he didn't understand it.

At least Eric's loud accusations had quieted the other fights on set while everyone else turned to stare at him and Eric. And Herb, red-faced, still standing out of camera range at the edge of the terrace.

"I'll chill when you stop flirting with my woman, Casey," Eric said with a growl, his usually calm demeanor uncharacteristically angry and insecure.

His woman?

"That caveman for fiancée, Saunders?" Jack asked.

Eric lunged at him again and he side-stepped the attack. The dude came at him again, but Phil the cameraman stepped between them, Steve Kosinski behind him, his brown hair bunched around his shoulders.

"For the last time!" Jack yelled, feeling the heat rise at his temples. "I'm not flirting with Rachel Daniels. It'd be a cold day in Hell when that happens and last I checked, Lucifer still hadn't bought a parka."

Eric's eyes sizzled with rage. "So, she's not good enough for you now? Is that it, Casey? Now that SanFran Confidential's back courting you? Now that you're about to become the highest paid actor on television?"

Jack's eyes narrowed and he held in a sigh. They'd all seen him talking on the phone to Evan Bellows yesterday. In front of his studio trailer. Moments before the world fell apart and Lucifer grabbed Berith. Challenging him to come down to Hell and take her back again.

He remembered the horrible devastation burning in Archangel Azrael's eyes at the terrible news. Jack hadn't been able to get Berith out of his thoughts, fearing what Lucifer had already done to the selfless angel of death who had redeemed herself in the eyes of Heaven. And betrayed Lucifer alongside him when they both escaped from Hell.

Lucifer wanted retribution and he'd gone to great lengths to get it. Regardless of what that vindictive bastard had planned, Jack was going in after her. As soon as the guard was ready to bitch-slap Luci on his home turf. Azrael insisted on time to prepare the guard before Jack and Talia went back to Eolowen to train for this fight.

Returning to Hell terrified him and he hadn't slept well since the news broke about Berith. He'd already been struggling with the aftermath of seeing his dad in Purgatory—and now Berith was Lucifer's prisoner.

As if that wasn't enough, Rachel was flirting with him again.

He had no idea what she was after either. But she was definitely after something. Was she trying to make Eric Saunders jealous enough to propose to her? Or was she after something more insidious? Was she back with Lare Dumont? Or worse...back with Lucifer? And back in the stealing souls business. He had no clue, but he had no interest in Rachel Daniels. Or anyone but Talia.

"Again, Eric," Jack said with a snarl, holding Eric's tawny muscled arm away from his face. "Happily married to Talia Smith and happily contracted to The Divine Newlyweds Show."

Finally, Eric's anger dissipated when Gianni moved between them, standing beside Phil. Looking concerned. At last, Eric stepped back from Jack.

"That's enough!" Herb yelled, red-faced and furious, hands clenched into fists.

This time, the entire cast turned to stare at him, tempers finally cooling.

"All right, people, ten-minute break to clear your heads," Herb announced. "Go!"

The cast scurried off the terrace set and scattered along the edge of the pond, including Rachel who backed away from Talia, a playful grin still on her face. Jack had no clue what game she was playing. But he knew Talia wouldn't put up with it.

"Jack?" said Gianni in a quiet voice.

Gianni looked concerned. No, worried. And judging by his expression, it was all directed at him.

"What's up, Gianni?" Jack asked, keeping an eye on Eric Saunders, in case he wanted to go for the title again.

"Everyone's saying they saw you flirting with Rachel off set." His voice was quiet but razor-sharp.

"What?" Jack cried, eyes wide as he struggled to keep his mouth from falling open. "When? I haven't spent a moment alone with her—and I have no intention of doing so." He shook his head. "Please tell me that doesn't include you."

Gianni shook his head. "No, of course not, but I'm concerned about all these rumors." He lowered his voice. "Or why anyone would possibly think you'd leave Talia for Rachel Daniels after everything she's done to you."

"Leave Talia?" he said, chuckling at the absurdity. "Are you high? I'd never, ever leave Talia. You know that!"

"Of course, I know that, Jack," said Gianni, looking Cary Grant-calm despite his frustration as he motioned toward the rest of the cast and then the crew. "But someone out there is spreading these insane rumors. We need to figure out who. And why. Before this entire show falls apart."

Dammit, Gianni had a point. Filming had gone straight to hell, just like the rehearsals. This *unscripted* scripted show had been a bad idea from the start and with all these fights, this season would be the show's last if something didn't change. Fast.

"Okay," said Gianni, crossing his arms. "Where do we start?"

"Oh my God!" someone shouted behind Jack. "Not another one."

That was Jennifer Collins' voice.

"Another what?" Herb asked.

"This…"

Someone gasped. Whispers hissed.

Jack turned to see Jennifer holding up a small clear plastic bag. A quarter of the bag was filled with white powder. Flake.

Gianni stared wide-eyed at the bag and then his gaze shifted to Jack who stormed across the set toward the silver Four Acre Studios van parked against the curb. Jennifer stood beside a stack of blue storage tubs that had been unloaded, frozen in place as she held out the bag to Herb. Dude's face had gone from red to pale.

They both turned to stare at Jack like he'd just robbed a 7-Eleven at gunpoint.

But he couldn't take his eyes off the plastic bag. Full of cocaine. And they kept staring at him. He gritted his teeth. Like that shit was his.

"Jennifer," he said, struggling not to stammer as he tried to hold in his shock. "That's not mine."

Jennifer glanced from Herb to Jack and finally Gianni who was standing behind him now.

Gianni laid his hand on Jack's shoulder, squeezing. "Jennifer," Gianni said in a clear, confident voice. "That cocaine is not Jack's. He's clean."

Herb's brown eyes were a mix of sadness and anger. "Jack, I—"

"So, am I gonna have to piss in a cup before takes now, Herb?" He crossed his arms. "That way you'll know I'm not a liar. Either you trust me or you don't. That shit isn't mine."

Herb went quiet and Jack knew that look. He wanted to rage and shout, but he held his anger tight under his tongue. Herb didn't believe him.

"Fine," said Jack with a growl, eyes narrowing. "Maybe Evan Bellows will believe me?"

He stormed past the studio van and headed toward the distant row of squat grey studio buildings. To his trailer.

"Jack, wait!" Herb called. "It's not that I don't believe you! It's—"

"I'll be in my trailer! Not doing flake!"

Jack broke into a run across the open, sunlit field, the summer heat roiling around him.

4

Kesien soared in a graceful arc down from the Heavens toward Earth, following the dark, smoky trail that Asmodeus had left in the clouds. That led straight toward Los Angeles, California. Right to Jack Casey and Talia.

He never imagined that he'd be forced to abandon his post entirely to pursue a Hell prince. But he couldn't let Asmodeus ambush Jack and Talia.

Sulfury residue clung to the clouds, the stench of brimstone strong as Asmodeus' trail descended toward the studio below. Where Jack and Talia had begun filming another season of the reality television show where they met. Where she'd saved his life. And his soul.

As an angel of death, Kesien had scoured most of the Earth, crossing over humans. From queens and presidents to drug addicts and alcoholics. Those human cases had even brought him here, to this very studio.

He just hoped he got to Talia and Jack in time. Before Asmodeus blindsided them with an attack. With their rare powers, they would be formidable adversaries for the Hell prince, but the human—Jack—was fragile despite his seraphim powers. If the battle lasted too long,

Asmodeus might succeed in dragging Jack back to Hell—with Talia powerless to stop him.

The thick, smoky trail wound through the bright summer sky, fleecy clouds interrupting the clear, serene blue as he descended through the white mists toward thick, velvety green grass below. Where Four Acre Studios stretched across the landscape, rows of squat grey buildings lining one side.

But the trail of dark smoke coiled away from the studio buildings, toward the outer plots of land where intricate sets, even a replica Midwestern town square, stood on the outskirts. Exhaust fumes and eucalyptus hung above the stink of brimstone as he followed the smoke toward a cluster of white trailers parked along the grey studio buildings.

The smoke looped and coiled over top of the trailers, floating far away from them until it curled around a two-story, windowless tan building at the studio's edge. A warehouse. Behind it was an old, beat-up tan trailer. Isolated from the others. Away from the sets and other buildings, it was shadowed beneath a stand of tall trees at the far end of a rolling meadow.

That led toward a tree-lined pond and concrete patio in the distance.

As Kesien swooped low, halo humming, charcoal grey wings spread wide, he felt Asmodeus' presence nearby. The cold, heavy darkness made him shudder. It wasn't as chilling as he felt in Lucifer's presence, but the Hell prince's proximity made his wingtips tremble and his skin crawl.

Asmodeus was here on the studio lot. Close to Jack and Talia.

Somehow, he had to take this Hell-creature down before Jack and Talia got ambushed.

Three times, he circled the beat-up tan trailer, using his angel senses to gather a picture of what was inside, but each time he got close, the images blurred and his angel senses blunted. Fear trembled along the curve of his wings.

What if he was too late? He winced. What if Asmodeus had already cornered Jack? Or mortally injured Talia?

His fury overcame his fear, propelling him over the trailer's rooftop and beneath the trees' dusky shadows as twilight settled like downy feathers against the Earth.

Quickly, he folded his wings against his shoulders and moved toward the trailer's only door. Did this trailer belong to Talia and Jack? Seemed in the wrong place though. Had Asmodeus already gotten to them? Like Samael and his former guard had ambushed the death angel guard at Eolowen?

No! He couldn't be too late this time!

Gritting his teeth, he leaped toward the door and blinked through it.

Into a dark, silent space. Cramped. Suffocating. And reeking of brimstone.

He pressed his angelic form flat against the wall, extinguishing his halo to conceal his presence as the darkness began to take shape. An old, dark leather sofa stood across from a table, four chairs, and a kitchenette. Ahead, a television hung dark on the wall above two grey leather chairs.

Where Rachel Daniels sat, blue eyes filled with fear as she struggled against the smoky trails of darkness binding her legs and arms to the sofa. Keeping her a prisoner inside this trailer.

Movement blurred to his right. Kesien turned.

Rachel Daniels stood beside him now, grinning, dressed in a tight, lacy pink dress and matching heels.

Kesien's gaze shot back to Rachel who was still bound to the couch. Confused, he looked back at the woman standing beside him. How could there be two of them?

In this other Rachel's leering smile, he saw a much darker presence. One that sent chills across his wings and made his heart ache at the unapologetic evil that bubbled up from her presence.

And then he knew.

Asmodeus, a cherub before the Fall, had shifted form to look like Rachel. To prey on Jack and Talia. They were completely unaware that the real Rachel Daniels was a prisoner inside this unused set trailer.

And Kesien was powerless to warn them.

A ripple of darkness startled him. He reached for his Eternean sword.

Moments too late.

But he realized that Asmodeus was posing as Rachel to lure Jack, unaware, into a trap and carry him away. Straight to Hell. Back into Lucifer's hands.

Somehow, Kesien had to stop this ambush before Jack fell into Asmodeus' hands.

And then Lucifer's.

A flood of dark energy rolled over him, knocking him to the floor. Thick, ropey strands of darkness coiled around his wings and arms and legs, pinning him to the dusty hardwood.

At seven feet tall, Asmodeus towered over him, long wavy hair the color of mustard seeds, skin pale and dusty red skin, and dragon-like eyes fiery with amusement. The monstrous Hell prince laughed at him.

"I've trapped my first angel of death since leaving Purgatory!" A Cheshire grin spread across Asmodeus' long, pointy face. "Don't bother trying to alert your guard. None of those Enochian angel notes will penetrate my dark wards, so don't bother singing them. I hate angel hymns. My wards have blocked you completely from their sight, so shut up and try to stay out of my way, huh?"

Kesien stiffened. He couldn't sing out a message to his guard and they couldn't detect his presence inside here. He had to figure out a way to warn the guard. Fast. Before Jack ended up dead or in Hell.

The stocky Hell prince nudged Kesien into a sitting position against the wall. "Now, you get to watch me lure Jack Casey here as Rachel Daniels." Asmodeus' fiery eyes narrowed. "Where I'll waste him for the bounty. Highest in Hell's history. You're going to be Lucifer's consolation prize—unless I decide to waste you, too. So, don't piss me off."

Kesien stared unblinking into the Hell prince's beady fire-orange dragon eyes.

"Lucifer demanded him alive for that bounty," Kesien replied.

"Why would you kill him and go against Lucifer's orders? He'll hunt you to the ends of Creation if you defy him."

"I do what I want," Asmodeus said with a growl, flashing pearly white teeth at him. "And I take what I want. Lucifer will still get Casey's soul. But I'm aching to kill an angel and some humans. That's like killing two birds with one stone." He laughed, a deep guttural sound that made Kesien want to rage. "Or lots of angels." He leaned closer to Kesien's ear. "After being banished to Purgatory by Lucifer for so long, I need to unwind a little. Focus my cherubim energies on a flesh and blood subject."

Kesien's eyes narrowed. "I hope you unwind into pieces, Asmodeus. Better yet, I'll help you with a little Holy Fire."

"You'll try, death angel," said Asmodeus as he gripped Kesien's upper arm. "And fail. Now, let's get you moved out of the way. Can't have you tipping off Casey when I get him inside here."

Closing his eyes, Kesien focused on his squad mate, Deemah, and sent out a silent prayer for help. Testing Asmodeus' wards.

Her response should have been instant. But not even a burble of angel tones fluttered back to him through the air currents. Not even a single note.

Asmodeus was telling the truth. Nothing penetrated the wards from either side. Kesien wondered if Lucifer knew that Asmodeus was already defying him. Could Lucifer even do anything about it? After all, he was still tethered in Hell. He couldn't come to Earth and stop his errant Hell prince.

Kesien groaned. Asmodeus had counted on that, too.

And there would be no help from Heaven. They couldn't even locate Kesien now, thanks to Asmodeus' dark wards. Even if Azrael's guard tracked him from the crossroads to Earth, they would lose his trail at the studio. And they couldn't break demon wards that they couldn't detect.

Somehow, Kesien had to break these shadowy chains and stop Asmodeus from luring Jack inside this trailer. And killing him.

Kesien tapped the well of Holy fire within him until the wave of anger and panic ebbed. He'd take a play out of Jack Casey's playbook and act out his part for Asmodeus. Until he could figure out a way to expose the Hell prince's trap. He'd pretend to be an ensnared, helpless angel of death while he did everything possible to communicate with Heaven or any angels here on Earth.

He turned his gaze to the forbidding, pale red demon.

"You've got the wrong bait, Asmodeus," Kesien said in a flat, almost bored tone. "Jack Casey isn't interested in Rachel Daniels. Everyone knows that." Kesien struggled against the shadow bonds again.

"See, you big, washed-out red dolt!" Rachel shouted. "I told you that, but you wouldn't listen."

"Idiot," Kesien mumbled. "If you'd bothered to study your prey, you'd know that he isn't in love with Rachel anymore. He'd never follow her inside here."

Asmodeus cracked a smile, his fiery eyes lighting with amusement. "He would with the right kind of bait," said Asmodeus, holding out his corpulent hand, palm up. "Like this."

The seven-foot demon cast a quick glare at him and then thrust his hand at Kesien's face. A clear plastic bag of cocaine materialized.

Kesien did his best to hide his shock as Asmodeus' heavy laughter echoed through the trailer. The Hell prince strutted around him and then dropped down on his haunches. He leaned back against the grey walls, grinning, still holding the bag of cocaine.

"See, angel of death," Asmodeus said in a quiet voice as he nudged Kesien with his elbow. "You've gotta have the right bait, according to Heaven. And I intend to tap into his coke addiction. That should lure him into this trailer and right into my hands. I've already stirred up some fights, got the humans wound up, and sent rumors flying."

Kesien did his best not to react to Asmodeus's threats.

"If that doesn't work, I'll shift into his father's image," Asmodeus said with a snicker. "That will be my backup plan in case the coke doesn't appeal to Casey. But his dad being released from Purgatory would definitely get Jack's attention."

"You monster!" Kesien shouted, gritting his teeth as he tried to lunge at Asmodeus.

But the shadow ropes held.

The pale red demon laughed and turned his back, dismissing Kesien.

"Casey's addiction and grief issues are all the bait I'll need if the coke fails," said Asmodeus as he patted Kesien on the head like a dog. "Why do you think Lucifer sent me, you witless angel? It wasn't to charm Casey back to Hell. Or ask him nicely. It was to deliver the annoying little bastard to Lucifer in Hell. One of these things will do the trick, so watch and learn, death angel!"

Again, Kesien called out to Deemah, trying to get her to hear his distress call. To get someone outside this trailer to protect Jack Casey and his seraphim powers. Fast. Before Heaven lost one of its best soldiers to Lucifer.

5

Jack didn't stop running until he reached his trailer. He unlocked the door and shuffled inside, sinking into the taupe sofa's soft cushions in the opulent space.

In moments, the trailer door opened. He expected to see Talia standing there, but it was Gianni, out of breath. The taller soap star closed the door and sauntered into the trailer like Cary Grant accepting an Oscar.

"You weren't kidding," said Gianni, glancing around at the upscale finishings. "Your trailer *was* nicer than ours."

Jack shrugged. "You know I didn't ask for this, right?"

Gianni slid his hands into the front pockets of his black dress pants and sat down beside Jack on the sofa. The collar of his tan dress shirt hung open where he'd taken off his tie. Jack unbuttoned the first three buttons of his blue-grey dress shirt and propped his Doc Martens on the coffee table.

"I know you didn't," said Gianni, "but the rest of us appreciated the upgrade."

Jack turned to stare at the impeccably dressed soap star, his hair Cary Grant-perfect despite the breeze. Jack knew his bangs were anything but orderly, especially after Rachel had thrown her arms around his neck and smashed her mouth against his.

"And you know that I didn't kiss Rachel and that coke isn't mine, right?"

He needed to hear that Gianni still believed him. In him.

"Of course, I know that," Gianni replied, sounding insulted and that made Jack smile.

"Talia and I are golden," he said, motioning toward the framed picture on the coffee table of his and Talia's first promo picture for the series. "She's the love of my life and I sure as hell wouldn't jeopardize her love to flirt with Rachel."

The conversation went quiet as Gianni studied him for a few moments, that reflective stare encompassing him. Gianni had more to say. He felt it in the weight of the taller actor's stare.

"Jack, you've been distant and distracted since you came back from that fight in Purgatory." Gianni's gaze was piercing, observing him for a moment or two. "What happened? Talk to me. I saw all of those demons and that archdemoness, remember? Tell me what's happening. Are you still battling demons?"

Jack nodded, his gaze falling to his hands as he tangled his fingers together.

"Something terrible's happened," he said, not even sure where to begin.

Gianni's eyebrows shot up, mouth flattening as the taller actor studied him, waiting in that patient way of his for the next explanation. This one was stranger than the last one.

"When I was in Hell," Jack began, struggling to explain all of this to Gianni, but he knew the dude was probably the only person on Earth that could understand any of it. "Berith, a fallen angel of death, helped me survive down there. She healed me and helped me convince Lucifer to let me join his fight."

"What?" Gianni's eyes widened. "Join the Devil's fight? Jack, you didn't!"

Already, Jack vehemently shook his head. "Relax, dude, I was playing the long con. It was the only way I could get Lucifer to take me on his march against Heaven and out of Hell. So Berith and I could escape. Despite her fall, Berith had a rare healing gift and she healed me several times. In Hell and back in Eolowen, the place where Azrael's death angel guard hangs. And because of her, Talia and I didn't lose each other when Lucifer marched on the Heavens."

Gianni's mouth gaped. "Lucifer marched on the Heavens? Isn't that end of the world?"

Jack released the breath he'd been holding. "It would have been if we hadn't stopped him." He paused, staring out the small window that overlooked the green, shaded lot behind the Studio 22 building. "For her repentance and for helping to stop Lucifer, Heaven redeemed Berith. Gave her wings and halo back. And her angel of death status. But now, Lucifer's grabbed Berith. Challenged me to come to Hell and rescue her."

"Jack! You can't!" Gianni cast a glare at him. "That's a huge trap set just for you."

He nodded. "I know Luci's still gunning for me, but Gianni, I have to save Berith. He'll kill her."

"He'll kill you. Jack! You know I'm right!"

Of course, he was right. Lucifer always got his revenge. But Jack couldn't let him erase Berith from existence either. At least the bastard was still tethered in Hell.

He ran his fingers through his light blond hair, struggling with the situation. At the end of the day, he couldn't live with himself if something happened to Berith. He had to rescue her.

"What if Lucifer had taken Izzy?" Jack asked, watching Gianni's expression. "Would you go in after her?"

Gianni's eyes narrowed. "You damned right I'd go in after her," he said in a determined voice. "I get it, Jack." His voice got quiet and sounded defeated. "Is Berith that important to you?"

Jack gave him a sharp nod. "She's like a mother to me."

"That makes a lot of sense," said Gianni, nudging him. "Because I've met your mother."

He laughed. "Good point. Seriously though, I owe Berith and I can't let her stay in Lucifer's hands. He'll kill her for her betrayal." He winced. "And for mine. But I have no clue who's trying to set me up with the bags of coke and why Rachel's flirting with me like she's gunning for an Emmy nomination."

Gianni's expression turned pensive. "Doesn't make a lot of sense, does it? I trust all of these people—well, except for Rachel."

Jack had no idea who was trying to discredit him on the set of *The Divine Newlyweds Show*. He had a list of enemies and bounty hunters that was miles long and that included Lucifer. But he had no idea who'd want to sabotage his new show. Was it Lare Dumont and Tyler Hughes? Acting alone or trying to collect Lucifer's bounty any way they could?

The trailer door began to rattle.

Jack's attention snapped to the door as Gianni scrambled to his feet.

"Is that demons approaching?" Gianni asked in a nervous voice.

Jack slowly got to his feet as the noise amplified. "Every demon in Hell knows about the bounty on my head, so it's possible."

Something blurred through the door.

Jack set himself, ready to summon a handful of murder marbles.

Gold light engulfed the space as something took shape.

"Wait!" Jack cried, grabbing hold of Gianni, keeping him from lunging at the materializing figure in front of them.

Archangel Azrael appeared before them in long grey death angel robes, wings extended, red-gold halo spinning like a top as he gleamed with golden light.

Jack smiled. "That's one of the good guys." He pointed at the archangel. "That's Archangel Azrael. He commands Talia's death angel guard. Berith is his…bae."

Azrael frowned, giving him a questioning look. "Bay? What's a bay, Jack?"

"B-a-e." Jack spelled it out. "The one you put before anyone else."

The corners of the archangel's mouth briefly rose and then fell back into a forlorn expression, an ache in his charcoal grey eyes that radiated. He looked rough, soot-grey wings drooping, silver-black hair flat against his head. And he'd let Gianni see him. The archangel had always been so careful, but right now, he was visibly distracted.

It hurt Jack to look at the him. Dude had spent millennia pining for his lost angel love. Finally gets her back and then Luci snatches her, threatening to tear off her wings while Azrael was trying to drag Archangel Samael's cowardly winged ass back to High House. It was a low blow and the Archangel of Death was suffering.

"This is the other reason, Gianni," said Jack, motioning at Azrael. "That's the love of Azrael's life out there, dragged back to Hell." He flashed Azrael his most confident smile. "And we're going to storm Hell to get her back. Crashing Luci's party in death angel style. With murder marbles and Holy fire."

When he glanced back at Azrael, he was smiling. It was brief, but Jack knew that smile meant the archangel hadn't lost hope.

"Thank you, Jack," said Azrael in a tired voice. "I appreciate your enthusiasm and optimism. I'm afraid I need to interrupt your filming schedule." He cleared his throat. "I need to speak with you and Talia right away."

Jack nodded. "I'll go get Tal."

Azrael held up his hand. "No need. She's on her way."

Gianni stepped backward, that look of awe still shining in his eyes at seeing an archangel suddenly appear in front of him. In full celestial light—well, full enough for human eyes. If the archangel had appeared in his full celestial light, it would have blinded him and Gianni.

"I'll leave you to your discussion, Jack," the taller actor said and poked Jack's shoulder with his fist. "Let me know if I can help. I haven't forgotten the archangel battling demons to rescue my love, Izzy, either."

"Thanks, dude," said Jack, walking him to the trailer door. "Appreciate the support. Tell Herb I'm...talking to Evan or something."

Laughing, Gianni shook his head. "I'm not going to cause Herb's head to explode. I'll tell him you need a half hour to—clear your chakras."

Jack glared at him. "Seriously, dude?"

"Okay," he said with a chuckle. "I'll tell him that you need to meditate—clear your head. And not because of the coke either, okay?" Gianni fanned the air. "I'll tell him Rachel's perfume gave you a migraine or something."

"Read my mind, dude," Jack said with a smirk. "Thanks for being in my corner."

"Always, Jack," said Gianni as he opened the trailer door.

Talia stood outside on the steps, waiting for him to exit. She reached out and squeezed Gianni's shoulder and then hurried inside, worry shining in those luminous, arctic grey eyes. When she saw the archangel, she blinked toward him and gripped his sleeve, looking frightened.

"Archangel! Are you all right?"

Azrael kept his head held high, but exhaustion and pain burned in his charcoal grey eyes. Those majestic archangel's wings still drooped a little. Like someone had told him the odds of rescuing Berith. He was still hurting and worried sick about her.

"Talia, I've returned to tell you both that preparations to storm Hell have begun."

Jack's heart felt heavy, his breath quickening. He was really going back there again. He'd already struggled through his return to the Garden, the beach house, and the escape room. But Hell? That was on a whole other level.

Last night's nightmares still haunted him—as much as Lucifer's phone call this morning. Even before Berith contacted him through his dreams, he still had nightmares about that place. Sometimes, the scent of sulfur or charred wood was a visceral reminder of what he went through down there. Regardless, he didn't have a choice. He was going after Berith.

"Muriel has begun drills with the guard," said Azrael, motioning toward the ceiling. "Master armorer, Zephana has set up a temporary forge at Eolowen to increase the protection of our Eternean armor. Oseira has returned to the grand hall from High House, to provide us healing until..."

Azrael's voice trailed off as his breath caught and he turned away for a moment.

"I thought I'd lost her for eternity," he said, his voice shaky, his back still to them as his wings twitched and his grey robes rustled. "And when she was returned to me, I—" He exhaled a heavy breath. "I was overjoyed. And now…" He paused, pulling in a quick breath. "Now…I can't bear her absence a second time. Help me bring her home. To Eolowen. To Heaven."

Talia walked toward him, laying a hand on the archangel's shoulder, squeezing.

"Jack and I are with you, archangel," said Talia, her soprano voice soft. "We'll bring Berith home."

"We've got your back, dude," Jack replied. "To Hell and back. We won't let Luci harm her."

"In four human days, the guard will be ready for you to train with us. For the descent. Be ready for my summons."

Talia gave Jack a worried glance. "We'll return to Eolowen immediately when you call for us, Azrael."

"Thank you," Azrael choked out, his back still to them. "And Talia, Pravuil needs to see you at Eolowen immediately. You need to awaken the transference power before our descent. We may need it down in Hell."

"I'll leave as soon as things here have calmed down, sir," said Talia.

"Until then," said Azrael.

With a blink, the archangel disappeared through the trailer wall and vanished.

Talia turned toward Jack, her grey eyes glassy. "I've never seen him so broken before."

Jack nodded. "He's hurting. Together, you and I can turn this around, Tal. With our combined powers."

Smiling, she moved toward him, sliding her arms around his neck. "I like the sound of that, lover."

He gently kissed her lips as Muriel materialized in the trailer, startling Jack.

Whirling around, he smashed his right hand into a fist, intending to summon a handful of murder marbles, but when he realized it was Muriel, he let the power cascade between his fingers, and fall like glitter to the floor.

"Talia! Jack!" she cried, sounding out of breath. She grabbed hold of Talia's sleeve, those death angel grey eyes wide and filled with apprehension.

"Scared the hell out of me, Muriel," he said and pulled in a breath as he let his hand fall to his side. "Angels need to learn about doors. And knocking!"

"Sorry," said Muriel, grimacing as her gaze flicked to him and then back to Talia. "Didn't have time to knock." She began to pace through the trailer, wings shifting against her shoulders, hands in motion. "We've got some big problems! And I didn't have the heart to bother Azrael with them. He's dealing with enough right now."

Talia stepped toward Muriel and stopped her in mid-stride.

"What is it, Muriel?" she asked, her gaze intense and focused only on Muriel. "Spill it."

Jack edged closer, dreading what she was about to say.

"Two things," said Muriel, her eyebrows pressing into a frown. "One, Asmodeus was spotted near the crossroads by a cherubim patrol. Apparently, Samael released him from Purgatory and Lucifer's banishment."

Jack's mouth went dry. A demon so nasty that Lucifer banned him from his operation. That said a lot. He cast a worried look at Talia who looked even more frightened now.

"I'll send a flock of Watchers out to search for Asmodeus," said Talia, nodding toward the door. "Since Oseira is still at Eolowen, ask her to send a squad of cherubim after him. They can handle one Hell prince—since this one was a cherub once. Now, what's the second thing?"

Handled that without even ruffling a wing feather. God, this woman impressed the hell out of him! Talia would handle that minor douchebag without having to trouble the archangel with it. His death angel wife never failed to amaze him. But he braced for more bad news.

Muriel stepped back from Talia. She brushed a lock of sable hair out of her eyes, glancing at him and then back at Talia. He stiffened.

"Two, Kesien's missing. Deemah thinks he's gone rogue, hunting Samael and his old squad."

"What?" Anger churned in Talia's eyes. "I gave him a direct order not to pursue Samael and his guard for now. I know he wants to bring them to justice, but we need him right now."

"Don't have to tell me that," said Muriel, hands on her hips, Eternean armor glinting in the trailer's warm lighting.

The air had traces of that *cool rain and roses* scent that he associated with Heaven. He smiled. And Talia.

"Get Deemah and Anahera working on pinpointing Kesien's location," Talia replied. "Sing out the moment you locate him."

"Babe, this isn't like Kesien," said Jack, stepping toward her and Muriel. "He's always followed his orders to the letter, even when he didn't exactly agree with them."

Talia nodded. "I know. That's what worries me. He's always described himself as the Maker's soldier to command."

"Until that douchebag, Samael pushed him over the edge after all the angelcide in Eolowen," said Jack, as he motioned toward the ceiling. "He feels played by people he trusted to have his back. I get it."

Talia folded her arms against her chest, a faraway look in her eyes. "I thought he understood that Samael and his former squad were in Hell. With Lucifer. Out of his reach."

Muriel sighed, wings flexing. "I thought he did, too. Then he went on patrol and didn't come back."

"Azrael told me he disappeared from a patrol," Talia replied, frowning. "And I want to know why."

"He see something that the others missed?" Jack asked.

He rubbed his hand across his clean-shaven jaw and thought back to their excursion into Purgatory with Zanth, the archdemoness. Kesien had been bordering on mutiny and hadn't been himself then either. Dude wanted to rampage through Purgatory, extinguishing Samael's halo and the rest of his old squad. Talia had to work hard to keep the usually patient and forgiving angel of death focused on capturing Samael and the Book of Secrets.

Had Kesien gone on patrol with the intention of pulling a fade? So he could go hunt Samael and his former squad mates?

With Azrael hurting and distracted and Talia back on Earth, it was the perfect time to slip away and go on the hunt for those dickhead traitors.

"Maybe," said Talia, deep in thought. "But I think the patrol was a good diversion for him to slip away. Still, it doesn't make sense." She turned around, her gaze shifting from him to Muriel. "He'd want to be there when we storm Hell. Because that's where Samael and his former squad are hiding. Going off alone to challenge the Gates of Hell makes no sense either."

Muriel sighed and leaned against the taupe wall beside the grey lacquer kitchen cabinets, wings settling around her shoulders.

"I agree, Talia. He knows Azrael is frantic to get this assault in motion."

Talia pressed her hand against her cheek, staring into the trailer's shadowy corners as the golden hour rapidly receded. Finally, she fixed Jack with her gaze.

"Jack," she said, studying his face with those intense, arctic grey eyes. "What did you mean by your comment about Kesien seeing something?"

He stepped toward her, taking her hands in his and caressing her long, thin fingers.

"What if he saw something on patrol?" he said in a quiet voice, squeezing her hands. "Something the others missed somehow? Something enticing enough to Liam Neeson his way through it."

Talia frowned. "Liam Neeson?"

"Yeah," said Jack, glancing at Muriel who was nodding at him. "You know? Being a one-man army to stop the worst kind of bad guys."

At last, Muriel smiled. "Like those movies where he says he has a certain set of skills or something."

Talia's frown deepened.

"What?" Muriel cried. "They were good movies. Liam Neeson destroyed those bad guys that took his daughter."

A cold wave of fear rolled over Jack. Bad guys...damn. He gripped Talia's hands tighter until she turned to look at him.

"Tal, the bad guys!" he cried. "Kesien went after the bad guys."

She shook her head. "Jack, no. Kesien wouldn't attempt to assault Hell alone. He's far too sensible than that."

"Not Samael or Hell, babe," he cried, feeling a deep sense of dread wash over him. "Or his former squad. Bigger prey."

"Lucifer?"

He shook his head. "Not that big. I'd bet my next paycheck that he went after Asmodeus."

The realization hung heavy as Talia and Muriel both got quiet.

"Jack...that's gotta be it," said Muriel.

Talia took hold of Muriel's arm. "Was he patrolling the crossroads?"

The look on Muriel's face told Jack everything. Of course! Kesien was at the crossroads! Probably saw this badass demon skulking along the roads and left formation to follow him. If this thing was too mean for Lucifer's taste, then Jack could only imagine what terrible things Asmodeus would do to one lone angel he encountered on the roads.

But Kesien wasn't stupid. He wouldn't be an easy mark. Still, Jack couldn't get the fact that Lucifer had permabanned this monster from Hell because he played too rough with the other demons.

"Tal," he said, dread in his voice again. "If Kesien went after Asmodeus alone, he could be in real trouble."

Talia nodded, a horrified look spreading across her face. "Muriel, get Oseira and the other cherubim to search for Kesien. We've got to find him quickly. Before he finds Asmodeus."

"I don't know, Talia," said Muriel. "She's been acting a little strangely since Samael's ambush on Eolowen."

"Strangely?" Talia replied. "In what way?"

Muriel shrugged. "I don't know. Forgetful. Distracted. Like she didn't know where she was a couple of times. But she was pretty stressed out by that attack. We all were."

"Regardless," said Talia. "We need the cherubim to find Kesien and quickly. Promise me you'll get her involved with finding Kesien, Muriel."

"I will," she said. "I don't want anything to happen to him."

Jack shuddered. He didn't know anything about this monster that Talia called one of the seven Hell princes. But if he was as mean a bastard as Lucifer claimed, then Kesien didn't stand a chance against Asmodeus.

"What if we use omnificence, Tal?" he asked. "To find Kesien."

She cradled Jack's face in her hands. "Excellent idea, my husband," she said and kissed him.

Someone pounded on the trailer door. "Talia? Jack?" It was Steve Kosinski, set coordinator. "Herb wants the whole cast back on set in another fifteen minutes. Sharp."

He glanced at Talia. Dammit! What now? Had someone found needles and syringes on the set? Monogrammed with his initials?

"Thanks, Steve, we'll be there," Jack answered.

Talia turned back to Muriel. "For now, get the cherubim to locate Kesien. First chance we get, we'll try to use omnificence to search for him. Sing out if you find him."

"Or Asmodeus," Jack said with a groan.

Muriel blinked through the ceiling and disappeared.

Finding Asmodeus wasn't the worst part. How much worse was smiting a Hell prince than a Devourer of Angels or one of Lucifer's lieutenants? Judging by the looks that Muriel and Talia had given him, he knew it would be worse. Much, much worse.

He glanced at Talia, but she was staring past him, eyes wide, mouth agape. Focused on something behind him. And she looked horrified.

6

TALIA TURNED AWAY FROM THE TRAILER DOOR, HER FRIGHTENED GAZE focused on the coffee table. The taupe walls and the narrow space felt claustrophobic. But the small clear plastic bag tucked into a crystal bowl on the coffee table terrified her more than a confining trailer.

Jack squinted, looking confused as she blinked across the maple hardwood floor and bent toward a bowl filled with several baseball-sized, silver-lacquered spheres.

Her breath caught as she picked up the bag of cocaine. The sight of it made her stomach drop and her heart clench.

Shocked, she turned around to him. "Jack…"

His eyes got wide, lips parting, but no words came out. He stammered a moment and finally pointed at the bag. It was the first time she'd seen him speechless in a while. And that made her even more nervous.

"Not you, too," he said finally with a groan.

She frowned. "What does that mean?"

"I hope you don't think I'm the one stashing those bags of flake around the sets," he said, a hand against his silk blue-grey dress shirt.

His shirt was almost the color of the ice blue minidress and flats that wardrobe had dressed her in for the scene by the pond. The ice blue matched her expression of shock that he'd ever include her in that group. And that made her worry. He probably felt like everyone was ganging up on him, silently accusing him of using drugs again.

Turmoil glimmered in his eyes, his gaze glued to the bag. Along with a faint hint of hunger that blossomed on his face. A flash of need. Of want.

As an angel of death, she felt it. And she feared that the sight of the drugs had awakened that sleeping dragon of addiction that he'd fought so hard to cage. It hovered in his beautiful pale green eyes with an intensity that alarmed her.

Would he decide to accept Evan Bellows' offer and return to his old show, *SanFran Confidential*? Where Lucifer had agents ready to ply him with enough drugs to overdose again. She winced. Or force the drugs into his system if he refused them. Like they'd done in the past.

She propped her hands on her hips, fixing him with her best angel of death glower.

"Jack Casey, I'm the one that saved you from the drugs, remember? And when you overdosed, I got your heart started again."

He cast a wary look at her and then at the bag as she slowly walked toward him, studying his eyes, his expression. Through their bond, she felt his anxiousness, saw the sweat break out across his forehead as he stared at the bag.

He was struggling. Fidgeting. Chewing his bottom lip, fingers twitching.

For the first time since Rachel had forced cocaine into his system at the Malibu beach house, she feared that he'd give into that niggling ache for the drug. And right now, it was a powerful shout in his ear. She worried that he'd relapse after nearly a year of being clean.

She held up the bag, his gaze following her movements. He'd stopped talking, all his focus on that bag.

"Jack!" she shouted, yanking the plastic bag away from him.

"What?" he asked, his gaze flicking from the bag to her face.

Like he was mesmerized by the drugs. Was that Lucifer's doing somehow? Some power that had been cast on Jack—something involving this banished Hell prince, Asmodeus? Or was it all Jack's addiction? She wished that Kesien was here. He'd had a lot more experience dealing with human addictions than she had—right now, she'd welcome his advice. She'd never handled addicts well and had failed to stop most of their premature deaths. Those failures even got her roped into that first wager with Lucifer.

Why had Kesien rushed off to pursue this Hell prince loose from Purgatory when the whole guard was preparing to assault the Gates of Hell? Why! And why alone? One angel of death was no match for Asmodeus. He knew that!

"I know how to fix this," she said, stepping back from Jack.

She rushed past him and the taupe couch, into the bedroom. A freestanding white shower stood to the left beside a rectangular, white basin sink. Across from the white-tiled shower was a little room with a small white toilet. She hurried toward it.

He rushed into the bedroom after her. "Talia!"

She snapped up the toilet lid when Jack grabbed her arm.

She met his hungry, desperate stare, afraid that he'd try to take the bag from her. Forcing her to use her angel of death strength to keep the bag away from him.

"Dump it," he said through gritted teeth, shaking. "All of it. I want it gone."

With a flick of her wrist, she emptied the bag into the toilet and flushed it all away. Only then did he let go of her arm.

She took him by the hands and turned him toward her, seeing the mask of sweat across his face, fear burning in his pale green eyes. He held onto her, still shaking.

"Tal…for a moment, snorting some lines was all I could think of." His voice was so pained and quiet. "What's happening to me?"

She wrapped him in her arms, her wings protectively draping around him as she held him close.

"Something is tapping into your addiction struggle, Jack," she said in a soft voice. "It could be Lucifer—going through Rachel, maybe? Or maybe even Asmodeus. Use your block to distance yourself from it."

A deep lament rattled through his chest, his skin so warm against her body as she felt him shudder.

"If you hadn't been here…" He pulled in a pained breath. "I might have bogarted that whole bag."

Her embrace tightened. She was afraid for him. Afraid to leave him alone.

"We can't stay here, Jack," she said in a soft voice. "Something is targeting your addiction issues and I won't watch you overdose again, do you hear me?"

She felt him nod against her hair. "I'll put up my block," he said in a tired voice.

"Especially when you're around Rachel or on set," she added.

He nodded again and she felt his confusion and worry rising.

"Around the flake, you mean," he said, bitterness in his tone.

"Yes," she said finally. "Because another bag of that poison could show up anywhere, Jack. Anywhere."

She couldn't deny that something was intentionally amplifying his weakness. Exploiting it. For the bounty on Jack's head? For leverage to get him to Hell? Or plain old spite? Had Lucifer found a way to exploit Jack's addiction from Hell? She shuddered. Through Berith?

Somehow, she and Jack had to get through this first round of filming quickly, so she could get him back to Eolowen. Distance him from the drugs and Lucifer's demon bounty hunters. Long enough to rescue Berith—without delivering Jack into Lucifer's hands.

Right now, that feat seemed almost impossible. They needed one of the Maker's miracles. And they needed it soon to keep Lucifer in check—and Jack safe.

"And yes, Jack," she said, turning his handsome face toward her. "We have to assume that Rachel is helping Lucifer again—maybe he forced her into it? So, you need to stay as far away from her as you can." She laid her hand against his cheek, caressing. "If she keeps hitting on my husband, I'm going to hit her back."

He smiled, those pale green eyes brightening.

"You saying you're jealous of Rachel?" he asked.

She leaned up and kissed him. "I'm saying that one careless murder marble could ruin her day if she keeps hitting on you."

The corners of his mouth quirked into that sexy little smirk. "I'm really liking Jealous Wife Talia. She's hot."

She wrapped her arms around his neck and blinked him backward. Beside the queen-sized bed.

Surprise lit his green eyes. She gave him her best seductive smile and slid her hands down his chest. Shoving him backward. Onto the bed.

"Hmmm…Jealous Wife Talia is hot," she said with a playful smile. "Let's discuss."

He laughed and pulled her onto the bed against him. With an anxious kiss, he rolled on top of her. Leaning down, he brushed a curl out of her eyes, his kiss long and smoldering.

It left her breathless. And wanting more.

"Discuss? Oh, I'd much rather demonstrate," he said.

His hands slid to the zipper at the back of her dress, unzipping it until the cap sleeves fell off her shoulders. His hot mouth was against hers in a white-hot kiss, his lean body pressing against hers, wings curling around her. The feel of his body against hers was intoxicating and she wanted to make love to him instead of film this horrible script. Or train with the guard. His hands caressed her thighs and slid up her hips toward her bra, unfastening the clasp in back as her breath quickened.

She pressed her fingers to the buttons of his shirt, using her angel powers to unbutton it. His dress pants were already loose as she unzipped them and slid them off his slim hips, revealing grey boxer briefs. He had such a beautiful body, tall, lean, and sculpted, and the feel of his hands against her skin made the angel light within her roil with heat and need. His hot mouth was against her neck, her skin sizzling with his kisses as he slid her bra free, his hands stroking her breasts. His touch made her forget everything but the heat of his fingers and his hot caramel voice whispering her name against her ear. She wrapped her legs around his calves, aching to feel the heat of his skin against hers.

But the pounding on the trailer door reverberated through the space.

Cursing, Jack smacked the bed with his palm and reluctantly rolled onto the edge as she struggled to pull her dress back on and zip it.

Again, the insistent pounding shook the trailer.

"This better be good," he said with a growl and zipped up her dress the last few inches.

After running his hand through his hair to smooth his bangs, Jack got to his feet, pulled on his pants and shirt, and then rushed to the trailer door. Talia stepped into her flats and hurried only a few steps behind him. He yanked open the door and Talia fought back her shocked look.

Director Evan Bellows stood outside, dressed in a short sleeve yellow shirt and tan slacks. His thinning, dark brown hair had a bald spot at the crown, but it was long across his forehead and at his nape. He held out his hands, looking defeated, desperation shining in his brown eyes.

"Jack...we need to talk," said Bellows.

7

Jack glared at his former director. Dude had shit timing. Besides, when the cast and crew of *The Divine Newlyweds Show* saw Evan outside his trailer door, they'd go apeshit. They were already pissed at him, accusing him of flirting with Rachel and stashing flake around the set. Falling into his old habits again.

He'd have to be a new kind of stupid to cheat on the love of his life. The one he'd fought for to his last breath. To Hell and back.

Much less with the woman that almost killed his career—and him. On Earth and in Hell.

"Dude, I'm due back on set any minute," he said. "I told you I'd think about it. You need to give me a little more time."

Evan's balding hair was windblown and he looked like he'd slept in his clothes. Like he'd rushed over here for some reason. Didn't make a lot of sense. Phil, his agent, told Evan to give him a week to decide and his old director seemed fine with that.

Until today.

"Jack, you know the clock is ticking," Evan replied, an edge in his voice, hands in motion as he paced in front of the trailer. "You know that. Lare's disappeared. There's no show lead. Sure, we can stall with a few episodes without him, but without a ratings draw like you,

SanFran Confidential is history." Evan reached out and gripped his sleeve. "Jack...you're the only person that can save this show." He shook his head. "Don't let it end like this. Please, Jack—give your fans what they want."

Jack pulled away from his hold. "They want Drum and Davy, Evan. Together. As partners again."

Evan sighed and folded his arms against his chest. "But if they can't have them back as partners, the fans still want Davy back on the show, Jack. Returning to the department—as the show's hero. They've been writing letters for two years, begging us to bring you back. The letters haven't stopped."

Hadn't stopped? Jack stared at him in surprise. He figured some of his fans would write a few letters and then give up after a couple of months. They'd been writing into the show for two years? A lump rose in his throat. He owed them more than a quick no to Evan.

"They're still writing in?" he said in a hushed voice.

All this time, he'd still believed bits and pieces of Rachel and Lare's lies, deep down. He'd never quite erased the programming they'd so expertly delivered to him while they were systematically breaking him down for Lucifer. He hated to admit it, but even now, those lies hurt—because he feared the kernel of truth behind them.

But he hated to disappoint those fans that had kept writing letters and petitioning the network. For two years! Not knowing the full story. Would they even want him back if they knew about his flake addiction? They had to know though. His firing from the show had been the hottest story in Hollywood that entire year, the rumors and undercurrents of his drug addiction were all over social media. In all the tabloids and magazines, too.

Evan nodded. "That's right, Jack. Still writing in...every single week. And Lare's ratings have dropped. Badly." He ran his hand over the balding spot at his crown. "Network's concerned. Questioning. Wondering if the show's run its course. Lare can't carry the show alone anymore. Drummond Turillo can't. They want you at the helm."

Was it because Lucifer had called in Lare's contract? Or had fans lost interest in a buddy cop series without buddy cops? If the network was ready to cancel the whole show, was there even enough story left for Davy to helm the show alone?

He stared down at his feet. It was such a huge career gamble. If he was wrong, he'd ruin both *The Cinderella Hour* and his career.

Again.

"Evan…" He propped his hands on his hips, wings rustling. He wondered if Evan could hear them even if Talia's angel of death magic hid them from view. "What if you're wrong? What if the network doesn't like the numbers and pulls the plug after a few more episodes? Then I'm screwed."

Evan's face brightened as he motioned Jack out of the trailer. "Would you just come over to Studio 18 and discuss it with me, Jack? Please? Look at the scripts. See the storylines for yourself. See the numbers—and the polls."

He owed Evan—and his fans—that much.

"Jack, I can guarantee you one season if you sign aboard again. Canceling it after a couple of episodes when they'd finally brought you back would kill the show with fans."

Evan had a point. And at two plus million an episode, that would be a cool forty-six million in his pocket. He and Talia could live the rest of their lives like kings on that.

He ran his fingers through his hair, not knowing what to do. He had to at least discuss it if it meant guaranteeing his and Talia's future on Earth. Even if it meant he had to walk away from acting afterward.

"All right," he said, glancing at Talia. "Let's talk."

"Jack, you can't," she said in a shrill whisper.

"No promises yet, Evan," he said, his gaze returning to his former director. "But it can't hurt to look at the scripts. See what storylines they're offering me."

The idea of not having to play himself appealed to him. Sometimes, that was exhausting. Like now, with most of the cast and crew treating him like a traitor. And a drug addict.

The hint of a smile warmed Evan's dark brown eyes as he motioned for Jack to follow him. "No, of course not!" Evan gripped Jack's arm as he led him out of the trailer. "I get it. Let's talk about these scripts. Discuss the storylines. Show you where the show is headed if you come home, Jack."

Home. He scoffed. They threw him out years ago and never looked back. Didn't even bother to check if he was all right. If he had a place to stay or food to eat. He winced. Like his mother a decade ago when his dad died.

For most of his life, home had only existed in his head.

The memory of Purgatory rushed back to him. Hugging his old man again after a decade. Talking to him man to man, something he'd been denied and had ached for all these years. He had to teach himself to be a man and he'd done a piss poor job at it, too.

He hadn't realized how deep that pain ran until he saw Dad standing there in the illusion of the cabin on San Juan Island, immersing himself in the ghosts of those summer vacations. When they'd all still been a family. Because those four fleeting years had been the last time they'd all been together. And happy.

Even now, the memory of seeing his dad again choked him up and sent pain through his chest, so raw and sharp that it felt like the night Dad died. When Jack was just seventeen.

God, he'd never felt that alone before. Until Lucifer dragged him off to Hell for an eternity away from Talia.

He never wanted to feel that alone again. Ever.

"We can talk about script approval, too, Jack," said Evan, tossing out another carrot.

Script approval? His eyes widened. Maybe they'd even let him direct an episode or two?

"I'll be back shortly, Tal," he called to her.

Talia's gaze narrowed and she looked frightened as she followed him out the door. "I'm holding you to that, Jack."

She was worried he'd fall back into those old patterns. The ones that had caused Pravuil to write him off and end his Book of Life and Death at twenty-six. And require saving. As bad as all of that had been, he was still grateful. Because if he hadn't needed saving, he would have never met Talia.

He paused, leaning over and giving her an anxious kiss. "I'm counting on it," he said with a smirk and lowered his voice to a whisper. "But seriously, if I'm not back in fifteen minutes, come and get me, huh?"

That made her smile. "I'm setting my stopwatch now," she replied in a whisper. "Already counting the minutes."

"Love you, Mrs. Casey."

She was grinning as he left with Evan.

As he followed Evan past the line of trailers toward Studio 18, Jennifer Collins approached from the other direction, that ubiquitous clipboard in hand. She stopped at the steps of his trailer, staring, mouth gaping, shock glimmering in her brown eyes.

Talia stood in the trailer doorway and greeted the show's set coordinator as Jack disappeared around the corner of the Studio 22 building.

Shit. Now, Jennifer thought he was betraying the show. And the entire cast and crew would know it by the time he got back to his trailer.

This was the worst shoot ever. He'd be lucky if any of the cast or crew spoke to him again after this conversation with Evan.

Including Herb who might just have a heart attack when he heard the news.

Evan was quiet as they walked in the shadow of Studio 22, veering around it to the sidewalk and heading right toward Studio 18. He remembered how strange it felt to walk away from Studio 18, where he'd been for years, and into Studio 22 after he'd been fired from his *SanFran Confidential* cameo.

Now, it felt unsettling to approach his old building again. It had been a while since he'd been inside these squat grey walls. Where the flake had flowed like winter in Vail and Rachel and Lare had been gaslighting him about everything. Feeding him coke like vitamins until he'd blackout and take out his lows on anyone and everyone. Including himself.

As he approached the door into Studio 18, he caught a glimpse of Roy the cameraman slipping around the building, camera on his shoulder. Rhonda was behind him with another camera.

Damn.

Were they filming him to take the evidence of his betrayal back to Herb? Show it to the rest of the cast along with the other dailies. It made him feel angry. And a little like the last days he'd been on *SanFran Confidential* when no one wanted him around. For anything.

"Come on inside, Jack," said Evan as he held open the studio door. "I've got the scripts all laid out in the rehearsal room."

Jack nodded and started inside.

"Stop right there, Casey!"

The sound of Lare Dumont's furious shout stopped him in his tracks.

Dammit. When was this douchebag going to give up and relocate his demon ass back to Hell where he belonged? Lucifer probably sent Lare to annoy him until he could send more bounty hunters. Or hurry Jack into trying to free Berith without preparing for the assault. So, Lucifer could torture him alongside her for eternity.

Regardless, he'd like nothing better than to bitch-slap Lare back to Hell. So, if his dumb ass wanted a fight with a dude that had seraphim powers, he'd give him exactly what he wanted.

Grinning, Jack whirled around as Lare Dumont rushed up the stairs at him. He shook his head.

Tyler Hughes stood behind Lare, glaring at Jack from a comfortable distance as Lare tried to intimidate him.

Evan looked startled by Lare's arrival. No, shocked. Especially after the dude had disappeared for months and then showed up like nothing happened. If Evan knew where Dumont had been, he'd lose his mind.

"Lare Dumont." Evan's brow furrowed and he looked pissed. "You'd better have one helluva good story about ghosting your hit show for months."

Lare's fierce glare didn't budge from Jack.

"Evan, better call waste services," said Jack. "Looks like something took a couple of ginormous dumps on the studio's sidewalk."

"What are you doing here, Casey?" Lare demanded, arms crossed as Hughes scowled at Jack.

"Cleaning up another one of your messes," he said in a weary voice and shook his head.

Lare gritted his teeth, pointing a finger at Jack. "Dammit! This is my show! You stay the hell away from it!"

Jack chuckled. "Was your show." He motioned over his shoulder at the open door into Studio 18. "Now, it's mine—if I want it."

"I'll kill you!" Lare shouted, eyes burning red.

Evan's eyes lit with terror as he shrank back from Lare and grabbed hold of the studio door.

Jack laughed, sending his former costar-turned-demon into a blind rage.

Dumont leaped at him.

They tumbled into the grass as Hughes rushed into the fight, his eyes also glowing red.

Lare Dumont threw the first punch, but Jack rolled out of the way. Dumont's fist thumped against the ground.

Jack kicked Dumont in the chest, propelling him backward as Hughes came at him. His fist connected with Hughes' jaw, dropping him to the ground.

Dumont grabbed Jack around the neck and hauled him backward. Throwing a punch that exploded against his chest.

For a moment, Jack couldn't pull in a breath.

He wheezed, dodging another of Dumont's leaps, and pulled in a shallow breath. Aiming low, his fist slammed into Dumont's gut.

His former costar crumpled from the blow. Dumont grabbed his belly and hit the ground hard as Hughes came at him again.

Ducking underneath Hughes, Jack flipped his former movie costar over his shoulder. Hughes skidded across the grass.

But the kidney punch dropped Jack to his knees. He gasped, the pain like a hot poker. Dumont hit him again.

Jack fell into the grass, writhing against the twin blows to his left kidney. His wings curled flat against his shoulders and he couldn't breathe.

Again, Dumont lunged at him.

Thrusting upward, Jack uppercut Dumont, stopping his forward momentum cold.

He landed another punch and then a left hook to the dude's jaw. Staggering Dumont.

The right cross dropped Dumont to the ground. And he didn't get up again.

Hughes kicked Jack in the right knee.

Swallowing a cry of pain, Jack weathered the blow. Turned. Landed a right hooks.

Hughes screamed and grabbed hold of his nose.

"My nose!" he yelped, his voice shrill and nasal. "You broke my nose, you bastard!"

Clutching his face, Hughes dropped down beside Dumont, trying to get his demon BFF back on his feet. But Dumont rolled back and forth in the grass, looking dazed.

"Casey!" Dumont shouted in a hoarse whine. "This isn't over!"

"You're welcome to try me any time, Drum," Jack replied with a snicker. "You know where to find me."

When Jack turned around, Roy and Rhonda were crouched on the sidewalk, cameras rolling. Along with a dozen paparazzi.

He groaned. Dammit! They'd filmed the whole thing.

Warm stickiness clung to his mouth and above his left eye. He brushed his fingers across one corner of his mouth, feeling his lip swelling. His hand came away bloody.

"Jack!" Talia rushed at him, hands against his face. "You're bleeding!"

"So are Lare and Hughes," he said with a crooked smirk. "And I made sure of it."

Guess his fifteen minutes were up.

Roy stopped filming and moved across the sidewalk to Jack. "Got every single punch that was thrown. Herb's gonna love this."

Jack shook his head. "Or fire me."

"Not a chance, Jack," said Rhonda, grinning as she patted her camera. "Best unscripted thing I've filmed since this season started."

Talia held onto him as he turned toward Evan and shook his head.

"Sorry, Evan. Don't think I belong on your show anymore—and neither does Lare. Don't want to brawl with my costar every day. I'm out."

He felt bad for his fans, but he hoped they were more Jack Casey fans than Davy Pierson fans. Because he wasn't going back to that hell. He'd spent enough time there in his short life.

"Jack, no!" Evan cried, rushing toward him, eyes filled with alarm, but Jack waved him off. "You haven't even read the scripts yet!"

"Doesn't matter," he said and smiled at Talia. "I made a commitment to The Cinderella Hour. And it changed my life forever. For the better. I'm going to see it through to the end, Evan. I owe them everything. I'm not walking out on them now."

Evan groaned, hanging his head. "I get it, Jack," he said in a defeated tone and cast a disgusted look at Lare Dumont struggling to stand up. "The show's got a lot of problems right now. I get that this isn't about money—that it never was about money."

"Take care of yourself, Evan," said Jack.

With his arm around Talia, he turned away from the studio door. And almost ran into Roy's camera. Roy grinned at him.

"Got that scene, too," he said and reached out, patting Jack on the shoulder. "One I think the whole cast and crew will want to see. Nice work, kid."

Jack felt the heat rise in his cheeks, the blood hot against his face.

Rhonda hefted her camera off her shoulder and poked Roy's shoulder, looking worried.

"Dammit, Roy," she scolded. "Kid needs some medical attention after that fight." She motioned Jack to follow her. "Come on. Let's get you to the set doctor."

Jack shook his head. "Does everybody think I'm a goat?"

Talia laughed as she put her arm around his waist. "Come on, kid," she said, holding him close. "Let's go find that set doctor."

"I'm your husband, not your goat," he replied, feeling a little light-headed.

Rhonda pulled out her phone and called the set doctor as they walked around the building, turned left, and strolled down the sidewalk back to Studio 22, Roy filming everything. Talia opened the studio door and he stepped through the threshold, unsteady as he moved past the set stage lit up with an array of lights for tomorrow's filming schedule. Steve Kosinski handed off a paper list to a production assistant and rushed toward him.

"Jack, are you all right?" he asked, motioning them toward the office on the far right. "Dr. Sarasin is waiting for you. Herb's pulling his hair out."

Talia opened the door into the tiny glass office on the right. The mint green room had a small black conference table in the center that seated six people and had whiteboards on all four walls. Dr. Sarasin, dressed in a short-sleeved lavender blouse and white pants, sat at the table, a small blue bag beside her.

Herb made laps around the room, passing each wall of whiteboards, and muttering to himself. He whirled around when he heard the door open.

"Jack!"

Herb rushed across the room and gently steered Jack out of Talia's hold and into an empty chair beside the set doctor. Jack dropped into it, feeling dizzy as blood trickled into his left eyebrow and eyelashes and dripped from his lip.

Dr. Sarasin's hazel eyes softened as she opened her bag and pulled out some gauze. Gently, she blotted the cut above his eye and then his lip.

"What the hell happened, Jack?" Herb cried.

"This, Herb," said Roy who rushed over with a tablet computer.

Herb looked horrified, shaking his head as the raw footage played. Jack heard his conversation with Evan fill the room as he and his former director walked along the sidewalk to Studio 18.

"Jack…why?" Herb sounded shaken. No, devastated. "You'd really walk away now? The show can't survive without you. You know that! Jack, please don't do this."

Jack winced and laid his hand against his head as the doctor blotted the blood from the cut above his eye.

"Wait for it, Herb," said Roy as he flashed a smile at Jack.

"What are you doing here, Casey!" Lare Dumont's voice crackled through the office.

"This is going to need stitches, Jack," said Dr. Sarasin as she reached into her bag.

Jack pulled away, but Talia stepped forward and picked up fresh gauze. "Let me put pressure on it while you prepare," she said to the doctor as she winked at him.

The gold light from her fingers warmed his forehead as Talia hid her healing light behind the gauze. He smiled. Knitting the gash together so he wouldn't need stitches.

"I'll kill you!" Lare Dumont's shout filled the room.

Herb was glued to Roy's tablet, watching the brawl in front of Studio 18 with a mixture of dread and fascination.

"Sorry, Evan." Jack's voice echoed through the room, blaring from the tablet. "Don't think I belong on your show anymore—and neither does Lare. Don't want to brawl with my costar every day. I'm out."

Herb gasped, his gaze shooting to Jack.

"You're—you're out?" he said barely above a whisper like he didn't believe it.

Jack nodded.

"Jack, no!" Evan's voice reverberated and Herb cringed, closing one eye as he kept watching the video roll past. "You haven't even read the scripts yet!"

"Doesn't matter. I made a commitment to The Cinderella Hour. And it changed my life forever. For the better. I'm going to see it through to the end, Evan. I owe them everything. I'm not walking out on them now."

Herb let out a peal of laughter and rushed over to Jack, ruffling his hair. "That's the most beautiful thing I've ever watched, Jack," he cried. "Brings tears of joy to my eyes." Then he got quiet and turned back to Jack. "You weren't acting, were you? For the cameras!"

"Of course not!" Jack yelled.

Herb laughed. "Kidding, Jack. I'm so relieved." He turned to Roy. "And I'm ecstatic about you and Rhonda capturing these—amazing unscripted moments. Those shots are totally going into the first episode."

"What?" Jack snapped up from the chair but grabbed hold of the table when the room tilted. "You're printing that shitshow?"

"You bet I am," Herb replied, a gleeful smile on his face.

Dude had lost his mind.

"Why?" Jack demanded.

It had nothing to do with anything divine or newlyweds.

"Because it's part of the conflict on the set and I'm putting in," said Herb with a decisive nod.

Jack grabbed a piece of gauze and pressed it to his mouth. "I'll be in my trailer," he said with a sigh. "Rehearsing the next scene—where I pass out."

Talia was at his elbow, an arm around his waist. "I'll make sure he's okay."

"Script's gonna change, Jack," Herb called to him. "We're incorporating the set drama, including the conflicts with Rachel and Eric."

"Great," Jack said with a groan as he opened the office door. "I look forward to the scene where she clocks me with those damned red-soled high heels of hers. After Eric pounds my face against the set floor, accusing me of flirting with Rachel. And I'd rather flirt with Lucifer than her."

Talia shook her head. "That I wouldn't want to watch."

"Me either, babe," said Jack, leaning on her as she led him out of the studio toward their trailer.

She helped him up the two steps into the trailer, past the sofa and kitchen, and into the bedroom. He tugged her toward the bed.

"Now..." he said with a grin. "Where were we?"

A devious smile curved across her face as she gently pushed him onto the bed.

"Right here," she said and tossed the blanket over him. "So you can rest, Jack Casey."

"From a fight with those two lightweights?" he shouted in protest.

Already, she was nodding.

"I didn't even call up a murder marble this time!"

She got quiet, studying him for a moment. "I know, but you're unsteady and look a little dazed, Jack. That worries me."

Frowning, he laid back against the pillow, his head pounding, the room tilting a little. Dammit, she had a point. He'd held off half of Lucifer's demon army before. Fought Lucifer blow for seraphim blow and was winning, too. He could splatter demons like water balloons. Why had a fight with two douchebags like Lare and Hughes banged him up like this?

A cold chill rolled over him. He reached back and frantically felt for his wings. Still there.

"My halo still on?" he asked.

She smiled. "Not sure how, but yes, it's still glowing a soft white gold, Jack."

Some of his panic had fled, but it spiked again. Had he lost the seraphim powers? Had the seraphim finally figured out a way to take back those powers he'd accidentally summoned from the healing stone back at the vineyard in Santa Rosa?

He held out his hand and summoned a murder marble.

"What are you doing?" she asked, scrutinizing him.

When the gold, marble-sized sphere appeared in his hand, he blew on it until it dissipated like smoke and vanished. Still had Talia's rare powers.

He extended his arms and called up a seraphim ward. It appeared like a bubble around him, humming with white light. He let it fade.

"Still have all my powers," he said finally.

But he couldn't deny that he felt weakened after this fight. Why? He needed to know why. Had Lare or Hughes done something to him?

"Oh, shit..." His voice trailed off as his hand shot to his left shoulder, wildly searching for a soul tether.

Had those two bastards tagged him with a new soul tether?

But he felt nothing connected to either shoulder.

"What is it?" Talia asked, sitting down on the bed beside him.

"Thought maybe Luci got those two douchebags to tag me with a new soul tether." He sighed and reached out, gripping Talia's hand. "Tal, I'm not sure what this is exactly. But something's off. I shouldn't be this tired or busted up after fighting Lucifer's clown brigade."

She was quiet. Too quiet.

"What's that about?" he asked, motioning at her.

"What?" she replied.

He pointed at her. "That. If you weren't worried, you'd have argued with me, told me it wasn't possible, that I was fine, or given me some other sound reason why this wasn't happening."

She bowed her head, nodding. "You're right. I haven't seen you like this since you were tethered. Something's wrong and we need to figure out what. Fast." She glanced around, her mouth opening, but no sound came out.

She was summoning someone with those angel notes that he couldn't hear.

"Which angel did you just text?"

"Kesien," she said, her tone sounding concerned again. "But I got no response. I'm worried, Jack. This isn't like him to ignore a direct summons."

Where was Kesien? Even he was getting worried about the dude. Had Lucifer gotten hold of him? Or had Samael? Either possibility was terrifying. If Lucifer had Kesien and Berith, the evil bastard might force them to choose one or the other. And the thought of doing that made him ill.

"Maybe we should search for him with omnificence now?" Jack said and motioned toward the front of the trailer. "You and Muriel both have been worried about him, yet no one's seen or heard from him. Including the cherubim. Not even a damned postcard that said, vacaying in sunny Revengeland. Going after my douchebag former squad. Wish you were here. Love, your angelbro, Kesien."

Talia's gaze was distant. Like she was either shooting the shit with Azrael or her squad. Or she was already using her rare angel powers to search for Kesien.

But her concentration was interrupted as Muriel appeared in the set trailer bedroom, looking distressed again.

"Talia!" Muriel called.

Her panicked expression scared Jack.

"What's wrong, Muriel?" he asked.

Talia glanced over at him and then back at Muriel.

"What?" he asked.

"You didn't make a joke," Talia said in an intense voice. "You're as worried as I am."

He nodded. She knew him too well.

"And you've got good reason to be," said Muriel, rushing over to Talia. "Talia, Asmodeus was seen along the crossroads."

"What?" She jumped up and took Muriel by the shoulders. "Then it's true. Kesien did see Asmodeus." She winced. "And he went after the Hell prince. Alone. That's why he's not responding to any of our calls."

"Samael must have brokered a deal between Lucifer and Asmodeus," said Muriel, a dire look on her face. "Lucifer must still have some use for him, but why delay us from trying to rescue Berith? That's what Lucifer wants—for Azrael and Jack to attempt to save her."

Talia's winter pale face turned ghostly white. "What if Asmodeus is defying Lucifer and trying to take control of Earth?" She shuddered. "Including killing Jack for that bounty?"

"Pravuil agrees," said Muriel, shrugging. "He thinks that Lucifer released Asmodeus from his exile to hunt Jack."

Talia shook her head as she sat down beside Jack again. "It means that he's probably hunting angels, too," she said, sounding ill.

Muriel dropped down beside Talia on the bed, looking like she'd eaten one too many Dove chocolates.

"What's that mean exactly?" Jack asked in a quiet voice. "Why send this thing to hunt me down when Lucifer wants me in Hell?"

Both Talia and Muriel looked up at him.

"He's either out there wreaking havoc to try and hurry you along," said Muriel in a dire tone.

Talia's eyes got glassy. "Or he's here, Jack. On Earth. Hunting you on his own and trying to collect your bounty."

Either way, that meant a bad time for him. Dude was a Hell prince, according to Talia. So, a lot more powerful than Zanth had been as Lucifer's archdemoness first lieutenant. Besides, this dude was so nasty that Lucifer banished his demon ass from Hell. No, this dude was trouble with a capital D. If Asmodeus was here on Earth, then he and Talia needed to find him and stop him. Before Asmodeus hit him. Hard. When he least expected it.

Great. Another high-level demon was gunning for him. Like reruns of his honeymoon—without them paying any residuals. That was terrifying.

"You think Kesien saw this demon whack job joyriding along Heaven's highways and got ganked following it to the next rest stop? After it caught the next non-stop flight down to Earth?"

Muriel and Talia stared at each other. In the mounting silence, Jack knew they were tossing around those angel notes, leaving him out of the conversation.

He frowned. "Why, that's a good point, Jack," he said. "Thanks for bringing that up, Jack. We'll look into it right away. Cool? Cool!"

Talia turned back to him, but she didn't smile. For a moment, he saw the data and information roll across her luminous grey angel of death eyes. She was using omnificence. Finally, her gaze returned to him.

"By High House," she said in a small, quiet voice. "Maybe Kesien is here…on Earth?"

"Did you locate him with omnificence?" Jack asked.

She shook her head. "No, I can't locate him anywhere. Either someone's shielding him with angelic or demonic power or…"

"Or what?" Jack asked.

"Or he's been erased from existence," she said in a shaky voice.

She cast a frightened look at Muriel and it had amplified when she turned back to him.

"We have to find him."

Jack's eyes narrowed. "I'm going to hope that he's being shielded so no one locates him. And not in that big demon's hands. So, what did this demon dude do that caused Lucifer to red card him?"

Talia stared at him in confusion, shaking her head. "Red card?"

Muriel shrugged. "Sorry, Jack. That an acting reference?"

"Soccer," he said with a sigh. "Okay, changing sports. What'd Asmodeus do to make Luci banish him for unnecessary roughness?"

"Football," Muriel said with a smile. "The other kind that you human weirdos play."

"Football? That game really doesn't involve using the foot at all." Talia looked perplexed. "I know you occasionally punt that pointy ball, but only as a last resort. Shouldn't it be called handball instead?"

Jack broke into a fit of laughter. Angels. Dealt with the Middling and Purgatory and demons and weird powers like murder marbles and omnificence. No issue. But the term football confused them because they only kicked the ball *some of the time.*

"Okay, I'll stick to basketball or baseball," he said finally.

"Or hockey," said Muriel. "That one's pretty straightforward. I like hockey."

"Okay, Luci gave Asmodeus ten in the penalty box?" said Jack. "For what?"

Muriel frowned and finally shrugged. "I'm not sure, Jack," said Muriel. "That's a question for Pravuil." She sighed. "Or Berith. Maybe Azrael knows, but I hate to bother him right now. He's pretty distraught."

"Agreed," said Talia. "Muriel, I'll ask Pravuil about Asmodeus' history, so we'll know how to engage this beast."

Jack nodded. "And soon. In case Asmodeus grabbed Kesien and is hiding his presence from us."

Nodding, she fixed Muriel with her gaze. "That's what I'm afraid of, too, Jack. Especially since I can't specifically locate Kesien's whereabouts with omnificence."

Muriel rose from the bed and extended her wings. "I'll get Deemah down here while you talk to Pravuil. Maybe she can fill in the gaps? She's been in Kesien's squad from the beginning."

"Thanks, Muriel," said Talia, getting to her feet.

Suddenly, both Talia and Muriel's gazes darted to the ceiling.

"What now?" Jack said with a groan. More of those damned angel notes he couldn't hear.

"Pravuil's calling me back to Eolowen," said Talia, turning back to him. "And…Azrael wants an update."

She looked frightened.

"About what?" Jack asked as he moved beside her and rubbed her shoulders.

"God's Scribe wants to talk about the transference power." She laid her hand against his face, caressing his cheek. "About awakening it."

He stared at her a moment, not liking the idea of her jaunting off to the spire with that dusty red monster hunting angels. And him.

"I'm coming with you," said Muriel, extending her wings as she stepped closer to Talia. "To update Azrael and then I'll come right back to guard Jack."

Having Muriel at Talia's side made him feel more comfortable.

"Good," he said, sliding his game face into place and forcing a relaxed, comfortable smile on his face.

When God's Scribe summoned her to Heaven, she had to go. As much as he hated to be apart from her. Especially with Rachel hitting on him and bags of cocaine appearing all over the set like party favors. But he wouldn't remind her of that right now. She already had too much on her mind without fretting over—or smiting—Rachel Daniels.

Her brow furrowed, sadness illuminating her luminous grey eyes.

"But I can't leave Jack alone," she said, pain shining in her eyes. "Not with a Hell prince searching for him and me unable to locate him with omnificence."

"I'll send Anahera and Daidrean down with Deemah to keep watch over your headstrong Hollywood hottie until I come back," Muriel said, smirking at Jack. "Er, husband."

Talia bit her lip as she glanced from Muriel to Jack. "Will that be enough protection?"

Muriel snickered. "He's got seraphim powers, Talia. And with three angels of death beside him, he should be safe until you and I return."

"What about from Rachel Daniels?" she asked crossing her arms against her chest as her wings flexed. "I don't like her hitting on my husband. And with the drugs appearing on set…"

She wasn't that worried about Rachel. It was the drugs that frightened her. No, not the drugs. The chance that he'd overdose—that's what was really troubling her. He took her hands in his and squeezed them.

"You're afraid I'll do a few lines, aren't you?" he asked, grimacing.

His loving angel of death wife didn't even blink at that statement. She shook her head. "No, I'm afraid I'll lose you, Jack," she said, gripping his hands. "To an overdose."

He was right. She would never forget his first—hopefully only—one. He pulled her into his embrace and gave her an urgent kiss. "I will flush every bag I find, babe. I give you my word."

Her eyes turned watery. "But what if Rachel—or something more powerful—tries to force it into you?"

Didn't have an answer for that one. He had no idea what he'd do if Rachel tried to mainline him with it again. The thought of that made him shudder. But why would Rachel return to her old ways now? Was Herb trying to stir up some familiar conflicts for the show's fans again? Increase the show's drama in absence of competitions and sexual tension? He planned to talk to Herb again. Pitch some of his ideas to return the show to the old format in a new way. To keep the old married couples exciting.

He shook his head, flashing his *everything's gonna be all right* smile at her.

"She won't," he said, stroking his fingers down her forearms. "Because I'm going to turn this show around."

Her eyes widened.

"That's right, babe," he said, pulling her close. "I'm going to give Herb his unscripted moments and the show its competitions back."

The worry returned to her luminous grey gaze. "How?"

He grinned. "By turning this buying-a-house segment into a dream home competition. It's going to become the Divine Makeover Show. Renovating the backyards, kitchens, and master bedrooms. The winner of the challenges will win an all-expense-paid renovation of their new place. And turn it into a newlyweds' divine dream home."

"Jack!" Talia cried. "I love it! It will be like designing my wedding dress and the bouquets."

He nodded. "Exactly, except it'll be our home."

Home. God, nothing had felt like home for a decade or more. Except when he was with Talia. He wanted them to have a place to call home, too. A celestial haven here on Earth. Demon-proofed and airy enough that Talia's squad could spread their wings a little and not take out a window or something. Room for him and Talia to stretch their wings. Together.

"A real home, Talia, not my shithole apartment. You and me. As a married couple."

Her eyes got misty. She threw her arms around him and held him close, kissing him hard on the lips.

"Could I help decorate it?" she asked in a quiet voice.

"Of course, babe! It's going to be your haven here on Earth. But if it's part of the show, we'll have to do it together, if that's okay?"

Her smile became a grin as tears brimmed in her eyes. "Like a real married couple," she said in a wistful voice. "It sounds divine, Jack. But only if we can get a place by the ocean. I want you to have that beach house again. The one you loved so much."

He wrapped her tighter in his arms, wings shifting, and held her against his chest.

"Best wife ever," he said against her ear. "I'd marry you all over again, Mrs. Casey."

"And I'd say I do all over again, Mr. Casey," she replied, nuzzling his neck.

"Can we do the honeymoon again, too?" he asked.

She nodded. "Minus all the demons."

He laughed, reluctantly letting her go. "All right, Mrs. Casey," he said and stepped back from her. "Go talk to Pravuil about transference while I convince Herb to do a season about renovating houses into dream homes. He can only fire me once."

"Muriel, get the squad here," said Talia, her gaze still on him. "I'm not leaving until they're here to protect Jack."

In the silence, he saw Muriel open her mouth, but no sound came out. More angel notes. Less than a minute later, Deemah appeared, long walnut hair trailing across her shoulders, gold shield of light in her hand. Anahera blinked into the room beside her, taller, short red hair windblown as she stood beside Deemah. And Daidrean dropped down from the ceiling, his dark brown hair shaggy, soft grey eyes looking a little sleepy as he stood beside Anahera.

"Squad reporting to protection detail," said Anahera in her soprano voice. "Hi, Jack."

"Hey there, squad," he said with a wave. "Any news on Kesien's location yet?"

A strained look tightened Deemah's features, worry shining in her grey eyes. "No, but we've got to find him fast. Before he finds Asmodeus. Or that monster finds him."

"Don't worry, Deemah," said Talia. "As soon as I return from a conference with Pravuil, I'll use omnificence again and search for his Enochian brand here and in the Heavens. And I'll search for his light, too. In the meantime, protect Jack at all costs. Blink him back to Eolowen if you have to, but keep him safe."

"Acknowledged," said Anahera.

"Be good, Jack," Muriel replied as she spread her wings.

"Do I have to?" he asked.

Talia, Muriel, and the squad turned toward him and shouted in unison. "Yes!"

"Love you, Mrs. Casey," he said, waving at her.

Talia smiled. "Love you, too, Jack."

Together, Talia and Muriel blinked through the ceiling and headed back to Heaven to meet with Pravuil. And awaken some rare angel power. Without him.

8

AMONG THE RUSTLE OF THICK, DEEP SHADOWS WITHIN THE SMOKY trailer, Kesien felt darkness oozing around him as all his senses awoke from a strange, sleep-like state. Angels didn't sleep, so these half-awake sensations made him uncomfortable.

No, it unnerved him. Had all of the angels on Eolowen's terrace felt like this before being erased from existence?

All around him, muffled sounds grew louder. Shuffling. Shifting. Things moving in the darkness.

He focused on his light, so dim against these heavy shadows, and let it rise. It pulsed through him, warming his face and hands, ruffling his wing feathers.

As the trailer took shape in the shadows, the shuffling sounds grew louder, and Kesien knew.

Asmodeus had returned. He felt him nearby.

Squinting, he tried to slough off this weird feeling of oblivion that had engulfed him and still clung to the edges of his senses. And was thankfully dissipating. Unlike so many of Azrael's guard, their celestial lights extinguished forever. That moment still ached through him and no matter how he tried to tamp it down inside, he couldn't move forward.

How long had he been trapped in this dark trailer, hands and feet bound, wings draped in shadowy bindings that held him down and stopped him from flying? From escaping.

He closed his eyes, feeling across the distance for Talia's Enochian mark.

Angels of death each left an Enochian brand upon the Earth that burned with their presence. Visible to other angels of death (and demons), it allowed them to locate each other. In absence of the brand, they found each other by uttering the angel notes in the Enochian tongue. The angel language they used to communicate with each other. Notes that humans couldn't hear. Demons could hear most of the notes (except the uppermost registers), but only a handful understood the language. He'd been calling out in that range for hours, but only darkness had greeted him.

He had hoped to get a signal out by bombarding Asmodeus' wards with a constant barrage of angel notes. But so far, nothing had penetrated the dark wards.

Where was Talia? Where was his squad? The guard?

Were they with Azrael running relentless drills across Eolowen's terrace and along the rolling meadows behind the grand hall? With Berith in Lucifer's hands, Azrael was so distracted and struggling to maintain that archangel detachment required to assault the Gates of Hell.

The archangel had even petitioned the seraphim to summon Abaddon back to Heaven. To help him plan this assault to rescue Berith and recapture the Book of Secrets. The whole guard knew that the Book of Secrets was the only reason Heaven was allowing Azrael and the guard to venture down into Hell. They wouldn't take such a risk for one angel of death.

If Talia and his squad were still on the Earth, their brands would burn in white Holy fire across it. Asmodeus' wards didn't even allow him to sense angel presences outside this trailer. Nevertheless, he had to keep pounding against the wards. And he had to keep searching. Talia and her rare angel powers were his only chance to escape Asmodeus. Before the Hell prince ambushed Talia and killed Jack.

Had that already happened? While he was trapped in this abandoned trailer?

Kesien sat still and listened for any sounds around him, trying to pinpoint Asmodeus' position. He felt the Hell prince sliding among the shadows within the trailer, his attention focused on the human presence. Rachel Daniels. These shadow bindings even prevented him from accessing her Book of Life and Death to know how this situation ended for her.

Until he had a way to fight back or alert his squad, he did his best not to draw Asmodeus' attention as he kept searching for the death angels' glow of Holy fire. Anywhere on the Earth. Where it burned brighter than the sun for all celestial beings.

He winced. Including Asmodeus. Could he see that Holy fire, too?

Gritting his teeth, Kesien balled his hands into fists and fought against the shadowy bonds restraining him. Trying to break free. Trying to locate the presence of even one angel's Holy fire.

Angelic Holy fire should have been immediately visible to him. Human-made walls and structures didn't stop angelic sight, but something interfered with his senses inside this abandoned trailer. This murky haze draped in shadows writhed around him like spirits. Like Hell creatures.

Something banged and rattled in the darkness. Rachel Daniels moaned. He felt her struggle against her own bonds even across the trailer.

Again, he called out to Talia in a series of angel notes, the tones trilling into a lilting melody that rose through the trailer in layers. Begging her to answer him.

But not a sound floated back to him.

"Talia, hear me!" He sang in the Enochian tongue, the melody soft and baritone-clear.

Not a single echo returned to him. Not one celestial symbol burned through this cloying darkness. Like he was the only angel left in the cosmos. He knew that couldn't be true, but it still terrified him.

The leathery beat of demon wings startled him as Asmodeus' dark, swirling form materialized in front of him and then stalked through the heavy blackness. Past him. Mostly shadow.

To his surprise, the Hell prince flicked on a thin light in the trailer, lighting up grey walls, a dusty glass coffee table, and the black leather couch. The furniture cast long, lean shadows through the narrow space until the light settled on Rachel huddled on the sofa.

Asmodeus hung over Kesien now, becoming corporeal. Grinning. His pale dusty-red skin was so bright against the shadows crowding out the thin light in the trailer.

"Your boss is training hard," said the Hell prince, his tone mocking. "Won't be enough to save that traitorous angel bitch, Berith though." Asmodeus laughed, the sound a deep rumble. "Or that waste of humanity, Jack Casey. Can't wait to off that little shit once and for all. Since Lucifer can't seem to get the job done."

"Betraying Lucifer isn't wise," said Kesien, his gaze unblinking as he studied the overconfident gleam in the Hell prince's red eyes.

"Casey dies," Asmodeus said with a growl. "I've been locked up forever, listening to enough whiny humans to last me an eternity. It's time for me to hit back at them."

Kesien grimaced. "Why Casey? When your boss wants him alive?"

It didn't make sense why Asmodeus was so dead set on killing Jack. As far as Kesien knew, Jack hadn't even encountered the banished Hell prince yet.

Why would Asmodeus purposely go against Lucifer?

"Do you know how many demons that little shit's ended?" Asmodeus' eyes burned like hot coals. "A human! And Lucifer wants him alive. Makes me sick! Even though all his demons want to shred that little bastard limb from limb. It's time to even the score."

Kesien felt the lies ripple from the Hell prince.

"Not smart, Asmodeus. He won't banish you again. He'll take you apart."

Asmodeus shook his head and began to pace. "I can handle whatever Lucifer throws at me. He's just trying to heave his muscle around Hell and convince his minions that he's still the deadliest power in the universe by killing Casey himself. Why else would Lucifer want him alive?"

And then it all made sense. Whatever Asmodeus did to cause Lucifer to banish him made the Hell prince an outcast to the other demons. Killing Jack was the only way Asmodeus could regain favor with the demons. Even if it meant going against Lucifer. But maybe Asmodeus didn't realize that Lucifer had all his powers back? He'd been in Purgatory a long time.

But no one understood—including Pravuil—why Lucifer wanted Jack back in Hell. It was more than Lucifer's limitless capacity for petty revenge or a show of force. Whatever Lucifer's reason, it was too dangerous to risk Jack's life and immortal soul by agreeing to Lucifer's ridiculous demand. Even with his seraphim powers. The entire guard was terrified that Lucifer would trap Jack back in Hell.

That would destroy both Jack and Talia.

Ultimately, Kesien knew they had little choice in the matter. They needed Jack and his seraphim powers down there, but at what cost?

Azrael was already building protections for Jack into the assault plan. And maybe with Abaddon involved, they could save Berith and the Book of Secrets without losing Jack in the process?

"Asmodeus, you do realize that Lucifer has changed, don't you?" Kesien replied.

He needed to see how much Asmodeus knew about Lucifer's transformation.

"He's stuck in Hell," Asmodeus said with a caustic laugh. "Tethered there for assaulting Heaven."

So, he had some information. Just not the most important piece.

Kesien clicked his tongue. "No wonder you're so arrogant. You do know that Lucifer engineered a Phoenix Shift, right?"

The smile slid off the Hell prince's dusty red face. "A what?"

"A Phoenix Shift."

The huge demon shook his bulbous head. "What's that?"

Kesien gave him a look of pity. "A rare event where a fallen angel regrows their wings and regenerates their halo. Along with all of their power."

Terror welled in those bright red dragon eyes and the Hell prince swallowed hard. "Lucifer's regained all of his power?"

Kesien gave him an emphatic nod. "All of it."

One last time, Kesien ignited all his angel senses and sang out a series of calls. But all that returned to him was the buzz of a distant lawnmower. And this cloying darkness.

Suddenly, he felt Jack's presence nearby. The churn of his seraphim energy hung in the air like heat lightning. His heart beat into his throat. Had Asmodeus captured him? Where was Talia? She wouldn't have left Jack alone. Unguarded. With Asmodeus so close. Or had Asmodeus' hold slipped—a little bit?

"Liar," said Asmodeus, poking Kesien in the chest with a dusty red, taloned finger. "If he's regained everything, he wouldn't be tethered in Hell, would he? Nice try, angel. If you'll excuse me, I've got a trap to bait."

The Hell prince lurched away from him and plodded through the trailer's heavy black shadows. Toward the human, Rachel Daniels.

Rachel gasped and struggled against her bonds, leather creaking. The thin light in the room barely reached her as Asmodeus hung over her.

And suddenly, the choking darkness dissipated again. Enough that Kesien saw all of the Holy fire brands burning around him—except Talia's Holy fire. Asmodeus' wards had slipped a little.

Quickly, he squinted, focusing all his angel senses, and tried to send out a call for help. But The shadows quickly strangled every note that he sang.

Feeling defeated, he gazed over at Rachel Daniels. Her face was smeared with red lipstick and black mascara streaked down her lightly freckled face as she struggled against the shadowy bands of darkness that wrapped around her and held her prisoner. Tears threaded down her face, auburn hair plastered against her forehead and cheeks as she glared up at Asmodeus.

Was Asmodeus acting alone down here? Or was Kesien's former squad helping him? Trying to take over Hell alongside Asmodeus?

Sickened, Kesien gritted his teeth as he searched for demons, for the members of his former guard. He wouldn't allow Reptev or Lix to ambush humans and the angels he cared about—not this time.

Instantly, he felt a flood of demons nearby. So many demons! They weren't congregated in the trailer, but they were out there. Ready. Waiting.

His anger burned hot. Lucifer's bounty. Half of Hell was out there, lying in wait for Talia and Jack while Asmodeus tried to lure them into his trap.

A cold chill washed across his wings.

No. Just Jack.

While Talia was back in Heaven, Asmodeus was using his cherubim abilities to shift into Rachel Daniels again and lure Jack into this trailer trap. Alone, Jack would be an easy mark if Asmodeus ambushed him through Rachel's form or hit his weaknesses. Like posing as his dad. Demons were experts at that. Those seraphim powers might not be enough to protect Jack this time.

Now, Kesien was afraid for Jack.

Smoky trails of mist and shadow strangled the trailer's light. But even in the fading glow, Kesien saw the mess that Asmodeus had made. Staging it to look like there'd been a huge struggle in here. Clothes were scattered across the floor and drawers pulled out, dishes and pillows strewn across the floor.

The trailer had been ransacked. Rachel probably put up quite a fight against Asmodeus, but she couldn't overpower a Hell prince any more than Kesien could defeat him alone. But with the Hell prince distracted, maybe he could break these demonic bonds holding his arms and wings immobile? And get help.

Rachel's desperate, strained voice pierced the silence.

"I said I'm not helping you," she said with a whimper. "I don't care what you do to me."

Kesien's eyes widened. Still refusing to help this monster...Rachel Daniels had some courage left to defy Asmodeus. He was impressed.

He focused the light inside him into his shoulders and forced it into his hands, his fingers. And made the light expand outward until it bled into the shadow bonds draping his wings. Trying to break them.

"I don't need your help!" Asmodeus' deep voice reverberated through the trailer. He sneered at her. "In fact, I don't need you at all, little human. I already have your form. That's all I need to break him down until I can control him. If I could just get that powder into his system, he'd be much easier to control." He shook his fist in her face. "The only reason I'm keeping you alive is to access your memories."

"You're wasting your time!" Rachel shouted. Raw, hoarse—and angry. "Planting it around the set may make the cast and crew suspicious, but he won't touch that stuff. I know Jack. He's way too smart for that."

Asmodeus' huge, shadowy presence hung over her now, ugly and menacing.

"I'm not worried," the big demon said with a laugh. "Posing as you, I'll get him to snort it. You'll see. If not, I'll just snap the little bastard's neck and be done with it. Damned Lucifer and his stupid bounty."

Asmodeus was a fallen angel, one of the cherubim until he fell with Lucifer. A chill raked across Kesien's wings. Even though Asmodeus had fallen, he could still shift form like other cherubim. He could impersonate anyone.

Like Rachel Daniels. Or Jack's dad. Jack wouldn't know the difference. And Kesien couldn't warn him.

The bonds draping his wings began to dissolve and dissipate into the thick shadows. It was working! He needed Rachel to keep talking long enough for him to free himself.

Rachel shook her head. "Not going to happen. Now, I know why Lucifer banished you. Because you're just plain mean—and you don't listen. Lucifer said alive, you big, stupid demon!"

Asmodeus backhanded her, splitting open her lip. A thick stream of blood trickled down her chin and dripped onto her torn white blouse.

"Shut up, human," he said with a growl. "You're weak and ignorant. And you know nothing about my world!"

Or the fact that he was attempting to steal control of Hell from Lucifer. Grossly overestimating his abilities, too.

Rachel smiled, her over-bright blue eyes sizzling with hatred as she glared at the huge demon.

"If I'm so weak," she said, nodding toward the shadowy bonds surrounding her, "then why are you so scared of me?"

Again, Asmodeus laughed, a deep, rocky rumble. "Scared of you? Why in Hell would I be afraid of you? Or Jack Casey? Or any human!"

Rachel's smile brightened. "Hurts not having a soul, doesn't it? Because when one of these angels—or Jack—takes you down, you'll be erased from existence while my soul will go on." She shook her head slowly, clicking her teeth. "You fell so far that you lost your place in eternity. Ooooh…that's gotta hurt."

Asmodeus screamed and rushed at her.

"Pick on someone your own size, Asmodeus!" Kesien shouted.

He couldn't let this monster kill Rachel Daniels either.

The massive demon halted only inches from Rachel and then wheeled around, turning toward Kesien.

"What was that, angel?"

He needed to take another lesson from Jack Casey right now. What would Jack say to this massive demon? To infuriate it more, set it off guard.

"I said, pick on someone your own size. But you can't because you're nothing but a little demonic bully, Asmodeus. Scared of humans now? You must have hit your head hard against the lava rocks when you fell from the Heavens into Hell."

A bass rumble thrummed through the trailer as Asmodeus growled and slid through the darkness toward him. In moments, the seven-foot-tall demon towered over him.

"Someone like you, little death angel? You my size?"

Kesien let the light within him settle in calming waves through his body, through his wings as he stared into Asmodeus' dark, vacuous demonic eyes that glimmered red with amusement. At that moment, he felt the shadowy bonds fall away.

He was free.

"Exactly like me, Asmodeus," he said, smiling, and launched himself at the Hell prince.

But Asmodeus hit him hard, throwing him against one of the trailer walls.

Kesien crumpled.

Recovering quickly, he flew out of Asmodeus' grasp and turned, shield of light gleaming in his right hand. He slammed it toward the seven-foot-tall demon's head.

Missed.

Asmodeus' dusty-red skin was like worn leather as the shadows shattered around him.

Kesien swung the shield again, bashing it against the demon's chest. The edge of the shield cut across Asmodeus' forearm. Inky black smoke floated up from the gash as the massive demon turned, grabbing hold of Kesien's wings.

Spinning him around.

Knocking the light shield out of his hands. The light shattered into shards and went dark.

Strangled by writhing bands of shadow that slithered up from the floor, Kesien fought, but there were too many shadows! They tangled around his legs and slid around his waist. The bonds encircled his arms and immobilized his wings.

"No! Talia! Deemah! I'm here!"

Kesien struggled, but the darkness was too heavy and the shadows overwhelmed him. Pulling him down, dimming the light inside him.

He screamed as the darkness gripped him in its iron hold, imprisoning him within the trailer again. And that horrible sense of nothingness slid over his senses again, numbing him until he blacked out.

9

AGAINST PARRISH BLUE SKIES AND CONSTABLE CLOUDS, TALIA LANDED on Eolowen's white stone terrace amid a flurry of angels of death sparring and running defensive drills. The entirety of Azrael's guard. Wings and swords were in constant motion, armor clanging as dove grey wings beat the air. Scent of roses and rainwater clung to the wind as she stepped between shield bashes and sword blocks, finally locating Azrael who sparred with Muriel.

Why was Muriel sparring with Azrael? She was supposed to update him and return to Earth to protect Jack alongside the rest of the squad. Azrael must have countermanded that request when she reported back to him.

Azrael's face was a mask of determination, charcoal grey eyes fierce against the clear gold glow of his Eternean armor. A sword of Holy fire guttered in his grip as he focused blow after blow on Muriel's shield of light.

When he realized Talia was there, he halted his sword swing.

"Talia! At last!"

Before she could speak, Azrael gripped her arm and lifted her into the air beside him.

Muriel followed as Talia spread her wings and soared over

Eolowen's grounds beside the archangel. Everywhere she looked, angels of death trained and drilled for the assault on the Gates of Hell. The thought of having Jack that close to Lucifer terrified her. And she worried about what Lucifer had already done to Berith.

They banked over the burbling stream and the stone white pergola blooming with roses, honeysuckle, and jasmine and sailed over Eolowen's long nave. When they circled back around to the round room, Azrael slipped through a roof portal into the room below. Talia followed, Muriel behind her. White curtains pooled on the white stone floors and wafted against the air currents.

She chuckled, remembering Jack's face when he found out those curtains were the doors and windows that Azrael had promised him. He'd only wanted to be alone with her after months of being separated. Without sharing the room with all of Heaven's angels.

When Talia landed, she found Archangel Pravuil pacing the room, wings carrying him around it, feet hovering above the white stone. Three curtains of light brightened the room, two of them displaying figures and paragraphs in glowing Enochian script. The third curtain of light was blank. Several books floated throughout the space and drifted beside the third curtain of light that stood beside the white bed.

Where she had once healed the love of her life after he'd spent months in Hell. She smiled. The memory of his beautiful, leanly muscled body tangled in the white sheets, wearing only a pair of blue boxer briefs was seared in her memory. That light blond hair disheveled and so sexy and those devastating, pale green eyes smoldering with pain and need.

She stared down at her wedding rings, missing him already, even though he was only a blink away. But with that bounty on his head, the drugs appearing on set, and Asmodeus hunting him, she hated being away from him—even for a short time. She touched the fabric of her ice blue dress and summoned her grey angel of death robes.

"Talia!" Pravuil cried, blinking toward her. "At last! We have work to do."

His white robes were crisp, billowing as the breezes flowed

through the space. His short white hair framed his face and made those yellow archangel's eyes look so bright. His long, graceful white wings expanded around his shoulders in a gentle arc of feathers as he folded his hands together and studied her for a moment.

"I came as soon as I could, archangel," she said and pointed with her thumb over her shoulder. "Had to make sure Jack was safe."

Pravuil's eyes narrowed and he shook his head. "Jack Casey's destroyed enough demons to repopulate Hell three times over! Those demons would have to be dumber than stumps to mess with him."

"Like Asmodeus?" Muriel asked.

Talia and Azrael turned to stare at her.

"What?" Muriel cried with a shrug. "How dumb do you have to be as a demon to get banished by Lucifer?"

Pravuil laid his hand against his chin, pensive for a moment. "Muriel's got a point," he said. "That's pretty dumb—especially for a Hell prince. Lucifer's a putz for trusting him to carry out anything— even a pizza."

Muriel snickered. "You've been around Jack too long, Pravuil."

Pravuil cleared his throat. "You're right. Jack's...colorful phrasing has a way of rubbing off, even on a Scribe."

"Scribe, what did Asmodeus do to get banished by Lucifer?" Talia asked.

Pravuil glanced at her and then Muriel. "Asmodeus rose quickly through Lucifer's ranks after promising he could escalate violence on Earth. And delivering. His shapeshifting abilities brought about mass shootings, suicide bombings, and massive increases in terrorism. Killed tens of thousands of humans. He was ruthless. Vicious. Kept your guard very busy crossing over humans and preventing premature deaths. And they were determined to hunt down this monster. Then Asmodeus staged a coup in Hell by shapeshifting into Lucifer, killing demons, and destroying a bunch of schemes that Lucifer had in motion. Thought he should be in charge."

Muriel's eyes widened. "He impersonated Lucifer and started a coup?"

Pravuil nodded.

"Brave...but incredibly stupid," said Talia. "I can't believe Lucifer didn't destroy him on the spot."

"Lucifer probably wanted to," said Pravuil, sliding his hands behind his back and underneath his wings. "But Lucifer didn't want to extinguish cherubim power that he could still wield. And control. Lucifer admires ambition—up to a point. But no one challenges him in his own domain or tells him how to run it. Lucifer banished him to Purgatory to face many of the souls he sent there. It wasn't easy to get a demon inside either, but Lucifer always finds a way. Anyway, Talia—Asmodeus is no match for Jack's seraphim powers. He should be safe with your squad watching out for him."

"That includes you, too, Muriel," said Talia, pointing at her best friend. "Please make sure he's safe down there. For me."

Muriel nodded. "As soon as Zephana finishes my armor upgrade—Azrael's orders. Then I'm heading back down. So, don't worry, Talia. Anahera and Deemah are with him."

Talia's brow furrowed. "What happened to Daidrean?"

"Looking for Kesien," Muriel said with an exasperated sigh.

Talia started to speak, but Muriel cut her off. "I know. Not enough to keep Jack out of trouble. I'll hurry."

Muriel lifted into the air currents. She shot through one of the ceiling portals, leaving Talia and Azrael alone with Pravuil.

Talia was worried. Azrael had barely spoken, pain radiating in his charcoal eyes and etched into his face.

"Azrael," she said, reaching out and caressing his shoulder. "There's still time to save Berith."

He nodded. "I'll let you and Pravuil work," he said and flew up through one of the roof portals.

Returning to training with the guard.

"I've never seen him so lost," said Pravuil, watching him fly over the grand hall and land in the meadow.

Talia turned back to God's Scribe. "He's hurting, Scribe. Berith was—"

"His reason for existing," said Pravuil, his gaze still focused on the portal. "I was there when she fell with Lucifer. For the longest time, I feared that he'd take a leap off those clouds and follow her."

"You were there when Berith fell with Lucifer?" Talia could barely speak.

"Of course, I was there," he said. "I'm as old as the firmament. Just like Azrael and Berith." Pravuil floated around the room again, wings extended. "Most of you younger angels question what happened because you weren't there during the Rebellion. Or during the Fall. Well, let me tell you, it was brutal."

Talia watched him traverse the room. "Scribe, I don't question what happened. I know what happened. I saw it all through the Book of Secrets. Through the story gems. Over a third of all angels fell that day. I felt their pain and regret. I think that every single fallen angel regrets that moment and wishes to change it. Even Lucifer."

"What?" Pravuil turned toward her. "They regret it?"

She nodded. "That regret burned through every single story, Scribe. Especially Berith's. I feel it sometimes in Lucifer's words. I know he regretted not having enough angels to win the Rebellion, but at the core of his anger, there is pain. Doesn't excuse what he's done, of course."

God's Scribe studied her for several long moments. "Lucifer will never forgive the Maker for choosing humans over his first creations: angels. His words. The Maker didn't choose one over the other. He made angels their mentors and He made humans to teach angels about His nature. They were created in the Maker's image after all. The Maker wanted angels to learn to love and dream, something He couldn't create in us. He wanted them to walk beside each other someday, but Lucifer twisted those words and selfishly brought down so many angels because of it."

"Well, it's time that we bring one of them back home again," she replied. "Berith redeemed herself. She earned her place back at Eolowen. The others will have to tell their stories to the Maker."

Pravuil motioned toward High House. "They'll have to do more than tell their stories." He turned toward the curtains of light as images of the Rebellion raged across them, making Talia wince.

"They'll have to show those stories, prove that they've earned redemption." He waved his hand and the images disappeared when he turned away and stretched his wings wide. "Unlike humans, they knew better."

Talia studied God's Scribe as he moved around the room, red-faced and restless. He was worried about Berith, too. And Azrael. Then she realized that even the Scribe didn't know what Lucifer was up to with all these theatrics and this sweeping challenge to Jack. He didn't seem comfortable with the guard storming the Gates of Hell for one angel of death either.

Or was it something else he wasn't discussing?

"Scribe," she said, turning back to him. "What's bothering you? This isn't the first time the guard—or Heaven—has clashed with Lucifer. Azrael's distraught, but he's still the most formidable archangel in Heaven. What's the matter?"

Pravuil turned away, hands folded as he landed in front of the blank curtain of light.

"Talia…I'm—I'm worried."

Her stomach sank. God's Scribe was worried. That made her wings quiver.

"About what, Scribe?" she asked in a quiet voice.

There were an infinite number of things to worry about, but she needed to know what most troubled God's Scribe.

"Talia, I have no idea what Lucifer's up to," he said in a quiet voice. "But I fear that he's somehow trying to bring about the end of the Maker's Creation." He turned toward her, his face a mask of concern. "Jack's world—the Earth."

Her stomach twisted into knots. "But why would he do that? Without Earth, he has no souls to make deals with, no souls to condemn. No wagers to make."

"Because, Talia," said the Scribe in a dark voice. "He was never meant to regain his power. Hell was meant to be his prison as much as it was for the damned souls that refused redemption."

She shook her head. "What does that mean?"

Pravuil bowed his head, pinching the bridge of his nose with his thumb and forefinger.

"I think that Lucifer intends to challenge the Maker's authority by ushering in the destruction of the Creation. Lucifer knows that destroying the Creation is the best way to hurt the Maker. Besides destroying risen souls."

Talia rushed toward Pravuil and gripped his sleeves. "But Scribe, only the Maker can open the Book of Creation and break the first seal."

Pravuil remained silent for a few moments. "As I've always been told. With every seal that's broken comes a flight of angels upon the Earth. Pouring out seven bowls of woe upon the Creation. Heralding the arrival of the Seven Travelers. Setting them into motion with each seal that shatters. The Angels of Death are the seventh flight, Talia, pouring the seventh and last bowl upon the Earth. And that's death."

She'd been told about how the seven seals would someday be broken by the Maker. As each Heavenly seal broke, it shattered a protective pillar in the Creation. When those pillars had all shattered, it would unleash seven flights of angels. First, they would trumpet the breaking of a seal and the shattering of its pillar. Then each flight of angels had to herald the arrival of horrible devastations upon the Earth through one of Hell's Seven Travelers. The thought of doing that to humanity brought tears to her eyes.

"But Talia," he said, his voice dark. "For angels of death, the sixth flight is your Armageddon."

"I don't understand, Scribe," said Talia, eyes narrowing as she shook her head. "What do you mean, our Armageddon?"

Pravuil bowed his head as he laid his palm against one of the curtains of light. "That sixth flight is called the Enochian Apocalypse because it ushers in the War of Light and Dark. Demons will battle angels on the Earth and in the skies above Earth. As the Seven Travelers lay waste to humanity. And the Light must win in order to save humanity."

For several moments, Talia couldn't speak. For all her existence, she'd heard bits and pieces about these events, but until now, she'd never dreamed that she'd see them come to pass. Was Jack's world doomed? Would he and his soul rise, leaving her behind here? In Eolowen. Separating them forever?

"If the Maker breaks that first seal, Talia," said Pravuil, turning toward her. "The rest will break, too. And there would be no stopping any of this. So, making sure that Lucifer remains tethered in Hell is our highest priority."

That part she understood. Keeping the Gates of Hell locked and Lucifer in Hell was the most important part of this assault. Azrael knew that, too. Then she knew. He had to be prepared to leave Berith behind if the assault meant releasing Lucifer. That's why he was so distraught.

She felt a chill rush along her wings. Did she now have the same directive? Did she have to be prepared to leave Jack behind rather than allow Lucifer to escape Hell?

Rage bubbled through her. She would never leave Jack behind. If faced with that decision, she would stay there with him. She refused to ever be separated from the man she loved more than her own existence. Never again.

"Are you trying to tell me that if it comes down to leaving Jack behind or releasing Lucifer, I have to abandon the love of my life?"

The silence in the room was palpable. When his gaze finally met hers, his eyes were watery.

"Yes, Talia," he said with a nod. "That's what I'm telling you."

She felt the despair rush through her body with lightning speed. "Scribe, if I have to make that choice, I won't be leaving Jack behind in Hell. I will be staying there with him."

Pravuil's aching sigh filled the room. "I knew that would be your answer, Talia. And I admire you for it. Azrael feels the same way." He ran his fingers across the nearest curtain of light and it sparked gold against his fingertips. "It's the same one I'd make, too, if I loved someone like you love Jack. Like Azrael loves Berith."

Talia shook her head and moved toward the conflicted Scribe. "Scribe, that's not the choice I'm making."

"What?" Pravuil's brow furrowed and he shook his head. "But this is about Jack—"

"No, this isn't about Jack," she said and crossed her arms, wings unfurling behind her. "This is about Lucifer. About rescuing Berith. I don't know what Lucifer's playing at with this taunting challenge, Scribe, but I won't let him make it about Jack. Or Berith."

The corners of Pravuil's mouth lifted for a moment. "What if you have to make a choice, Talia?"

"Then I choose love, Pravuil. I choose light. I may not be able to stop whatever game Lucifer's playing, but I will never again allow that monster to force me to choose a lesser future. Either love frees all or it shatters alongside the rest of Creation. But I won't be forced to choose."

"That's what I call moxie, Talia," said Pravuil. "It might be the rarest angel power in existence. The one that saves us all."

She wiped the tears out of her eyes. She refused to let Lucifer separate her and Jack ever again.

"Now, I came here to awaken this transference power, Pravuil," she said with a nod at him. "Where do I start?"

Pravuil reached out and caressed her cheek. "Right here with a blank book and an unread story gem," he said. "So, we can figure out what Lucifer's trying to do with the transference power."

The flutter of wings distracted her. When she looked up, Oseira, one of the cherubim stationed at High House, descended through a rooftop portal and landed in the center of the room. Her white robes billowed around her, dark tawny skin warm against her bright, hawk-like yellow eyes. That seemed distant. Her short dark hair framed her oval face as she glanced at Pravuil and then Talia.

"Oseira, welcome," said Pravuil, turning toward her.

"Good to see you, Oseira," said Talia.

The cherub stood motionless, her yellow, hawkish gaze moving around the room. She didn't speak as she studied the curtains of light, Pravuil, and then Talia again. Staring. Watching. Observing.

What was the matter with her?

"Oseira, are you all right?" Talia asked, stepping toward her.

The cherub nodded. "Forgive me," she said in a slow but lilting tone. "I'm studying the effects of preparing for this assault on Azrael's guard. And I have a lot more results to gather. Excuse me."

Without another word, the cherub shot through a roof portal into the crisp blue sky and flitted across the meadow toward the rest of the guard.

"Oseira hasn't been herself since she left High House to heal for the guard," said Pravuil, glancing from the roof to Talia.

Had they performed some sort of reeducation process on the cherub? That thought made Talia shudder. She'd ask Azrael about it later. Right now, she needed to investigate transference and hear the stories about it.

"I can see that," said Talia as she moved toward the floating books and the empty curtain of light. "Now, you were saying about transference?"

"Yes! Yes! Let's look at transference now."

Pravuil plucked one of the books out of the air. A story gem reader. The large, oversized book required Talia to hold it with both hands. It had six empty gem sockets on its sky-filled cover that was dotted with puffy clouds scuttling slowly across it. A soft breeze blew across the cover's landscape, smelling like cool rain and rose petals. Like Heaven.

An empty gem socket perched in each corner of the cover and two empty sockets anchored the book in the center. It reminded her of the Book of Secrets with all its gems, but she remembered the moving field of stars on the cover. And being able to reach through the starfield to find things.

The cover on this reader was solid and wouldn't let her hand pass through it. Maybe because no stories had been committed to it yet?

God's Scribe held out a bright violet-purple gem the size of his palm. The story gem pulsed with an almost neon glow inside.

"This gem has never been read before," he said, extending the gem to her. "The story belongs to Gadreel the Fallen Watcher. I gathered the story after…after the exodus from the Garden. But it was so long ago that I don't remember all the details about her story."

Gadreel the Fallen Watcher...Talia remembered that name. Remembered that she had been a Watcher assigned to watch over the Tree of Life in the Garden, but she let Lucifer corrupt everything in the Garden.

"She was the Watcher in the Garden," said Talia with wide eyes.

Pravuil nodded and pressed the warm gem into her hand. "Place it in the first center socket and listen to Gadreel's story. She talks about her rare gift of transference."

"Didn't she fall with Lucifer?" Talia asked.

Pravuil shook his head. "I'll explain after you've heard her story."

With the fallen angel, Procel still among his loyal followers, Lucifer had an angel with rare powers that could easily awaken the transference power. If they had the elements from the Creation.

She pressed the story gem into the empty socket in the center of the book. It snapped into the socket and began to hum, still glowing with that inner light. The gem's violet-purple light washed over the cover, turning the blue sky purple as Talia pressed her palm against the stone.

The stone burned with light, glowing like a hot coal, and giving off sparks that became images both still and moving. The empty curtain of light fluttered, capturing everything as the book's pages fluttered.

"Let it open and write Gadreel's story in the reader, Talia," said Pravuil, standing beside her now.

Nodding, she let the book float into the air. Wind blew open the cover, pages flipping until the book opened on the first page. It hovered in front of her as inkwells appeared above it. Inks of every color spilled across the page until thick gold light engulfed the book, burning away the excess ink. Leaving behind words and phrases that filled each page. As the ink spilled onto the next page, the words from the previous page glowed, floating into the air in front of her.

Talia read each page as it hovered above the book and then drifted back after she'd read the last word. Beside her, the curtain of light showed her the events as they happened.

A massive sprawling tree with heavy roots, delicate green leaves that sparkled with light, and glimmering fruits that Talia had never seen before. The tree towered above the Garden wall, above all the other trees except the Tree of Knowledge beside it, and above the humans there. The Maker's first experiment.

But the tree's fruit was forbidden because of what it granted. Of things to come. Of things beyond life in the Garden. Of promises yet to be made.

A young Watcher with light brown hair, sad brown eyes, and a shy smile soared above the Tree, wings spread, circling it. Watching. Keeping the humans at a safe distance from its sprawling branches and the nearby Tree of Knowledge beside it.

Until one day, Lucifer visited the Garden.

He was relentless. Insisting that she was hiding the truth from them. Lying to the humans. That it wasn't fair. They deserved to know everything.

So, she watched. While the humans picked fruit from both trees. And ate it, learning who and what they were. They became fearful. Of the angels. Of the Garden. And finally, they became fearful of the Maker.

As they fled from the Garden, terrified of the Maker's anger at what they had done, Lucifer laughed in delight. It broke the Maker's heart to close the gates on the Garden forever. At that moment, Gadreel knew that all of it had been her fault.

She remained at the edges of the lonely Garden, far from the Maker, and cast her guilt and anger onto the trees, scattering it among the flowers, and hiding it throughout the vegetation. Denying her role in destroying the Garden. Until she realized that everything in the Garden was now dying. Dying because she had transferred her guilt and anger there. Only after the Rebellion tore through the Heavens did she understand that she had awakened a rare power. Transference.

To find Transference, you must understand that wood is fuel and fire is rage. Guilt. To awaken Transference, you must locate a piece of intact wood from the destroyed Tree of Life's trunk and burn it in the first flame that lit the Hellfires.

Already, the inks began to dry up and blow away, leaving the parchment pages empty. Or making them appear empty. Talia knew that only her rare angel powers allowed her to read these books and the stories to imprint on the pages. Images that flashed across the curtain of light began to dissolve.

"Pravuil!" Talia cried.

God's Scribe blinked beside her, a hand on her shoulder. "What did you discover, Talia?" he asked.

She pointed at the book. "According to Gadreel's story, I need a piece of intact wood from the Tree of Life and the first flame that lit the Hellfires. I need to burn the wood with this flame in the Garden to awaken transference."

Pravuil drifted through the room, deep in the thought.

"Wood from the Tree of Life…okay, those pieces still exist. In both High House and the Garden. And the first flame that lit the Hellfires… hmmm, let me think."

He pressed his hands against his forehead as he floated through the space, mumbling to himself.

"Yes, I remember that first flame when it lit the fires below. I captured that Holy flame and cataloged it in the Archive. I remember now."

Both pieces required to awaken transference were found in the Archive and High House. Both locations coincided with Samael's raid. She felt a chill rake her spine. Those traitors had awakened transference the night that they stormed High House and the Archive. That had been part of their plan all along.

"Pravuil," she said, nodding toward the book. "I wasn't the first to awaken this rare power."

He frowned, moving closer. "What does that mean?"

She motioned toward the distant spires of High House. "When Samael's guard defected that night, they broke Samael out of High House and took wood from the Tree of Life. Then they attacked the Archive. To steal part of that first flame of Hell. So, Procel could awaken transference. It was part of their plan all along."

"Those traitorous swine!" Pravuil shouted. "And they've had it all this time, doing Maker only knows what with it."

Talia wondered if they were using it on Jack. To shift more

addiction pain onto him and increase his struggle against it. And to weaken him.

"If you give me part of the first flame that lit the Hellfires, I'll carry it to the Garden and awaken the rare power. I have a bad feeling that Lucifer has been using it on Jack for some time. It would certainly explain his addiction issues right now."

Pravuil picked up the Book with Gadreel's story gem and turned toward her as he extended his wings. But Talia grabbed his shoulder.

"Scribe, wait," she said, studying his yellow eyes. "You said you'd tell me about Gadreel's fall after I'd read her story."

God's Scribe nodded and stared past her a moment. "I did, didn't I? Her story is a sad one, Talia. In time, she realized that what happened in the Garden had been her fault because as a Watcher, she'd failed. She didn't understand that she, too, had been under Lucifer's influence. She wasn't strong enough to stop Lucifer from infiltrating the Garden and getting the first humans to eat the fruit on the tree. But instead of seeking help, she went into the Garden and ate fruit poisonous to angels."

"Pravuil, that's horrible!" Talia cried, feeling sick.

Pravuil nodded. "We found her the next day, her eyes empty, wings still. Light gone. Beneath what remained of the Tree of Life. If only she hadn't hidden what she'd done. We would have shown her that Lucifer had been too powerful. That it wasn't her fault."

An angel erased herself from existence rather than face the consequences of her actions. A very human reaction. Talia wished that she could have helped Gadreel. Shown her that what happened in the Garden wasn't her fault.

"Lucifer has so much to answer for, Scribe," Talia said through gritted teeth.

"Yes, he does," said Pravuil as he lifted into the air. "Wait here, Talia. I'll return with the flame shortly.

Talia watched the Scribe shoot through a portal in the rooftop and blink across the horizon toward the Archive.

10

It seemed like forever until consciousness returned to Kesien. He groaned and struggled to sit up, wings shifting, but the shadow bonds made any movement difficult.

"Hey? You all right over there?"

Rachel's voice startled him as the ransacked trailer came into sharp focus, shadows almost strangling the thin sunlight pouring through one small window to his left. Where the voice had come from. A hint of sulfur hung in the air, mixed with traces of some overpowering floral perfume.

A perfume that belonged to Rachel Daniels.

"Hey, angel?" she called out. "You all right?"

Asmodeus had made every celestial creature visible inside the trailer. Including Kesien.

"I'm okay," said Kesien with a groan, his head feeling heavy and foggy. "Are you okay, Rachel?"

"I'll live," she said.

Kesien nodded. "Same."

"Wait a minute," Rachel cried. "How do you know my name? Are you one of those angels of death?"

"I'm part of Talia's squad."

She exhaled sharply. "Talia, huh? Bet she had a lot to say about me."

"Only if you hurt Jack again."

"Never again, angel. But that big fat demon's in for a world of hurt if I get hold of him."

Kesien chuckled. He loved how passionately and colorfully some humans spoke. Like Jack Casey. She'd been with Jack for a while—and it showed.

"Agreed. By the way, Asmodeus is shapeshifting into your form and impersonating you all over the studio lot."

"What?" Her voice became sharp, a growl underneath her words. "I swear if he causes me any bad publicity or does any stills from my left side, he's a very dead demon."

Kesien laughed as he struggled to break the shadow bonds surrounding his hands. "He's too busy trying to ruin Jack Casey for Lucifer. Or trying to become a hero to Hell's demons. I'm not sure— maybe both."

"Poor Jack," said Rachel and Kesien heard the sincerity in her voice. "Lucifer's never going to leave him alone. And it's all my fault."

He'd heard some of the stories and read others in Jack's Book of Life and Death, but he hadn't heard much about Rachel Daniel's part in all this chaos. Much less hearing it in her own words.

"Your fault?" he said. "How?"

"That story would take a lifetime to tell," said Rachel, scoffing. "Let's just say that I sold Lucifer my soul to become rich and famous. To extend my contract, I gathered souls for him. Jack's didn't go according to plan though."

"What does that mean?" Kesien asked.

He knew bits and pieces of that story from his new squad. Of how Rachel had groomed Jack, a wide-eyed kid who'd landed the part of a lifetime in Hollywood, into a coke addict who lost everything. When he refused the drugs, she forced them into his system and left him destitute enough to either overdose or kill himself. But somehow, Jack held on. He turned his life around after meeting and falling for Talia during her first wager with Lucifer on the first season of this show they were filming.

"You're an angel of death," Rachel snapped. "I'm sure you know all about how Talia saved his soul in those wagers with Lucifer and then later, Jack saved Talia when she fell from the Heavens."

Kesien nodded in the half-light. "I wasn't in Talia's squad until later, but yes, I've heard the stories. I also know how he sacrificed himself to keep Talia from being dragged to Hell. When he ended up there, he had to face you in one of Lucifer's cage fights. And he forgave you which broke Lucifer's contract."

Rachel was quiet for several moments. "All true," said Rachel finally. "But what you probably don't know is that Jack has been Lucifer's target since he was a child."

Kesien froze. Was that true? "Are you sure about that?"

"Lucifer tore Jack's family apart. On purpose. Turned his mom into an ice queen. Made his dad an alcoholic and die young. Turned his sisters against him. Leaving Jack alone in the world."

"Why?" Kesien replied, his voice sharper than he realized.

Why would Lucifer expend so much energy and focus on one human? It didn't make sense.

Rachel laughed. "Don't you know? He'd planned it for years. Decades. All part of some Phoenix Shift he orchestrated. To get his wings and power back. After he discovered Talia had rare angel powers, he knew that she had to be his test for the Phoenix Shift. To make sure it worked. So, he had to ensure that she'd lose the wager."

Had Lucifer really ruined Jack's entire life just to win a wager? And get his power back? Of course, he did. Lucifer hated humanity. All of it. Blamed his fall on humans. And now, he hated Jack most of all.

"Lucifer's a monster."

Rachel chuckled. "Can't argue with that. He set up Jack to die in that first wager. Sacrificed. He never expected Jack and Talia to fall in love and foil his plans. Or Jack to become his biggest nemesis."

"Bet he never expected Jack to end up with seraphim powers either," said Kesien as he let the light flare into his hands, trying to break the shadowy bonds shackling him again.

"Seraphim powers?" Rachel cried. "Jack?"

"It was an accident that Heaven is still trying to fix. So, Jack is a very real danger to Lucifer's plans. That's why Lucifer is still trying to end him. And anyone else that crosses him. Like you, Rachel."

Again, she was silent for several moments. "You're right. But I earned my trip to Hell. I belonged there after everything I did to Jack." She sighed. "And the others. There were so many others before Jack and I saw them as quotas, not people. But Jack? Jack was special. I never wanted anyone like I wanted Jack. Maybe if I hadn't sold my soul, we'd have made it? But I wanted to be famous so badly. My soul was long gone when he stepped into my world, my contract expiring."

Poor Jack. Thinking he'd just gotten his dream come true, not realizing he'd stepped into a viper's nest and set in motion his premature death.

"You should have seen him, angel," said Rachel, her tone wistful. "He was the most beautiful thing I'd ever seen. That anyone had ever seen. Still is. But back then, people would just stop and stare at him. He was that beautiful. Casting director for SanFran Confidential almost fainted when he did his screen test. She could barely speak to him. And even if he hadn't been that gorgeous, he could act. Boy did he have the talent! Just blew away directors, turning scenes and characters on their heads every time he stepped in front of the camera. He was a natural."

Kesien smiled. "Jack sounds pretty amazing."

"At twenty, still just a kid, he had it all, angel," said Rachel, a smile in her voice. "Until Lucifer and I took it all away from him. And still, he saved me. I owe Jack. Big. That's why I need to get out of here and warn him…before it's too late."

Maybe if they worked together, they could break these shadow bonds. Her with physical force and him with his angel light.

"Why don't we work together?" Kesien offered. "Help each other break these bonds and ambush Asmodeus?"

"You're an angel! Why would you need my help?"

"Because Asmodeus is a lot more powerful than me. He's a Hell prince. Without seraphim powers, I can't overpower him. But if we work together, we might be able to escape before he comes back."

Rachel was quiet again. "Eric doesn't even know that's not me," she said in a forlorn voice. "Will even he give up on me after this?"

"He hasn't left yet, Rachel. Look, Asmodeus needs to keep you alive while he impersonates you, so he's not going to kill you yet. But me? He has no use for me. I can go a few rounds with him, give you enough time to escape. But I can't do that if I can't move. You in?"

"What's your name?" Rachel asked finally.

"Kesien," he replied. "You in, Rachel Daniels?"

"If Jack trusts you, then so will I," she said. "Yeah. I'm in. How do we break these bindings?"

"Are your hands tied in front or behind your back?" Kesien asked.

"In front," she answered.

Perfect! Strike one, Asmodeus.

"Okay, I'm going to try one of my angel abilities, Rachel," said Kesien, his voice calm and steady despite the sudden rustling sounds that touched his ears.

Asmodeus was back! Maybe she hadn't heard him yet?

"It won't break these bonds, but if the light's with us, it will put me right next to you. Then we'll have to work fast, okay?"

"He'll be back soon," Rachel said with a groan. "He's never gone long."

The beat of those leathery wings touched Kesien's ears. He had to do this now. And hope for the best.

"Brace yourself," said Kesien as he measured the distance from his place against the wall to the black leather sofa.

It wasn't far. Close enough for an angel of death blink maneuver.

He steadied himself, focused his Holy fire forward—toward the sofa—and blinked.

His body lurched through the shadows and dim lighting, everything a blur until he felt the whump of leather against his body.

When he opened his eyes, he was beside Rachel on the sofa. Her face was bruised and swollen where Asmodeus had knocked her around, makeup smeared, and eyes red. Hand and finger bruises dotted her arms where he'd roughed her up.

Should have disabled his ability to use blink. Strike two, Asmodeus.

She stared up at Kesien for a moment, her eyes watery. "It worked," she said in a hushed voice. "But I didn't expect you to be…so—beautiful."

He chuckled. "I'm an angel, remember?"

"Angel of death," she corrected him. "You can reap me anytime, Kesien. Wow…"

"We don't reap souls from the dead," he said. "We guide them into the next realm."

"Whatever you say, stud," she replied.

With a sigh, Kesien turned his body so his hands were touching hers. Deemah and Muriel would tease him unmercifully when they heard this story. If he told it.

"Okay, Rachel, I'm going to focus all my light onto these bonds, but I need you to use your human strength on them, too. Together, we can break them."

"Sure thing, handsome," she said and he felt her grab hold of the shadow bonds wrapping his hands and wrists.

The trailer door handle rattled, sending a spike of fear through Kesien. Rachel froze. His body jolted, wings shuddering as he pushed all the light inside him downward. Toward the shadowy shackles restraining him.

"Now, Rachel," he whispered. "Pull with everything you've got!"

He pulled in a breath and held it as Rachel gripped the bonds surrounding his hands and yanked. Hard. Once. Twice. The third pull made the shadowy rope fall apart in her hands.

"It broke!" Rachel shouted in a whisper. "It really broke!"

Kesien's hands were free, the shadows falling away.

He turned, grabbing hold of the ropes on his right wing, as the trailer door opened. Rachel pulled hard on the ropes as he flooded them with his Holy fire.

Snap! His right wing was free.

But the voices stopped him cold. He froze.

"Look, Asmodeus—you need us!"

That voice.

Anger flooded over him. It was Lix. His former squad mate. The stories were true. They were on Lucifer's side. And now working with Asmodeus.

"I don't need some turncoat angels helping me with anything," Asmodeus' voice was husky and loud, almost a growl. "I got Jack Casey right where I want him."

"Yeah, free and still causing Lucifer damage," said another voice, a sharp tenor.

Kesien gritted his teeth. Pharzus. Was Reptev with them, too? The three of them were inseparable. He sighed. There had been a time when the four of them had been inseparable. Until Samael started his rituals and Kesien refused to participate. Along with Deemah, the fifth and newest member of that squad.

"Watch your mouth, angel," Asmodeus said with a snarl, "or I'll end you fast."

"But you want this fast and decisive, right?" Lix again.

Kesien shifted his left wing toward Rachel and flooded the ropes binding it with light.

"Pull!" Kesien whispered in a sharp tone. "With everything you've got."

Rachel tugged on the bindings hard as Kesien's light began to burn through them.

"Of course," said Asmodeus, "but first I need to see what Casey's carrying around. See if it's really seraphim powers."

"What if it is?" Pharzus again.

"Then I move to plan B."

"Which is?" Lix asked.

"I get Lucifer involved."

Liar. Kesien had heard Asmodeus' plans. He intended to kill Jack. Become a hero to the demons and stage a coup against Lucifer.

Muffled voices grew louder as Kesien slammed his light against the bonds, Rachel still pulling.

"Come on, Asmodeus," said a third voice, a loud baritone. Reptev.

It made Kesien sick. "We can help you ambush Casey. Take him down for good."

Something popped and the shadow ropes began to break apart.

And Kesien was free!

"All right, Reptev," said Asmodeus, and the voices moved away from the trailer door. "Talk to me."

Kesien spread his wings and lifted off from the floor, hovering above the sofa. It worked!

He landed on the floor in front of Rachel. He wasn't sure if he could blink through the walls and escape because of the shadows surrounding the trailer, but he wouldn't leave Rachel alone here. Not with a monster like Asmodeus.

"Don't leave me here," Rachel cried. "We had a deal."

"Of course," said Kesien, reaching out and squeezing her bound hands. "Now, we break your bonds. But after I do that, we're going to have to do a little play-acting. Your specialty. I'm going to create some fake shadow rope and we're going to both pretend to be captives until both of us can escape. Okay?"

She nodded, tears rolling down her bruised, freckled cheeks. "Acting is my life—and I'm pretty damned good at it, stud. I'll play along for a little while. Until he leaves again."

While his former squad discussed how they could ambush Jack Casey, Kesien worked with Rachel and broke her shadow bonds. Quickly, he fashioned some fakes with his angel powers and draped them around his wings and Rachel's hands and feet.

When the trailer door rattled again, Kesien blinked back to the wall and slid into position. Moments before Asmodeus entered the trailer. Alone.

The huge demon moved through the trailer, checking Rachel's bonds, and then he planted himself in front of Kesien. For a long time, he stared, studying Kesien's bonds, his wings, and his face.

Looking for anything out of place, Kesien realized. But he wouldn't give Asmodeus anything to divide his attention. He wanted the demon to be satisfied and leave them alone again. Long enough for them to get out that trailer door.

"Pharzus!" Asmodeus shouted. "Get over here."

The former angel of death and former friend landed in front of Kesien and his eyes widened, but he didn't make a sound. His black hair was short and framed his oblong face, aquiline nose, and wide mouth. His dark grey gaze flicked from Kesien to Asmodeus, but surprisingly, he didn't let on that he knew Kesien.

"Watch this angel for me," he said. "He's already tried to escape once. Make sure he's here when we get back."

"When you get back?" Pharzus questioned.

Asmodeus nodded and slid back from Kesien. "Yeah, Reptev, Lix, and I are going to collect a bounty." The huge demon pointed a finger at Kesien. "You move even a foot from this wall, I'll know it, angel. And if you're not here when I get back, the girl and Casey will both die. I guarantee it."

Kesien stared at Pharzus as Asmodeus headed out of the trailer. To ambush poor Jack. And Kesien had no way to warn him.

11

IT FELT LIKE AN ETERNITY BEFORE PRAVUIL RETURNED TO THE ROUND room, carrying what looked like a glass snow globe partially wrapped in white silken fabric. But its surface was frosted and she couldn't see what was inside it. It was about five inches in diameter and had a strange orange glow to it that flickered and guttered.

He extended the globe to her still draped in a fabric that seemed to grip the glass.

Carefully, she accepted the globe and removed the cloth. As soon as it was free from the white draping, it floated in the air in front of her.

"A protective measure in case it's dropped," said Pravuil. "The celestial silk keeps it anchored, but if it's removed—or dropped—the sphere floats. Also helps when we reshelve items in the Archive. The globe turns transparent when touched by authorized users." He motioned for her to take the sphere. "Go on, pick it up."

Talia gripped the sphere in both hands. Like a fogged mirror hit with hot air, the frosty sheen vanished, revealing roiling red and orange flames. Writhing. Angry. Unforgiving as they licked at the container, the flames' tips turning blue and white.

"The flames were created during the Rebellion," said Pravuil. "The embodiment of Lucifer's rage and fury. And his followers. When they were thrown from the Heavens, the flames arose. But Lucifer and his fallen angels feed the Hellfires with their anger and thirst for vengeance. Hell couldn't burn without it."

Surprised, Talia stared at God's Scribe for a moment. Lucifer kept Hell burning with his unrepentant rage and unending search for vengeance?

"If Lucifer stopped raging, would the fires go out?" she asked.

Not that Lucifer would ever give up that fury or his quest for vengeance. They were dear old friends to the King of Hell.

Pravuil shrugged. "Perhaps…if all the Hell creatures gave up their rage and vengeance. And the souls there gave up their hate and anger. Lucifer's far too blinded by resentment and a false sense of betrayal to ever give up that rage though. Like the damned souls that he presides over."

Talia ran her index finger across the surface and the flames followed the tip of her finger across the globe. Attracted to her touch? It made her uneasy.

"Why does it follow my fingers?" she asked, glancing up at the Scribe.

Pravuil slid his fingers across the left side of the sphere and the flames followed.

"It craves consumption, Talia," he said. "It needs fuel to feed. Without it, that flame would extinguish itself quickly. That's why it's encased in that sphere. You must keep it enclosed until you have wood from the Tree. Break the globe with the wood when you're ready to awaken the power."

She nodded. "I'll make sure it stays sealed until I'm ready," she said. "Thank you, Scribe."

"Always a pleasure, Talia," he said and extended his wings. "Sing out when you've awakened the power and I'll meet you back here. We need to understand what transference does before you and Azrael's guard assault the Gates of Hell."

She wrapped the cloth back around the globe and cradled it against her grey angel of death robes.

"Now, hurry to the Garden and gather a piece of the Tree," said Pravuil as he floated toward the ceiling. You'll need to awaken the power where it once stood."

Talia stretched her wings and rose through the room to a portal on the roof, but the wash of gold light caught her gaze. She stared at the white stones of the terrace as the memory of Samael's guard's betrayal rose around her.

Images flashed. Of angels of death cut down by the traitorous guard. Lights erased from the Heavens. It made her chest ache and brought crystalline tears to her eyes.

A piercing shriek rang out, sending a chill through her. She turned.

The memory of Berith's abduction permeated Eolowen.

Like a black mist, a horde of demons rose out of the stones, from the green grassy meadow. The storm of demons swirled around her as more poured onto the terrace.

Overwhelming Berith. Overwhelming the guard.

She felt the crystalline tears rush down her face and shatter against the rooftop. Overwhelming Azrael.

His pain rang out across Eolowen's nave, tangled in the willow tree, and shot along the burbling stream as it rose in frantic shouts. Screaming Berith's name as he swung Holy fire swords through swaths of demons. Trying to get to her.

The last sound across the meadow, before the storm of demons subsided, was Berith's forlorn call.

One word. Azrael.

The hand against her shoulder shook her out of the memory and she heard the soft beat of wings. Her own. And Pravuil's.

"Talia...what is it?" he asked in a soft, concerned voice. "What's the matter?"

Still, the crystalline tears flooded her cheeks and shattered against the rooftop.

"I still feel all of the angel deaths here, Pravuil," she whispered, her wings quivering. "And I saw..." She pulled in a heavy breath. "I saw the demons overpower Azrael and take Berith." She was shaking. "It was horrible."

Pravuil pulled her into an embrace. "I forget about all the rare angel powers you possess, Talia," he said in a soft voice. "I should have realized that you would soon experience those moments for yourself. And that you'd still feel the angelic deaths around you. See, Berith was trying to use resurrect to bring as many back from oblivion as she could when…when a storm of demons attacked."

"I had no idea," she said. "I thought that too much time had passed to bring them back."

Pravuil let her go. "For the healers, yes. But apparently, with yours and Berith's rare gifts, resurrect can be attempted as long as you still feel their essence, still see that sparkle of light."

Talia gasped. "Scribe, I can still see the resonance on the stones. If that's true, then I have to try!"

She handed him the globe and flew down to the terrace.

She weaved around pairs of angels of death sparring until she found a smear of light on the stones. Dropping to her knees, she laid her hand on the light and reached inside for the resurrect power.

At first, it came softly. A frosty breath of blue light illuminated her fingertips from the Creation's first drop of water. Next, a wash of green light from the Creation's last grain of sand. Sparks of yellow light shot from her fingertips, born from the Corridor of Pervasive Light. And finally, blood-red light dripped from her fingers, oozing across the smear of light. Covering it with the blood of life.

The terrace began to rumble.

Angels of death scattered, shuffling backward as a column of white light shot up from the terrace stones and burned like a roman candle. Until the outline of an angel took shape. Wings elongated and unfolded.

Irinas stepped out of the light and gasped, her grey eyes wide as she gazed around the terrace. Her shoulder-length sable hair fell against her tawny face and she gazed at the silent, shocked guard surrounding her.

"Eolowen," she cried in a clear alto voice. "By the Maker…I'm home."

"Irinas!" Azrael rushed through the shocked angels as the archangel laid his hand against her radiant cheek. "How?"

Smiling through his glassy charcoal gaze, Azrael turned to Talia. "Talia...did you—?"

She nodded. "I used resurrect, archangel." She held out her arms and turned in a circle. "It's not too late for most of them."

Irinas hugged her. "Thank you, Talia," she said and pressed her hands together. "To have your light extinguished and then...relit again. I—have no words except thank you."

"Everyone, off the terrace!" Azrael commanded. "Let Talia work."

As crystalline tears clinked against the stones, Talia sought out every glimmer of light across the terrace and called up resurrect. Bringing angel after angel back from oblivion.

For hours, she churned through her well of Holy light, resurrecting angels. Several times, when her halo dimmed, Azrael and Muriel let her draw light from their halos until she'd recovered every lost angel of death's light. Exhausted and drained, she collapsed against the wall, wings drooping.

"Did I get them all, archangel?" she asked, her voice barely above a whisper.

He dropped down beside her, his charcoal grey eyes wet with tears as the entire guard crowded around her. Muriel knelt beside her, stroking her hair.

Azrael nodded. "All but one," he said with a painful smile.

His pain spiked through her. He meant Berith.

She reached out and gripped his arm. "Patience, archangel. I'm not done yet." She motioned at the crowd of over two hundred angels of death shining against the Parrish blue sky in their Eternean armor. "We're not done yet."

Muriel grinned. "Talia's right, sir. We're just getting this party started...to quote another absent member of the guard."

"Soon as we locate Kesien and finish our training," said Talia, determination burning in her grey eyes, "there's gonna be Hell to pay."

Azrael sighed, amusement shining in his eyes. "Another Jack Casey quote."

"He has a way of rubbing off on you, doesn't he?" Pravuil replied as he landed on the terrace.

"Thank the Maker," said Azrael as he gently picked up Talia off the terrace. "Talia needs some time to replenish her Holy fire. Scribe, get Oseira back here to make sure our restored angels of death receive any needed healing. The rest of you, back to training."

Talia tried to get Muriel's attention, wanting her to return to Earth and check on Jack, but she felt the world turn white as she lost consciousness.

12

"Herb, will you just listen to me for five minutes?" Jack insisted, hands in his pockets. "That's all I ask…five minutes."

In faded Levi's, blue Vans slip-ons, and a distressed, pale yellow Henley, Jack stood in front of the small black conference table, waiting for Herb to say something. The small glass office at the back of the dark studio set was private, but he'd interrupted a meeting with set coordinators, Jennifer Collins and Steve Kosinski.

Seated at the conference table, whiteboards on all the walls, Steve and Jennifer watched in silence, glancing from Herb to Jack and back again. Steve looked frozen, to-go coffee cup in hand. Jennifer sat with her hands in her lap, coffee cup untouched beside her.

Herb glanced past Jack toward the table as he rolled up the sleeves of his coral dress shirt, black dress pants wrinkled, balding head shiny under the fluorescent lights. The room smelled like coffee and Jennifer's vanilla cologne as she shrugged at Herb. Steve looked surprised and had a deer caught in headlights look as he drank his coffee.

"All right, Jack," said Herb, fixing Jack with his gaze. "You've got five minutes and then we've got to fix our shooting schedule."

They looked terrified. Like he was going to give his notice or check into rehab or something.

Grinning, Jack grabbed a black dry-erase marker off the table and rushed over to the whiteboard. The marker squeaked across the dry-erase board as he drew the generic floor plan of a house and labeled each room: kitchen, family room, master bedroom, deck, and guest room.

Already, Herb was frowning.

"Is that the floor plan of your new house, Jack?" Jennifer asked, pressing her teal glasses up the bridge of her nose, her hair pulled tight into a ponytail, clipboard in her lap. She wore black leggings and a gold tunic.

He shook his head. "Haven't bought anything yet."

Steve laid his hand against his close-cropped beard, brown eyes bright, and long brown hair loose at his shoulders. He wore faded jeans, Doc Martens, and a jean shirt.

"Is that your dream house?"

Again, Jack shook his head.

"Jack, I don't have time for a game of Pictionary," Herb snapped, looking grumpy as he sat back down at the conference table. "And I need to get Jennifer and Steve out there setting up scenes. What are you drawing?"

Still grinning, Jack pointed at the whiteboard. "I'm drawing the layout of your new show format, Herb. And it's gonna make the network cry money."

"A house plan?" Herb's frown bordered on a glare.

Jack nodded. "But not just any house plan, Herb," he said. "It's the start of a new competition for all four couples."

"What competition, Jack?" Steve asked.

"Competitions were scrubbed for the new show, Jack," said Jennifer, looking worried like he'd had a psychotic break with reality. "Don't you remember?"

"The competition I'm proposing," Jack replied and tapped the whiteboard. "The current script is gonna get us all fired. So, I propose a new format."

"Fired?" Herb shouted.

"He isn't wrong, Herb," said Jennifer as she laid her clipboard on the table. "Have you read today's pages? The new script supervisor quit over it this morning."

Herb gasped. "What? Shirley quit?"

Jennifer nodded emphatically. "Union's sending us a new one this afternoon."

"Forget about the old script!" Jack shouted.

Herb's attention returned to him, but he was red in the face now. Jennifer looked terrified. Steve covered his eyes, shaking his head, looking ill.

"Here's your new format," said Jack, tapping the whiteboard again. "Each couple buys a fixer-upper house. Potential dream home. They each work with a designer and carpenter, do the work themselves… work a little divine magic, turning three or four rooms into dream renovations. Each week, we let the fans vote on their favorite reno. Least favorite reno sends one couple home. Winner gets a celestial reno on their entire house. Boom! Fans love the show again. Network cries money. Profit."

The silence in the room was heavy. Maybe he'd explained it too fast? He fidgeted, twirling the dry-erase marker around in his hand. Or maybe they just hated it? But anything was better than this unscripted scripted disaster they'd already filmed.

"Did I go too fast?" Jack asked in a quiet voice, holding out his hands.

"Jack…" Steve rushed over to the whiteboard, his gaze flicking from the drawing to Jack.

"You hate it, don't you?" he said finally.

"Jack…this is—fantastic!" Steve cried.

Jennifer nodded, hugging her clipboard. "I love the idea! This will play well on the screen." At last, she smiled. "It's like the old show, too. Our fans will love it."

"Well, Herb?" Jack replied, turning around.

But Herb was rushing toward him.

"Jack! I love this!" He spun Jack around and then hugged him.

"This brings back the competition from previous seasons and sets up a new kind of tension. Network's gonna love it, too! I know it."

"What do you want us to do?" Steve asked Herb as Jennifer crowded in beside him, hugging her clipboard.

Herb slid his phone out of his pants pocket. "Let me pitch this to the network. If they greenlight it, we'll need a couple of weeks or so to retool the sets, rewrite the scripts, and hire four designers. Should be fast since the network already runs two or three renovation shows." He turned to Jennifer. "Get the cast settled on a brief hiatus. Steve, you handle the crew hiatus—and the new script supervisor." He pointed at Jack. "And Jack, you stay away from Evan Bellows until this is settled."

Jack laughed. "Dude, I already passed on that offer, remember?"

"I'm still working that fight into the show, Jack," said Herb. "Now, go relax in your trailer with Talia while I get your pitch moving."

"Done. Let me know how much money the network throws at us, Herb," he said with a smirk. "Hope it's enough to send Evan a fruit basket."

Herb laughed. "You'll be the first to know, Jack."

"Later," said Jack. "Gonna break the news to Mrs. Casey."

He hurried out of the office, ran past the empty set, and dashed into the July heat, the door to Studio 22 closing behind him.

Dammit, Talia was still at Eolowen, dealing with another rare angel power. He frowned. And trying to find Kesien. He couldn't tell her until she came back…and he had no idea how long that could take. He hoped Kesien was okay. He missed that calm, patient angel of death calling him kid.

An airplane whined overhead, a mower buzzing nearby. He wanted to spread his wings, fly up to Eolowen, and help Talia awaken this new power. But he couldn't. He was stuck here dealing with the human messes he'd made. Right now, he needed to find Gianni and tell him about the new format he'd pitched. He'd stop by Gianni's trailer, call Banks—he sighed—and Rachel over. Tell them the news after he told Gianni.

The air smelled like eucalyptus and fresh cut grass as Jack hurried toward the row of trailers behind the building, rehearsing in his head what he'd say to Gianni. God, he hoped Gianni and Banks wouldn't get pissed at him for changing the show.

Maybe they'd even thank him?

He walked past his trailer and stepped up to Gianni's trailer door. He reached out to knock on the white door, but something slammed into him. Hard. Knocking him off the second step and onto the asphalt.

Dazed and seeing stars, he struggled to get up, strained to clear his fuzzy vision.

Something hit him hard again. Slamming him across the pavement. Behind the trailers.

Blood dripped across his throbbing face, jaw swelling, and knees raw and aching from the pavement's bite.

A shadow blocked out the sun.

He looked up.

Into the leering, dusty red face of Asmodeus moments before the huge demon hit him again.

13

Forced to wait for her Holy fire to regenerate, Talia reclined on the round room's small white bed and watched Oseira examine the more than two dozen angels scattered along the curved white stone wall. Angels that Talia had resurrected from Eolowen's terrace. Soft scents of jasmine and honeysuckle wafted through the room as angels flitted in and out of the space.

As Talia watched the cherub work, laying hands on each angel, she noticed the slightest hint of a shadow around Oseira's hands, barely dimming her healing light. Turning it a soft gold. Like the first breath of tarnish on a gold coin.

She'd never seen a shadow like that before. Especially on the cherubim. She'd asked Pravuil to make sure Oseira was all right. God's Scribe had used his archangel energies to scan her for injuries and dark influences but found nothing. He promised to keep a closer eye on the cherub and had even informed High House, but Oseira had done nothing to warrant further scrutiny. That's how the seraphim phrased it, according to Pravuil. Besides, as soon as Oseira was done healing these angels and ensuring the guard was ready to assault Hell, she would return to High House. Pravuil said that the seraphim would observe her more closely when she was back in the spire.

Talia hoped the cherub healer would be okay. She seemed confused at times, sometimes struggling to complete basic healing tasks, things that had been second nature to her when Lucifer marched on Heaven.

After Oseira had healed and cleared the last angel of death, Oseira blinked onto the rooftop and flew over the willow tree toward more squads that trained in the meadow.

Talia sat up on the bed and stretched her wings, her halo back to its bright gold again. She had let her light refill all day and now, she felt well enough to travel to the Garden. Was this how Jack felt during a power drunk, she wondered?

She spread her wings and lifted off the bed, blinking onto the terrace, but Azrael met her there.

"Heading off to the Garden already, Talia?" he asked, looking forlorn but focused.

She nodded. "I just need the sphere and I'm ready to fly."

Azrael motioned to one of the death angels in the guard, Laialus. His long grey hair blew in the wind as he carried the silk-wrapped globe in both hands. He held it out to her.

"Thank you, Laialus," she said with a nod.

As she cradled the artifact against her grey robes, Azrael laid his hand on her shoulder. His gaze was intense.

"You know I can't let you go alone, Talia," he said. "Not after the storm of demons that took Berith." His intense gaze shot past her, drifting toward the crossroads. "We have no idea what Lucifer's planning."

"Where's Muriel?" Talia asked, glancing around the terrace.

"I sent her back to Earth," he said and motioned over his shoulder. "To make sure that Jack's safe. And to keep looking for Kesien. Try to pick up his trail and see where it stopped. It's been days, Talia. I'm worried."

She was worried, too. It had been days. Had Lucifer ordered Asmodeus to grab Kesien? Had that horrible Hell prince dragged Kesien to Hell alongside Berith, ready to sacrifice him? She knew that Eolowen had been warded by the seraphim after Berith was taken, but

Kesien left his post when he saw Asmodeus at the crossroads. Where was he now?

Cherubim patrolled alongside death angel guards throughout Heaven, to hopefully prevent any more angel abductions. And that included the Corridor of Pervasive Light. She didn't know how Lucifer penetrated Heaven's defenses long enough to grab Berith from Eolowen's terrace, but Kesien was a different matter.

He'd gone off alone and put himself in harm's way. She was furious at him. But worried sick.

"I know," she said and bowed her head. "I'm worried, too."

Azrael let go of her shoulder. "Until we locate Asmodeus—and Kesien—none of my guard travels alone. And that includes you, Talia."

His wings unfolded and spread like a fan behind him.

"That's why I'm going with you."

Her eyes widened. "You, sir?"

"Yes, me," he said. "I want to make sure you're safe in the Garden. Lucifer may try to stop you from awakening this power because it could be a window into his plan."

The archangel was right. She'd never even considered that possibility.

"I've requested cherubim patrols to fly over the Garden while we're inside, so I doubt Lucifer will try anything." Azrael flexed his soot-grey wings wider and hovered above the terrace. "But just in case, let's hurry."

Talia cradled the globe against her robes with her left arm and lifted off the terrace, dove grey wings extended.

"I'm ready, sir," said Talia.

Azrael banked across the meadow, flying over the willow tree, and turning toward the horizon. Where the Garden stood, open and abandoned.

Talia flew close, following the archangel's path until she found an updraft. She floated on the warm currents that carried her alongside the archangel's flightpath across the sparkling white rooftops and spires of Heaven. Toward the crossroads and the road to Purgatory.

All along their route, the skies were dotted with angels. Patrolling.

She hadn't seen this many patrols since Lucifer marched on Heaven. But apparently, the seraphim felt that Lucifer was still a credible threat against them. Enough to have cherubim prowling the roads in lion form and protecting the skies in eagle and angel forms. And agreeing to send a sizeable force to assault the Gates of Hell. Talia had seen the destruction Lucifer could inflict firsthand, so Heaven's defensive preparations made her feel safer.

But her worry for Jack deepened. He was back on Earth alone with only Muriel and Anahera to protect him. Deemah and Daidrean would assist, but they were still frantically searching for Kesien. Granted, Jack had seraphim powers, but if he overused them, the power drunk would incapacitate him. That's what she feared most. She had to get back to Earth and make sure the love of her life was safe.

Asmodeus terrified her. He was hunting Jack right now, waiting for the right moment to strike. If that monster knew she'd returned to Eolowen...

Her whole body shuddered at the thought and she increased her speed, wings furiously beating the air until she sailed past Azrael, banking left over the crossroads. Turning toward the distant walls of the Garden.

If Asmodeus killed Jack—or dragged him off to Hell—she'd never see him again.

"We need to hurry," she called to Azrael.

Azrael blinked beside her. "Agreed. I'm worried about Asmodeus, too, Talia. As a Hell prince, he'd like nothing better than to unseat Lucifer and rule over Hell."

"What?" Talia cried, surprised by the archangel's comment. "He couldn't unseat Lucifer."

Azrael nodded. "No, of course not, but Lucifer only promotes his most ambition demons." The archangel's face pinched in a frown. "And the most bloodthirsty. He leverages their ambitions—and desire to kill—to maintain control. When he could no longer control Asmodeus, the cherub launched coup while impersonating Lucifer. Of course, Lucifer banished him. Now, Lucifer's holding freedom over that demon's head to make him obey. But that won't last long."

Talia grimaced. "Long enough to hurt Jack."

"Asmodeus is too weak to tangle with Lucifer—and Jack—for long. Even before Lucifer regained his power, Asmodeus was no match for him. He was a cherub before the Fall, so he's still formidable, but not seraphim-level."

"Either way, Lucifer will get what he wants from Asmodeus," said Talia. "But that monster could still kill Jack."

Azrael nodded and then blinked across the sky ahead of her. Talia followed with two blinks until she caught up to him as he landed in front of the Garden's entrance. Where the doors had been thrown open. Blown apart after Lucifer's powers returned and he escaped Jack's trap.

Talia winced. After killing Jack.

She thanked the Maker again for giving her the power to bring Jack back from that.

Still, she shivered at the memory of feeling Jack take his last breath. Exhaling sharply, she carried the globe into the Garden, Azrael beside her.

The archangel was tense, a stony expression on his face, wings taut and twitching, gaze steely as he scanned the murky Garden. The overgrown brush and dried-up vegetation cast shadows throughout the dimly lit space, rotted fruit husks littering the ground, giving the walled space a fermented, sweet smell. It had the perpetual feel of twilight, the sunlight never quite piercing the rot and gloom of the Maker's ruined experiment.

Brush crunched as she passed through the ruined orchards of long ago on both sides and headed toward the remnants of the Tree of Life. Its blood-red leaves still stained the ground red in a circle where Jack had lain dying. That moment still brought crystalline tears to her eyes. They rolled down her cheeks and disappeared into the knee-high grass.

"I know how difficult returning to the Garden is for you, Talia," said Azrael, his gaze traversing the dim light and shadows that shifted with the wind. "I will never forget Jack's sacrifice here either."

After tricking her and Muriel into leaving the Garden, Jack shoved the archangel out the doors and fused the locks, trapping him inside with Lucifer who would have overpowered Azrael, too. Even in his weakened state from the Fall, Lucifer was still tremendously powerful.

"The memory still lingers here, sir," she said. "It will forever haunt the Garden—and me."

He rubbed her shoulder and stopped in front of the red circle that stained the overgrown grass. And turned to face the entrance.

"I'll keep watch, Talia," he said. "Hurry."

Talia dropped to her knees beside the circle of leaves and set down the globe. Already, it began to glow, flames leaping, sensing the nearness of the Tree of Life's remains. Most of the great trunk had turned to dust, but small sections remained, looking dry and bleached like bones. Almost smooth. It reminded her of the driftwood on the island beaches where she and Jack had honeymooned by the Puget Sound. Another memory she would never forget. Despite the demon attacks, she had precious memories of walking those beaches at sunset in his arms.

She missed him so much right now, hating to be this far away from him. Worrying about his safety. She ached to feel his arms around her or hear him call her babe or Mrs. Casey. By the Maker, she loved that man! She hoped Muriel and Anahera were keeping a careful watch over him.

After sifting through the piles of dust where the massive trunk had fallen and rotted away, Talia found a small four-inch hunk of the tree trunk. It would be enough to awaken transference.

She moved back to the globe and unwrapped the white silky fabric. The sphere floated up from the ground and drifted about three feet above the red circle, flames licking against the clear glass globe, trying to escape and consume the wood. Eager to burn down the Creation with hatred and rage.

Talia gripped the sliver of wood in her right hand. As she lifted it toward the globe, intending to smash it, voices whispered across the periphery of her senses. They rose all around her in layers, drowning out even the wind.

Then she felt a presence. Heavy. Dark. Multiplying.

"Azrael…" she said in a wary voice. "Something's in here with us."

Azrael moved closer, enfolding her in his great archangel wings. "I feel it too, Talia. Hurry and finish this!"

Abruptly, the wind died. Brush rustled. Shadows shifted.

She glanced past the globe.

Into a sea of red eyes that had surrounded them. Blocking the entrance to the Garden.

From the overgrowth, a small, leathery red demon shuffled through the tall grasses and stopped about twenty feet from the red circle. And spoke.

"Azrael! Talia! What a grand surprise! Fancy meeting you both here."

That voice went right through her and she felt her anger rise.

Lucifer.

14

THE WORLD FROZE AS JACK FELT ASPHALT RAKE AGAINST HIS CHEEK. AND the flutter of angel wings around him.

Talia's squad had amazing timing.

But that thought was crushed as two angels of death dropped from the shadows and pinned him against the hot pavement.

"That was too easy!" a sharp tenor voice crowed.

"Frankly, Casey," said a deep, rumbly voice. "I'm disappointed. I thought this would be fun and at least last a few minutes."

Through the din of feathers and icy shadows, Jack realized that voice belonged to Asmodeus. And he had a couple of cowardly angels of death sitting on his back.

Something burned against his forehead for a moment and then faded into a warm touch that finally ebbed. Like something had grabbed hold of his brain and squeezed it for a moment. It hurt like a migraine and then vanished.

Cupping both hands, he called up two handfuls of murder marbles as he peered through a charcoal grey wing feather at Asmodeus' hulking frame.

"Too easy, huh?" said Jack with a sneer. "Well, let's do another take. This time, with special effects. Bitch."

Jack flung both handfuls of murder marbles. They exploded, knocking the angels of death backward. Into Asmodeus. The force knocked all three of them across the asphalt and into the side of Gianni and Izzy's trailer.

Spreading his wings, Jack pulled himself up from the hot pavement and called up a sword of Holy fire in each fist.

"This better, Asmo?" Jack asked with a shrug. "Or do you prefer Deus? Hey, that's kinda short for douchebag, isn't it? And Asmo rhymes with—"

"Shut up, Casey!" Asmodeus growled and pointed a dusty red finger at him. "You think those swords scare me? You're wrong."

Jack flung both swords at the two angels of death that stood there gaping at him. The Holy fire blades sliced through their wings, setting feathers on fire. Shrieking, they threw themselves onto the ground and rolled, trying to put out the fire.

Then Jack called up a basketball-sized sphere of Holy fire. "Don't be so salty, Asmo. Those blades were meant for your angel of death dudes. Friends of yours? Now, for you, I've got something much more intimidating." He shifted the ball of Holy fire back and forth in his hands. "Because if this Holy fire doesn't scare the Hell out of you, you're too stupid to live. No wonder Lucifer's already tired of your shit."

Asmodeus glared at him, baring pointy white teeth. "A puny human has managed to summon some Holy fire. Big deal. That might scare some lowly angels of death, but I'm a prince of Hell, Casey." He thumped his chest with a meaty hand. "Nothing scares me—especially a winged human."

Jack grinned. "How about a winged human with seraphim powers? That scare you? 'Cause I'm packing enough Holy heat to melt an entire legion of demons, dude. And that includes one puny Hell prince. Catch."

Jack tossed the massive ball of Holy fire to Asmodeus. Dude was unfortunate enough to catch it. A heartbeat later, it exploded in the huge demon's face. Knocking him halfway across the studio lot. Into a smoking black crater about four feet across.

The Hell prince lost his hold on freezing time and the world moved around Jack again. That's when he felt the blood dripping down the side of his face. He hurried up the two steps into his trailer and slammed the door. Locking it. He needed Talia's squad to ward the trailer—now that Asmodeus had become bold enough to attack him in the middle of this crowded studio. Talia was going to be furious when she found out. She'd make sure the trailer got warded. He might be able to keep a ward at the door for a short time, but demons could get through in a bazillion other places. And he'd be too power drunk to stop them.

He gazed around the trailer, fearing another ambush, but no red eyes stared back at him from the shadowy corners. He rushed through the trailer, snapping on lamps and turning on lights. That's when he felt a gnawing pain in his gut. Hunger? No, he was craving something —bad. Salt?

He moved toward the kitchen sink and his gaze fell onto the box of powdered donuts on the light grey quartz countertop.

Or was it sugar he craved?

Jack...

He turned at the sound of the taunting whisper. Cold fear snaked down his spine. He wasn't alone in here.

"Asmo's a little busy putting out fires right now, like the wings of his angel of death bros," said Jack as his gaze flicked through the trailer. "They're on fire. Literally."

Couldn't be the Hell prince or his sidekicks.

He watched for the slightest movement. The faintest shift in the light. Or the afternoon shadows creeping along summer's hard edges. The room had no tinge of sulfur or brimstone, but the hint of woodsmoke made him tense.

"And Luci's passport's still expired," Jack called out as he moved toward the bedroom.

Jack...

Again, the voice hung just above the soft huff of the air conditioner and muffled movements outside his trailer as the studio activities flowed past.

"Whoever you are, call my agent," he shouted as he entered the bedroom, moving past the shower toward the bed. "I don't answer calls outside Heaven's or California's area codes."

His mouth felt dry, that ache in his gut intensifying. He felt cold, chilled—achy. Like he was hungover. His gaze narrowed when he saw something small and white lying on the comforter.

And then it hit him.

Like he was strung out. And needed a hit or two to make him feel normal again.

Memories of addiction washed over him in sharp waves as he dropped down on the bed and examined the small white thing there.

His heart hammered his rib cage. It was coke...another bag of flake!

And every cell in his body hungered for it. In a way he hadn't felt in a year.

He froze, staring at the bag like it was a poisonous snake. But that horrible ache amplified through his gut, the need to feel that euphoria, that rush blasting through him again. That feeling of being on top of the world. Of being able to do anything.

He licked his lips and reached toward the small plastic bag. He could almost smell the pungent traces of gasoline through it, feel that amped-up rush surge through his body.

No. It had been a year since he'd touched the stuff. He pulled his hand back.

Go ahead, Jack... The voice hissed around him. *You need it, don't you?*

Anxiety was a sour ache in the pit of his stomach alongside the gnawing craving that trembled through him. God did he need it! Right now.

Just a couple of lines. To steady his nerves. Get him back on track. That's all.

He hesitated and then scooped up the bag. He held it in his palm, feeling the burn and call of its contents, eager to feel it flood through his veins. The siren's call washed over him like a tsunami, begging him to open the bag. To fix this.

Cradling the bag like it was an injured sparrow, Jack rushed into the kitchen and set the bag on the grey quartz countertop. He shoved his hands in his pockets and fished out his car keys. God, just a quick key bump or two to steady him, and then he'd do some proper lines. A credit card and a rolled-up bill would do the job.

Frantic, hands shaking, he knocked over the box of powdered donuts, spilling them all over the sink and countertop as he struggled to open the zip closure on the small plastic bag.

Something behind him went bang and thump as he dipped his apartment key into the fine snow-white powder.

His fingers shook as he lifted the key up toward his nose.

One quick key bump! No one will care. It's just one. To steady his nerves after fighting that massive demon. He'd earned it.

The sweet smell of gasoline washed over him. God, he'd missed that familiar chemical scent. Missed that rush of electricity scouring his veins, surfing his system with an amazing high, and all the confidence he'd ever need. Laughter buzzed against his ears and he almost didn't care.

Almost.

It took every ounce of strength inside him to punch through his anticipation, his obsession. And hit the brakes. Hard. For all he was worth.

His hand shook as he struggled to force the key back, away from his nose.

No. No! What was he doing? One key bump would put him back on the treadmill again. Back on the bullet train about to jump its track.

All aboard! Next stop oblivion!

His breathing was heavy, pulsing, as sweat flecked his face and soaked his bangs.

He glanced at his wedding ring.

No. He couldn't do this to Talia. He couldn't hurt her like this. And he couldn't disappoint Gianni.

Even his mother's disillusioned voice shrieked in his head. "Jackson Seeger Casey, don't you dare! All of this will be your fault. Do you hear me?"

Where was all of this coming from? He felt like it had been hours since he'd done a line, not a year.

"Jack, no!" the voice behind him shouted. "Don't!" It was Gianni.

With bruising force, Jack slammed his hand against the countertop, scattering the flake off his apartment key. Into the sink.

He screamed in rage, in frustration, and dropped his keys on the counter. He dumped the bag of cocaine into the sink, tossed it down the drain, and turned on the water. Shaking all over, he backed away, pressing his face into his hands.

Dammit! Now, Gianni thought he was a liar. He felt sick.

The flash of light startled him.

He looked up through the small window over the sink. Into the eyes of a photographer. Grinning. Paparazzi.

Dear God...dude had snapped a shot of him about to key bump himself into losing everything.

A hand gently pressed against his shoulders as they heaved, the sorrow bubbling up.

"Jack? Talk to me," said Gianni in a kind, patient voice. "What's going on?"

He couldn't talk. All he could do was motion at the window with one hand and cover his face with the other.

Gianni smashed his eyes closed. "Dammit! Tell me that wasn't a photographer."

When Jack didn't respond, Gianni steered him away from the window and over to the sofa. Gently and slowly, Gianni slid Jack's hands away from his face. He looked shocked.

"You're bleeding, Jack," Gianni said finally. "Tell me what's happening. And don't worry. Somehow, we'll fix this, okay?"

Jack gulped air, trying to say a dozen things at once, but all that came out was a moan.

"I need to know if you did some coke, Jack," said Gianni, his gaze unblinking.

Emphatically, Jack shook his head. It took him a moment or two to find his voice.

"No. Dude, I–I didn't. I didn't! I don't know what's the matter with me. It hit me like a bullet train when I saw the bag of drugs on the bed." He moaned and smashed his eyes closed. "And now, some dickhead paparazzi is texting TMZ to sell them a photo of me snorting flake. In ten minutes, it'll be everywhere. I just killed the show, my career, and my marriage all in one aborted key bump."

Gianni didn't say a word and it was killing him. "Dude, right now, I really need to hear you say that you believe me."

With all the calm and poise of Cary Grant, Gianni reached up with a paper towel and blotted the blood still clinging to the side of Jack's face.

"How did this happen?"

His best friend didn't believe him. He wanted to crawl in a hole and bury himself. And he couldn't face Talia. Not after this—this mess. What would he say? How could he justify this? He sighed. He couldn't justify it. That was the whole problem. God, he felt sick all over.

"Jack? How did this happen?"

Gianni's insistent voice drew his attention back and he squinted at his best friend. Who looked at him without judgment. Without condemnation. It was a simple inquiry, but why was he feeling so anxious and out of control?

He stared down at his hands, knuckles scuffed and bleeding, scrapes along his arms.

"Asmodeus ambushed me before I got into my trailer," he said.

Gianni's eyes widened, the first emotion creeping into his face and those warm brown eyes. It was fear.

"Who is Asmodeus?"

"More of a what, really."

"A what?" Gianni stared at him a moment. "Jack, please tell me that's a Greek Uber driver or your second favorite classical pianist."

Jack ran his hands through his hair. "It's a seven-foot-tall Hell prince that Lucifer sent to end me."

Gianni went from puzzled to terrified in less than two seconds. He grabbed hold of Jack's shoulders and shook him. "Are you telling you were just attacked in here by a seven-foot-tall demon that's in line for Hell's throne?"

Jack shook his head and Gianni sighed in relief.

"It was outside and Luci would never hand over his throne to one of his Hell princes. Especially one he banished for unnecessary roughness."

"What?" Gianni cried, his mouth agape.

"And Asmodeus wasn't alone. He had a couple of turncoat angels of death with him."

"There were THREE of them?"

Jack nodded. "Yep, but it's cool. They're all cowering and licking their wounds. Didn't you see that crater outside?"

"That was you?" Gianni cried, looking incredulous.

"Not my fault. Asmodeus was dumb enough to catch a huge ball of Holy fire."

Gianni began to pace in front of the sofa. "Jack, they could be on their way back here at any moment. You're in terrible danger! Why would Heaven leave you alone to face all these horrors like this?"

Finally, he whirled around and dropped down on the couch again and Jack saw anger burning in his brown eyes as he fidgeted. Kind of like if Cary Grant had starred in *Lethal Weapon*.

"Talia had to return to Heaven and investigate some rare angel power," said Jack. "Transference or something like that. And her squad has a member missing, so they're searching for him right now."

Gianni grabbed him by the shoulders again and shook him. Hard. "Jack! Lucifer is still hunting you. Lucifer still has a bounty on you. Every demon on the planet is probably still trying to get at you. Why would they leave you alone like this?"

Jack bowed his head. "Wish I knew, Gianni," he said in a defeated voice. "Maybe they thought that with my seraphim powers and my wings, I'd be fine while they handled this other stuff?"

"With a seven-foot Hell prince gunning for you?"

When Gianni put it like that, it didn't make sense. Unless someone had carefully orchestrated all the pieces into position. To get him alone. And make him an easy mark for Asmodeus. He winced. Or the drugs.

"What if it was all orchestrated, dude?" Jack asked.

Already, Gianni was nodding. "It had to be." He slid his phone out of his pocket. "That's why I'm not letting you out of my sight until Talia returns. Those demons probably got you alone, so they could turn up the heat somehow on your addiction, push you into doing coke again."

Damn! Gianni was probably right about that, too. He'd never even considered that they'd try that shit again—like Lucifer did to him on the set of *The Prince Charming Hour*.

"Dude, they could kill you. I can't—"

Gianni stood up from the sofa and crossed his arms. "I'm staying, Jack! And you're not talking me out of it."

Jack stumbled up from the couch, but the piercing sound of *Sympathy for the Devil* screeched from his pocket.

He froze, his heart pounding, the nightmares coming back to him. Hazy memories of the beach house. Flash of horns. Burn of red eyes.

"That's—that's Lucifer, isn't it?" said Gianni, his voice barely above a whisper as he pointed at Jack's pocket.

For a moment, Jack couldn't breathe, his throat closing. Finally, he pulled in a wheezing breath and slid his phone out of his pocket. His hand shook as he brought the phone to his ear. And turned on his game face.

"You've got to have better things to do than blow up my phone, Luci. If not, get a hobby already. Travel. Oh, wait…"

"Pardon the interruption, Jack," Lucifer's enthusiastic British accent made him shudder this time and all he wanted to do was hang up the phone. "I'll hold the line while you…do yours. Or have you finished your one-man party yet? It's so nice to see you finally loosen up and overdose. I've been so bored waiting for this moment. Do hurry up and kill yourself, so I can end the rest of humanity. I do have a schedule to keep."

Jack responded with a caustic laugh. "Not sure what you think's happening here on Earth, but you need to hire better demons. 'Cause that douchebag Asmo is lying to you. If I were you, I'd take that traitorous little bitch out before he steals your throne."

"Really, Jack? You're going to go there? Who was the traitorous little bitch that pretended to be part of my operation and then trapped me in the Garden?"

"Oh, clearly me," said Jack with a smirk. "Was just taking a page out of your playbook, Luci. 'Cause I hate hot weather almost as much as I hate you. Like you expected anything less from me? Go ahead! Believe everything Asmodeus says and hell, while you're at it, start believing in Santa Claus and the Easter Bunny. But don't say I didn't warn you. Remember, you banished that little bitch to Purgatory for a reason."

Lucifer exhaled sharply. "I do hate it when there's an actual point amongst all your feeble human ramblings."

"And another point, Luci," Jack said, watching Gianni's expression turn more horrified as the conversation continued. "This dude tried to kill me. Directly going against your orders. Can't believe you'd stand for that from a minion. Much less one you banished."

For several long moments, Lucifer was silent.

"Fear not, Jack, I'll sort all of it out when you return to Hell. And I will kill you last because I want you to watch all those angels of death get erased from existence, especially dear, sweet Talia. Who seems to be stuck in the Garden at the moment. A pity she may not make it out of there, Jack. Hope you kissed her goodbye before she left."

His heart hammered against his rib cage. Talia was in trouble! That's why she hadn't returned yet.

Had Lucifer trapped her in the Garden? If he left right now, maybe he'd get there in time to save her.

"Sleep well, Jack," Lucifer said and began laughing maniacally as the phone went dead.

"Jack, what is it?" Gianni rushed toward him. "You're as white as a sheet."

He lowered the phone from his ear, feeling shell-shocked as he turned to stare at Gianni.

"It's Talia," he said, struggling to say it out loud. "Lucifer said she's trapped in the Garden. I've got to go there and rescue her."

He shoved his phone in his pocket and flexed his wings. Gianni tackled him before he could lift off the floor and threw him onto the couch.

"Lucifer told you that so you'd rush there and get captured, Jack! I won't let you fall into that madman's trap trying to rescue her when she probably doesn't need rescuing."

Jack grabbed hold of Gianni's sleeve. "But what if she does? And I do nothing?" He bit his bottom lip. "Gianni...I–I can't lose her."

"Jack...you won't," said Gianni, still holding onto him. "But you've got to trust me. You're a little out of your head right now. I think that demon attack did something to you."

"Why do you say that?" Jack demanded.

"I've never seen you like this before, Jack. Not even the night when you overdosed. Or when you were coming off the flake. At your lowest addiction point, you weren't this anxious and paranoid." He gave Jack a sharp shake. "They've done something to you. Amplified your addiction struggle. Intensified it so you'd give in and do the drugs again."

Jack stared down at the floor as he thought back to the fight with Asmodeus and ran through it again, blow by blow. Had they done something to him? Then he remembered that moment when something had burned against his forehead. And his head throbbed like a migraine for a few moments then stopped.

"Wait a minute!" Jack cried, holding up his hand. "I think you're right, Gianni," he said and laid his hand against his forehead, feeling for a bump or a gash. "Is there any sort of injury on my forehead? A cut? A bruise?"

Gianni stepped closer and scrutinized his forehead and face. Finally, he shook his head. "There's a cut on the side of your face, but that's it."

Jack ran his fingers across his forehead, dead center, where he'd felt the burning pain. "I remember, during the fight with Asmodeus, his two turncoat angels of death pinned me to the ground. I felt something burn against my forehead. For almost a minute, my head ached like a migraine. Then it all stopped. Could they have done something to me during the fight?"

Gianni steered him over to the taupe sofa and squinted, examining his forehead. "I see a faint red mark there, but no sign of any sort of damage."

"I really need to consult with Talia on this, Gianni." He glanced up at the ceiling. "If she doesn't divorce me over the flake. And that damned photo."

He got up from the couch and walked the floor now, terrified that Talia was being killed by a million demons at that moment.

"Talia's not going to divorce you, Jack," said Gianni, walking beside him. "She may kill you, but never divorce you."

"What if she's in trouble, Gianni?" he said, pacing, wings twitching. "And here I stand, just letting it happen."

Gianni slid his arm around Jack's shoulders. "Keep the faith, Jack. Lucifer is just trying to upset you."

"There was no trying involved, dude," said Jack as he kept pacing up and down the trailer. "Worked like a charm."

"Promise me that you won't do anything until morning, Jack," said Gianni, still walking beside him.

He couldn't make that promise. If Talia was in trouble, he was going after her.

"Promise me, Jack!" Gianni shouted. "You're under the influence of something. Let it wear off first."

Talia would never forgive him if he let Lucifer lead him into an ambush. He had no choice but to trust Gianni's instincts. No matter how much it hurt.

Gianni pulled out his phone and called Izzy while he paced the trailer alongside Jack, telling her he'd be back in the morning.

So, his long night began. And he was worried sick about Talia.

15

TALIA GLARED AT THE LITTLE RED DEMON THAT LUCIFER HAD SPOKEN through, wanting to erase him from existence. Like those traitorous angels of death that had turned on the guard. Extinguishing dozens of them before they flew off to assault High House and the Archive. But she thanked the Maker that she was able to finally bring them back. Finishing what Berith had started. Talia prayed that Lucifer wouldn't harm her.

Azrael chanted a series of angel notes that drifted up through the Garden, alerting the nearby patrolling cherubim as Talia stepped forward, into the red circle of leaves. Toward the little red demon.

"I don't want to hear anything from you, Lucifer," Talia replied, glaring at the smile that curved across the demon's scaly face, those red eyes blazing bright in the Garden's eternal dusk.

"Not even a word or two about Jack? Surely, you must wonder how he's doing? Alone and so very far away. And so lonely—now that his playdate with Asmodeus has ended. Poor Jack must be distraught. And with all those drugs appearing on set? Why he might do something rash. Like…overdose."

A cold chill washed across her heart. Asmodeus had found Jack! Was he hurt? Or worse? She did her best not to show Lucifer any sort of reaction. Had that monster killed him? Or forced those drugs down him—enough to overdose?

"Oh, yes…let all of that sink in, dear Talia. You might return to the show's set as a widow. Would definitely change the show's format, now, wouldn't it? And that nauseating happily ever after they're always pushing. Turn it into a real crime drama—like SanFran Confidential. Oh, wait…"

Talia felt the tears sting her eyes, but she pushed back hard, to keep them from falling. No, she had to trust that Lucifer was lying and that Jack was fine. She wouldn't give Lucifer the response he sought.

She stared at the little red demon and let loose a peal of laughter. "Jack's just fine, Lucifer. Don't you worry. I'm sure he outmaneuvered Asmodeus and is sleeping soundly in his trailer as he waits for me to return."

"It's good to have dreams, Talia," Lucifer fired back. "But I don't think Jack Casey has slept soundly since his senior year of high school. Especially tonight after what Asmodeus and part of Samael's guard did to him."

Talia tamped down her fear and held onto her smile. "Winded him at best, annoyed him at worst. Jack wouldn't even break a sweat with those opponents."

"Perhaps not, Talia," Lucifer continued, the empty-eyed little red demon's unending stare making her uncomfortable. "But after Procel focused his new power through those angels of death onto Jack, I fear that his addiction is now out of control. And it may just cost him his life." A guttural laugh filled the Garden. "And his soul. There's a whole spoke of Hell dedicated to addiction and obsession for a reason."

"Lucifer!" Azrael shouted. "What did you do?"

"Well, I just told you, dear Azrael. Procel used Jack to practice his new rare angel power. You know? Transference." Lucifer began to laugh again. "And he just transferred a magnification power to Jack, increasing his addiction to cocaine about seven-fold I believe. Terrifying actually. I've never seen a man so paranoid and anxious before. And hurting for flake as he calls it."

Talia did her best not to show surprise or pain. Lucifer would magnify every moment and use it against her.

"And how convenient! What with all that cocaine appearing on set? He's in the right place at the right time. To overdose." Lucifer chuckled, his smug, amused tone raking down her spine and she struggled to hold it together.

"Jack has no interest in doing cocaine, Lucifer," Talia replied. "It'll never happen."

But internally, she was terrified. If they hit Jack with something that amplified his cocaine cravings, he might just break down and use again. Her heart hurt and she feared for him.

"A shame that your squad's all tied up, searching for a missing member," Lucifer continued. "Otherwise, they might have been there to stop poor Jack's backslide into drug use. Of course, don't take my word for it. Check social media." He laughed maniacally again. "Check the tabloids. They should all have photos by now. And Jack Casey won't be able to act his way out of this...oh, what does he call it? Shitshow."

Azrael stepped in front of her and pointed at the empty-eyed little demon.

"I'm coming for you, Lucifer. Soon."

The little demon grinned. "Oh, I'm counting on it, Azrael. And I look forward to every moment."

In a puff of smoke, the little demon disappeared as a flock of cherubim appeared at the Garden entrance. Some cherubim swooped low in eagle form while the others in angel form stormed through the overgrowth, routing demons.

Azrael whirled around and gripped Talia's arms. "Hurry, Talia," he said through gritted teeth. "We need to finish this. Now."

Fighting back her anguish, she turned toward the globe, a sliver of wood from the Tree of Life in her fist. Quickly, she drew back her arm and smashed the wood against the globe. That shattered.

Flames coiled around the wood, chewing through it.

Sparks flew. Ash filled the air. In the thick, black smoke, Talia felt something come to life.

It oozed through fire and smoke, through charred wood, through shattered glass that floated above the red circle of leaves. And slammed into Talia's hands. In a wave of red rage and blue vengeance that became a surge of purple flames, the fire burned down her arms and into her feet. The heat was stifling, her skin inflamed, her lungs filling with smoke.

In a burst of heat and light, the flames disappeared as her Holy light absorbed all of the released energy. And she felt the thrum of a new power churn within her. She still needed to test it, to make sure she had truly awakened transference.

Concentrating on fallen tree limbs to her right, Talia focused her attention on a bare spot beneath a stand of dead saplings.

She watched, surprised, as the tree limbs lifted from the ground and shifted across the Garden to rest beneath the dead saplings. Next, she focused her fear for Jack's safety onto Azrael and pushed it toward the archangel with a flick of her hand.

"Archangel, how do you feel?" she asked.

He squinted at her. "Feel?" he asked. "Why? Are you finished here? I think we should go and check on Jack." He crossed his arms, looking concerned. "After Lucifer's bluster, I'm afraid Jack's hurt or incapacitated."

Quickly, she waved her hand in the air, dissipating the fear. In moments, the tension drained from the archangel's face.

"How about now?" she asked.

The archangel looked puzzled. "I was deeply afraid for Jack just now. But I'm certain that he's okay." He frowned. "Was that your doing?"

Talia nodded. "I used transference to send my worry for Jack to you. Then I transferred it back again."

"The power's working, Talia," said Azrael. "Now, let's return to Eolowen and have Pravuil evaluate this new rare ability. That way, you can return to Jack and ease that horrible fear you're carrying. I felt it."

With a nod, Talia flexed her wings and rose into the air. Azrael flew beside her as a flock of cherubim passed overhead, patrolling the ruined Garden alongside one of the death angel squads. The demons had fled and then dissipated into smoke, but Talia didn't want to be here when they returned. She glanced back at the shadowy walled place.

Or if Lucifer decided to contact her again.

Following Azrael closely, she zipped out of the Garden and sailed along the tree line toward the crossroads. Azrael stayed beside her on the left as she banked over another forest and veered right over the crossroads. Toward the distant meadow that framed the back of Eolowen, the grand hall. Where Pravuil waited for her to return and demonstrate this rare angel power. That seemed more kinetic than the other powers she'd awakened.

But Pravuil needed to observe the power, see its capabilities, and understand how deeply it could penetrate. Lucifer had alluded to transference allowing him to magnify Jack's addiction. She needed to know if that was possible—and whether Lucifer had been lying about Procel using it on Jack through Samael's death angels.

She blinked across the meadow ahead of Azrael and he let her go. He was watching her back, she realized, making sure that nothing ambushed her. She cringed. Like Asmodeus had done to poor Jack. The thought made her ache all over.

After banking over the pergola, she flew over the willow tree and landed on the round room's rooftop. She dropped down through the portal and found Pravuil hovering against the far wall, studying some of the books in the room. Waiting for her return, she realized.

"Talia, you're back!" he cried, blinking to meet her.

He gave Azrael a nod when he landed behind her.

"Watched her back the whole time, I see," said Pravuil with a knowing smile.

Azrael nodded. "I refuse to allow Lucifer the opportunity to grab more of my guard. Especially this one. Who's very special to me and the guard."

Talia turned toward Azrael, seeing a mixture of pride and pain in his charcoal gaze. Berith's abduction was killing him. She threw her arms around him and hugged him tightly.

"We'll bring her home, sir," she whispered. "Don't you worry."

He nodded and let her go, wings folding against his back as he slid out of the way. He leaned against the opposite wall, wings flat against his shoulders, arms crossed, observing. He needed to see how transference worked and how Lucifer might use it against them somehow. Either way, he wouldn't get in the way of Pravuil's evaluation.

"I can already sense the new power within you, Talia," said Pravuil, glancing over at Azrael.

"She absorbed the power quickly and was able to immediately use it, Scribe," said Azrael. "There was no delay."

Pravuil turned his gaze back to Talia. "Tell me, how did you use it?"

With an encouraging nod from Azrael, Talia held out her hands. "I felt it in my hands at first. Then my whole body seemed to absorb the energy. First, I tried to physically transfer something to another place. Fallen tree limbs. Transferring them was easy."

"Good, good, Talia," said Pravuil as he floated above the floor, wings in gentle motion. "What else did you try?"

Again, she glanced at the archangel and then back to Pravuil. "I transferred an emotion from me to the archangel."

Pravuil raised an eyebrow. "An emotion?"

She nodded. "I transferred my fear for Jack's safety to the archangel without telling him what I transferred."

"Did it work?" Pravuil asked in a quiet voice.

"Yes," she said with a smile. "The archangel had a sudden bout of fear and wanted to make sure that Jack was safe."

"By the Maker!" Pravuil exclaimed. "It works!" His excitement quickly fled. "But why did Lucifer go to so much trouble to have Procel awaken it?"

A very good question. Lucifer wouldn't have gone to all the trouble to transfer emotions and feelings remotely from Hell to Earth or Heaven. It seemed like a novelty at best. No, there had to be something he'd gain by using the power. But what? And who did he plan to use it on?

"I keep asking myself that question, Pravuil," said Talia as she floated through the room, wings whispering against the breeze. "It seems like something that's just an amusement for Lucifer. What could he do with that power? Something strategic? Something deadly?"

Pravuil was pensive as he stared out the portals.

"Other than using it to harm humans and less powerful angels," said Azrael, frowning as he moved away from the wall, "why did Lucifer go to all that trouble to obtain it?"

"Would he be petty enough to go to all that trouble just to harm Jack?" Talia asked.

Pravuil and Azrael stared at each other a moment and then turned toward her.

"Yes," they both said in unison.

"My angel instincts tell me that power was gathered for a greater purpose," said Azrael as he paced through the room. "But to do what? It makes no sense to me, Pravuil."

God's Scribe shook his head, squinting at the text in his hand. "Me neither, Azrael," he said, "but we've got to keep digging on this one. Figure out what Lucifer gains with this rare power. And why."

"Talia!"

Muriel dropped down from a portal on the roof and landed with a thump against the stone floor.

Talia rushed toward her. "Muriel, what are you doing here?" she demanded. "You had specific orders to guard Jack. Who's with him right now?"

She bowed her head. "No one. I'm sorry."

"No one!" Fear and anger shot through her body and thrummed against her wings.

"We thought we'd picked up Kesien's trail, so Anahera and I went with Deemah. We followed it to Earth and the studio where you guys are filming."

Talia's eyes widened. "So, Kesien did follow us."

Muriel nodded. "But somewhere near the filming locations, his trail disappears. We think Asmodeus grabbed him. It's the only thing that makes sense after—"

"After what?" Talia demanded, glaring at her best friend.

Muriel gave her a sheepish look and stared down at the floor. "After Asmodeus attacked Jack. But Talia, Jack knocked that demon into next week. Along with those two former members of Kesien's squad."

Talia gasped and exchanged a shocked look with Azrael who moved toward Muriel, laying a hand against her wings.

"Muriel—Kesien's former squad is with Asmodeus?"

She nodded. "They ambushed Jack, but he handled them with his seraphim powers. So, if we find those former squad members, we'll find Asmodeus. And Kesien. I'm sure of it. Deemah's sure of it, too." She sighed and poked the floor with the toe of her Eternean armor boot. "But Talia, we need your omnificence power to locate them. It's the only way to find him now."

Now that they had something tangible to track—like Kesien's former squad—omnificence just might work this time. She should be able to locate angels that could move freely about the Earth. Angels that might not be shielded from their senses by a Hell prince. Or affected by a demonic ward.

"Will you try?" Muriel asked in a hopeful tone.

"Only if you promise to get someone down there to watch Jack. Now. Until I can get back to him."

Muriel grinned. "Deal. Deemah's going to lose her mind if we don't find Kesien soon."

Talia sighed. She understood that feeling well. If she didn't get back to Jack soon, she was going to go on a rampage.

"Locate Kesien and get back to Jack, Talia," said the archangel, motioning her toward Muriel. "We'll keep investigating this rare angel power and contact you if we uncover anything."

First, she was returning to check on Jack. Only when he was safe would she use omnificence to locate these rogue angels and use them to lead her and her squad to Kesien. But only when she knew that Jack was okay.

"Let's go, Muriel," Talia replied and unfolded her wings.

Muriel frowned. "Aren't you going to use omnificence first? To find Kesien's squad members?"

Talia shook her head. "Not until I know Jack's safe. Besides, I may need Jack to use his omnificence alongside mine. He's got a knack for using his, so I want to be thorough."

"Fine," said Muriel, lifting off from the stone floor. "But he's probably going to be cranky after Asmodeus ambushed him."

Talia smiled. She could deal with Jack being cranky as long as he was okay. But she worried that Lucifer had called Jack on his phone and filled his head with all kinds of horrible images again.

"I will happily deal with Jack at his crankiest, Muriel," said Talia as she shot up through the portal and beat her wings against the air currents. "As long as he isn't hurt."

"I hope he's fine," said Muriel as she blinked across the Heavens.

Talia blinked after her, frantic to reunite with her husband.

16

As the steamy July evening settled against the studio lot, Jack paced the trailer, his heart racing along with his thoughts.

How long had Talia been gone? A day? Or was it longer than that? What was the matter with him? Why couldn't he remember?

He couldn't remember what day it was or when she'd last been in his arms. And it terrified him. Lucifer's banter was garbage, he knew that, but something inside him wouldn't turn loose of the possibility that Talia had been ambushed by demons and dragged off to Hell like Berith.

He couldn't take it if Lucifer took her. He'd lose his mind.

"Jack, I've lost count of how many trips around this trailer you've made," Gianni remarked from the taupe couch where he'd planted himself, looking like Cary Grant posing for the cameras. "Talia is okay. You have to believe that."

Every part of him wanted to believe Gianni, especially his aching heart, but didn't the dude understand? Lucifer called him to gloat for a reason. To shove it in his face that something had happened to Talia.

And it was driving him crazy!

Finally, Gianni jumped up from the sofa and stepped in his path, stopping his obsessed pacing.

"Jack," he said, shaking his head. "You're doing it again."

Jack frowned, flexing his wings and then his fingers. "Doing what again?"

"Obsessing over that phone call from Lucifer," said Gianni, concern flickering in his warm brown eyes. "Once isn't like you, but twice? What's going on?"

Jack barely heard him, his attention settling on all the horrible things that Lucifer could have done to Talia by now. He glanced around the trailer. One line. That's all he needed to make this all go away. Just one.

He chewed his bottom lip, his gaze traveling around the room, looking for one of those small plastic bags, a little flake. Just a couple of key bumps.

Dammit! What had Lucifer done to Talia?

"Jack!" Gianni shook him. Hard. Forcing Jack to look at him.

Jack tried his best, but he couldn't stay focused. His gaze wandered again.

"My God...you're looking for drugs, aren't you?" Gianni looked horrified.

Jack chuckled, his gaze in motion again. "That's ridiculous! I'm looking for..."

"What, Jack?" Gianni demanded and gripped him by the shoulders. "What?"

He glanced over at the kitchen counter, then the coffee table, and finally, over at a small bookshelf outside the bedroom. Not a bag of flake anywhere.

"Dude, my keys!" Jack cried with another chuckle, looking away. "You see my keys anywhere?"

Gianni's kind brown eyes narrowed. "On the kitchen counter, Jack," he said, anger sharpening his tone. "Right where you dropped them."

He licked his lips, his body feeling hollow and jittery. God, he needed a line! Bad. Just one line.

He turned toward the kitchen. His salvation perched beside the dish soap in a small plastic bag. He lurched toward it.

But Gianni was faster.

The taller soap star snatched the bag off the counter before Jack could get to it.

Jack's gaze darkened, wings twitching as he glared at Gianni. "Give that back, dude."

Gianni held it out of his reach. "Forget it, Jack. I'm not letting you throw away a year of being clean."

He gritted his teeth, pointing at Gianni. "Dammit, Gianni! Give me the damned bag!"

"Or what?" Gianni demanded. "You gonna use those seraphim powers on me?"

That wasn't a bad idea. Jack held out his right hand.

"How about a well-placed murder marble?" Jack replied and then pointed at the bag. "Now, give me the flake, dude."

Gianni laughed, shaking his head. "Nice bluff, Jack, but I know you'd never toss one of those at me."

Jack's eyes narrowed. Dude was right. He wasn't that good of an actor. Even his game face couldn't convince Gianni that he'd use a murder marble on him. He'd use it on himself before he'd hurt his best friend.

"Still want this, Jack?" Gianni asked, dangling the small bag just out of Jack's reach.

He nodded, but the ache against his forehead made him hesitate.

"You sure about that?"

Jack squinted, rubbing his forehead, feeling a little lightheaded now. No, he didn't want that. Flake had ruined his entire life. Of course, he didn't want that.

He backed away from Gianni, shaking his head.

"No," he said with a growl, mouth flattening into a grimace as he stumbled backward, backing away from that little plastic bag filled with his ruin. He felt the kitchen counter at his back. "Flush that shit, dude. Now. Before my resolve breaks."

Gianni stared at him a moment and finally smiled. "Welcome back, Jack."

Jack nodded, his mouth dry, the memory of that gasoline and ether scent making him ache all over just to taste it.

The taller soap star moved to the sink and turned on the water. He opened the bag and dumped the contents. White powder circled the drain and then disappeared with a gurgle.

Only when it had disappeared from his sight did Jack's muscles go slack. He turned away and bumped the box of powdered donuts again, already on its side. Angry, he shoved it toward the sink, knocking open the lid. More powdered sugar scattered across the countertop and the sink's edge to taunt him.

He turned away, feeling drained, his body still aching for the drugs as he moved over to the sofa, legs shaking, and sank into the cushions, wings folding against his shoulders. With a moan, he pressed his face into his hands.

"What's happening to me, Gianni?"

"Jack, you're being controlled," said the soap star softly as he moved toward the coffee table. "It's not your fault."

Gently, he sat down on the sofa and put his arm around Jack's shoulders.

Jack glanced over at his best friend. "Dude, if you hadn't been here, I'd have been setting up lines all over that quartz countertop with a cheese knife and a spatula."

Gianni shook his head. "No, you wouldn't. Tonight, I've watched you say no to it twice now. Saw you dump it down the sink once and heard you tell me to dump it a second time. You're stronger than whoever's trying to control you. Remember that!"

He rubbed his forehead again and the memory of that fiery touch against his skin and ensuing migraine rushed back to him. Along with the tense moments when he'd almost snorted that key bump earlier. And then struggled with his feelings of guilt and grief afterward.

What was happening to him?

"Gianni," he said in a small, tight voice. "Dude...help me. I don't know if I can stop myself a third time."

"You can, Jack," said Gianni, patting his shoulder. "But don't worry...I'm not letting you out of my sight until Talia returns."

Jack felt sick. "What if this thing catches me alone again? And I…" He pulled in a sharp breath. "I give in?"

Already, Gianni was shaking his head no. "Something's trying to control you. I don't know if it's Lucifer or that demon that ambushed you, but we need to find a way to shut it down. This isn't your fault."

Right now, Jack had to believe that. He knew he wasn't himself. He couldn't concentrate on anything for more than three seconds and his flake craving was overpowering his worry over Talia. Even at his worst, when he thought that he'd lost Talia forever, the drugs had never come before her safety.

He sighed. "Until whatever this is wears off—and Talia returns—will you stay with me, dude? Make sure I don't do any drugs?"

"I already called Izzy and told her I was staying here with you tonight, Jack," he said and rubbed his shoulder. "But I promise you, I won't leave until Talia's back. She'll know what this is and how to counteract it, so hang in there."

Jack nodded, but his heart hurt. How had he gone from worrying about Talia to craving flake to looking for a fix? It made him sick. He didn't remember Gianni calling Izzy either. He felt like he used to feel after waking up at Lare and Rachel's beach house. With time missing. And an unsettling feeling that something dark and ugly, something he couldn't remember, had happened to him.

He didn't want to think about that right now either.

Gianni's brow furrowed and he sat up straighter on the sofa. "You know what, Jack? It's strange, but you've been exhibiting acute withdrawal symptoms since I got here."

Jack felt his temper flare. "What are you saying, dude? I didn't do any flake if that's what you're insinuating. Today or any other day."

Had he done some lines and not remembered it? That thought chilled him to the bone.

"No, Jack, that's not what I mean," said Gianni, motioning around the trailer. "Even if you had just done drugs in here or an hour or so ago, you wouldn't be having withdrawal symptoms yet. Not for several hours, maybe even a day. That's why your behavior is so strange. It's like someone's doing this to you somehow. Inserting these symptoms."

Jack tossed that around in his head for a moment, staring at his hands.

Gianni was right. It would be at least the next day before he felt any sort of withdrawal after using. He remembered those days when Rachel had forced him to go cold turkey after claiming she couldn't get any flake. Deliberately pushing him into an awful withdrawal. Like she was enjoying his suffering. He remembered those times vividly. But Gianni was right. These symptoms felt forced. All he could do was wait them out.

IT WAS ALMOST midnight and Jack had lost count of how many laps he'd completed around the trailer again while Gianni watched his third nature show. He'd just turned on some show about wildebeest migration when Jack heard the flutter of wings.

Like an apparition, Talia blinked through the ceiling and landed in the trailer. A moment later, Muriel landed followed by Anahera.

"Talia!" Jack shouted and rushed toward her.

"Jack!"

He threw his arms around her and held her, his body trembling. Her wings folded against her back and her arms slid around him, holding him so tight he could barely breathe. His mouth found hers and he kissed her frantically, urgently, tangling his fingers in her hair.

When his wave of panic had passed, he felt exhausted. She brushed the hair out of his eyes, but he took hold of her left hand and held it, not wanting to completely let go of her.

"Jack, you're shaking," she said, brows furrowing as she scrutinized him and her fingers traveled across his face.

Checking for injuries, he realized. When her fingers slid across his forehead, he flinched. She felt it immediately, tilting his head to the side. Her angel senses were recording every bruise and bump.

"God, I missed you, Tal," he said in a painful whisper, his voice quivering. He put his arms around her again and held her close, his mouth against her ear. "Lucifer was talking so much shit…I was terrified that he'd taken you. L–Like Berith."

She held him out at arm's length, her luminous grey eyes watery and filled with concern. "Oh, Jack—I'm sorry he worried you." She squinted at him. "Did Asmodeus do this?"

Jack nodded. "Dude and his angel mascots only got one hit on me though. Okay, two, but I kicked all of them to the curb." He squeezed her hands and bowed his head. "I'm glad you're okay, Tal. I've been goin' out of my mind with you gone."

She ran her hands through his hair, stroking, but her fingers slid back to his forehead. Where those douchebag angels had hit him in the forehead. Hard.

"I kind of like worried Jack Casey," she said and gently kissed his lips.

He met her bright gaze. "Like how?" he asked, the corners of his mouth quirking into the hint of a smile as he stepped closer. "That's cute, kiss-on-the-cheek like? Or that's hot-as-hell, shove-me-down-on-the-bed like?"

Talia glanced around the room and then smiled at him. "We'll discuss later, lover," she said and nodded toward the bedroom.

"I like how this conversation's shaping up," he said with a smirk, but he felt the guilt churning in his stomach.

He had to tell her about the drugs. When she found out about the paparazzi photos and the approaching shitshow, she'd be furious. At him. He'd be lucky if she let him sleep in the same county much less in the bed beside her.

His gaze fell to the floor and he let go of her hands, shoving his hands in his jeans pockets as he began to pace.

"Uh, Talia…" he began, trying to find a way to tell her without her demanding a divorce. "Something uh—happened while you were away."

She was quiet for a moment and Jack heard Muriel and Anahera blink out of the trailer. Cowards.

"You're scaring me, Jack."

In a moment, she wouldn't be scared. She'd be furious. He glanced over at Gianni, looking for a supportive gesture, but his best friend's attention was glued to the wildebeest migration. Damn. All his friends were cowards.

He ran his hands through his hair, still not looking at her. "In a moment, you're gonna be furious. Just promise you won't smite me."

She stormed over to him and grabbed him by the arms, spinning him around to face her. "Jack Casey, you look me in the eye and tell me what's going on."

He sighed and met her intense grey gaze.

"Something bad happened tonight," he said in a quiet voice, feeling sick. "That I caused."

She stiffened but nodded for him to continue.

"I…" He struggled to find the words to tell her about the drugs, but they caught in his throat. "I…"

Talia's eyes were wide, her wings twitching, face tense as she stared at him, waiting for him to drop a bomb.

"You what, Jack?"

He winced, covering his face with his hand. "The drugs, Tal," he began. "I found another bag in the trailer." He rubbed his face. "And I was weak," he said with a moan and turned away again. Toward the kitchen.

He felt her hand against his sleeve.

"I was just going to do a line. One key bump. God, the craving was eating me alive. And I had the flake ready to snort…but dammit, I couldn't do it." He struck the kitchen counter with his fist, scattering more powdered sugar from the donuts. "I washed it all down the drain, but Tal, a paparazzi got a shot of me through the trailer window. Almost doing coke. By morning, that photo's gonna be all over the world. Network's probably gonna cut me loose over it, too. And I…I can't fix it this time. Please don't divorce me."

"Jack Casey," Talia said in a stern voice and spun him around again, her grey eyes piercing. "I love you and I am not going to divorce you just because you stumbled."

He stared at her in surprise. Stumbled? He screwed up. Everything.

"Tal…I did more than stumble." He sighed. "I came within a breath of snorting that whole bag."

She laid her hand against his cheek. "And yet somehow, you stopped yourself."

"Twice, Talia," said Gianni, rising from the sofa. "He asked me to flush another bag down the sink. Which I did."

Jack winced, feeling sick all over. "But what will happen with the next bag? I may bogart the whole thing and go on a bender for days. Like my dad used to do."

God, he really was just like his dad, wasn't he? Maybe his mother was right about him?

Talia shook her head as she leaned up and kissed him. "Jack, there's something you don't know."

"What do you mean?" he said.

Talia reached up and tilted his face toward her. She leaned up and gently kissed his forehead.

"Lucifer unleashed a fallen angel's rare power on you today. That's what this bruise on your forehead is about."

"What rare power?" he demanded, feeling the anger sizzling through him.

She kissed his lips. "Transference, lover. He used it to magnify your addiction dramatically, to get you to take all these drugs around the set, hoping you'd overdose."

His anger burned hot, but it quickly cooled to fear. If he'd given in to even one line, he'd have done that whole bag. Because before, one line was never enough. Once he got started, he couldn't stop until he'd blacked out or amped himself into blissful oblivion.

If Lucifer had a way to magnify his addiction, he didn't stand a chance of resisting it. Dude was still winning.

"See, Jack," said Gianni, grinning. "I told you it wasn't your fault."

"Tell that to the paparazzi," Jack said with a groan.

Talia wrapped her arms around him. "I will," she said. "Tomorrow. After we've found Kesien."

"Talia's right, Jack," said Gianni. "If we stand together as a cast, then people will assume the paparazzi faked that shot somehow."

Jack turned toward the taller soap star. "Stand together as a cast?"

Gianni nodded.

"Right," Jack snapped. "Maybe you, me, Talia, and Izzy? Probably Banks. But Rachel? Eric Saunders? They'd throw me under the bus for a dollar-off coupon at Disneyland. And you know it."

Talia folded her arms against her chest, looking concerned. "Jack's probably right about that, Armand."

"Forget Rachel and Eric, then," said Gianni, ramping up quickly. "The crew would stand with us, too."

Jack shook his head. "Jennifer thinks all these bags are mine, Gianni. And Steve thinks I've been stashing them around the set to do a quick line between takes. Even Herb's been looking at me funny like I was picking it up from craft services or something. Yeah, we'll have a dozen breakfast sandwiches, a dozen bags of flake, and four carafes of coffee. Sure, I'll sign for that. Just put it under Herb Rutherford. Right."

"Then we'll go talk to Herb," said Talia. "Tell him the whole story."

"He needs me on the show, Tal, but not that bad. It's not worth his reputation as a director. Or his time trying to manage a shitshow like this."

"You gave him that reputation, Jack," Gianni replied. "Trust me, he'll want to fix this."

"I'll offer to do a drug test," said Jack, leaning against the kitchen counter. "I can prove I'm clean. Tabloids will twist it no matter what though."

Gianni nodded. "You're right about that, Jack. I don't think we have much choice but to talk to Herb."

No matter how much he hated the idea, Jack knew he had no choice. If he got fired, he got fired. Another drug scandal would end his career. There'd be no coming back from that a second time. Maybe Azrael would let him move into Eolowen?

"Okay," said Jack in a heavy voice as he began to chew his bottom lip again. "We tell Herb everything tomorrow. It's not like he isn't gonna know about that photo. Probably already knows."

Gianni patted him on the back. "Don't give up hope, Jack. We'll make this right tomorrow—today, I guess. It's already after midnight. Now, try and get some sleep, okay? Izzy and I'll be here first thing tomorrow and together, we'll go to Herb."

Jack reached over and hugged Gianni. "Thanks for still being in my corner, dude," he said. "Means a lot to me."

"Always, Jack," said Gianni with his best Cary Grant smile.

He said goodnight to Talia and headed back to his trailer. Only then did Muriel and Anahera creep back into the trailer.

"Everything okay?" Muriel asked in a timid voice.

Anahera nodded, her short red hair bright against Muriel's long sable hair. They still looked like deer caught in headlights as they glanced from him to Talia.

Smiling, Talia wrapped Jack in her arms, her wings cradling him.

"It is, now that I'm home," she said and kissed him softly on the lips.

He held her tight, not wanting to let go. Every time he felt her arms around him, he was home.

"God, I love you, Talia," he said, his voice breaking as he laid his head against her shoulder.

Anahera smiled.

"Looks like everything's all right again," said Muriel. "Except for Kesien."

Jack frowned and lifted his head. "What? You still haven't found him? What gives?"

Talia shook her head. "We tracked him down to the studio here, Jack, but then his trail goes cold."

"It just disappears," said Muriel, a hand on her hip. "Deemah and Daidrean haven't stopped looking for him since they got to Earth."

"We still think Asmodeus has him," said Anahera in a soft voice. Tall and willowy, she was almost a head taller than Muriel and as tall as Jack.

"Damn," said Jack with a sharp whistle. "If that douchebag has him, then we need to take this Hell prince down fast. Before he and his angel of death mascots hurt Kesien. Like they did at Eolowen."

Muriel and Anahera bowed their heads, the hurt radiating from their grey, angel-of-death eyes.

"That was so brutal," said Muriel.

Anahera nodded. "Berith was trying to bring them back with resurrect when Lucifer's forces grabbed her."

"And there was nothing any of us could do to stop it." Muriel's face brightened. "Until today."

"What do you mean?" Anahera asked, glancing at Muriel.

Talia let her wings fold against her shoulders, her light grey eyes glowing with pride.

"I finished the resurrect cast on the terrace, Anahera," she said. "Brought all of them back again."

"What?" Anahera cried, rushing over to her. "You recovered them all?"

Talia nodded as Anahera hugged her. Muriel was beside her, grinning now. She hugged Talia, too.

"Wow, that's fantastic, Talia," said Anahera.

Jack leaned over and kissed Talia. "That's my wife!"

Muriel's wings fluttered. "Can't wait to find Kesien and tell him that. That moment broke him."

Jack couldn't imagine how painful that moment was for Kesien, knowing that his former guard had been responsible. It changed Kesien, turning him into an angry crusader, relentlessly pursuing those douchebags. To a point where he wasn't thinking straight. Maybe now he could search for these bastards with a clearer, calmer outlook?

"I just hope it brings back the chill, patient, and collected angel dude that I still admire," said Jack.

"Agreed, Jack," said Muriel. "Kesien needs to give himself a break and understand that none of that was his fault."

Talia nodded. "Maybe the resurrection of those extinguished angels will help him understand that?" She studied Jack a moment and then took hold of his arm. "But right now, you need some attention."

He grinned and tugged her past Muriel and Anahera, toward the bedroom.

"That's right, Mrs. Casey," he said, kissing her again. "I need some attention."

He led her into the bedroom and sat her down on the bed. He slid his arms around her, but she just smiled and shoved him back on the bed.

"I love our discussions," he said, pulling her against him. "Tell me again how much you like worried Jack Casey?"

"Oh, I love him more than anything," she said, her smile widening.

He frowned. "He taller than me?"

She shook her head.

"So, let's talk about this hot as hell, shove me down on the bed discussion point. For science."

"Oh, that was only half the story, Jack," said Talia, running her fingers through his hair as she leaned closer.

"What's the other half?" he asked, grinning.

"This," said Talia and pressed her hand against his forehead.

His whole body arched as pain twisted through his head, down his neck, and through his chest. He smashed his eyes closed, the pain so intense he couldn't utter a sound. He gripped the comforter in both hands, writhing against the fire and pain that wound through his body and slammed into his feet.

He cried out in pain, the agony washing over him in waves. He gritted his teeth, Talia's warm hand the only thing anchoring him to reality. The pain seemed to go on for an eternity until everything went dark.

Sometime later, muffled sounds rasped at the edges of his consciousness. Bringing back the sharp pain. A soft rustle as pain gouged his temples. Voices funneled through water as needles stabbed the back of his head. Frantic huff of his breathing was in time to the thrumming ache pounding against his temples.

Something warm pressed against his forehead, forcing the sharp pains to recede. Like something had unhooked itself from inside his brain.

"Jack?" called the muted soprano voice, the notes soothing against his ears.

He tried to answer, but at the first sound out of his mouth, his head began to pound. He couldn't move. Couldn't reach up to touch his head and relieve the pain.

Her name rose soundlessly on his lips, over and over until he whispered it in little bits of sound that didn't rattle his head and shoot pain down his neck and spine.

"Jack, are you all right?" Talia's voice was sharp, insistent.

Gingerly, he opened one eye. Muriel and Anahera stood protectively around him, wings unfurled and draped around him beneath Talia's dove grey wings that cradled him.

"Jack, answer me, please," she said, gripping his right hand.

Can't, he mouthed, but no sound escaped. And he was glad. Any sound he made would bore through his brain and knock him unconscious again.

Then he felt the warmth of her healing light washing over him in golden waves. Slowly, it dissolved the sticky threads of pain that clung to every part of his body. When the pain grew distant, he tried to answer her again.

"That some kind of weird angel of death foreplay?" he asked.

Muriel burst out laughing, and Anahera joined her.

"What?" Talia cried, her cheeks turning red.

"I don't kink shame," he said in a scratchy, weak voice. "Just hope it was good for you at least. For me? Not so much."

Talia looked all kinds of embarrassed and confused.

"Talia, he has no idea what just happened," said Muriel, still laughing. "Might want to tell poor Jack what that was."

Anahera nodded. "He has no idea, Talia."

Jack gave her a sharp nod.

"Sorry, lover," she said, still blushing. "That was my new transference power. I used it to remove Procel's connection to you, the one magnifying your addiction issues."

"Connection, hell," Jack snapped. "Those were meat hooks. And every one of them hurt like hell when you pulled them out."

Talia stroked his hair. "I'm so sorry, lover. This power is so new to me. I had no idea how painful removing Procel's attachment to you would be. I thought it would be quick."

He struggled against the dull ache and stiffness to slide his arms around her. "It's okay, Mrs. Casey. It's over now. Thank you."

Tears collected in her eyes, turning to crystals that cascaded against his chest.

"I'm so sorry that I hurt you, Jack," she said. "I—"

He laid two fingers against her lips and ran his other hand through her silky black hair.

"I'm fine and I love you, Tal," he said and then slowly kissed her lips, pressing gentle sips down her neck and back to her mouth.

But already, his eyes were closing.

The rustle of wings touched his ears.

"Talia! Thank the Maker!" Was that Deemah's voice? "I'm pretty sure Asmodeus has Kesien, but I need your rare angel powers to know for sure. We need to hurry—before they destroy him."

"Gotta—help," he muttered through thick lips. "Kesien, Tal…"

"Just rest, Jack," said Talia against his ear as everything began to dim. "I need to use my omnificence now."

He tried to respond, but everything turned black again.

17

WHILE JACK SLEPT, TALIA CALLED UP HER OMNIFICENCE POWER INSIDE the trailer. Daidrean stayed beside Jack to make sure Asmodeus—or Lucifer—didn't try to harm him. He even cast a ward around Jack, to make sure no one tried to use transference on her husband again.

With wings encircling her, Talia gathered Muriel, Deemah, and Anahera into a circle. She moved to the center of the circle and knelt on the grey and gold rug in the living area. Her squad called up an angel of death ward and its gold light washed over her in protective waves. Ensuring that nothing dark—or from Hell—interrupted her.

Closing her eyes, Talia reached into the well of rare angel powers she carried, feeling its currents roil until a river of information flooded her head. Torrents of images, landmarks, and words became a whirlpool surrounding her. Steadying herself, she dipped her hands into the rushing flow of omnificence that raged around her like a hurricane. And searched for Kesien's Enochian brand. They should have been able to see it burning from everywhere. The fact that it was dark was disturbing.

But somewhere in this murky, churning maelstrom was his mark and somehow, she had to find it—and him—before Asmodeus erased him, scattering his light forever. Preventing her from ever resurrecting him. Unlike Eolowen's terrace where the death angels' lights had endured, still intact. Talia knew that Asmodeus would ensure that Kesien's light was never found.

She felt it. There were reasons that Lucifer had banished this monster. And those same reasons made Lucifer recall him. To wreak maximum harm and pain. She couldn't take the chance and allow Asmodeus to erase Kesien from the universe. She was an angel of death. And she feared no Hell creature—especially a soulless monster like Asmodeus.

But finding Kesien's mark in this flood of lights and images would take time. Like finding one star in the Heavens without knowing its location. An almost impossible task. Jack would have said that finding it would be like searching for one off-color bulb on the Vegas Strip. Even with this rare omnificence power, searching for Kesien would require time and patience on her part.

She knew he was close. Very close. But Asmodeus had strangled any light surrounding Kesien when he captured the angel of death. So, omnificence was the only way to locate him right now—through his former squad's location. She was glad that Jack was sleeping. He'd have insisted on helping her by using his omnificence power. They could find Kesien much faster with their combined powers, but Jack would have drained his Holy fire and fallen into a terrible power drunk.

For hours, Talia knelt on the floor and searched the Earth for Kesien. She knew he was probably nearby, but with Asmodeus shielding his presence, she had no choice but to use omnificence. As slow and painstaking as it felt.

She was peripherally aware of her squad shifting around her, realizing that Muriel had spelled Daidrean who was guarding Jack and Deemah had spelled Anahera in the circle.

Wards flickered and went out around her and then reappeared, conjured by her squad mates. She noticed sunlight filling the trailer as it made a slow trek across the maple hardwood floor, dust motes drifting like snow as she peeled back layers and layers of information and locations.

At times, her halo dimmed and flickered, but one of her squad mates always took hold of her halo and fed her light from theirs. Keeping her going.

Soon, Jack padded barefoot through the trailer, that light blond hair disheveled and sexy from a night's sleep. A hint of blond stubble shadowed his jaw, those sleepy, pale green eyes blazing through her as he sat nearby. He only had on a pair of light blue pajama bottoms, lean chest bare, large green coffee mug in hand.

He knew she was using omnificence and she half-expected him to kneel beside her and call it up, trying to help. But she knew that Muriel had probably talked him out of it, explaining that only a celestial being could pull off this search. She'd been at it, motionless, on her knees, for hours. Humans weren't built for that and as he lingered near her, she saw that realization sink into his gaze. He had that restless, helpless look on his handsome face, shifting that coffee mug from hand to hand because he didn't know how to help her.

In a short while, he disappeared, showing up with damp hair, faded Levi's, those blue slip-on sneakers, and a navy blue Henley.

A knock at the door momentarily caught her attention as Muriel joined her squad mates clustered around her and relit the wards.

Behind her, she heard Armand Gianni's voice.

"What's Talia doing, Jack?" Armand asked.

"She's using a rare angel power to locate her missing squad mate," Jack replied in a quiet voice. "It can take a long time to sift through these mountains of images and information. She's been at it forever—and I can't even help her."

She heard that little hitch in his voice, telling her that he was concerned for her. She loved him, even more, when he showed those little signs of worry. He loved with his whole heart and soul and she'd never felt that kind of love from anyone. Ever. Until she met Jack Casey.

Then he was standing behind her.

"Muriel, tell Tal that Gianni and I are headed over to break the bad news to Herb and hope I don't get fired." He chuckled. "If they do fire me, this might be Gianni's big break."

"That's not funny, Jack," Armand replied.

"It won't be to Banks, but Rachel might love it."

"Forget Rachel," said Armand.

"Love you, Mrs. Casey—be back soon!" her beautiful husband called out from the trailer door. "Hey, while you're searching for information, see if there are any job openings at the Pizza Playpen by my apartment. Gianni said he'd give me a reference."

"Jack, stop!" Armand shouted as Jack let the trailer door bang shut.

Talia's heart sank a little. She hoped there was a way to straighten out all of this paparazzi business. Jack's passion was acting and she would hate to see that taken from him again.

As the sun moved along the hardwood toward the bedroom door, Talia searched for the angels of death in Kesien's former squad. Reptev. Lix. Pharzus. She focused omnificence downward until she located all three of these death angels' marks. And then searched around them. Near them.

Until a brief gold spark emerged in the wake of their movements.

Gently, she eased her touch toward it, the rush of images and places slowing. She held her hand steady, hovering, forcing the currents to freeze as she shifted them past the three angels of death.

Buried in the murk and eddies, Kesien's Enochian mark gleamed like a polished gold coin.

Holding her breath, she reached toward it, gripping it in her fist as she pressed deeper into the flow. Focusing time and place downward into a spiral that got sharper and closer. Oceans and continents. Countries. States and cities.

California rushed up at her and she held her grip around Kesien's mark as it began to burn brighter as oceans, mountains, and desert gave way to the city of angels.

She pushed against it, forcing it closer. Burbank. Four Acre Studios.

Holding her breath, she watched Kesien's mark glow like a sunrise as the Studio 22 building appeared, trailers behind it.

Then, farther out, behind a warehouse building stood an old

abandoned trailer near a wooded lot. In the deepening shadows engulfing it, she saw Kesien's mark blaze with Holy fire.

There! She'd found him.

"Found him," she announced, her tone stiff with concentration. "An abandoned trailer behind a warehouse and beside a wooded lot."

Slowly, she let the currents and waves recede and called on her Holy fire. It surged through her, burning away any fatigue. She stretched her wings as the wards around her fell.

Deemah's eyes were watery as she extended her wings. "Let's go get him."

Talia glanced around the trailer. She had no idea how much time had passed, but Jack hadn't returned yet. He was with Armand and the crew. He would be safe until she returned from rescuing Kesien.

"Swords out, squad," she ordered. "Shields forward. Let's go lay waste to some demons."

"And some traitors," Deemah said, her gaze narrowing as she drew her Eternean sword from the sheath at her side."

Anahera, Daidrean, and Muriel drew their swords, and one by one, shields appeared in their hands.

"Let's bring Kesien home," said Muriel with a nod.

Talia summoned a sword of Holy fire in each hand. "All right, squad, Supremes formation."

"It's like having Jack along with us," said Muriel.

Laughter filled the trailer as they assembled in a roundel formation and blinked through the trailer ceiling, flying into the afternoon sun. Toward the abandoned trailer.

Already, Talia felt the presence of demons and angels in that trailer. They were in for a fight just to get inside.

The abandoned trailer blended into the warehouse's tan paint, making it almost invisible. Combined with the wooded lot, the trailer completely disappeared from view. The perfect place for Asmodeus to fortify and hold an angel of death hostage.

"How many times have we flown over this broken-down husk?" Deemah asked as they banked around the warehouse to approach the trailer from the trees behind it. "And all those times, he was trapped inside it. I should have known. I should have felt his presence."

Talia shook her head. "Deemah, even if we landed on the rooftop, his brand would be invisible. There's no way you could have sensed him through all of these demon wards and shadows."

Muriel motioned toward the trailer with her shield. "Talia's right. These aren't ordinary demon wards, Deemah. These are generated by a Hell prince which is right up there with archdemons."

Using her highest-pitched angel notes, Talia instructed the squad to land on the trailer roof. The moment her feet touched the roof, shadows churned and writhed against her Holy fire. Trying to drain it.

Quickly, she ordered them away and they lifted off the trailer, landing among the leafy green trees.

"All right, those aren't just wards," said Talia as her squad huddled around her, shields clutched in their hands. "They're absorbing all light—and trying to feed off our Holy fire."

"Meaning?" Anahera asked.

Talia pointed toward the trailer. "Meaning that any effort we expend trying to break through will result in all of us being weakened."

"We wouldn't stand a chance in there by the time we broke through," said Muriel, hands on her hips. "If we broke through."

"Exactly," said Talia. "We have to find a way to destroy those dark energies."

"Or bring an army," Deemah said with a sigh.

"That's our second option, Deemah," Talia replied. "If we can't break these wards quickly, we summon a cherubim patrol or an archangel. But I'd rather not trouble Azrael with this right now. He's got enough on his plate."

"Couldn't agree more," said Muriel as she stared at the trailer. "Because whatever's deployed around that trailer is chewing through our angel light like a Great Dane."

Was it their angel light or their Holy fire? Or both? Talia needed to know the answer.

"Stay here," she said, stretching her wings wide. "I need to test something."

"Be careful, Talia," said Muriel.

She nodded at Muriel and then blinked into the air, wings extended. She turned in a graceful circle and then descended toward the trailer, a sword of Holy fire extended. When she landed on the rooftop again, she pressed the sword's fiery blade against the shadows.

The Holy fire cut through them cleanly. But all around her, shadows crept like assassins toward her wings. Toward her angel light.

Immediately, she took flight, shooting across the bright summer-blue sky toward the patch of woods. She landed without a sound.

"It would appear that the shadows are attuned to angels. Those defenses actively assault anything with angel light, but my sword of Holy fire cut right through those shadows."

"Angels of death can't summon Holy fire," said Muriel. "Unless we all have Talia's abilities, we'll be incapacitated before we break through."

"Even if we could, we couldn't sustain it long enough to break through," said Anahera, frowning as she stared at the trailer, a hopeless expression flickering in her charcoal grey eyes. "It would take a seraph to break through those defenses. Only they have a Holy fire blast powerful enough to defeat these Hell shadows."

Talia grinned. "Fortunately, we have one on hand."

Deemah raised an eyebrow. "A seraph? Here?"

Muriel poked Deemah. "The dude himself. Jack Casey."

At last, Deemah smiled. "Do you think Jack has enough Holy fire to break through these shadows?"

"It may take most of his seraphim energies," said Talia. "But yes, I think if I support him, he can do it."

Muriel was grinning now. "Rescued by power drunk Jack! Kesien will love this." She rubbed her hands together. "And I can't wait."

"He will love that," said Deemah, and then she gritted her teeth. "After I knock him into the next century for going rogue like this."

"Get in line, Deemah," said Talia. "Azrael may assign him patrol duties at anime conventions for eternity after this stunt."

"How about we make him guard Rachel Daniels for the rest of the year?" Muriel offered, crossing her arms against her chest.

"Now, that punishment has real flare, Muriel," said Talia. "I'll consider it. Now, let's get back to my trailer and get Jack involved."

The squad put away swords and light shields as Talia blinked into the air. They followed in tight formation as Talia raced across the sky toward her trailer. And Jack.

18

JACK AND GIANNI RUSHED INTO THE SQUAT GREY STUDIO 22 BUILDING, weaving around the paint and set crews as they tore down the remnants of the show's old set. Jack ducked under the yellow couch that two crew members carried inside. Gianni followed, dodging more crew carrying white wicker end tables into the building. Jack and Gianni veered right, out of the line of furniture headed into storage at the back of the building. The smell of fresh paint mixed with sweat and warm sawdust.

Jack felt the crew staring at him as they moved back and forth through the cavernous, dark-walled space. He sighed. Staring at him like he had horns.

Well, that cinched it. That paparazzi photo had already jetted across the globe and back again. Exploding across the studio. He cringed, imagining all the bad memes of him that must be making the rounds across social media. He felt sick. Ashamed.

Lucifer had to be loving every moment of this shitshow.

He pulled in an anxious breath, his gut roiling with nerves, and headed toward the small glass offices in the back of the studio. Where Herb was probably conferencing with the studio execs right now, discussing his severance package.

Was there anything at all he could say to Herb that could possibly fix this?

Footsteps clacked behind them. Jack turned.

Jennifer hurried toward Herb from the other offices. She was dressed in fuchsia leggings and a purple tunic, her black flats tapping against the painted concrete floor. Her fuchsia and purple glasses sat low on her nose as she stared at the floor, looking forlorn, and clutched that clipboard against her chest. She stopped in mid-stride when she saw him.

"Jack!" Her eyes were as wide as the swath of devastation he'd wrought with that one photo.

"Hi, Jennifer," he said in a pained voice, glancing from the floor to his hands. "Herb available?"

She shook her head.

Jack sighed. "Jennifer, I can see him through the glass. Look, I know I—"

Gianni grabbed his arm and stepped in front of him. "We know it looks bad, but Jennifer, Jack's innocent."

She didn't respond as she glanced from Gianni to him. How could she? She'd already seen that photo. He winced, her expression like a sword thrust to his gut. And she believed it.

"Look," Jack said and held out his hands. "I know how bad that photo looks. And I know the whole crew thinks I'm in my trailer snorting coke every day like it's Christmas candy. But dammit, I'm not. I know what it's like living paycheck to paycheck. I know what it's like to not eat for a week because you only have enough to pay the overdue rent." He brushed his bangs out of his eyes. "That tabloid report is false. And I'll take any drug test you want to prove it."

Jennifer pointed over his shoulder.

He turned. Herb stood behind him, looking sad and angry. Like a disappointed father and Jack felt guilt stab him in the gut.

"Jack," he said and Jack heard the recrimination in his voice.

How could you? He heard the unspoken words behind it and he wanted to melt into the floor.

"Herb, I..." He bit his lip, feeling his eyes begin to sting.

But nothing would come out. He couldn't justify it. He couldn't refute it. And dammit, he couldn't fix it. He didn't know what to do. Or how to make any of this right.

He covered his face with his hands and slid down the wall. Feeling worthless. Feeling defeated.

"Herb, Jack's innocent," said Gianni. "Someone's been working very hard to hit Jack in his weak spot. He's been clean for nearly a year. But someone's been stashing cocaine all over the set, hoping he'll break and return to doing coke again."

Herb shook his head, hands on his hips as he glanced from Jack to Gianni. His tan dress pants and blue dress shirt were rumpled, eyes bloodshot, and puffy bags under his eyes.

Like he'd been up all night.

"Network's furious. It's out of my hands, Jack."

"Then stand up for your stars!"

Jack uncovered his face and looked up.

Jennifer stamped her foot against the floor and then threw her clipboard against the wall. It skittered across the floor and stopped against a paint can. She folded her hands into fists, shaking as anger flared in her big brown eyes.

For a moment, Herb could only stare. Jack had never seen such an angry outburst from her before. None of them had.

"What was that, Jennifer?" Herb said finally, eyes narrowing in confusion.

"I said stand up for your stars!" She pointed toward some shelving off to her left. "Get studio security onto the set. Find out who's planting the drugs." She pointed at Jack next. "Jack Casey made this show a ratings juggernaut, Herb! We could have made more money as baristas that summer when we cast The Cinderella Hour. Our sets were recycled cast-offs. Our budget was nonexistent. Scripts written on paper from the studio recycle bins. We would have lasted about four episodes without him." She stomped her foot. "Tell me I'm wrong!"

Herb ran his hand across his forehead, glancing from Jennifer to Gianni and then Jack.

Finally, he shook his head. "You're not wrong, Jennifer." His voice was tired. "We owe Jack Casey everything for making this show a success."

She folded her arms against her chest. "But…you're going to stand by and do nothing. Let the network fire Jack and kill the show."

Herb stuttered, but his words turned into a jumble of company policy and other garbage.

"Well, Mr. Rutherford," said Jennifer as she pushed her glasses back onto the bridge of her nose. "Just so you know, if the network fires Jack, the crew walks with him. Steve's over at the set teardown right now, but he said he's through if Jack goes."

Jack's mouth gaped and he couldn't speak.

"What?" Herb stared at her, looking shocked. "Jennifer, you know this decision is out of my hands."

"Herb," said Gianni in a firm tone, "I can't speak for anyone else, but Izzy and I are out, too, if Jack gets fired over this."

Jack swallowed the lump in his throat. They were standing up for him instead of throwing him under the bus.

"That includes the camera crew, too," Phil called across the room as he and Rhonda carried scaffolding through the building. "Kid's innocent. Can't you see that?"

Rhonda hefted a black metal bracket onto her left shoulder. "And he's worked his ass off to make this show a success. That makes him worth fighting for."

Jennifer pulled the pen from behind her ear and shook it at Herb. "And don't forget who came up with the new format for the show. The one the network fell in love with and greenlit just yesterday."

Jack got to his feet. The network loved his new idea? Only until this morning apparently.

He walked over to Jennifer and hugged her until her face turned bright red. Then he turned around to face Herb and shook his hand.

"Thanks for everything, Herb," he said in a sobering and defeated voice. "I'll clear out my things from the trailer." He held out his arms. "I'm sorry…I don't know what else to say besides I'm clean."

"Jack, don't go," said Jennifer.

There was nothing left to say. Herb had already made up his mind. It was out of his hands.

He patted Gianni on the shoulder and plodded past him. Toward the exit.

"Jack, wait," Herb said and grabbed hold of his arm.

Jack turned.

"Look, I don't know if I can fix this," said the balding director, looking flustered and stressed. "The decision is out of my hands, but as soon as I'm off this call, we'll talk. Maybe there's something we can do? Give me a chance to at least try and fix it, okay?"

This was just wasting everyone's time, but he owed Herb that chance. Finally, he nodded.

"Armand, don't let him out of your sight until we've had a chance to talk, okay?" Herb held up his hands. "And please, no one do anything rash yet. Jennifer, tell Steve and the crew to keep working. And make sure Phil and Rhonda know I'm working on this mess, too."

"Okay, we'll wait until there's some kind of official statement," said Jennifer as she went to retrieve her clipboard. "But Herb, we're totally serious about leaving."

Gianni laid his hand on Jack's back and motioned him toward the door again.

He'd wait for the official axe in his trailer. All of this chaos from one damned photo.

If he'd been a bigger star, they'd have sent him to rehab, no questions asked. He'd just go post his *mea culpa* on Twitter, announce his rehab stint, and then return to the show. Even if that worked here, he refused to play that part. He wasn't snorting coke and he'd never lie and claim he was.

"That went well," Jack said with a groan as they headed outside and turned right toward the row of trailers.

Gianni laughed and shook his head. "At least we know the crew believes in you now."

"Yeah, that was a real surprise," he said with a smile. "Jennifer was amazing. Phil and Rhonda, too. Even Steve Kosinski spoke up."

Gianni patted him on the shoulder as he unlocked the trailer and shoved open the door, the afternoon sun filling it with warm gold light.

"We owe Herb a little time to fix this," said Gianni as Jack stepped into the trailer ahead of him. "Let's see what happens."

Jack nodded. "Guess there are worse things than getting fired. I should be used to it by now."

He knew there were worse things. He'd seen them, endured them, but right now, the thought of getting fired was a sharp ache in his chest. And it brought back all the bad memories from last year. Almost a year ago. Next month, he'd turn twenty-seven. It had been one crazy year.

He closed the door and Gianni plopped down on the couch, but he couldn't sit. He was too restless. He paced the maple hardwood, blue Vans sqwicking, mind racing.

Gianni picked up the television remote, turned on the TV, and flicked through the channels. He paused on a nature show and Jack frowned. More wildebeests.

"Dude, what's with you and the wildebeests?"

Gianni shrugged. "I don't know. I'm just fascinated by their incredible survival instincts. Constantly crossing croc-infested rivers and surviving."

"Kind of like auditioning in Hollywood. And that includes my callback for SanFran Confidential," Jack said, shaking his head.

The knock on the door startled him. He cast a confused look at Gianni and moved to answer the door.

"That can't be Herb already," said Gianni, casting a wary look at Jack as he shut off the television and followed Jack to the door.

Or maybe it could? He was so fired.

Jack sucked in a breath and opened the trailer door, staring in shock. Evan Bellows stood outside in a grey suit and white dress shirt, looking stressed and desperate.

"Evan?" Jack replied. "What are you doing here?"

Surely even Evan Bellows had seen the TMZ photo. Had he come to gloat? Congratulate Jack on his imminent firing?

Evan bowed his head, bald patch at the crown of his dark hair showing.

"Jack, forgive me, but I just had to try one more time to convince you to come home to SanFran Confidential. The show needs you—and you know it."

Jack motioned him inside. He hoped his former director wouldn't still be here when Herb showed up. Herb might just keel over dead at the shock.

"Your timing is weird, Evan," said Jack, thrusting his hands into the pockets of his Levi's as he tried to quell his urge to pace.

Evan turned toward Gianni, staring.

"Forgive me," said Jack, holding out his hand to Gianni. "Armand Gianni, costar of The Divine Newlyweds Show and star of Crossing Paths." He gestured at Evan. "Evan Bellows, director of SanFran Confidential."

Evan shook Gianni's hand briskly. "A pleasure to meet you, Mr. Gianni."

"You as well," said Gianni with a quick shake of the director's hand.

Evan turned his gaze back to Jack. "Jack, I know about the photo, okay," he said, holding out his hands. "And I don't care."

Jack wanted to bust out laughing. Evan didn't care. How was that even possible? That was the whole reason they'd fired him from *SanFran Confidential.*

"Wait a minute," Jack said with a frown as he began to pace. "You don't care? Dude, you fired me for doing coke, remember?"

"We'll have you apologize to your fans, admit your problem, and then send you to rehab in Malibu. It'll be fine."

Jack bristled. "No, it won't be fine," he said with a growl. "Because I didn't do any flake, Evan. And I'm not gonna apologize for something I didn't do."

"You're an actor," Evan quipped and patted Jack on the back. "Play the part of a sympathetic drug addict, go to rehab, spend a week at the beach, and come back a changed man. That should be easy for you."

Easy wasn't the problem. He wasn't going to let the world think he was back on drugs when he was clean. Full stop.

"Not happening, Evan," he said. "I may get my ass fired from my hit show because of a bad picture, but I'm not gonna lie to my fans. I'm not gonna let the world think I'm back on drugs."

Evan slapped him on the back. "Jack, they've never stopped thinking you were on drugs. Perceptions never change. You should know that."

He crossed his arms against his chest. "Maybe so, but the difference is I'll know."

"You were always so self-righteous, Jack. Even when you were in Hell. Well, I think our little experiment has proved that you're still a breath away from binging on coke. I'll make room for you in the Obsession and Addiction spoke of Hell. Right beside Berith. Where both you traitors belong."

The cold chill that slammed through Jack made him freeze in mid-stride. He whirled around, staring at Evan Bellows. A surge of fear rooted him in place. But that wasn't Evan Bellows talking.

That was Lucifer.

One thing was clear: whatever he'd just let into his trailer wasn't Evan Bellows. And now, he'd endangered his best friend's life.

Evan began to twist and elongate.

Gianni stumbled backward and shoved Jack behind him as Evan Bellows shifted form into Asmodeus, a seven-foot-tall, dusty red demon that wanted to kill him outright. And now, he had Lucifer riding around in his head.

This day got better and better.

"Come on, Luci," Jack replied. "We both know you sent Giggles the Clown here to try and dust me with flake a bunch of times. But the only way you could do it was to turn up the volume so high on my addiction that even the paparazzi could hear it. And I still tossed the flake. All that time stuck in your playpen has made you rusty at turning humans, Luci. Face it. Even with the Phoenix Shift, you're still a disappointment to dear old dad."

"Jack!" Gianni shouted, elbowing him in the gut. "Now isn't the time to pick a fight with the Devil and his seven-foot-tall, shapeshifting demon bodyguard."

"I prefer Lucifer," said Lucifer in a flat tone through Asmodeus, in his own voice now, that British accent prominent.

"Over what?" Jack snapped. "Douchebag? Dickhead. Oh, Devil! Sorry, knew it started with D."

"JACK!" Gianni was flustered and pissed at him, but Jack couldn't stop the rage from flaring through his body. Or out his mouth.

Lucifer released a tortured sigh. "All right, enough talk. Kill him."

"Giving up that pleasure, are you, Luci?" Jack taunted. "Guess it was too much for you to accomplish—given your advanced age."

"Jack Casey, if you don't shut up, I'll kill you myself!" Gianni shouted, a murderous look churning in his brown eyes.

His portrayal of a psychotic Cary Grant made Jack laugh.

Lucifer began laughing, too. "See, Jack, even your best friend wants to kill you. I can't wait for your return to Hell. You'll never know another moment's peace for eternity. And I'll love every moment of your uninterrupted misery."

Gianni grabbed Jack by the shoulders and slammed him backward, against the wall of the bedroom. Then shoved him into the bedroom, locking the door behind them.

"Nice acting, Gianni," Jack said with a smile as he helped Gianni shove the dresser in front of the door.

Gianni did a quick bow. "I'd like to thank the academy and all the ways I'm about to die for this performance." He sighed. "Dammit, Jack, that's the King of Hell out there."

Jack nodded as he and Gianni shoved the bed up against the dresser.

"Yeah, riding around in a seven-foot-tall shapeshifting Hell prince."

They ran over to the small window on the far wall. Jack unlocked it and shoved it open.

"I'll vault you out and you pull me through," said Jack.

"Hurry," said Gianni, glancing over his shoulder.

Jack gave him a boost up to the window and he shimmied through it, climbing onto the roof. Then he reached through the window.

"Give me your hands, Jack," he said.

The sound of a buzzsaw roared behind Jack.

Gianni froze as a shower of wood, fabric, and padding rained down on Jack. And a massive shadow turned the room to midnight.

Shit. Asmodeus had already chewed through the furniture. Wincing, Jack turned around.

Asmodeus stood in front of the destroyed bed, an angel of death standing on either side of him. The door was off its hinges, the dresser and bed in pieces.

"Oh, Jack, that pathetic little performance gave me almost a whole minute of entertainment. I can't wait to see your other tricks before Asmodeus kills you."

Game face, dude, he told himself as he flexed his wings, halo brightening.

Show time.

"Asmo here might manage to kill me—if he accidentally falls on me. Otherwise, you're gonna have to suck it up and buy that Netflix subscription, after all, Luci, because this cheap entertainment just isn't doing it for you. I hear they have all the seasons of The Cinderella Hour streaming now. Would give you a chance to catch up. See how big of a douchebag sore loser you really are."

"Asmodeus," said Lucifer, sounding unaffected. "Make sure you kill him slowly. I want to watch him suffer. For a very long time before his soul arrives."

The hulking red demon lumbered toward Jack as both angels of death took flight.

"I had the high score for months on Duck Hunt when I was a kid," Jack replied and summoned two handfuls of murder marbles. "Just sayin'. Dad's Nintendo was epic."

He flung a handful of murder marbles at each angel of death.

Murder marbles exploded, throwing both angels through the wall and into the living room. Moaning, they didn't get up.

Jack turned back to Asmodeus. "Shields up, Scotty," he said, setting himself.

He summoned a bright white seraphim ward that settled around him. And a writhing, basketball-sized sphere of Holy fire in both hands.

"Sorry for the repeat performance, Asmo, but hey, I could use the residuals right about now." He lifted the Holy fire over his head. "Splattering this dumbass red demon in three…two…one."

With the snap of his wrists, Jack flung the sphere at Asmodeus with both hands like he was shooting a layup.

"Stream this, bitch. Still watchin', Luci?"

The massive blast of Holy fire tilted the trailer onto its side as it flung Asmodeus through the living area and against the trailer's farthest wall, putting a massive dent in it. Jack got flung into the bedroom wall, his wings softening the blow.

But the huge Hell prince crumpled. And didn't get up.

Jack climbed over the broken furniture and rushed past the writhing angels of death. He stopped in front of Asmodeus, the demon's dusty red body still smoking.

"Sorry, Asmo," he said with a smirk. "Y'know, you should give up vaping. It's really bad for you. Looks like you'll have to kill me yourself, Luci."

"Ah, well," said Lucifer as Asmodeus struggled to pull breath into his demon lungs. "I'm sorry, but I can't pencil you in until next week, Jack. Responsibilities and all. No hard feelings? I promise to end you slowly myself. Do the job right."

"No hard feelings," said Jack, bending down to examine Asmodeus closer. "I have some free time next week, Luci. We'll do lunch. At your place. Toss around a few balls of Holy fire. Splatter some demons. Wreck the joint. Y'know, it wouldn't kill you to serve some good booze at this fiesta. Some top-shelf tequila. Hundred-year-old scotch. Hope you bring enough for all of Azrael's guard this time."

"Oh, I will, Jack," said Lucifer as Asmodeus sputtered and wheezed. "Enough for all of you, I promise. Can't wait."

"You bring the piñatas and I'll bring the murder marbles," said Jack, getting to his feet. "And the pain. Lots of pain—all for you."

"Wrapped, I hope. I do love presents, Jack," said Lucifer. "Until next week."

Smoke drifted up from Asmodeus as the huge demon collapsed against the crumpled boards of the hardwood floor.

Damn. Hope the insurance was paid up on this trailer. And how in hell was he going to clean a seven-foot Hell prince off this maple hardwood? They didn't make a Swiffer big enough for this job.

"Jack! Jack, where are you?"

Talia's clear soprano voice rang out above him.

He turned around as Talia landed in the middle of the smoking trailer. He glanced behind her. The two angels of death had fled, leaving Asmodeus half-dead on the xylophoned maple hardwood. Muriel landed behind Talia, setting Gianni down in the living room. He stared at the devastation in shock.

"Jack, what happened?" Gianni asked. "You didn't follow me through the window."

Talia was in front of him now, throwing her arms around him, and holding him close.

"Jack, are you all right?"

He kissed her and gripped her hand. "Well, Asmo showed up at the trailer posing as Evan Bellows. I should have known better, but it took me off guard and I let him inside."

Muriel muttered under her breath as Anahera, Deemah, and Daidrean landed in the middle of the chaos.

"Aw, I missed the fight," Muriel said, her bottom lip protruding into a pout.

Daidrean kicked a hunk of the roof out of his path. "Me, too. Demon's already down."

"That's terrifying, Jack," said Talia, holding his hand tighter. "It could have been so much worse though. What if it had been Lucifer?"

He chuckled, brushing dust out of his blond hair with his left hand.

"Um, actually...Lucifer was riding around in Asmodeus' head, Tal. The two of them and two angels of death tried to kill me and Gianni. Angels of death escaped though. Lucifer said he'd pencil in killing me for next week though. Good thing we're crashing his party about then. I'd hate to disappoint him by not being there. I want to see his face when we rescue Berith."

"Jack, you've got to stop taunting Lucifer," Talia demanded.

"He started it," Jack replied.

"He could kill you!" Talia fired back at him.

Gianni punched Jack's shoulder with his fist. "I might kill you if you don't stop. You're going to get run over, Jack."

Jack shrugged. "Anyway, Asmodeus is down. You find Kesien?"

She reached up and stroked his hair. "We did, but we need a hot blond actor with seraphim powers to get us through Asmodeus' defenses."

"He been in anything I've seen?" Jack asked.

Talia nodded and put her arms around him, kissing him hard on the lips. He returned her affection with an urgent kiss that made him ache all over.

"We need to hurry," said Muriel.

Reluctantly, Talia let him go. "Ready, Mr. Casey?"

He nodded and flexed his wings and they extended like sails around his shoulders.

"Anahera, call down another squad," she directed. "To deal with Asmodeus and get this trailer back together in a hurry. And to make sure Armand Gianni is protected."

Gianni held up a hand. "No need, Talia."

She frowned. "Why not?"

"Because I'm coming with you."

Jack shook his head and crossed his arms. "Dude, no—it's too dangerous."

"How can it be worse than facing the Devil inside a seven-foot-tall shapeshifting demon?"

Jack turned back to Talia, rubbing the back of his neck. "He's got a point, Tal," he said in a quiet voice.

"All right, Jack," she said. "He's probably safer with us. Daidrean, help Jack fly Armand to the abandoned trailer."

With a nod, Daidrean moved beside Jack. Gianni stepped between their extended wings. He and Daidrean lifted into the air with their arms hooked around Gianni's waist, carrying him out of the smoking trailer. Talia followed as Anahera called out for another squad.

THE SQUAD LANDED in the wooded lot beside the abandoned trailer. Jack and Daidrean gently set Gianni down between them and waited until Anahera returned.

"Report, Anahera," said Talia as she turned toward the tall, red-haired angel of death.

"The other squad has Asmodeus restrained," said Anahera. "And they're putting yours and Jack's trailer back the way it was before Asmodeus and Jack wrecked it."

"Hey, Lucifer started it!" Jack replied, crossing his arms.

"Thanks, Anahera," said Talia, her wings shifting against her shoulders.

Jack knew that Anahera's good news had eased Talia's worry as her wings relaxed against her back.

"All right, squad," Talia said in a commanding tone as her gaze settled on Jack. "Shields and swords out. Someone give Armand a sword, please."

"He can use mine," said Deemah with a wink at Gianni. "I much prefer shield bash anyway." She unsheathed her clear gold Eternean sword and extended it to Gianni, hilt first.

Grinning, Gianni accepted it. He tested its weight and balance, taking a few practice swings. He sliced through a small tree branch hanging above his head in a clean cut.

"Beautiful...I've never held a finer sword."

"And you won't, dude," said Jack, pointing at the blade. "That sword's made from a rare celestial metal shaped by the finest archangel bladesmith in Heaven."

"Seriously?" Gianni stared at the weapon with reverence now.

Jack nodded.

"Okay, squad, the plan is simple," Talia announced, her gaze encompassing all of them. "Jack will use his seraphim powers to break through the shadow defenses. When they're down, we storm the trailer through the front door—the only door. Expect heavy numbers of demons to respond. Especially with Asmodeus in the guard's custody."

She turned toward Jack and laid her hand against his face, stroking. "Lover, we need all the Holy fire you can muster. It will take a lot of Holy fire to cut through those defenses. They're attuned to angel light. They'll drain an angel's entire well of energy before she can break through." She leaned up and kissed him softly. "But you don't have angel light."

He smirked. "But I have a shit-ton of murder marbles and Holy fire."

Muriel chuckled.

"Squad," Talia continued, "Jack will most likely have to expend his entire cache of Holy fire."

Jack frowned. All of it? That meant a power drunk. That's why she let Gianni come along. To watch out for him because of the power drunk.

"That's why Gianni's along, isn't it?" he said in a quiet voice.

She nodded. "Armand, I need you to be Jack's designated driver because he's going to be very power drunk."

"I'll keep him safe, Talia," he said and checked Jack with a shoulder bump. "Even though he's a pain in the ass to watch."

"Welcome to our world," Muriel quipped, making Talia and Anahera laugh.

Jack shrugged. "Admit it, you'd be so bored without me."

"Kid's got a point," said Deemah.

"Not your goat," Jack snapped.

Deemah laughed. "I can't wait to hear Kesien say that again."

"Me, too," Jack replied. "All right, let's do this." He glanced at Gianni. "Dude, stay behind the squad and don't do anything I'd do, okay? It'll get you killed, trust me."

Gianni smiled and held his sword in a defensive position. "Wow, Jack Casey becoming the voice of caution? That frightens me more than the demons."

"Me too, Armand," said Muriel, calling up a gold shield of light. "Me too."

"While hearing these strange words of caution from my husband is frightening, he's right," said Talia. "Don't do anything in there that Jack Casey would do—unless you have his seraphim powers."

Jack feigned a look of shock and laid a hand against his chest. "I'm feeling targeted here."

Talia wrapped her arms around him and held him close, kissing him. "Ignore him, Armand."

"Yes, Armand," said Muriel with an eye-roll. "I've watched him take on greater demons alone when ordered not to by archangels. And he's locked angels of death out of fights, taking on Hell creatures by himself. And that includes Lucifer. So, Jack Casey is not your best example on how to fight demons."

Gianni gave him a look of disdain. "Really, Jack? Are you high?"

"Wishing for a couple of key bumps about now," he said with a sigh, hands on his hips, feeling the urge to pace—or splatter some demons. "But no. Just trying to protect people I care about."

"Stupid brave is the term we use, Armand," said Muriel and lightly smacked Jack in the back of the head.

"Jack's incredibly brave," said Anahera, "but he takes way too many chances with his life." She nodded at Talia. "The look on Talia's face says it all."

Talia was nodding along with her squad and Jack saw how pale she looked. And frightened. For him, as usual.

"Stupid brave," Talia said as she reached out and tweaked Jack's clean-shaven chin. "And I can't help but love him for it."

"Aw, I love you, too, Mrs. Casey," he said and wrapped her in his arms for a quick kiss. "All right, squad leader," he said, brushing his lips against her ear. "Let's do this."

She stepped out of his embrace and stretched her wings to their full length. "Let's go, squad. Supremes formation."

Jack busted out laughing. "I love this woman," he said and waited for the angels of death to gather in a circle behind Talia.

Gianni raised an eyebrow. "What's Supremes formation?" he asked.

Jack patted him on the back. "It's a circle, my dude, but the name—long story."

Muriel called up her gold shield of light and turned back to Gianni. "No long story, Armand," she said with a sideways glance at Jack. "That's Jackspeak for roundel formation."

"Well, that explains everything," Gianni said, grinning. "Thanks, Muriel. Actually, I kind of like it."

"Me, too," she whispered. "Just don't tell Jack. It'll go to his head that Azrael's whole guard calls it that now."

Jack stood up straighter. "Sweet."

"Wish Azrael was here," Muriel replied.

"Why's that, Muriel?" Anahera asked.

"I wanted Gianni to hear Jack call Azrael dude when he's power drunk."

Jack felt his face burn. He shoved his hands in his Levi's pockets and kicked at the ground.

"That's Jack," said Gianni. "Never a dull moment." Gianni nudged him with his shoulder. "And I wouldn't have him any other way."

"Me neither, Armand," said Talia. "Jack, are you ready?"

He took his place behind Talia, closing the circle. Gianni was to his left, deftly holding Deemah's sword.

"Ready, Mrs. Casey," he said, his gaze shifting toward the abandoned trailer. "Let's do this."

19

Talia shot into the air, wings in furious motion as she circled the treetops and then blinked across the sky, landing on the ground in front of the abandoned trailer. The rest of the squad surrounded her, still in roundel formation with Jack and Armand on flank. She needed to keep Armand as far back from the action as possible. To keep him safe.

Pressing index and middle fingers together, she turned them counterclockwise in a small circle, freezing time. With a quick blink, she returned to her squad and touched Armand's forehead, unfreezing him. For an instant, he looked confused, but then he reset his stance and shifted the Eternean sword across his body.

Quickly, she blinked back to the trailer again, trying to sense the level of demonic presence beyond these thick, writhing shadows.

She had no idea how many demons would assault them once Jack broke through the demonic blockades surrounding this old trailer. Even with omnificence, she couldn't get a clear map of the demonic energies inside. Asmodeus didn't realize that allowing the other angels of death to move freely in and out of this trailer had allowed her a brief glimpse of Kesien's brand. But nothing else escaped the tangle and pull of this dark ward. She had no idea who—or what else —lurked in there. Forcing them to enter blind.

They had to be careful. Especially Jack.

After he emptied his seraphim powers, he would be an easy target —especially when the power drunk settled on him. She and the squad would have their hands full with legions of demons. She needed Armand there to protect Jack—to shout if demons flanked them. But she worried that Lucifer might try to harm Armand in a power play to capture her or Jack.

She'd already conveyed that fear to her squad, so everyone agreed to keep one eye on the humans. Protecting them from being crossed over—a thought that terrified her.

"You ready for me to hammer these defenses?"

Jack startled her and she jumped, turning around to face him. "Sorry, lover," she said and laid her hand against his smooth face. "I was just planning how to keep Armand safe." She caressed his cheek. "And you."

"Me?" he asked, looking surprised.

"Yes, you," she said, nodding at him. "After you've expended your seraphim powers."

"Good point," he said quietly and glanced at his hands. "I'll be pretty worthless once the power drunk hits me. Sorry, babe."

"We all have limits, lover," she said and let go of him. "Even angels of death. Go ahead and deal with the defenses whenever you're ready."

He leaned over and kissed her and then approached the trailer door.

Talia stood as close to him as she dared, but just out of range of those angel-light-absorbing shadows.

"Can you see the shadows, Jack?" she asked.

He nodded and stretched his hands toward the trailer, fingers splaying as he closed his eyes, concentrating.

Muriel and Anahera kept watch, checking around them and overhead. They moved Armand between them with Deemah at his back. Putting him in the vanguard position within the roundel formation. Keeping him guarded and safe.

"Wow, these are intricate, babe," Jack muttered, scratching his head. "You weren't kidding about using all my Holy fire to break through."

"Is it possible—with only a single stream of seraphim power?" she asked.

She hoped Jack's energies would be enough. If they needed more seraphim energy, she'd have to return to Azrael and he might recall her whole squad. Forcing them to leave Kesien to Lucifer's mercy as they tried to get one of the seraphim to attack the defenses. With no guarantee that the seraphim would comply.

For several tense moments, Jack stared at the shadowy energies encasing the trailer. Finally, he glanced over at her.

"I think I can bust an opening in this thing," he said, his pale green eyes narrowing as he stared at the door. "A small one. Enough to get us inside."

"Wonderful!" she cried, reaching out and hugging him. "Ready?"

He nodded. "Ready."

"Squad, assault the target on Jack's signal."

She had to let Jack make the call because only he would know how long he could hold this barrier open if he couldn't completely break through it.

Folding his wings against his back, Jack reached toward the trailer door. He pulled in a breath, held it, and called up a burst of Holy fire. And flung it at the door.

It crackled across the trailer in tiny red and blue arcs that surged across its surface in a wave, encasing the trailer a moment and then vanished. White smoke trailed away.

"Wow, you weren't kidding about this thing being locked up demon-tight!"

He rubbed his neck a moment, his attention hyper-focused, and then he pointed his hands at the door again. With a deep breath, he hit the thick, writhing shadows with another burst of Holy fire. Larger than the last one.

Energy crackled, sparked, and then rushed over the trailer's surface. Leaving a thin hole around the trailer's door handle.

For a moment, Jack hesitated and then reached for the door handle. He turned it in his fist.

"It's slow going, Talia," he said, not turning toward her. "But I think I can cut through to the door and get us inside."

She reached up and kneaded his shoulders. "I knew you could do it, lover." She kissed his cheek and let go as he lifted his hands toward the shadows again.

"It's working," she announced to the rest of the squad. "But it's going to take Jack some time, so shields to the sun, protect Armand, and watch for demons."

———

THE SUN BEGAN to sink behind the studio buildings as Jack staggered back from the trailer. His bangs were damp with sweat, eyes glazed with exhaustion. He pointed toward the trailer, his breathing labored. He'd hit the door over and over with Holy fire bursts. Throwing them at the trailer, one after another until his arm hung limp at his side. He gripped his right shoulder, rubbing it as he stretched and flexed the arm, wings rustling with every movement.

"Shadows are down," he said in a weak voice and let go of his shoulder. "Should get you through the front door into demon central now. Tell Kesien...you're welcome." He looked pale and a little unsteady.

Jack dropped to his knees, wings flat against his back, looking dazed.

With a gasp, Talia rushed toward him. In a moment, Armand was on his right, concern bright in the soap star's big brown eyes as she slid her arm around Jack and kneaded that sore shoulder with a burst of healing light.

"Lover, you did a great job," she said and brushed his bangs out of his eyes. "Just rest now while we go in and—"

"Babe," he said, groaning as he forced himself to stand up. "If you give me a few minutes, I'll go in with you. I've still got some seraphim energy left."

"Jack, no," she insisted. "You're exhausted."

He waved her off. "I'm fine. Just need to rest for a minute or two."

She watched him carefully, studying his face, his hand movements, and checked for any slurring or loss of coordination. But she didn't detect anything other than weariness.

"I don't want to have to worry about you in there, Jack," she replied. "This is going to be a battle. I need you battle-ready."

He saluted her. "Private Casey reporting for duty, ma'am. Just point me at those demons."

"Muriel?" she called.

Muriel dropped down on her haunches beside Talia. "What's up?" She looked at Jack. "Power drunk hitting yet?"

"I don't think he's steady enough to go inside," said Talia, watching him carefully.

Jack listed a little to the right but quickly regained his balance. He did a couple of jumping jacks and then dropped to the ground and did three push-ups.

"Does that pass muster, General Smith?" he asked.

"Jack doesn't seem power drunk," said Muriel then she cracked a smile. "And believe me, when he is, you'll know it."

Muriel was right, of course. Talia hadn't seen him power drunk since their honeymoon, but there was no mistaking it. And right now, Jack was fine. Tired, a little unsteady, but fine. And if he still had seraphim powers left, his presence might make the difference inside. To free Kesien.

"All right, Jack," she said and squeezed his hand. "We may need you in there, but stick close to Armand. I want you out of there at the first sign of a power drunk. Understood?"

He saluted again. "Orders received and understood, Mrs. Casey."

"Assemble, squad," said Talia in angel notes. "And keep the humans to our flank. Out of demon reach."

Jack sighed. "Kiddie table again."

Muriel ruffled his hair. "Sorry, Jack. You're on the fragile list at the moment."

"Fine," he said, crossing his arms against his chest. "I'll be in the back, conserving my seraphim powers. But I've still got murder marbles."

Muriel was grinning as she got into position on Talia's right as Talia approached the door.

Deemah stood on her left, shield raised, anxious gaze fierce. Talia knew she was worried sick about Kesien and determined to free him. To the back, Anahera stood on the left in front of Jack, shield and sword out, watching for demons. Daidrean crouched on the right in front of Armand, Eternean sword in one hand and shield in his left hand, tilted toward the sun.

With slow, steady movements, Talia approached the trailer. The defenses had been weakened by Jack tearing a hole in them, but they were still present. Still siphoning angel light but at a greatly diminished capacity. That meant that she and her squad had to hit everything hard and fast. A long, drawn-out battle here would leave her and the squad drained of angel light. Like it or not, she needed Jack in there. His seraphim powers might just make the difference.

"Opening the door," said Talia as she gripped the door handle.

She closed her eyes for a moment, concentrating on her well of Holy fire. It was mostly full. Then she pulled on the handle and gently opened the door. It didn't make a sound as she let it rest against the side of the trailer.

With a quick hand motion, Talia signaled for the squad to follow and slipped through the threshold into the trailer's strangling darkness.

Her squad moved on kitten feet, moving inside, and fanning out in the oppressive darkness that hung like spirits around them.

Talia held her breath until Daidrean entered, followed by Armand, and finally Jack.

Without warning, the trailer door slammed shut behind them as things rustled in the blackness.

"Kesien?" Talia called. "Kesien, answer me."

"Talia? Is that you?"

She felt a wave of relief wash over her at the sound of Kesien's calm, patient voice. He didn't sound hurt or ill.

"Are you all right?" she asked.

In the uppermost register of angel notes, she heard Kesien.

"We're fine. We managed to break our bonds, so the moment you say go, we'll move."

"We?" Talia sang out in the highest crystalline angel note she could utter.

"Asmodeus took Rachel Daniels," said Kesien in his highest angel notes, keeping the demons from hearing him. "He's been impersonating her since filming began, doing awful things to Jack. Once she's free, those things will stop."

"We captured Asmodeus," Talia told him.

"But Talia—"

Kesien didn't get a chance to finish his sentence. A heavy rumbling rocked the trailer as something landed hard against the rooftop, bowing it downward.

"Aw, shit," Jack exclaimed. "Tal...I think Asmodeus wasted your other squad."

The seven-foot-tall Hell prince tore open the trailer's roof, like opening a box of cereal, and dropped through the ceiling. He landed on the floor, rocking the trailer back and forth as he leered at Talia.

"Lucifer's chew toy is almost correct, angel," Asmodeus said with a growl in his voice. "Unfortunately, they are too metaphysically challenged at the moment to be considered an actual squad."

"You shapeshifting sonofabitch!" Jack shouted, but Armand and Daidrean grabbed him before he could lunge past them at Asmodeus. "Before this is over, you're gonna be the next sealant on my trailer's hardwood floor." He pointed at the massive demon. "Lucifer's chew toy," Jack sneered. "At least I serve a purpose. You're not even going to be a memory in that other squad's head after this—once Talia brings them back."

"I doubt that, Casey," Asmodeus replied with a laugh.

Jack glared at him. "It's called resurrect, bitch. And you're not on the list."

Asmodeus lifted his corpulent arms and gestured around him. "I'm going to enjoy putting you down, Casey."

"You mean you'll try," said Jack, eyes narrowing.

"I wanted to waste you back at your trailer, but Lucifer insisted on testing your powers." Asmodeus gave Jack a hungry, malevolent stare. "He'll have to settle for your soul now because you aren't leaving this trailer alive. And thank you, angels, for giving me three humans to consume. They should give all my demons a full belly."

"Three? Dude, either you're counting skills are sus or you're holding more than Kesien in here."

From every dark crevice and shadowy corner, demons rose. In a sea of red eyes and pointed gnashing teeth, the wave of demons rolled over them.

"Shields!" Talia shouted.

Moving as one, Talia and her squad dropped to the floor and held out their shields, repelling the legions of demons.

"Kesien," Talia called out in angel notes. "You and Rachel get to us. To the door. Now."

"On it," said Kesien.

Talia couldn't hear anything above the rustle and scritch of the massive horde of demons. But out of the corner of her eye, she caught sight of Jack flinging handfuls of murder marbles in a circle around them.

"Hold shields!" she shouted. "Prepare for a blast."

Explosions cascaded around them, rocking the trailer. But still more demons emerged and rushed toward them.

Something blurred past in a haze of grey and feathers after the last murder marble exploded. A gold shield of light swiveled into the air as Talia felt two presences beside her. One angelic and the other human.

"Kesien!" Talia cried when she saw the tall, curly-haired angel beside her.

Deemah threw her arms around him and hugged him, her shield still overhead, repelling demons and Asmodeus' bursts of dark power.

"Deemah, by the Maker," Kesien exclaimed as several demons smashed against his shield. "I never thought I'd see you again."

"Thank you," said Rachel, her voice shaky. "I thought that red monster was going to kill me."

"Thank us after we're safely out of here," said Talia. "These demons have us pinned down at the moment."

A massive sphere of Holy fire sailed over the squad's head.

"Fore! Playing through!"

Jack hit the large sphere with another smaller ball of Holy fire and it shattered into dozens of golf-ball-sized orbs of Holy fire. Twice the size of Jack's murder marbles. Jackspeak for oblivion spheres.

"Stay down!" Talia shouted. "Shields to the sun!"

A cascade of explosions ripped through the trailer in waves. Punctuated with the shrieks of hundreds of demons.

"How are you doing that?" Asmodeus sputtered as Jack cut down the bulk of his demon forces.

"Seraphim powers, bitch!" Jack yelled.

Again, Asmodeus summoned legions of demons that rolled across Talia's squad like a locust plague. The squad's shields of light dimmed, but they held.

"Talia, our shields can't take another force like that!" Muriel shouted.

But another basketball-sized sphere of Holy fire sailed across the trailer. Jack threw a baseball-sized Holy fire orb at it, shattering it into another few dozen Holy fire explosives that fell like rain on the demons.

When they ignited, the blast tore through the trailer with splintering force.

The trailer rolled three times and abruptly stopped.

Death angel shields turned a dim, deep gold, flickered, and went dark. But they flared back to life when Jack grabbed hold of Muriel's shield, infusing it with seraphim power. It burned white-hot, the brilliance seeping into the other shields until together, they were brighter than a searchlight.

When the smoke cleared, only ruins remained of the trailer. Everything had gone still. And not a single demon skulked through the debris.

"Had enough, douchebag?" Jack shouted.

Asmodeus thundered through the trailer, looking shaken as Talia and her squad scrambled to their feet. They surrounded the huge demon as Kesien escorted Rachel over behind Jack and Armand.

"You okay, Rach?" Jack asked in a quiet voice.

That made Talia bristle. Despite everything she'd done to him, Talia still heard a hint of concern in his voice.

Asmodeus made no moves to attack them and no other demons remained after Jack's two Holy fire bombs had concussed through the trailer.

"I'll be okay, Jack," Rachel replied in a pained voice. "Thanks for the rescue." She squinted at him. "Why'd you bother?"

"Asmodeus does a terrible job of impersonating you," said Jack. "I much prefer your version of Rachel Daniels to his."

Rachel smiled as she reached up and brushed her fingers across Jack's cheek. Talia wanted to smite her right then and there.

"Thanks, Jack," she said. "Means a lot to me."

"Take Asmodeus into custody," Talia ordered. "Again."

Daidrean and Muriel moved toward the huge, hulking demon.

"You really think you've won this fight?" the seven-foot-tall demon asked.

Talia ignored him, praying that Jack wouldn't poke the bear any more than he'd already done.

"Looks like it," said Talia as Deemah joined Daidrean and Muriel. "Secure him long enough to get him far away from Earth. We'll let High House pass judgment."

Daidrean and Deemah began to wrap Asmodeus' feet and hands in ropey white light.

"I'll contact Azrael," said Muriel. "See what he wants done with Asmodeus."

"Thanks, Muriel," said Talia as she turned toward Anahera and Jack.

Armand was behind Jack. He opened the trailer door and motioned Rachel outside. She walked with a limp, her face bruised and cut.

Asmodeus had knocked her around. She couldn't wait to remove him from the Earth and get humans out of his line of sight. It was bad enough that he'd erased a squad of death angels. She wouldn't give him the chance to erase another one. She just hoped that she could resurrect them.

Jack turned toward the door, Daidrean behind him.

But the sounds of scuffling made Talia turn as Muriel's strangled shout sent a wave of terror through her.

"Anyone else moves and I end this one."

Jack and Daidrean froze.

Asmodeus glared at Talia, pointing. "You. Call off your squad. Now! Or you'll lose all of them."

He dragged Muriel against his corpulent, dusty red body, bending Muriel's wings down at a painful angle as he dragged her past everyone. And moved toward the trailer door.

When he was level with Jack, he stopped, gripping Muriel by the throat. Glaring at Jack with a hatred that nearly stopped Talia's heart.

"All right, Casey," said Asmodeus, his hold on Muriel tightening. "It's show time. You get to watch me erase this angel from existence. Or…you can give yourself up. Die now or die next week at Lucifer's hand. Your choice."

"No way, Jack," Muriel choked out. "Don't. You dare."

Asmodeus slammed his meaty fist against Muriel's head.

"Stop it!" Jack gritted his teeth, his pale green eyes filling with fury.

"Make me," Asmodeus fired back at him. "What's it gonna be, Casey?"

Jack's eyebrows pressed into a hard line and he glanced at Muriel and then Talia.

For an instant, she saw his pain. Felt his regret. Then he turned back to that huge demon monster.

"Jack…" She tried to push past Kesien, but he held onto her. "Jack! Don't!"

She blinked out of Kesien's hold, but Jack was out of her reach.

Surrendering.

Asmodeus dragged him forward.

"JACK!"

Deemah and Kesien were holding her back now.

"Talia, it's too late," said Kesien. "We'll have to find another way to save him."

Asmodeus slammed his fist against Jack's chest, knocking Jack to his knees as Muriel crawled away from the hulking demon. Anahera blinked to her and gathered her in her arms, lifting her up and out of Asmodeus' reach.

With a sharp inhale, Talia blinked out of Kesien's hold.

"Talia, no," Kesien said with a gasp.

She landed in front of Asmodeus and Jack, blocking the exit.

"Take me instead," Talia demanded, fighting not to let the tears well in her eyes.

"Sorry, angel," Asmodeus said with a toothy grin as he dragged Jack toward the trailer door. "You don't have an amazing bounty on your head. Lucifer only wants this one. So, I'll be taking my prize and leaving. Now."

"No." Talia tried to block his path again, but Deemah and Kesien got in her way. "Jack, no!"

The trailer door sprang open with a rush of wings and a flash of golden halo.

Something slammed into Asmodeus in a tremendous burst of Holy light. Knocking the huge demon halfway across the trailer.

At about seven feet tall, the willowy angel stood in Asmodeus' wake, holding onto Jack. The angel wore flowing white robes, his wings pearly white. His hair was long and white, eyes a soft archangel yellow.

He was beautiful. Powerful. And familiar somehow.

"It's over, Asmodeus," said the deep baritone voice with a commanding timbre and such presence.

A voice she recognized from her wedding.

Abaddon! Redeemed. As he had looked before he was sent to monitor Hell and Lucifer. Where he became twisted. A red-eyed demon. Until Jack saved him.

And now, he'd returned the favor.

Abaddon held Jack up as he stared down at Asmodeus and

summoned glowing white ropes that wrapped around the Hell prince, immobilizing him.

When Abaddon was within five feet of the hulking red demon, Asmodeus lunged at him, knocking Abaddon and Jack to the ground.

Abaddon recovered quickly and summoned the white fire of his powers. The force of the white fire hit Asmodeus hard. He crumpled under the blow, a hole through his dusty red chest. Even for a celestial being, that had been a killing blow.

Talia heard Abaddon sing a series of angel notes and in moments, a flight of angels landed all around Asmodeus.

The redeemed archangel turned to Talia and laid a hand against her face. "Talia, Asmodeus has been neutralized. I will take him back to Heaven myself and see to it that he's punished. If he survives."

With shaky movements, Jack struggled out of Abaddon's hold and steadied himself with a hand against the wall. But Muriel swept past Jack, looking mesmerized as she stared at the redeemed angel. The third time she tried to speak, the words gushed out.

"Abaddon! Thank you!" Muriel sighed, struggling for more words. "I—I...thank you."

She couldn't stop staring at the redeemed archangel. She seemed transfixed by his presence. By the fact that he had saved her.

Abaddon smiled, reaching out and taking her hand. "I'm learning to help others. It was an honor, Muriel." Then he turned to Jack who looked pale and shaken. "And that includes humans." He extended his hand to Jack. "Especially one who saved me from a very dark existence."

Jack shook his hand. "Aby. Dude, I can't tell you how glad I am to see you."

"I took your advice, Jack Casey," said Abaddon, his light shining bright against the shadowy demonic trailer. "I saw the world that humanity had to offer. And I wasn't disappointed. I was enlightened. So, I knew that I had to see everything in the Creation. And protect it from the wicked. When the time came. Thank you."

"What will happen to Asmodeus?" Talia asked.

"I'm not sure if he will survive the blow I dealt him," said Abaddon as he engulfed the Hell prince in pure white light. "But I'll take him straight to High House. Let the inquisitors deal with him."

Abaddon bent down and flooded Asmodeus with more white light and then like a shooting star, the two beings shot through the wall and blinked toward the Heavens.

With a heavy sigh, Talia glanced at Jack, feeling her anger burn deep, and motioned toward the trailer door. Already, the shadows dripped down the walls and puddled along the floors from Abaddon's neutralizing powers.

"Let's get these humans back where they belong," Talia ordered, casting a scowl at Jack who looked pale except for the bruise swelling on his left cheek.

He looked conflicted. Sad. But she was in no mood for kindness right now. Or excuses. Or Jack Casey's sexy, pale green eyes searing through her in an apologetic stare. She was furious at him and there was no way she'd let him water down her anger with his smoking hot looks.

Talia blinked through the abandoned trailer's open rooftop to avoid Jack, asking Kesien to make sure he and Armand got back to the trailer. While she went ahead to try and resurrect the squad that Asmodeus had erased.

SHE HAD JUST RESURRECTED the fifth angel from the mess that was their trailer when Jack limped inside behind Armand and Kesien. Muriel laid a hand on Talia's shoulder.

"Talia," she said in soft angel notes. "Don't be too angry at Jack. He was just trying to save me."

"No promises, Muriel," she snapped and looked away. "I can't lose him. He knows how I feel, yet he just hands himself over to a Hell prince wanting to kill him. Never thinking about me. If he loved me, he'd do everything in his power to stay with me. Not offer himself up as a sacrifice."

Muriel's brow furrowed, pressing into an angry line. "Talia...no matter how angry at him you are, you can't question how much he loves you."

"Yes, I can."

"Jack Casey went to Hell for you," Muriel said with a glare. "Never expecting to escape. He fought that possessed bodybuilding firefighter to his last breath to stay with you. And he triggered that reeducation power, erasing himself from your memory to save you from Lucifer. He loves you more than his own life. His own soul. Be mad at him all you like, but don't you dare forget how hard he's fought for you. That's not fair, Talia."

Muriel blinked across the room to Anahera.

Talia turned away from the trailer door. From Jack. But she couldn't halt the flood of tears stinging her eyes, turning to crystal, and hitting the floor. He loved her. She knew that. And she loved him. That's why she was so angry. For the moment, she had to push her feelings aside. Get this trailer back together in a hurry. She pressed her index and middle fingers together, turning them clockwise to unfreeze time.

"All right, squad," she called out to the angels of death inside the ruined trailer. "Let's fix what Asmodeus destroyed. I was able to resurrect the five angels he erased and I sent them back to Eolowen to Azrael."

Her squad mates cheered as she turned and cast Holy fire along the floor. Reassembling the maple hardwood back into its pristine installation. Kesien and Deemah resurrected the kitchen, down to the spilled box of donuts on the counter. Muriel and Anahera recreated the bedroom. Daidrean repaired the trailer's exterior while Talia completed all the fixes to the living room and the door. Jack and Armand were in the bedroom, making the bed, and putting everything back into the right place.

After a half hour, the trailer was back to its pristine state.

The knock at the door startled her.

Talia opened the door, surprised to see director, Herb Rutherford. He barged into the trailer, his tan pants and blue dress shirt wrinkled, tan leather loafers a little dusty.

"Talia," said Herb as he made his way to the living room as angels blinked through the walls and ceiling. "Where's Jack?"

Herb never saw even a wing feather as he collapsed onto the couch, looking dejected and stressed.

"He's in the bedroom," she answered. "Why?"

Armand was already headed down the hallway toward them, Jack behind him.

"Herb, what's up?" Armand asked, moving nonchalantly into the room.

Jack had his hands in his Levi's pockets, his gaze moving around the room.

"Look," said Herb, wringing his hands. "I'm trying to fix this, I really am, but that TMZ picture's pretty damning, Jack."

The picture! In all the commotion, she hadn't even had a chance to hear what Jack had to say about the photo. Or the bags of drugs all over the set. Much less how the paparazzi had managed to snap a picture of him doing coke.

Jack began to pace along the hardwood floor. He looked distraught. She wanted to go to him, tell him everything was all right, and hold him in her arms. But she was still furious at him for offering himself to Asmodeus in exchange for Muriel. Didn't he know that she couldn't lose him?

Armand offered a few ideas to Herb, but Jack stomped on any suggestion that involved him admitting to doing drugs.

"You could go into rehab, Jack," said Armand. "Two months later, you're out and back to work."

Jack stopped pacing, his face screwing up into a look of misery. "You want me to lie and say I did drugs when I didn't? Forget it."

"It's not lying, Jack," said Herb. "It's acting."

"Not to me," Jack growled.

As Jack resumed his pacing, the room fell silent. Herb looked lost. Armand looked frustrated. Jack looked devastated.

With her arms folded against her chest, Talia walked into the kitchen and stared out the small window. This was where the paparazzi must have taken the photo. Jack had been standing in front of the sink. Must have been holding the bag of drugs in his hands when they snapped the photo. How could they discredit the paparazzi photo? She couldn't just use her angel powers to change it. That kind of interference got Azrael in trouble before, so she couldn't do that.

Was there another way to fix this? Without divine intervention?

She glanced around the sink, at the refrigerator to her left, and the stove to her right. She stared at the grey quartz countertop, her gaze flicking past the powdered sugar scattered across it. And the box of six donuts that stood on its side beside the sink. Placed back in its original location by her squad.

Crumbs and sugar from the powdered donuts were everywhere. They'd left a trail of powder all the way to the sink. And left a white mess along its edge and across the countertop.

She'd clean this up later. After she'd seen the photo.

Quickly, she used omnificence to call up the paparazzi photo and it materialized in front of her.

At first, it made her wince, realizing how close Jack had come to returning to his old habits. His old life.

She studied the image more closely, enlarging it. In the photo's bottom, right corner was the box of spilled powdered donuts. In frame. Right at Jack's elbow.

Her gaze shifted from the window to the donut mess as an idea began to take shape in her head.

She materialized a cell phone in her hand with the paparazzi photo of Jack on the screen.

"Herb!" she called. "Come over to the window."

She heard Herb's heavy, anxious footfalls cross the room into the kitchen. She pointed to the window and the mess from the box of donuts. As she did that, she used her new transference power to push an idea into his head. About a publicity stunt gone wrong.

It wasn't perfect, but it might cast enough doubt to fix this with the network.

"Herb, look at this photo closely," she said.

He leaned toward the screen, squinting.

Talia pointed at the box of donuts at Jack's elbow.

"Look! Do you see the box of spilled donuts in the photo?"

He looked at her and nodded. "What about it?"

She pointed at the kitchen counter where the box had spilled powdered sugar in trails across the countertop.

"We point out the donuts, insist that Jack had powdered sugar, not cocaine. Claim that Jack was poking fun at himself using the powdered sugar, not cocaine. He was about to post the selfie on his social media, but paparazzi got there first. A bad joke and he apologizes, but he wasn't doing drugs."

Jack stared at the donuts and then at the photo. Finally, he looked up. "Herb, that's just dumb enough to work."

Herb took out his phone and snapped several pictures of the donuts and the sink. He made Jack take a donut out of the box and stand at the sink while he went outside and snapped some photos. When he returned, he patted Jack on the sleeve.

"Don't worry, Jack," he said and offered a smile. "I'll explain this to the network. When I show them my photos and the paparazzi shot—with the donuts in their frame—they'll back off from firing you. It wasn't unanimous anyway."

"Thanks, Herb," said Jack.

Gingerly, Jack turned toward her, looking sheepish and fearful. Nervous. "Thanks, Tal," he said in a timid voice like he was afraid to speak to her.

"Of course, Jack," she answered.

His mouth twitched as some of the taut muscles in his face relaxed.

"Okay," said Herb, moving toward the trailer door. "Everyone sit tight for a couple of days while I deal with the network. I'm putting the whole filming schedule on a two-week hiatus anyway. We need time to get everything in place for the new renovation challenges. I'll have Jennifer text everyone when we're ready to resume filming."

"Appreciate it, Herb," Jack called after Herb and closed the door.

Armand stepped past Jack. "I'd better tell Izzy what's happening. See you tomorrow?"

Jack bowed his head for a moment. "Listen, Gianni...Talia and I have to disappear for a while."

"Berith?" Armand asked.

Jack nodded. "We'll be back as soon as Berith's safe."

"You promise?" Armand asked, frowning.

"Promise," said Jack.

Armand hugged him. "Both of you, be safe," he said and shook his finger at Jack. "And Jack, no heroics."

"Take care of yourself, Gianni," Jack replied.

"You and Izzy take care, Armand," said Talia as she reached out and squeezed Armand's hand.

Armand and Jack stared at each other for a moment and then Jack hugged Armand back. "Give Izzy my love."

"Will do, Jack," said Armand.

The taller soap star hurried out of the trailer, leaving Talia alone with Jack.

She'd never seen Jack so nervous as he turned around to face her, hands shoved into the pockets of his jeans. Like the very first time that he'd spoken to her on the set of *The Cinderella Hour*. He chewed his bottom lip, his gaze anywhere but her eyes as the misery on his face built. Finally, she broke the silence.

"Azrael wants us at Eolowen to train right away, Jack," she said, her tone calm.

He nodded emphatically. "Sure thing. Right away. We can leave whenever you want, Tal."

"In the morning should be fine."

"In the morning, huh?" he repeated as he tugged at the collar of his navy blue Henley.

She nodded, waiting for him to say something. Apologize. Beg her forgiveness. Assure her that he would never sacrifice himself again. Proclaim his undying love for her all over again. But he stood there with his hands in his pockets, chewing his bottom lip, silently dying inside.

Finally, she couldn't stand it anymore.

"Jack," she said, crossing her arms. "Don't you have something to say to me?"

He winced. "I love you?"

By the Heavens, he was so devastatingly handsome with that windblown light blond hair, that sexy smirk curling the corners of his lips, and those pale green eyes burning holes through her. She wanted to throw him onto the bed and make love to him. But she had to make him understand that he couldn't keep sacrificing himself like this. Especially when she couldn't stand to exist without him.

She shook her head slowly. "Try again."

He frowned. "But Tal, I do love you."

She moved toward him. "If that's true," she said and poked him in the chest, forcing him to take a step backward. "Then why did I just watch you give yourself up to Asmodeus? Willingly. Completely ignoring how much I love you and how devastating that moment was for me."

"Tal, I'm sorry," he said in a pained voice and held out his arms. "I couldn't watch that bastard kill Muriel. I just couldn't."

She stomped her foot and pushed him backward. "And I couldn't watch that bastard kill the man I love! More than my own existence! You, Jack! You!"

"Babe, I'm so sorry," he said, his face pinched, those pale green eyes looking so sad and conflicted. "I never meant to hurt you."

She pushed him again. In front of the bedroom door.

"Well, you did, Jack Casey!" she shouted. "Very deeply. I almost lost you today. If you decide to sacrifice yourself again, think long and hard about your death angel wife who loves you more than anything. And don't!"

She smashed her mouth hard against his and kissed him so urgently that tears sprang to her eyes and rolled down her cheeks, turning to crystals.

He looked stunned. Shaken. Speechless. Those pale green eyes alight.

She marched over to the bed, grabbed a pillow, and slammed it against his chest.

"Think about that tonight, Jack," she said and slammed the bedroom door in his face. "On the couch!"

20

Jack was stunned. Dazed, he carried the pillow over to the taupe sofa and grabbed a grey blanket draped over the back of the cushions. Talia hadn't been that furious at him for a while—and it made him feel horrible. He plopped onto the sofa, draped the blanket over him, and laid his head on the pillow that smelled like roses and cool rain.

He sighed. Like Talia.

The trailer looked brand new again, back to its high-end finishes, pristine taupe walls, white trim, and maple floors showroom perfect. Kitchen had that fresh renovation sparkle. Even the stainless-steel sink looked polished and right out of a magazine—except for the donut crumbs and powdered sugar dusting the edges.

She'd put everything back together. Like she always did. He hoped that included their relationship. Because right now, he didn't know how to fix that. Apparently, he had a knack for tearing things apart.

He thought about the fight with Asmodeus as he flipped through channels on the big screen television, passing Gianni's nature show about wildebeests as he tried to find something to watch. To keep his mind occupied. But he felt the power drunk creeping toward him.

Soon, he'd be alone and power drunk, watching wildebeests go airborne and dodge a bazillion crocs in a river.

Kind of like the day he'd had.

Regardless, it was his fault. And he probably deserved it.

But what could he have done? Asmodeus forced him into trading himself for Muriel. He was the only one in the room that hulking red bastard would have traded her for anyway. Dude had already eliminated five of Talia's death angel guard. He wouldn't have hesitated to make Muriel his sixth kill of the day. Jack couldn't have lived with himself if he'd stood there and let Asmodeus kill Muriel.

He didn't know that Talia's resurrect power had intensified enough for her to bring all those angels back from destruction at Eolowen. Much less the ones that Asmodeus killed.

That power was mirrored in him, too, but he'd never tried to resurrect an angel that had been erased from existence.

Maybe Talia could have brought Muriel back? And maybe she couldn't? At that moment, he couldn't take that chance. His only bargaining chip had been the fact that Lucifer wanted him alive, no matter what he'd claimed tonight. Asmodeus even said the dude had been testing his powers.

Why'd Luci think they'd changed?

The couch looked brand new, but it was stiff and narrow. Cold—even in a July heatwave. Cold without Talia beside him. Without her arms around him.

This was the first time she'd ever banished him to the sofa for the night. Granted, she'd had many opportunities, but tonight was the first time he'd seen that distance in her eyes. Wanting to be as far away from him as possible. And right now, with the power drunk beginning, it hurt. A lot.

His head felt heavy, his vision blurring as everything got all oozy and out of focus. Like he'd done three or four shots. The room began to shift a little, gaining a bit of spin. More fun ahead. He knew this one would be rough after all the Holy fire he'd tossed around in that trailer and at that demon Hell prince.

His stomach lurched, the television's movement making him sick. Studio lunch was about to come up. Hard.

He jumped up from the couch, blanket tangling around him, and pitched into the floor.

Again, the room tilted, like fifteen shots kind of tilting. And the kitchen felt like it was a million miles away.

On hands and knees, he crawled toward the kitchen counter and pulled himself up to the sink. Hovering over it, he turned on the water, struggling to keep himself from hurling. Couldn't. Everything came up. Again and again, until he had dry heaves.

When he could catch his breath, he rinsed the sink and washed his face, holding onto the counter with one hand, his legs like rubber. He grabbed a bottle of water out of the refrigerator and staggered his way through the thick drunken haze back to the couch.

But the room twisted and spun into blackness, the couch miles away. Determined, he stumbled toward it. But darkness overtook him.

Sometime later, he felt the cool hardwood floor against his cheek and ice-cold water seeping into his Henley. The pool of chilly water felt good against his heated skin.

He tried to get up. Couldn't catch a wave in all that spin. His mouth felt like sandpaper as he laid his head back against the hardwood and closed his eyes while wildebeest migrated across the television behind him. Distorted. Loud. Until even the television sounds merged into the swirling maelstrom inside his head and finally went dark.

One thing he hated more than being blackout drunk was the hangover that followed. Maybe he'd get eaten by one of the TV crocs before morning and avoid the second half of this seraphim pain-fest. He never wanted to overuse his seraphim powers again.

Or anger Talia enough to spend another night on the couch. Too bad he couldn't even find the couch. Shivering, he curled into a ball and moaned, trying to stop the wild spinning that had overtaken him. Deep in the dark, swirling depths of the power drunk, he was grateful when unconsciousness put him out of his misery.

SOMEWHERE BETWEEN THE last fading jabs of the power drunk and the first gut punch of the worst hangover he'd ever felt, bright golden rays of sunlight warmed the cold hardwood floor.

His head pounded like John Bonham and Neil Peart were dueling drum solos on his cranium. It thrummed in his ears and reverberated against his eyelids, rendering him completely useless. He was shivering, curled into a fetal position, and hoping Lucifer would end him before he had to open his eyes.

No such luck.

In the blur of noise and sickness permeating his body, he heard distant muffled voices. He'd left the television on. Correction: he'd been too sick and power drunk to turn it off.

Or maybe Sir David Attenborough had finished narrating the wildebeest migration and was behind him, describing the rare sighting of a fallen Hollywood star in his natural habitat. Alone. Hungover. Curled in a fetal position on the floor. Begging Lucifer to end him. Sounded about right.

He hoped Attenborough was describing the croc-infested waters he'd fallen into and his impending demise.

Dude, make it quick. Before he had to open his eyes or try to get up from this floor.

Through the muted tangle of noise and voices, he felt a hand against his head.

Damn, Attenborough. Don't drag it out! Send in the damned crocs already. End it.

The same word repeated over and over, through a funnel, but he couldn't make it out. It was only one syllable.

Croc...Croc...Croc.

Nature show had an onscreen cheering section for the crocs. Damn. Nature shows were brutal. No wonder Gianni was rooting for the wildebeests. Probably didn't have a cheering section either. Poor little dudes. If he lived through this hangover, he'd have to donate some bucks to save the wildebeests.

Croc...Croc...Croc.

"Attenborough," he said in a whisper. "Crocs are winning. So, end it."

That whisper lanced his temples and stabbed his chest. He groaned, the rumble in his voice making everything shudder and ache.

Why wasn't an angel of death hovering over him right now? Crossing him over? Then he realized that required him to open his eyes. But even one eye was a struggle.

"Stop cheering for the crocs already," he muttered, his voice one long moan.

The voices were right on top of him now. This time, the word changed.

Jack. Jack! JACK!

"Attenborough, cross me over already," he moaned.

Someone laughed. "What is he saying?" A warm and calm male voice. Gianni?

"I don't know," said an achingly clear soprano voice so beautiful he wanted to melt into every note. Talia. "He's out of his head. And it's my fault—I made him sleep on the couch, knowing he hadn't gone through a power drunk yet."

Someone chuckled. "This is much more entertaining than the TMZ coke footage." Muriel?

"Let's get him to the couch." Gianni?

"Too many crocs," Jack replied. "Just ask David Attenborough. They've got their own cheering section."

More laughter. "He is totally out of his head." Muriel again.

"It's not funny," said Talia, sounding upset. "Help me get him off the floor."

Dammit, she was still pissed at him. He'd managed to upset her again. She was probably going to divorce him after yesterday.

"Don't divorce me, Tal," he moaned. "I'm really sorry. Ask Attenborough and the crocs."

Someone lifted him out of the floor. The rush of air made him shiver, his teeth chattering. It was a deep, bone-chilling cold. Like the kind he felt last night when Talia kicked him out of the bedroom.

In moments, he felt something soft underneath him. And a warm blanket covered him. He felt a warm hand press against his face until the balmy Caribbean feel spread over him like a heated blanket.

And the pain and sick feeling began to recede. Enough for him to open his eyes.

Talia knelt beside him, using her angel healing abilities. But he couldn't read the emotions swirling in her light grey eyes. Behind her, Gianni and Muriel grinned at him.

"Attenborough?" Gianni replied and gave him a confused look.

"Sir David Attenborough," he said in a rough voice.

Gianni was shaking his head. He had on a jean shirt and dark blue jeans that looked pressed. Every hair on his head was perfectly placed in that familiar Cary Grant way of his.

"Where did that come from?" he asked and propped his hands on his hips.

"Your fault," Jack snapped. "That damned wildebeest show you were watching is the last thing I remember before I had to hurl."

Gianni was almost in hysterics laughing at him now. "Is that what you were babbling about? That's hilarious, Jack!" He glanced at Muriel. "You're right. Jack needs his own show."

Frowning, Jack shook his head. "Solo?"

Both Muriel and Gianni nodded, but that word made him sad. He stared down at the sofa and cast a quick glance at Talia. Looked like she was still not speaking to him.

"That might depend on Talia?"

He pulled in a shaky breath and turned his attention to her, waiting for her response, but she kept her concentration on the healing light she was using on him. Like he was some helpless dumb animal—a wildebeest—that she had to heal. He wanted to curl up in a ball again. He didn't know how to fix this and it was eating him up inside.

It took every ounce of strength he could muster to sit up. Breaking her healing light connection.

He scrambled to his feet, the walls swaying, and tried to make it to the trailer door. Her distance and silence made him ache all over. He couldn't handle it anymore. If she wanted no part of him, he had to get as far from here as he could. But the trailer tilted again and he pitched into the floor.

"Jack!"

He shoved the hands away from him and crawled across the floor to the trailer door.

"Jack, what are you doing?" Gianni asked, stepping in front of him.

"I've gotta get out of here," he said through gritted teeth, his chest aching.

"Why?"

"Talia hates me," he said, his voice hitching. "I can't be here knowing that."

Talia blinked in front of him and dropped to her knees, grabbing hold of his arms. Forcing him to look at her.

"Hate you?" she cried, her face taut and pale. "Jack, I love you."

"I don't know how to fix this, Tal," he said, staring down at his hands. "I love you more than my own life, but I don't know how to fix this."

Gianni dropped down beside him. "Jack, couples fight. We can't always see eye to eye. I'd never seen so many sparks between two people until I saw you and Talia together. And I was always in a state of denial, watching how you two never fought or disagreed on anything. I was so relieved when you and Talia had a fight after my wedding. I was beginning to think you two weren't human."

Talia looked away.

"Jack," Gianni continued, a hand on his back. "What is it that you can't fix?"

"Talia was furious when I surrendered to Asmodeus to save Muriel," said Jack.

"So was I, Jack," said Gianni. "But after I thought about it for a while, I realized that you didn't have a choice."

Talia whirled around and fixed Gianni with her best angel of death glare. "Didn't have a choice? Of course, he had a choice."

Gianni smiled. "Talia, do you think Jack could have just stood there and watched that demon destroy Muriel?"

"Of course not, but why did he have to sacrifice himself? Why?"

Gently, Gianni took her hands in his and squeezed. "Two reasons." He glanced at Jack. "Jack, correct me if I'm wrong."

Jack shrugged.

"One, Asmodeus was only interested in Jack, Talia. He wouldn't have made that trade for anyone but Jack. And Jack knew that. The second reason is that he didn't want you in that demon's hands, Talia. Jack would die if anything happened to you."

Jack nodded emphatically. "Tal, I couldn't watch Asmodeus kill Muriel. And I still had enough seraphim powers to end Asmodeus. So, I took him up on his trade, intending to waste him at my first opportunity."

Talia turned toward him. Listening to him at last.

"Jack, I had flashbacks of Lucifer dragging you off to Hell again," she said, her voice quivering. "Everything in my body screamed in pain when he took you. And I couldn't take it. I love you and I can't lose you. Don't you understand that?"

"I'm so sorry, babe," he said, his voice shaking. "I didn't do it to hurt you. I was just trying to save Muriel." He sighed, bowing his head. "I'm sorry. If you want me to go, I will."

She threw her arms around him and pulled him against her. "Jack Casey, I don't want you to go! I want you to stay at my side forever." She pulled in a pained breath. "I thought you were going to leave me forever in that abandoned trailer. And it broke me."

He wrapped his arms around her and tilted her chin up, kissing her lips in a deep kiss.

"So, tell me how I can fix this, Tal," he said, reaching up and stroking her silky black hair.

"Stay with me like you promised," she said in a small quiet voice. "You made a vow. You're my husband. Now until forever, remember?"

He entwined his fingers with hers and brought her left hand up to his mouth, kissing her wedding ring.

"Happiest day of my life," he said. "I never want to be without you, babe. I want to spend the rest of my life with you. And my eternity. I changed my whole existence to be with you."

Tears funneled down her cheeks as she reached out and stroked the feathers of his wings. Then she ran her fingers across the white-gold gleam of his halo.

"You did, didn't you," she said through her tears as they turned to crystal and shattered against the floor.

He cupped her face in his hands. "And I'd do it all over again, Mrs. Casey. Every moment and every sacrifice."

She reached up and laid her hands on top of his, squeezing.

"Forgive me?" he asked in a quiet voice.

Nodding, she kissed him hard on the lips. He returned her kiss with every bit of strength he could summon. He held her tightly, never wanting to let her go.

She pointed a finger at him. "But you promise me, right now, Jack. When we assault Hell's Gates, you promise me that you won't sacrifice yourself to save Berith. I won't relive the pain I went through when you were dragged off to Hell. Promise me."

"I promise, babe," he replied. "Luci's not my type."

His joke made everyone laugh and diffused the tension in the room.

Gianni patted his shoulder. "Be careful when you go after Berith, Jack. I expect to hear the full story from you when you and Talia return for filming. So, no sacrifices down there—unless it's Lucifer."

"Thank you, Armand," said Talia, smiling at last.

"Dude, trust me, I'll tell you every last miserable detail when we come back from there. With Berith."

Gianni moved toward the trailer door with all the poise of Cary Grant back from his first official demon hunt. Could have been a whole new career path for Gianni. Or a new reality TV show if he got tired of this show. And Jack. Cary Grant, Demon Hunter for Hire. Cool show, bro.

"Take care of yourself, Gianni," Jack called to him.

"You, too, Jack. And I know you'll watch out for Talia."

He nodded. "Won't come back without her."

She leaned over and kissed him again, warming his body, and easing his apprehension.

Talia helped him to his feet and directed him back to the sofa where she continued healing him.

When she'd finished, he was feeling coherent again, the power hangover almost manageable. He'd just taken Talia's hand in his when Kesien and Deemah blinked through the ceiling and landed in a wash of gold light.

"Looks like you survived your talk with Azrael, Kesien," said Talia as she cast a glance at Jack.

He and Kesien were both in the dog house today. With Sir David Attenborough narrating it.

"Welcome back, dude," said Jack. "Glad you're okay."

Kesien gave him a quick nod. "Thanks, Jack." He turned his gaze to Talia, looking contrite. "And Talia, my apologies for going off on my own like that. It was reckless and thoughtless. I didn't think about my squad or the guard or the fact that I was abandoning my post. I ask your forgiveness for my reckless behavior."

Talia laid her hand against Jack's hair and caressed it. "You're forgiven, Kesien," she replied. "As long as I have your assurance that you won't go off on your own like that again. That you'll tell your squad what's happening and keep them informed at all times."

The tall angel of death bowed his head, those black curls in perfect order now that he was out of Asmodeus' hands.

"I give you my word, Talia. I've learned my lesson."

Talia cast a sideways look at Jack and he looked down at his hands. She was still hammering her point home at him. Those were words she'd wanted to hear from him. A contrite apology.

He looked up at her and brushed his fingers across her cheek. "Tal, you have my word, too," he said. "I'm sorry for being thoughtless and I learned my lesson, too."

But she was already shaking her head at him. "Jack Casey, we both know you have yet to learn your lesson about anything. And I know that there will be a next time. Because I can't change you. All I can do is love you." She kissed him. "And banish you to the couch when it happens again."

Jack laughed. "You know me too well, don't you?"

She nodded. "I'll just make sure to banish you to the couch after your power drunk is over. And to keep an extra guard over you."

He slid his arms around her neck and pulled her close enough to breathe in her intoxicating roses and cool rain scent.

"Let's go back to that *loving me* part," he said, smiling, and brushed his lips against hers. "How does that work...exactly?"

"Didn't your dad have that talk with you, Jack?" she asked, holding in her smile.

"Burnt to the ground by my death angel wife," he said with a chuckle. "I'd marry you all over again, Mrs. Casey."

She ran her hands inside his Henley, stroking, caressing his chest. "And I'd marry you over and over again, Mr. Casey. Now until forever."

"So, about that *loving me* part again," he said in a hushed voice.

"We'll discuss that later, lover," she said and turned back to Kesien. "Kesien, where's Muriel?"

"She went on patrol with Anahera," he said. "After they went to check on Rachel Daniels. Anahera is about ready to smite her. Muriel —not Rachel."

Talia's eyes widened and she exchanged a confused look with Jack. "Why?"

Kesien's smile lit his charcoal grey eyes with amusement. "Because she hasn't stopped talking about archangel Abaddon since he dropped into the trailer and took down Asmodeus. Saving the day."

"I surrendered myself to Asmodeus to save her and she thanks Abaddon for saving her. That's just great." Jack's eyes narrowed and Talia couldn't help but laugh.

"Being a sacrifice is a thankless job, Jack," said Talia with a chuckle. "See why you need to give it up?"

Kesien motioned toward the ceiling. "I just left Azrael and he wants the squad back at Eolowen right away. To begin training." He looked apprehensive. "Azrael said it's time. We can't wait any longer."

"I'll call the guard home," said Talia, but she turned one last time to Kesien as he spread his wings, intending to blink away from the trailer. "By the way, Kesien, the members of the guard that we lost that day…"

Kesien's expression darkened and he flinched, wings twitching as he nodded. He still looked deeply disturbed by what happened.

"A loss I'll never get over," he said and bowed his head a moment.

"I used my resurrect power and brought them all back," she said. "High House has probably already cleared them and let them return to the guard."

A shocked look gleamed in his charcoal grey eyes, his lips parting. "You brought them back?"

Talia nodded. "Berith tried. Until Lucifer grabbed her. But my resurrect is stronger. I was able to bring them all home again."

Kesien's eyes grew watery and he looked too moved to respond. Instead, he bowed his head and laid his hand against his heart. Then he blinked through the ceiling, wings spread wide.

Talia rose from the sofa, letting her wings open around her shoulders as she sang out notes that Jack couldn't hear. Calling all angels of death in the guard back to Eolowen.

With shaky steps, Jack stood up from the couch. He walked over to Talia and slid his arms around her waist from behind. He laid his face against her shoulder and wings, holding her close, breathing in her roses and cool rain scent.

"I love you, Talia," he whispered. "And I promise I will walk out of Hell beside you. With Berith. You have my word."

She reached back with her left hand and stroked his hair.

"That's all I want, Jack," she said in a sobering voice. "You beside me. Now until forever."

"Done, babe," he said and nuzzled her cheek. "I'm going to take a shower and change clothes."

She held onto his hand until he let go, disappearing into the bedroom to clean up and change clothes. When they got to Eolowen, he would start training for the assault on Hell's Gates alongside her squad. And try to save Berith.

21

TALIA LANDED BESIDE JACK ON EOLOWEN'S TERRACE AS DOZENS AND dozens of angels of death trained around them. More than three hundred angels of death crowded the meadow behind the grand hall, sparring, drilling—readying for the assault on Hell.

Apprehension roiled in the pit of Talia's stomach as she watched angels flit past in all directions, some training with swords and others with shields. Some did acrobatics and speed drills, wings in frantic motion in the skies over Eolowen. Others taught defensive and offensive tactics to their squads, testing each other in skirmishes.

The entirety of Azrael's guard filled the meadow and the terrace, joined by two Archangels of Death, Sidriel and Turiel, and their guards. Archangel Ramiel and his Watchers had also joined the assault. Azrael's guard was the largest, but with Archangel Sidriel and Archangel Turiel's forces, the combined guards' ranks had swelled to over four hundred angels of death.

Archangel Zephana and her forge angels had worked hard to equip all of the death angel guards with Eternean swords and armor. And the Watchers. Once the seraphim had sanctioned Azrael's mission, all three guards of death angels came together at Eolowen to support him. To stand with him at the Gates of Hell. Every angel of death understood the threat that Lucifer still posed by blatantly kidnapping an angel of death right out of Heaven. Off Eolowen's terrace. And none of them had forgotten Archangel Samael's treachery.

Azrael stood on his dais, Sidriel, Turiel, and Ramiel behind him as he oversaw sword and shield drills among the top squads in each guard. These squads would go into Hell first and secure the gates from Lucifer's hellhound guardians, Cerberus and Orthrus, and massive packs of hellhounds. Talia knew that her squad, with Jack as vanguard, would be at the front of that assault. They had to be ready for anything.

The heavy thump of shields against Eternean armor echoed across the meadow, clash of swords sharp and jarring. Every angel of death wore clear gold Eternean armor and grey short robes underneath. She smiled. Except for Jack who insisted on wearing his faded Levi's beneath that short robe. At least she'd talked him out of wearing his checkered Vans and into armored sabatons.

At the edge of the meadow, Watchers trained for ranged assault, arrows snicking through the air and thumping into white canvas targets all along the pergola and the white stone walls. Everything had a bright, intense sheen beneath the Parrish blue skies. But for the first time, it reality hit her. Heaven's angels of death were going to war again. Against Hell. Against Lucifer.

But none of these preparations and training exercises had given her a sense of readiness. This was Lucifer and Hell. He had spent an eternity learning how to thwart Heaven's standard tactics and taught those maneuvers to his demons and fallen angels. Besides, Heaven had battled Lucifer twice before, so the guard had to be better than standard. Better than the best soldiers in Heaven because Lucifer knew how to fight Heaven's best soldiers. He'd led them once. Trained them. Focused them. Fought beside them as the Maker's most powerful angel.

When Lucifer marched on Heaven, Jack's seraphim powers staggered Lucifer. Like hers and Jack's rare mirrored powers had surprised him.

What could they throw at Lucifer that would stun him now? Set him off guard long enough to rescue Berith? Somehow, they had to outwit the King of Hell. He had all his powers back. And he was just waiting for Azrael and the death angel guards to enter his domain.

And Jack. She sighed. Especially Jack.

She was terrified to have him enter Hell again. How badly would it trigger his horrible memories of that place? Would he freeze up? Become an easy target for Lucifer to erase? Or would she lose him forever down there?

No one really knew what powers Lucifer regained in his Phoenix Shift—no one but Lucifer. All she knew for certain was that Lucifer didn't have the power to sever the soul tether they'd attached to him during the assault on Heaven. If he'd had that power, he'd have broken his tether on the spot or shortly after.

"Wow, Tal," said Jack, his gaze moving from the meadow to the terrace. "There must be over two hundred angels of death out there, skirmishing and training to kick Luci's ass. And a shit-ton of Watchers, too."

"More like four hundred," she said, watching the drills running throughout the grand hall. "Not counting the Watchers." It made her proud to be part of the guard, but Lucifer's unpredictability terrified her. And so did his duplicity and misdirection. Not even Pravuil dared to speculate what Lucifer sought by kidnapping Berith.

"That's a lot of angels," he replied, sounding a little overwhelmed by the presence of so many angels.

The seraphim had remained ominously silent concerning Lucifer's end game, but they were wary enough to keep ample numbers of cherubim patrols in the skies and along the pathways and airways across and around the lower Heavens (what Jack called Angeland). The lower spires of Heaven (and all the angels here) existed to defend the portal that led to the Maker's treasured risen souls. And His throne.

Like most of the angels around her, Talia had never been on the other side of that portal. She'd never seen the Maker's throne or all its angelic soldiers of light and throne angels. Humans had depicted them strangely. All wheels, eyes, and wings. But Talia knew that they traveled at speeds she couldn't even imagine. Supposedly, they had more wings than seraphim. They were protected by shields of Holy light that ringed their angelic forms. That glowed like starlight around them. And their blinks were infinite. Making them appear like the strange ancient drawings of throne angels. Maybe someday, she would encounter them.

Even with the most powerful angels stationed at the Maker's throne, Talia knew that all angels below them existed to protect that soul portal. At any cost. And all of those risen souls—along with souls yet to rise like Jack's, Purgatory, and the Middling . And maybe even hers.

She glanced at Jack, wanting to wrap him in her arms and apologize properly to him for yesterday. He'd scared her to death. Again. And she had done her best to get that message across to him. But now that he was at Eolowen again, she saw the subtle change in his demeanor. His game face had slipped a little after seeing the war preparations in action. Like he'd been when they were preparing for Lucifer to march on the Heavens. She knew it was driving him crazy not knowing what Lucifer had in store for them in Hell. He'd pushed Jack hard, gloating about kidnapping Berith and delighting in his taunts to come and rescue Berith. Testing the strength of Jack's seraphim powers.

Lucifer knew exactly how Jack's time in Hell had scarred him. He counted on it. Sometimes, it made her ache all over when she watched Jack's eyes glaze over and the memories rush past. In those moments, he looked terrified. Sickened. Devastated. She knew that he hadn't told her everything that had happened down there. Always trying to spare her pain, but she only wanted to help him through it. Protect him. Ease his pain. He'd sacrificed himself to save her from that agony and after watching him in that abandoned trailer, she feared that he'd do it again in Hell. To save Berith.

She couldn't take that again. And he wouldn't survive a second captivity down there.

Somehow, she had to keep a squad on him at all times, make sure that he didn't get the opportunity to sacrifice himself. She couldn't lose him. He meant everything to her.

Azrael blinked across the terrace and hovered in front of her, wings spread wide, sword of Holy fire in his right fist.

"Talia!" he cried. "Jack! Welcome home to Eolowen. As soon as you get into your Eternean armor, join in with the drills and sparring. Your squad will be the first to assault the Gates of Hell, so we need you to train immediately."

"Sir, I—" How did she explain to Azrael that fighting Lucifer this time required more than standard death angel guard tactics?

"Azrael, is this just a warmup for the guard?" Jack asked as he studied the drills and weapons training in motion all around him.

Azrael raised an eyebrow. "Warmup? I don't follow you, Jack."

Jack gestured at the angels of death around him. "I don't mean to tell you how to fight demons and I know these drills will take apart legions of Luci's minions. A good warmup for the guard, but when we get to those gates, Luci's gonna take us apart if we try to hit him with these same ol' same ol' fights. Even with the new armor and Eternean swords in every death angel's hand. He's expecting every move we're perfecting right now. And he already knows how to counter each one."

"Jack," said Azrael in a stern tone, hand on his hip, charcoal grey eyes igniting like embers as he bristled at Jack's comment. "We've battled Lucifer for millennia. You've fought him for a year."

"And that's why you've fought him to a draw," Jack replied.

Azrael's grey eyes narrowed, lips pressing into a tight, angry line. He didn't appreciate Jack's candor right now. And he found Jack's comments arrogant—even though she knew that Jack didn't mean them like that. Not at all. She knew it was concern that made him speak up, nothing more.

"We have to achieve a level of precision and endurance—"

"Sir, Jack's right. Lucifer will expect these tactics from the guard." Talia summoned a sword of Holy fire that guttered in her hand. "We need more weapons of Holy fire like this and we need to hit him in ways he isn't expecting. Keep him guessing and adjusting long enough to grab Berith."

Talia felt Jack's arms slide around her, holding her close. "Mrs. Casey's onto something. We have to convince Luci that we're assaulting Hell to win. To bring it all down. When what we're really after is Berith. We fight like we have nothing to lose just long enough to grab Berith and run. It's not like Luci can follow us."

She loved the feel of Jack's arms around her and the sound of his hot caramel voice thrumming against her ear. She could melt in the timbre of his voice. In the molten pool of his pale green eyes.

Azrael tapped his fingers against his lips, his gaze far away as he landed on the terrace and paced around it, wings twitching at his back, the red-gold of his halo burning bright in the crisp afternoon sunlight. She hoped that he was considering what she and Jack had proposed instead of getting ready to shout at him for his human arrogance. Azrael seemed to be deep in thought though, appearing almost energized.

It was simple but it might work. Make Lucifer think the guard was fighting to end everything he had created in Hell, giving everything they had to his defeat. Just long enough to find Berith and retreat. They had to make Lucifer believe that this wasn't about Berith. That it was about kidnapping an angel of death right out of Eolowen. And it was, but they didn't have the forces to bring down Lucifer's operation.

Jack was still the one unknown factor. None of them—Jack included—understood what Lucifer gained by getting Jack down to the Gates of Hell. Why set this strange showdown into motion?

It was a trap from every angle. But what did he gain? What did he want from Jack?

"Talia!" Azrael cried, rushing back to her. He gripped her shoulders, grinning. "You're right! That's the way inside. Making Lucifer believe that our response is bigger than one angel." He turned to Jack. "And Jack, that is the way we divert Lucifer's attention. Long enough to grab Berith."

"How do we do that though?" Jack asked, his gaze intense and Talia could almost see the thoughts racing through his head. "How do we keep him off center with tactics he isn't expecting?

"Abaddon, Jack," said Azrael. "We will have Abaddon at the front of our assault when we hit those Gates. When Lucifer sees his former first lieutenant transformed and all the archangels, he'll know that this assault isn't about Berith anymore. Besides, Abaddon can ensure that those Gates remain closed behind us—and that they open again only for angels of death."

"Having Abaddon join the fight is perfect, archangel," Talia replied.

"When he shows up at Luci's door with those yellow eyes and huge sparkling white wings, Luci's gonna lose his shit."

Azrael frowned. "Why is that, Jack?"

"Because," Jack said with a smirk, those pale green eyes alight. "He's gonna know that Dad let his ex-con older brother come home and live rent-free while Luci's paying to live in a friend's basement. He'll lose his shit."

Azrael smiled as amused expressions rose on the faces of the other archangels behind him.

"Thanks for that…colorful confirmation, Jack," said Azrael.

"Sure thing, Azrael," Jack replied, looking pleased.

"Never a dull moment with Jack Casey on the field," said Kesien in crisp, clear Enochian notes as he flew past with Deemah, shields and swords in motion as they sparred on the white stone terrace.

Talia smiled, wishing Jack could hear them.

"I've never seen the guard so happy," said Anahera who sparred with Muriel to the left of Kesien and Deemah.

"If Jack calls Azrael dude," said Muriel with a grin, "they're all going to lose it though."

"Babe?" said Jack, turning toward Talia. "Can we use omnificence to pinpoint Berith's location in Hell? We need to know exactly where she is down there before we hit those gates. So we can do a quick grab and go."

"I'll have to consult with Pravuil," said Talia with a shrug. "With all those dark energies, chasms, magma, and heavy rock walls, it may be difficult."

She'd never used omnificence like that before and she didn't think Lucifer could shield all of Hell from omnificence's probing either. But regardless of shielding, Hell's landscape might be difficult to penetrate with omnificence. Especially now that Lucifer had all his powers back. She needed to be sure.

"Has transference awoken in Jack yet?" Azrael asked.

Jack grimaced. "Don't think so," he said, brushing his bangs out of his eyes. "Not sure what it does or how it feels though, so I can't be sure."

Talia gently rubbed his neck. "We'll investigate transference when I speak to Pravuil. He'll want to see you use it too, Jack."

"If I have it," he replied, shrugging.

So, he hadn't felt anything awaken in him? If he didn't receive transference, it would be the first rare power that hadn't been mirrored within him. Was he reaching his limit?

Her eyes turned misty. Or was their bond weakening?

That thought terrified her after their fight on Earth. And her completely forgetting about his power drunk and not even checking on him until the next day. She still felt awful. But she'd been so angry at him for surrendering to Asmodeus that she couldn't think about anything else.

She'd sent him to the couch to make sure he understood how much that had hurt and frightened her.

"Do you want us to run drills with the guard until we can talk to Pravuil, sir?" Talia asked Azrael.

"First, get into your Eternean armor," said Azrael, pointing toward the grand hall. "You'll find them in the armory where Zephana is working feverishly to get all the armor's protection upgraded. She's almost finished. Then see if we can infuse some of the seraphim's Holy fire into the weapons. Show Lucifer that he hasn't had a fight like this one."

"Good idea, Azrael," said Jack as his gaze moved toward Eolowen. "A show of Holy fire force might show Lucifer that this isn't a fight he wants to have. Especially with Abaddon on board. We don't need Luci to hesitate for long. Just long enough for us to grab

Berith. Hopefully, with omnificence, we'll know right where to find her."

"I hope so, too, Jack." Azrael nodded toward the grand hall. "Now, both of you, go. Get into your armor and see about that Holy fire. Then join the guard's drills."

"As soon as we check in with Pravuil," she said.

She extended her wings and lifted into the air, Jack beside her, his silvery grey wings in motion. Together, they flew over the terrace and landed on the round room's rooftop. Jack hesitated a moment when she dropped through a portal to the floor and then followed.

Pravuil floated through the austere white room, surrounded by dozens of books that floated above the white bed against the far wall. White curtains billowed from the windows and pooled along the stone floor. Jack glanced around the room and she wondered what he was thinking about, what memories had sparked in him. But his gaze quickly flicked to the books.

Several were tomes the Scribe had called forth from the Archive. Big dusty books with heavy dark bindings, their titles etched in crisp gold Enochian script. Empty story gem readers floated through the room, too, their empty gold sockets shiny against the crisp Parrish blue skies and the white stones.

"Talia and Jack," said the Scribe, turning in the air currents until he was floating in front of them. "Good to see you both."

Talia hovered a few inches off the stones, but Jack had his feet firmly on the floor, wings flat against his back. His white-gold halo gleamed against the white stones. Sometimes, it faded against his light blond hair and looked dull against those pale green eyes, that inner fire making them burn so bright.

"How are you, Pravuil?" Jack asked, shaking the Scribe's hand.

"Trying to unravel Lucifer's machinations. Again. My function as the Maker's Scribe has become secondary to dealing with Lucifer's moods and schemes."

"I can't imagine dealing with that for eternity," said Jack, a knowing look on his handsome face. "He's so damned full of himself. So arrogant."

The Scribe gave Jack a sour look. "You don't know the half of it, Jack." He gave a sharp nod. "But I suspect that you know Lucifer better than most of these angels."

Jack kicked at the stones with the toe of his checkered Vans, those faded Levi's hugging his lean body in all the right places. He had on a forest green Henley that made his pale green eyes look molten.

"Unfortunately, I know more about that insufferable douchebag than I ever cared to know."

Pravuil laughed. "My sympathies, Jack."

Jack rubbed the back of his neck and glanced at Talia when the Scribe's attention shifted to her.

"All right, Talia," said Pravuil, his wings elongating behind him, gold eyes intense. "Have you learned anything about transference since awakening it?"

"It's painful to remove its connection from someone," said Talia, glancing at Jack.

"Those connections are like grappling hooks in your brain," Jack said, nodding.

"But easy to remove unlike a soul tether," said Talia, still perplexed by Lucifer's focus on it. "I just can't understand why Lucifer needed transference, Scribe. As far as I can tell, it's a basic kinetic power and I'm surprised that it's considered such a rare angel power."

The Scribe scratched his head, short white hair a little windblown as he glanced at the books surrounding him.

"I've pulled everything from the Archive I can find about transference, but there just isn't much documenting this power." He glanced at Jack. "How about you, Jack?" the Scribe asked. "What have you learned?"

Jack shrugged. "I think this power skipped me, Scribe."

Pravuil's brow furrowed, those gold eyes darkening. "You don't have it?"

"Sorry," Jack said, shaking his head. "Not sure why, but it didn't awaken for me."

Pravuil looked surprised. Then worried. And that frightened her.

"Scribe? What are you thinking?" she asked, shifting closer to him.

"A few possibilities," said Pravuil as he slid his hands behind his back and floated to the floor. "One, Jack hasn't had time for it to awaken yet. Especially after all that show of Holy fire yesterday against that putz, Asmodeus."

"You know about that?" Jack asked.

Pravuil nodded. "Story spread like Holy fire across the Heavens when Abaddon brought Asmodeus to the Spire. Handed him off to High House."

Talia wondered what the seraphim's inquisitors would do with Asmodeus. If the former cherub-turned-Hell prince survived his injuries.

"The second possibility," Pravuil continued, "is that Jack is no longer mirroring your rare powers, Talia. The third possibility is that Lucifer's somehow interfering with Jack's ability to mirror the power."

"How are either of those possible, Scribe?" she asked.

She felt fear spike through her. How could Lucifer block Jack's ability to mirror her rare powers? Or most unsettling, why would Jack no longer be mirroring her rare angel powers?

"Maybe Lucifer is using transference to block the power from Jack?" Pravuil added. "Probably unlikely, but the possibility might exist. Most likely, Jack just needs a little more time for it to awaken."

"More time?" Talia cried as she landed beside Jack, her attention focused on the Scribe. "Why would he suddenly need more time when the previous power awakenings were immediate."

"Jack drained his powers yesterday with that massive show of Holy fire, Talia," said the Scribe as he glanced from her to Jack. "He needs time for the well to refill before he can awaken a new power. Like when you used resurrect to recover our angels of death from Samael's treachery. You had to regenerate your Holy fire before awakening transference. That's the most likely possibility here."

Jack held her close. He looked frightened and that surprised her.

"Scribe, the other two possibilities," said Jack, his eyes narrowing. "Why wouldn't I be mirroring Tal's powers anymore? And how could Luci be blocking me suddenly?"

With a sharp inhale, Pravuil laid a hand on hers and Jack's shoulders.

"Jack, we don't understand how you've been mirroring them in the first place. So, trying to understand why you don't awaken an ability would take time that we don't have right now."

A deep sadness burned in Jack's face and she felt his embrace tighten around her.

"Is—is it our bond, Scribe?" he asked finally in a quiet, frightened voice. "Did *I* break it?"

Her heart hurt at his question. After yesterday, he thought that he'd damaged their relationship.

At last, the Scribe smiled and shook his head. "No, Jack. I can tell you right now, that bond is undisturbed."

"Yes, it's rock solid, lover," she said and held him closer.

She felt him exhale sharply, the tension leaving his taut muscles. She pressed a quick kiss against his lips, making him smile.

"But I still wouldn't rule out some dark ugliness from Lucifer, so keep your guard up," said Pravuil. "I'd have kicked him out of Heaven way before the Garden. The Maker gave him way too many chances to hurt Creation."

Jack's smile broadened. "I'd have kicked him to the curb, too, Scribe."

He patted Jack's shoulder. "Now, don't you worry about Jack, Talia," said the Scribe as he plucked one of the story gem readers out of the air. "I'm sure the reason is all that Holy fire expenditure. He's human, remember? Sometimes, it takes things longer to rebalance for them."

Pravuil reached into the right pocket of his pearly robes and slid out the purple story gem with Gadreel the Fallen Watcher's story. The one she used to discover the parts of transference. He locked it into the center socket and Talia watched the words appear above the book. He turned toward one of the portals that opened onto the terrace. And pulled a translucent curtain of golden light out of the air. It was as tall as Jack and about three feet wide. When Pravuil pointed the book at it, the words spilled onto the curtain of light.

"Let's look at Gadreel's story again," said the Scribe, growing pensive as he stared at the Enochian language undulating across the curtain of light. "There were two parts of Creation needed to awaken this one and little information on how to use it."

"Her description was very brief," Talia replied. "Almost nothing after gathering Hell's first flame and a piece of wood from the fallen Tree of Life." Talia drifted around the edge of the curtain of light, studying the glowing words of Gadreel's story.

"Whoa," said Jack behind her as he stared at the curtain of light.

But he couldn't see the words. They were in the Enochian language.

"What's the matter, Jack?" she asked.

He stood beside her now, staring at the curtain, looking worried. "So, to awaken this power," he said, running his fingers through his bangs, "you burned part of the felled Tree of Life with Hellfire? That's some really dark shit for an angel to awaken, don't you think?"

She hadn't thought about the symbolism. After all, the items were elemental like resurrect. And she'd combined the pieces similar to resurrect. She shuddered. But none of the other powers consumed one element with the other. She'd been too focused on getting out of the Garden with the power. Anticipating that demon attack. But now that she had time to analyze the pieces, she knew that Jack was right.

"It's one of the darkest rare powers that Talia has awakened," said Pravuil.

"And yet, you and Tal think this power is kind of lame compared to the others?" Jack asked.

Pravuil cast an uncertain look at her and then turned to Jack.

"It's not exactly the way you're putting it, Jack," said the Scribe, "but it is definitely more simplistic and less powerful than the other powers."

"How, dude?" Jack asked as he stared at the curtain like he was trying to gather some sort of meaning from the symbols. "That first flame of Hellfire—wow. There's gotta be some hard-hitting retribution mixed with deep dark rage in those flames. And they consumed wood from the Tree of Life? This tree that contained all this essence of life and being and knowledge? A symbol of Creation. That Luci destroyed when he destroyed the whole Garden."

Frowning, Pravuil looked at Talia, his face scrunching into a look of confusion.

"Not sure what you're getting at, Jack," he said finally.

"Dude, to awaken that power, dark had to consume light." Jack began to pace around the room, looking a little unnerved. "Evil had to consume Good. Leaving this harmless-looking power behind that lets you move shit around and make people do stuff for you."

Talia blinked toward him and laid her hand against his cheek, halting his pacing.

"Jack," she said in a soft tone, trying to calm his agitation. "I'm afraid we don't understand what you think this power does. Can you describe it in another way?"

Jack scoffed. "Talia, it isn't what this power does, it's what it is. Lucifer doesn't have Vassago's power of possession without permission anymore, right?"

"No, of course not," said Talia, a cold feeling of dread beginning to creep through her chest. "He forced Vassago to use it for him."

"But now, he has something that can bend someone's will to do his bidding. It isn't transference of objects and thoughts." He exhaled sharply. "Dear God, Talia—it's a transference of will. His will. Through that fallen angel of death, Procel who awakened it. He's replaced Vassago with Procel."

Stunned, Talia stared at Pravuil in horror as the realization hit her hard. The Scribe had gone quiet as he came to grips with Jack's revelation.

"By the Maker…" Pravuil gasped and couldn't speak for several moments.

Frantically, he plucked books out of the Archive and out of the air, opening them, and throwing them at the curtain of light.

"I'm pooling every detail we have about transference, Gadreel the Fallen Watcher, and the pieces of the power."

Pravuil was rattled now, his hands shaking as he tossed book after book into the curtain of light. Each time, the curtain sparked, absorbing the information until after the tenth or eleventh volume, Pravuil blinked across the room to the curtain and pressed both hands against its surface.

Finally, with despair shining in his gold eyes, the Scribe turned toward them, his brow pressed into a hard line against his eyes, his mouth pinched.

"It's all inconclusive, but Jack, based on the nature of both of those elements, I can't discount it. That may be transference's ultimate power. Transfer of will."

Talia felt cold dread rush down her back and chill the tips of her wings. Would Lucifer transfer his will to Jack? Or her? To all of them? Trapping them in Hell forever.

22

thought of Lucifer gaining access to a power that allowed him to force his will onto someone. The white stone walls began closing in on him and he couldn't breathe for a moment.

The ramifications of this new rare power were terrifying for Heaven and humanity. But everything had been so chaotic with Lucifer misdirecting everything like the universe's best magician. Talia and Pravuil never got a chance to analyze it before or after Talia had awakened it.

And Lucifer had been counting on that.

Herding them. Pushing them. Attacking them from every angle. To keep them guessing and running and from spending too much time on any one thing—like another rare power that looked harmless.

Damn. How could he or anyone stop this vindictive bastard? And he had the distinction of royally pissing off the universe's most deadly supervillain. To a point where this dude shouted his name in his sleep and focused all his efforts on erasing Jack from existence. Or torturing him in Hell for eternity.

Lucifer wanted to lure all of them to Hell so he could destroy them. And they were just going to show up to the party with apples in their mouths. Like good sacrifices.

"Talia, what are we gonna do if Luci pops transference, takes over half the guard, and kills the other half before eliminating the survivors? Leaving you, me, Azrael, and Aby to fight him on his home turf."

Was there any chance at all of bringing Berith home in the face of this new power? One that for some reason, he didn't have. Leaving Talia to duke it out with the King of Hell alone.

He'd never felt such anxiety and fear before. It was consuming him as he began to pace the room, his heart racing, and his mouth going dry. He began to shake all over, his breath coming in gulps. Like a full-on panic attack.

His pacing was frantic and he shoved his hands in his Levi's pockets, trying to move faster than the dread and fear rushing after him like harpies.

"Jack, what's wrong?" Talia cried.

He didn't turn toward her. He felt like his head was going to split open or his heart was going to explode from the stress. What were they going to do?

"Jack, talk to me." She blinked ahead of him, holding out her hands to stop him from pacing, but he couldn't stop, couldn't tamp down this panic exploding inside him.

He struggled for a breath as Pravuil blocked his path, wings spread wide.

"Talk to us, Jack," said Pravuil, squinting at him. "What's going on?"

He'd never had a panic attack before they started filming *The Divine Newlyweds Show*. He gulped in a breath of air and tried to force it into his lungs, but he was hyperventilating now.

He'd never had a panic attack like this one.

Wait a minute! He'd never had a panic attack before Lucifer's crash dummy awakened this transference power.

Furious, he grabbed one of the books out of the air and heaved it against the stone wall.

"Dammit!" he shouted, his voice echoing through the round room.

"Talia—that bastard played me again! Stuck those meat hooks right back into my head again."

Talia looked horrified.

Lucifer had been transferring anxiety and panic to him through that damned fallen angel, Procel. Making him pace and freak out and get salty over every little thing.

Two could play that game.

He closed his eyes, gathering together all those dark thoughts and his out-of-control anxiety into a single, compressed image in his head and forced it outward. Back where it came from. Right down that transference conduit to Procel.

His body burned with heat as he wrestled against an opposing force trying to stop him. He pushed harder, throwing a ball of Holy fire behind it and shoving it down Procel's throat.

Something went thump!

"Jack!"

The thump was him hitting the stone floor hard. When he opened his eyes, Talia and Pravuil were standing over him. Talia dropped down beside him, her hand against his overheated forehead. His hair was damp as he stared at Talia for a moment.

"Transference just awakened," he said with a smirk. "Right in Procel and Lucifer's face."

Pravuil gave Talia a look like Jack was out of his head and dropped down on Jack's other side.

"Lie still, Jack," said Talia, fear burning in those luminous, grey angel of death eyes. "Let me use my healing light on you."

Gently, he laid his hand against hers and shifted it away from his face.

"I'm fine, babe," he said and sat up. "Actually, I'm better than that. Now, that I've got that douchebag Procel out of my head."

Pravuil's eyes got so big that Jack thought they might explode.

"Procel?" Pravuil said with a gasp. "In your head?"

Jack nodded as Talia slid her arm around his waist and helped him to his feet.

"I've been feeling overwhelmed with anxiety and little panic attacks since Talia and I returned to Earth to film The Divine Newlyweds Show."

Talia's concern darkened to a look of annoyance. "You never told me that."

He leaned over and kissed her. "Because I didn't realize that none of it was mine until now. Babe, when did you ever know me to pace obsessively?"

A quizzical look touched her face and he could almost see her rolling back through her memories of him. She bit her upper lip, still churning through her thoughts until finally, she stopped, frowning as she fixed him with her gaze.

"Not like you've done on the set this season, Jack. You haven't seemed yourself since we got to the set, but I never could put my finger on what or why."

He nodded, kissing her again. She noticed but hadn't said anything. He knew that she would have paid attention to that, confirming that he wasn't crazy. About the anxiety and pacing at least.

"It felt wrong to me, too, but I couldn't control it," he said, glancing from her to the Scribe. "Like the drug cravings. And I didn't connect all the dots until just now. So, I packaged all those bad vibes along with a ball of Holy fire and returned it C.O.D. to Procel and Lucifer just now." He grinned, laying his hand against his ear. "I think I can hear Lucifer cursing my name from here."

Pravuil's eyebrows lifted. "Then it worked?"

Jack nodded and Talia threw her arms around him, holding him close.

"Jack, I'm so sorry I didn't say something. You've been suffering through all of that for weeks and I—"

He kissed her. "Not your fault, babe. We didn't understand this new power, didn't know what it was capable of—or how Luci planned to use it. Now, we know. And the good thing is, we both have it now. We can use it right back at them."

At last, she smiled and her brooding expression softened. Like she'd let go of feeling responsible. Of feeling like she was to blame. When a pensive look made her gaze distant, he wondered if she'd already gone back to death angel mode, focusing on how to fight back against transference.

"But Tal, we have to be able to protect Azrael and the guard from transference, too," said Jack. "Any ideas, Pravuil?"

Pravuil held up his index finger. "Maybe. Let me talk to Zephana. See if she can infuse the armor with some sort of shield that can block this rare power."

The Scribe blinked to the rooftop and disappeared in another blink.

Jack pulled Talia into his arms and gave her an urgent kiss. "Still mad at me?" he asked. "About last night?"

She shook her head, a sad look turning her grey eyes glassy. "Just afraid, Jack," she said in a sobering tone. "Afraid that you'll leave me forever. And that would destroy me."

He started to speak, but she cut him off with a poke to the chest.

"So, think about this if you're faced with another sacrifice, Jack Casey. I don't want to exist without you. Saving me at your expense will destroy me."

He bowed his head, feeling a little overcome. "But I want you to go on no matter what, Talia. That's why."

She shook her head hard, her raven black hair whipping around her shoulders. "You're my reason for going on," she said in a quiet. "Without you, I'm broken. And lost. Don't you understand? Being without you is my hell."

He wrapped her tightly in his arms. "Message received, Mrs. Casey. I won't do anything to separate us. Okay?"

"Promise me."

"Didn't I already promise?"

"Promise me again," she insisted.

He smiled. "I promise. Again."

She kissed him with enough force to knock him off his feet. "Now, let's go train with the guard."

Feeling weak in the knees, he glanced at the white bed behind him. "I've got a better idea."

She kissed him softly and let him go. "Sorry, lover, the four hundred plus angels of death surrounding us cancel out that idea."

"We could blink down to the trailer for a bit," he offered with a smirk.

She tugged on his silvery grey wings. "Come on, let's get our armor and hit the practice field. Keep your mind on the assault, Jack. I don't want you distracted.'"

"Fine," he said with a sigh as Talia extended her wings and blinked to the rooftop.

Grudgingly, he unfurled his wings and rose behind her, up through a rooftop portal, and out onto the terrace.

FOR DAYS, Jack trained alongside Talia and her squad. He pushed himself hard to keep up with the angels of death, but by the third day, he stumbled, unable to match the stamina of all these celestial beings. He stepped out of the squad-against-squad exercises, but as the only vanguard in play, his absence didn't halt the drills. He collapsed against the terrace's curved outer wall and watched Talia, Muriel, Anahera, Kesien, and Deemah lay waste to the other squads. They were still Azrael's best.

Azrael stood on the dais, preening, looking like a proud father as Talia and her squad defeated every squad they faced.

Jack was drenched in sweat underneath his grey robe, his hair damp, and his face a mask of perspiration as he fought to catch his breath. The Eternean armor felt heavy, his Levi's clinging to his legs beneath the greaves, vambraces making his wrists and forearms stiff. Eternean armor was celestial, so it was light, but it was still armor. Hot and uncomfortable for a human. Besides, he missed his sneakers.

Oseira, one of the cherubim healers, moved around the terrace and examined the angels of death who waited there for the next round of exercises. Oseira's yellow eyes were hawkish, her features transforming out of the eagle form she had taken across the meadow.

Her dark brown eagle feathers faded to tawny dark skin, her short dark hair windblown.

She paused beside an angel or two, laying hands on them, and then moved on to the next angel. But she seemed confused at times. Like she couldn't remember how to summon a power or use her healing light. He watched her for several minutes as she cast her healing light on angels throughout the terrace. When she'd taken care of everyone, she shifted form into an eagle and took flight into the meadow to heal more angels.

Abruptly, Jack felt a presence. He turned.

Pravuil stood beside him on the threshold of the portal leading into the round room. His pearly wings curved around his shoulders, his gold eyes narrowing as he watched Oseira.

"Something wrong, Scribe?" Jack asked, peering up at him, one hand over his eyes to block the sun.

"Oseira still seems a little off-kilter," said Pravuil in a wary tone. "I'm concerned."

"What happened to her?" Jack asked, watching her shift into human form and begin healing angels in the meadow.

"She was on patrol in High House when Samael's guard ambushed the cherubim guard and attacked the spire. First line of defense. Two of her patrol got erased by Samael's turncoats. She almost made three, but the seraphim saved her. They saved several cherubim that night." He bowed his head, wincing. "Wish they'd been at the Archive, but thank the Maker that Talia was able to bring them back. I owe Talia so much."

"I owe Talia everything," said Jack as he turned his body toward the portal where Pravuil huddled, watching the preparations.

"Heaven owes Talia a great debt," said the Scribe. He reached down and patted Jack on the head. "And her fearless, headstrong husband. Both of you have given so much. This time, Heaven needs to make sure you're both protected from Lucifer's reach." He groaned. "That just got a lot longer."

"Yeah," said Jack, leaning his head against the white stones. "That's going to make the assault on Hell's Gates much more stressful. As if that was even possible."

"As soon as the assault force moves against Hell, I am taking Oseira back to High House. Have the other cherubim make sure her injuries are healed and it's safe for her to resume her duties."

"Good plan, Scribe," said Jack, turning back to watch the squads continue sparring. "Hope I live to hear how she's doing."

Pravuil chuckled. "You will, Jack. Otherwise, Talia will lay waste to Lucifer and Hell. In that order."

"Marrying her was the best decision ever," said Jack, flashing Pravuil a grin.

"Funny, she says the same thing about you, Jack," said Pravuil. "Heaven knows why."

Jack laughed as Pravuil blinked back into the round room to continue his research.

When Talia's squad emerged as the winner again, all the squads shifted across the meadow and the terrace. In the distance, the Watchers continued with their archery drills, the dull thunk of arrow strikes punctuating the sharp clank of swords, softened by the whisper of hundreds of wings.

The sound of angel wings had a different quality to it, not like birds taking flight. No, it was hushed, airy, almost like the wind or softly falling snow, and it had a delicate quality. Fragile. Like a soap bubble or a rose in full bloom where one touch would cause the bubble to burst or the petals to fall.

For what felt like an hour or so, Jack relaxed against the wall and watched Talia's squad defeat every squad they faced. He knew that they would be the first squad in with Azrael, the other archangels, and Abaddon leading the charge. As the vanguard of Talia's squad, he'd be saving all his Holy fire to slam in Lucifer's face. Hopefully keeping Luci distracted long enough for another squad to rescue Berith. He didn't care who rescued her as long as she escaped that douchebag's hands.

Jack didn't hear the command (damned angel notes), but Azrael called a break and all of the squads dispersed, filling the sky with angels of death. They flew in all directions, but Talia and her squad blinked over to the wall and sat down beside him.

"Dudes, you totally tore through all the competition out there," said Jack as Talia sat down beside him and put her arms around his neck.

"It was a lot slower without you, Jack," said Kesien who sat down beside Talia and leaned against the wall. "But we managed."

Jack laughed. "I'll bet."

Muriel sat down on Jack's left and stared out across the meadow. Anahera knelt beside her.

"Where's Deemah?" Jack asked, glancing around.

Kesien smiled and nodded toward Daidrean who sat in the grass.

"I think Deemah's taken a liking to Daidrean," said Kesien.

They both seemed deep in conversation and very close. Kesien seemed happy for her though, so he didn't say anything. He'd always thought that Deemah had a thing for Kesien, but maybe he was more like a brother to her. Like Muriel saw him.

Jack glanced at Muriel and she kept staring. He bumped her shoulder. Finally, she glanced over at him.

"How you doing, Jack?" she asked.

"Fine, but you seem a little distracted," he said. "What's up?"

Anahera giggled and Muriel glowered at her.

Jack exchanged a confused look with Talia and turned his attention back to Muriel.

"Don't be offended if she zones out on you," said Anahera, smiling as Muriel glared at her. "Her attention span has faltered—unless you're Abaddon."

Muriel's face blushed three shades of red. "Don't you—have armor to polish, Anahera?"

Her response made Anahera laugh, but Muriel shot a withering glare at her that would have crossed over an average human. Jack was a little surprised. Was it because the redeemed archangel saved her from that bastard, Asmodeus? Or was she really into Aby?

"Crushin' on Abaddon, Muriel?" Jack asked. "You need me to set you up? Aby and I are bros after he tried to kill me at my wedding."

Muriel had a funny look on her face, but it darkened to annoyance when Anahera started laughing.

"Why's that funny?" Jack said to Anahera. "You've seen Aby lately. Dude's amped now that he's an angel again."

"You saw him at the trailer, Anahera," Talia replied, leaning across Jack and toward Anahera. "Beautiful long white hair, sparkling white wings, and sunlit-gold eyes."

Hearing Talia admire another man made him feel a little funny.

"He hotter than me?" Jack asked her.

She shook her head, wrapping her arms around his neck and kissing him. "There's nobody hotter than you."

Muriel was unusually quiet. Jack nudged her. "Muriel, I'm serious. Aby is lonely after being stuck in Hell for so long. He's trying to recapture what makes the Heavens and the world beautiful. And he needs someone that can show him those things."

The anger in her eyes softened and she lowered her voice so that only Jack could hear her.

"But I'm the sidekick, Jack," she said in a sad whisper that made Jack hurt all over. "I'm the backup. You think someone like that is going to notice me?"

Jack put his arm around her and pulled her into a hug. "Yes, I do," he said. "And you know why?"

She shook her head and he felt her desperate need to hear that answer.

"Because when you show him all the things that are beautiful about Heaven and Earth, he'll see that they pale against the true beauty. And that's you, Muriel. I see that light every time I look at you. And he will too if you give him a chance."

Muriel smiled at him and turned to Talia. "Talia, if you divorce Jack, I call dibs."

Talia shook her head. "Sorry, Muriel, he's stuck with me."

"Now until forever, Mrs. Casey," he said and kissed her.

Suddenly, all of the angels lurched to their feet, and with wings spread, they took to the air.

"I'm the vanguard of this squad!" Jack shouted. "And yet, you still put me at the kiddie table?"

"Sorry, Jack," Azrael replied. "Take your place with your squad."

"More drills?" Jack asked.

Azrael nodded.

Jack pointed his finger toward Talia who was halfway across the meadow with her squad and blinked into the center of the squad.

"Sorry, lover," Talia said and hugged him. "Forgot you couldn't hear Azrael's command. I need to remind him not to do that during the assault."

"Yeah, not hearing his commands could go badly for me down there," Jack replied.

"Don't worry," said Talia, grabbing hold of his breastplate and pulling him close. "I'm not letting you out of my sight down there. I'll sing out every command in notes you can hear."

He pressed a lingering kiss against her lips. "Looking out for me, Mrs. Casey?"

"Always, Jack," she said and returned his kiss.

For several hours, they worked through more drills and exercises and then sparred with a few more squads until Azrael called them all to the terrace.

Azrael stood on his dais alongside Archangels Sidriel, Ramiel, and Turiel. They clustered around him, wings unfurled and blowing in the breeze.

Sidriel's long white hair flowed to her waist, a thick sweep of bangs across her forehead. Her light grey eyes and ebony skin were a sharp contrast to Ramiel's short, spiky white hair that settled against the collar of his grey robes and his wide-set, pale yellow eyes. Turiel's white hair was shaggy like a lion's mane that settled around his shoulders, tanned skin giving his grey eyes a brightness that matched his white hair.

"Angels, we have a difficult job ahead of us," Azrael began as he addressed three guards of death angels and the Watchers. "We have to answer the atrocities that have befallen the Heavens, events that threaten every angel, every human, and every soul." He pointed toward the spires. "Some of our brethren, turned by Lucifer and Archangel Samael, stormed the High House spire and the Archive to steal the Book of Secrets and release Samael. Shortly after, they stormed this great hall and kidnapped a redeemed angel of death."

Sidriel stepped beside Azrael on the right and held out her arms. "We lost so many angels during both attacks. Fortunately, though, Azrael's captain of the guard possesses rare angel powers that, thank the Maker, brought them home again. But we cannot let this evil stand. We cannot allow Lucifer and his demons to ever again set foot on these hallowed grounds and snatch another angel. Or a human from Earth. Or a soul from their eternal home."

"Guards," Turiel called out, taking a position on Azrael's left, hands behind his back. "We are going to answer Lucifer's assault with one of our own. With archangels leading, we will assault the Gates of Hell and take back this kidnapped angel. And show Lucifer that his evil won't stand."

"The plan is simple," said Azrael. "Zephana and her forge angels are infusing all your weapons with Holy fire and blocking light against a rare angel power. By tomorrow, they will all be finished. Archangel Abaddon will lead the charge with four archangels backing him up: myself, Sidriel, Ramiel, and Turiel. Behind us, the best death angel squad from each guard will fight through demons and hellhounds to the Gates of Hell. At flank, three more top squads will keep the way out clear of demons and obstacles. With Watchers providing critical cover and ariel damage support. Abaddon will get us through the Gates and then close them until we return with Berith. Any questions?"

When the meadow fell deathly silent, Jack knew that they were conversing in angel notes.

He stepped forward. "Just a public service announcement," he shouted across the meadow. "Sing out lower, so even the lowly human can hear and follow along. And not get himself killed."

Azrael motioned toward Jack. "In case you haven't met him, Jack Casey is our not-so-secret weapon. His seraphim powers will be critical when we face Lucifer. He may be soul tethered in Hell, but

Lucifer has regained his full seraphim powers. And he won't hesitate to use them. Jack is the vanguard of my top squad, the one that will assault Hell's Gates first. So, rest and regenerate your light. At dawn tomorrow, we head for the crossroads. And the road to Hell. Dismissed."

As the angels of death dispersed, taking to the skies and blinking across the meadow, Jack felt the weight of Azrael's words.

Tomorrow. At dawn. They were assaulting Hell's Gates.

The realization was sobering and he felt uncertainty roil through his gut. He had no idea what they would face, but Lucifer's taunting challenge still unsettled him. And with those gates being hellhound central, especially with Cerberus and his brother, Orthrus guarding them, they would face legions of demons and hellhounds before they ever got to the monster hellhounds with two and three heads.

He smiled. But maybe he could even those odds a little?

"Talia, I need to make a quick trip back to Earth," he said as he slid his arms around her.

Surprise lit her luminous grey eyes. "Whatever for, Jack?"

"Just need to pick up something," he said. "I won't be long."

She looked worried, but finally, she nodded at him. "If you're not back in an hour, the squad and I come looking for you."

"Promise?" he asked, giving her his best *everything's gonna be okay* smile.

She leaned up and gave him a sizzling kiss that burned into his feet.

"Promise," she said.

"Kiss me like that again and I'll be back in half that time."

She laughed, caressing his cheek. "I'll wait until you're back." She winked at him. "In the round room—since things in Eolowen will be quiet until dawn."

"I hear that Pravuil went to High House with Oseira," he said and brushed his lips across hers. "Probably won't be back until after we leave to assault Hell. Leaving the round room totally empty."

"A half an hour it is," she said and kissed him hard.

"Done!"

He blinked into the air, wings spread wide as he flew toward Earth, using seraphim blinks.

When he got to Four Acre Studios in Burbank, he landed at his and Talia's set trailer. He hurried inside and grabbed a green duffle bag out of the closet, and launched back into the air. One more stop and he would be back in Talia's arms, he told himself as he circled the shopping center below.

23

TALIA STOOD IN FORMATION WITH HER SQUAD AND JACK AS VANGUARD, heading the long column of angels that stretched from the end of the rolling green meadow to the stone walls of Eolowen. Three of Heaven's best death angel guards and a huge force of Watchers stood around her, wings fluttering in the breeze, burnished Eternean armor gleaming in the sun like a burst of Holy fire. Swords guttered with Holy flames, the only sound on the wind because Heaven was in silent contemplation on this dawn morning, holding its collective breath at the outcome of the guard's assault on Hell's Gates. Jasmine and roses were fragrant against the gentle winds that smelled like cool rain, fleecy clouds scuttling along the air currents that wrapped warm tendrils around the spires and coiled along the road leading to Hell.

Azrael stood stoic in front of the assault force, his charcoal grey eyes steely against the sun as the warm yellow sky washed aqua, Heaven's Parrish blue brushing across the sunrise. His face was taut, mouth set in a determined clench, head held high, soot-grey archangel's wings fluttering like a battle flag as he gripped the edges of his grey robes underneath his Eternean armor.

Beside him, Sidriel faced the sun, long white hair falling into waves against her shining clear gold armor and ebony skin. She looked calm but determined, her ash grey wings fluttering against the wind. Ramiel was to her right, spiky hair matching the twitch of his pearly wings as he clenched and unclenched the hilt of his sheathed sword. He seemed as tense as Azrael. But Talia understood. His Watchers were critical support, but they were never meant to be frontline soldiers like angels of death. Turiel was at Ramiel's right, hands pressed together in prayer, his lion's mane of white hair like a cloak hood around his shoulders.

They were all waiting for Abaddon, she realized. She felt the archangels' edginess, felt their unease. Abaddon was crucial to this fight. He had to hold Hell's Gates open for the guards and then close the Gates to keep damned souls and Hell creatures from escaping. Then he had to open those Gates one last time, allowing the assault team a path out. To escape Hell.

The silence was palpable, the archangels' nervous wait spreading quickly across the field to every Watcher and every angel of death. No one spoke or sang a single angel note. They all weathered the mounting moments of uncertainty in silent contemplation. Waiting for Azrael to set the rescue mission in motion.

"Maybe his alarm didn't go off? Or there's a line at Starbucks."

Jack's comment, intended only for her, carried across the meadow until it reached every angel of death and every archangel.

Talia tried to maintain her composure, but his comment made her and Muriel chuckle. Anahera's giggle joined theirs, amplified by Kesien's quiet laugh. Deemah couldn't hold back her snicker either as Talia's entire squad began laughing. Their amusement quickly infected nearby squads until the entire force of death angels' laughter filled the silence.

All the archangels turned around, their sharp stares laser-focused on Jack.

Jack stood up straighter, owning it, making it worse. She smiled. As usual.

"Maybe he burned his toast? Ran out of strawberry jam."

Azrael's stone façade broke, a smile lifting the corners of his mouth as a chuckle spilled out until all the archangels were smiling.

"Thank you for the...comic relief, Jack," said Azrael. "I think we all needed that moment." He focused his gaze on the entire assault force now. "As Jack pointed out with that much-needed levity, we are waiting for Abaddon's arrival. Until then, hold position."

Jack leaned toward Muriel. "Thought the entire complement of Heaven's death angels were going to smite me. I think I just did my own life review."

Muriel busted out laughing. She glanced over at Talia. "Talia, I don't care if you divorce him or not, I'm calling dibs. I'll duel you for him."

Jack nodded at the flicker of white light that passed overhead. "I think you've got dibs on someone else, Muriel. Give him a chance. Maybe buy him a new alarm clock as an icebreaker?"

A blush rose on Muriel's pale face, her light grey eyes brightening. Talia knew Muriel better than any angel in Heaven. She knew that Muriel had had a crush on Jack since that first season of *The Cinderella Hour*. She'd never shown interest in anyone before Jack, but after Abaddon saved her from Asmodeus, Talia saw the unmistakable sparkle of a crush in Muriel's eyes. She was infatuated with the redeemed archangel. Who had just blinked across the meadow and landed in front of the archangels.

At the sight of him, Muriel got quiet and her gaze shot toward him, ignoring everything else on the field.

Talia caught Jack's gaze and motioned toward the archangels and he was already nodding. She smiled at his faded Levi's underneath his grey angel of death robe and Eternean armor. But then she noticed the green strap across his chest, attached to a green duffle bag.

"Jack, what's that?" she asked, pointing at the bag.

That sexy smirk curved the corners of his mouth upward and she wanted his mouth against hers and the heat of his kiss burning through her.

"You'll see."

By the Maker, he was such a tease and she wanted to wrap him in her wings and hold him for an eternity. No matter what happened in

Hell, she wouldn't let him get more than a step away from her ever again.

"Promise me, Jack," she said, a wave of fear trembling through her wings. "That you won't do anything down there to separate us."

"Didn't we already talk about this?"

She shook her head. "Not like this."

She put her arms around his neck, feeling the heat of his skin ripple through her as she pressed soft kisses against his throat, along his jaw, and against his mouth. She wanted to lose herself in the pale green glow of his expressive eyes that scorched her heart like a blow torch.

His hands caressed her neck, sliding into her hair, sending waves of heat spiraling through her body. Her kiss was frantic, his warm cedary scent like a heatwave against her senses. She pressed her face against his neck, sipping, nibbling his ear.

"Tal," he whispered, his hot mouth brushing across her ear. "You keep that up and I'm not going to be in formation much longer. Not that I'm complaining, but Azrael might smite me."

She laughed and let him go. Reaching up, she ran her fingers through his soft, light blond hair that smelled like cedar and soap.

"Now until forever, Jack," she said to him. "Remember that when we reach Hell's Gates."

He gripped her hand a moment. "Mrs. Casey, it's my first and last thought every single day."

Her eyes stung, getting watery as she squeezed his hand, but Azrael's call to attention forced her to let go and turn toward the archangels. Jack and the rest of the squad snapped their gazes forward, anxious energy buzzing across the field as Abaddon stood behind the archangels, facing all three guards. His sparkling white wings caught the sunlight and reflected it with heavenly radiance.

"It's time," said Azrael, a heaviness in his voice as he addressed the field, hands behind his back, soot-grey wings rippling in the breeze. "Form on squad captains and maintain your positions and proximity until we reach the path into Hell's outer caverns. Keep sight of Abaddon at all times until we break into squads en route to the Gates.

Drawn weapons and shields are mandatory when we reach the caverns. Keep a sharp eye out for demons and hellhounds."

He paused a moment, staring past the angels of death. At Eolowen. Like he was trying to memorize the placement of every stone and recall every memory he'd made here with Berith.

"There's an angel of death in danger out there. Trapped in Lucifer's grasp. I thank every one of you for following me down there to save her. You all knew this mission was voluntary and yet every single member of three death angel guards showed up here to fight evil." His voice got tight and broke, forcing him to pause and pull in a breath or two, quickly regaining his composure. "And words fail me to adequately thank you for your courage and support."

Muriel's eyes were watery. Anahera bit her lip as tears slid down her cheeks. Talia couldn't hold back a crystalline tear that rolled down her cheek and disappeared into the thick green carpet of meadow grass.

He glanced at Talia and then Jack.

"As Jack Casey and Talia have taught my guard, over and over, love frees all. Like it will today. Thank you and Godspeed."

Azrael turned toward Abaddon, nodding.

"Guard, move out in squad formation." Abaddon's baritone voice thrummed across the silent field so bright with the burn of halos as the sea of dove grey wings whispered into motion.

Talia rose into the air. "Supremes formation, squad," she said in a confident voice. "Form around the vanguard."

She felt Jack reach out and take hold of her hand, squeezing, and then letting go as they rose over the green meadow toward the crossroads. And the road to Hell.

Momentarily, the assault force blotted out the sun as they flew low over the rolling hills, keeping the winding path in sight that led from Eolowen to the crossroads. Abaddon flew a few feet ahead of Azrael and the other three archangels, his focus on what lay ahead of the assault force. Ramiel's Watchers had been placed in the center of the column to insulate them, allowing them to safely launch aerial attacks.

The column banked left over the quiet, still crossroads and headed along the wide road to the right. As soon as they left the crossroads, where several roads converged, and flew along the right-hand road, the scent of brimstone sharpened the warming air. And Heaven's Constable clouds began to churn and rise into towering thunderheads that darkened the crisp blue sky.

As she turned toward the road to Hell, she caught a glimpse of Pravuil take to the air with Oseira beside him, headed toward the spires.

Thunder was a soft rumble ahead, the occasional flash of lightning increasing as the assault force flew on through the rapidly changing landscape. Trees thinned out, growing gnarled and misshapen, their leaves turning burnt orange and rust as the green grass thinned and faded into powdery ashen soil. The terrain began to look surreal as the sky turned storm grey. Bare rock tore through the barren soil like bones breaking through skin as the plains turned hilly. Jagged, sharp cliffs and overhangs appeared ahead as the road swerved abruptly left.

Toward a rising mountain range, dark with caves and crevices that flashed with red eyes as lightning crackled across the skies in great blue forked bolts.

As the terrain changed and darkened, Talia felt the shift in mood across the guards. And the Watchers.

Formations tightened. Ranks closed. Squads drew shields.

And Talia felt Jack's apprehension growing. She knew how hard this was for him to come back here. He still had nightmares about Hell that mixed with the flashbacks that had increased since they'd started filming *The Divine Newlyweds Show*. She slowed her wing beats, drifting into the center of her squad's formation until she was beside Jack. Already, she felt the fierce, frantic beat of his heart. His face was a mask of sweat, gaze in constant motion, pupils eclipsing much of his pale green irises.

She felt his fear, sharp and thick inside him. Like a knife blade.

"Jack," she whispered in his ear as she gripped his hand. "You're okay. We won't let Lucifer get hold of you again."

He nodded, inhaling a quick breath.

She leaned toward him, pressing a gentle kiss against his taut lips. "Use your block. In case Procel's still targeting you with transference."

He nodded again, swallowing hard as he closed his eyes.

In moments, she felt his block in place, and instantly, some of his fear dissipated. She wanted to clobber Procel. And then Lucifer, who delighted in torture.

"Thanks, babe," said Jack, a hint of relief in his voice.

She rubbed his shoulder a moment and then returned to her position in front as the rest of her squad closed ranks, pressing as close to Jack as they could and still fly. She sang out two angel notes of thanks that Jack couldn't hear. Her squad was very protective of Jack and for that, she was grateful.

All around them, jagged mountains towered into the dark skies, lightning shattering the grey haze as thunder shook the landscape in dark, foreboding rumbles. The dry heat was stifling, honing the air currents into a blade against her wingtips. Sulfur tanged the air, pungent and primed, like the air could light on fire at any moment. Talia worried for the Watchers in this environment. Angels of death were used to rapidly shifting terrains and that included Hell, but she knew that Ramiel had prepared them for this fight. Ramiel was one of the few archangels that had supported Azrael and her guard throughout everything. And she knew that he always would.

Sidriel was a new convert to Azrael's cause. Disgusted by her colleagues, Raziel and Samael, Sidriel approached Azrael and asked to join his fight. She had been one of Azrael's biggest supporters since then. When Archangel Turiel heard about Berith, he showed up at Eolowen with his entire guard and offered Azrael his support.

The rest of Heaven's lower reaches had been uncomfortably silent about Berith's abduction—including High House—but Talia understood. The Rebellion was still a difficult subject and every angel in existence had been affected by it. And the Fall. A third of all Heaven's angels fell with Lucifer.

Some angels would never forget those losses and Talia understood that. Those angels would defend Heaven against any breach by

Lucifer and his forces, but they wouldn't assault the Gates of Hell for a redeemed fallen angel.

Leaves fell like rain across the road from dying trees, the sulfurous air charged with lightning and mounting dark presences, wind spinning dry brush across the road like tumbleweeds. Plumes of ash swirled into dust devils that gyrated across the dead terrain. Against the afterglow of electric purple flashes of lightning, ozone smell rising, Talia saw the gaping, pitch black hole in the ground.

The way into Hell.

She'd flown along this road so many times when Lucifer dragged Jack to Hell. Trying to find some way back to him. Trying to find a way to save him.

Abaddon didn't hesitate when he saw the entrance. He landed on the rim of the gaping blackness as the storm roiled around them.

Angels of death landed in formation, maintaining the same positions as Azrael had ordered for the entire assault force. Communicating with angel notes, all three guards and the Watchers landed in a precision shift and held positions in the column that had been assembled at Eolowen.

Azrael, Sidriel, Turiel, and Ramiel locked wings in a roundel formation around Abaddon as they faced the abyss.

Abaddon's tall, shining frame was a beacon against the storm and the growing dark as winds whipped and ash plumes hung like fog around them.

Like the approach of a massive storm, Talia felt legions of demons rise from the ground and out of the ashen haze. But she kept her squad in formation protectively around Jack.

"Shields and swords out," she said in a deadly calm tone as she scanned the horizon, searching for a flash of red or a shadow of movement. "Vanguard, maintain center position."

"It's the babysit-the-human-with-seraphim-powers command," Jack replied. "Was waiting for that."

"Watchers, bows out!" Ramiel called out in angel notes. "Defensive perimeter formations."

"All guards, tight squad formations," Azrael ordered in angel notes, his gaze flicking from the column of angels to the blackness below. "Form on your vanguard. His seraphim powers are critical, so keep Jack Casey safe."

Poor Jack. He couldn't hear their commands.

She called out to the entire column, reminding them that their seraphim power support couldn't hear their commands, and then she repeated Ramiel's and Azrael's commands, so Jack heard. He glowered when he heard Azrael's orders.

"Jack Casey," she said in a scolding tone and laid her hands against his crossed arms.

He looked away.

"As extraordinary as you are, wielding my rare powers, and a host of seraphim powers, you are still human. And fragile. And a critical component of this assault. So, yes, we're going to protect you like we would Abaddon, our field commander. You and Abaddon are the two most important angels in this assault."

He met her gaze with a smile. "Angels?"

She nodded, studying him. "Halo? Check. Wings? Check. Rare angel powers and seraphim powers? Looks like an angel to me."

"Not sure how Jack keeps that halo though," Muriel muttered and the squad broke out laughing.

Jack chuckled. "Only because they don't know how to remove it."

Muriel gave him an emphatic nod as Kesien patted him on the back.

"Don't worry, Talia, we'll keep the kid safe. Because he's going to do the same for us with those seraphim powers."

Jack cast a sideways glance at Kesien who towered over Jack at six foot eight or so to Jack's six-foot height.

"Not yer goat," Jack snapped, looking away.

Deemah laughed and poked Kesien. "You're doing that on purpose now, aren't you?"

Kesien's smile broadened as he shrugged.

"Godspeed, angels," Abaddon called out, his voice carrying across the terrain.

But the command to move forward, into the abyss never came as legions of demons surrounded them in the gathering storm.

24

FOR A MOMENT, JACK FROZE. HIS NEXT INSTINCT WAS TO POUND THE shit out of these legions of demons with all the Holy fire he could fling. But he quelled that thought when Abaddon's commanding baritone voice filled the battlefield.

"Wings aloft!"

He didn't think. He spread his wings and blinked into the air. In a breath, the entire column of angels floated above the churning maelstrom of demons writhing like eels in hot ash.

Abaddon hovered in formation with Azrael, Sidriel, Turiel, and Ramiel.

"Watchers, unleash!" Abaddon commanded.

A hail of flaming arrows descended on the demons below. They screeched and shrieked as Holy fire burned through their ranks, devastating the legions. Extinguishing the thousands of glowing red eyes that covered the landscape.

And still more came.

"Again!" Abaddon commanded.

Bows twanged and arrows snicked through the air, felling more demons, and setting the legions on fire. The Holy fire turned them all to ash.

"Ground formation!"

At Abaddon's next command, the whole column descended. Ash crackled as puddles of red demon goo steamed.

Jack set himself, crouching, wings extended and ready for another leap skyward. But only bone-rattling thunder and wind shook the ground.

He gazed around him, making sure Talia was okay. She was to his right, gaze flitting around her and then back to him. Muriel was to his left with Kesien, Anahera and Deemah clustered behind him.

"Maintain squads and move forward," Abaddon called out as Azrael and Sidriel stepped down into the abyss' darkness. "Flank, maintain tight formations. Sing out at the first sign of Hell creatures."

Together, the two archangels penetrated the swirling blackness of the abyss. The road that led to the Gates of Hell.

"That was too easy," said Jack, feeling like the whole attack was being orchestrated.

Lucifer was playing them. If Luci wanted to wipe them out, they'd have encountered a lot more than these legions of benchwarmers. No, Lucifer wanted them to reach the Gates. Getting out again would be a very different story. One he dreaded.

He waited for Ramiel to follow and then Abaddon. When Abaddon disappeared into the heavy darkness, Jack's heart bounced into his throat, and played John Bonham's fifteen-minute drum solo from Zeppelin's *Moby Dick*. Jack had a hazy memory of that brown album cover always laying on the coffee table or the couch, his mother always picking it up and complaining to Dad about his clutter. Dad loved that album.

The last place Jack ever wanted to return to was Hell. And he feared that Lucifer had already ended Berith and had a trap ready to enslave his soul for eternity. Or Talia.

When Talia reached the lip of the abyss, she turned around to the squad. "We enter in pairs," she said, pointing at Muriel. "Muriel, you and I go in first. Kesien, you and Jack next. Anahera and Deemah on flank. Protect the vanguard. We don't know what's ahead, so enter and hold position until we're all inside. Acknowledge."

All around Jack, the squad acknowledged her orders. Then he felt her gaze settle on him.

"Jack…acknowledge those orders."

"Acknowledged," he replied.

"Dim halos, ready shields, and follow us down."

Jack's heart did an encore drum solo as Talia and Muriel waded into the liquid darkness. It swallowed them up quickly and his pulse became a solid surge until he heard Talia call out to him and sing some angel notes he could actually hear. Couldn't understand them, but no one got alarmed. That made him relax his urge to gather a handful of murder marbles. But he had no idea what she'd said.

"Dumb it down for the kiddie table, will ya!" he called out as he approached the mouth of Hell beside Kesien.

"She instructed the next pair to enter," said Kesien.

Kesien seemed calmer than he had since Purgatory, but there was still a restless tension within him that hadn't been there before Samael's treachery. He expected that tension and hyper-alert behavior here, but he wondered what Kesien would be like once the dust settled on this assault. Something had changed in him and Jack knew he wouldn't give up trying to bring his former squad to justice. Couldn't blame the dude. That was some ugly betrayal and Kesien was all about fairness and justice.

In moments, the blackness swallowed up Jack and then Kesien. Jack struggled to breathe, his muscles taut and corded until he reached the bottom. The thick, cloying blackness writhed around him as the distant orange-red glow of lava illuminated the subterranean cavern with a dangerous glow. As his eyes struggled to adjust, he made out Azrael's commanding presence among the shadows and heat. Sidriel, Turiel, and Ramiel were beside him, all of them holding formation around Abaddon.

As soon as the top three death angel squads, one from each guard, went through the mouth to Hell, Abaddon would give the signal to proceed with Watcher ariel support to protect all the squads. Jack knew that Talia's squad would be the first one to assault the Gates. This was Azrael's operation after all.

Jack reached out in the darkness and gripped Talia's hand. "No matter what happens in here," he said in a soft voice, "know that I'll love you to my last breath, Talia."

She shook her head. "Oh, no, you don't, Jack Casey. Don't you dare go talking about last breaths down here."

He brushed a curly lock of raven black hair off her forehead and leaned over, kissing her in a slow, lingering kiss.

"Jack, you're scaring me," she said, her grey eyes wide and bright with fear.

He smiled, shaking his head. "Not saying my goodbyes, Talia. Just want you to know how much I love you."

She relaxed a little, but she still had a wary glint in her eyes. "That's better."

Hope he lived through this assault. He'd better. If he didn't, she'd kill him.

When the third squad appeared out of the darkness and moved into the cavernous tunnels ahead, Abaddon motioned the force forward. Jack frowned.

Dude sang out those orders, didn't he?

He let this one go, but if not hearing those orders got him captured by Lucifer, someone was gonna get bitch-slapped.

The tunnels bore deeper into the earth as the rock became black and volcanic. More and more lava ran alongside them in thickening yellow-orange trails. As the tunnels began to widen, the tubes crossed over other tunnels above and below them. So far, nothing had approached them, but at every creak and rumble, Jack felt his muscles strain and his jaw clench.

Waiting for the next shoe to drop. He just hoped it wasn't dropped on him.

Abruptly, the tunnel widened, big enough to accommodate the entire assault force. The heat was oppressive as steam hissed from the lava trails and created pockets of fog along the tunnel.

Ahead, as the mist hung thick and spirit-like, the tunnel crossed another big, wide tunnel.

The hair on the back of Jack's neck stood up. One thing he'd learned about demons was that they loved crossroads. For ambushes.

"Squad, close ranks," Talia said, barely above a whisper.

A heartbeat later, Azrael's clear, commanding voice echoed through the tunnel.

"All squads, close ranks. Shields out."

As the archangels brandished shields, keeping Abaddon behind them, Jack felt Talia and her squad squeeze in close, the gold light from their shields casting an eerie glow through the too-quiet tunnels.

Jack called up a shield of light in his left hand, but the feral growl behind him made him halt and turn, shield raised.

Assassin demons!

Shadows frantically paced the perimeters, disappearing into the mist only to appear across from them.

"Ready swords and shield bash," Talia ordered.

"My pleasure," said Deemah, a growl in her voice.

They all faced outward from Jack, watching for the momentary materialization of the assassin demons in shadow panther form.

Behind them, shadow panthers materialized and ambushed the third squad. Long, sinewy bodies that were part smoke part muscle—and all teeth. The squad behind them crouched, shields raised, deflecting the panther attacks.

Ahead, a scuffle reverberated as a shadow panther's caterwaul sent shivers through Jack.

He called up a handful of murder marbles in each hand.

"Everybody, shields up!" Jack shouted and tossed murder marbles right and left.

Explosions cascaded up and down the tunnel. Shadow panthers screeched. Assassin demons splattered, leaving red blotches along the black stone walls

"Good work, Jack," Azrael called out. "All clear, let's keep moving."

"Murder marbles for the win," he said as Muriel ruffled his hair.

"They never get old, Jack," she said and took her position in front of him.

Again, they moved as a squad behind Abaddon and the archangels through the upper caverns of Hell.

As they continued along the widening tunnel, the heat increased as the tunnel sloped downward again. Jack had no memory of this part of Hell. Half the time, his vision had been completely blocked by the legions of demons surrounding Lucifer. He just remembered his grief and the sweltering heat that got heavier and more oppressive as they descended. Until he blacked out and woke up in a small crevice. He shivered. On the locked side of Hell's Gates.

Somebody yanked him backward, shaking him out of his memories. Confused, his gaze shot up until he located Talia and Muriel in the dark tunnel. Standing a few feet in front of him.

"Jack, did you hear me?"

Talia.

"Sorry, babe," he answered, shaking those awful memories out of his thoughts. "What did you say?"

He glanced at Kesien who still looked agitated when he let go of Jack. Talia looked afraid.

"What's wrong?" he asked.

She pointed down at his feet.

He glanced down. At a gaping break in the stone. And a drop that tumbled off into eternity. He broke into a cold sweat, gasping as he grabbed hold of the wall and his gaze flicked to Talia, but he couldn't respond.

"If Kesien hadn't grabbed you, you'd have fallen to your death just now."

Jack pulled in a heated breath, the staggering height giving him vertigo. "Sorry," he said in a sheepish voice. "Bad memories of this place. Can't shake 'em out of my thoughts."

Talia's expression was a mixture of terror and anger. "Try, Jack," she insisted. "Focus on what's in front of you, not what's passed."

Her tone was harsh and it stung. But he wasn't a soldier or an angel. He knew she was angry because she was scared, but it still hurt.

"I said I was sorry, not stupid," Jack snapped and let his wings flatten against his back.

He regretted that the moment it came out of his mouth. His gaze fell to his faded Levi's tucked into his Eternean sabatons and then down to the huge drop-off, judging the distance. He spread his wings and lifted into the air, clearing the gap.

Talia turned back toward the squad. She opened her mouth, but nothing came out as she got them moving again.

He bristled. The rest of the squad followed whatever orders she gave, gathering closer around him.

Guess he was now excluded from hearing the squad commands as well as the assault force commands. He'd just have to guess what to do from here and hope he didn't fall to his death farther down the next tunnel.

Without warning, the tunnel plummeted into a sharp angle downward as Azrael and the other archangels dropped like stones. Abaddon managed to stop in time.

"Column, halt!" Abaddon ordered.

"Azrael!" Jack shouted, extending his wings as he sprinted forward.

He blinked into the air and hovered above the drop a moment and then dived into the chasm below where the archangels lay motionless.

"Jack, don't!" Talia called out behind him.

When he landed, he found Azrael and the other three archangels tangled in a heap against a stalagmite. Inches from a river of lava that was the only light visible below.

"Jack...no—" Azrael choked out, wincing.

But the hot, fetid breath hammering his neck forced him to turn around. And look up.

Into the corpulent faces of three greater demons. Devourers of Angels.

They were surrounded.

Jack felt his fury ignite. He could almost hear Lucifer's laughter echo through the chasm.

"Azrael?" Abaddon shouted from far above. "Are you all right?"

"Don't—try to rescue us," Azrael stammered. "We're surrounded by three Devourers of Angels. It's too dangerous!"

Jack lifted his hand toward the eight-foot-tall greater demon with its frog feet and stringy limbs that grabbed Archangel Ramiel and held him aloft, trying to chew off his wings. And called up a burst of seraphim energies that knocked the demon backward.

"Jack!" Azrael shouted. "Get out of here—now! They'll kill you!"

The other two Devourers lifted Azrael, Turiel, and Sidriel into the air. Their wings hung at odd angles. Broken by the fall and the Devourers.

Why didn't the angels get it? These things didn't like the taste of humans. He was their best weapon against these things.

Jack lunged at the Devourer holding Azrael, knocking it sideways, but it didn't release the archangel. It was desperate to feed.

Jack decided to indulge it. With murder marbles.

He buzzed its head until it dropped Azrael and grabbed hold of him with both sticky fists.

"JACK!" Talia's shout was frantic as it reverberated through the crevice below.

He shoved a fistful of murder marbles down the Devourer's gaping maw and curled into a ball, wings covering his head.

The murder marbles exploded, blowing apart the Devourer, and propelling him into the air. He spread his wings wide, banked over Azrael, and rammed the Devourer trying to bite off Sidriel's head. It stumbled backward and fell.

Jack blinked past it, throwing himself in front of Ramiel before the damned demon bit him in half.

The Devourer dropped Ramiel and shoved Jack in its mouth.

"Okay, you asked for it," Jack snarled and conjured up another handful of murder marbles.

He dropped the handful down its gullet, punching the insides of its rancid mouth as he dodged its razor-sharp teeth until the murder marbles blew through the top of its head. Jack fell onto the rocks, covered in demon innards.

He shook it off and blinked into the air. Toward the last Devourer that had cornered the three archangels as they tried to rescue Sidriel.

She screamed when the Devourer bit into her left wing.

Jack hauled off and sucker punched the greater demon in the head. Twice. Until enraged, it dropped Sidriel and swiped at him.

He let it snatch him out of the air.

"Jack, no!" Azrael shouted.

Azrael and Ramiel pounded on the Devourer as it dragged Jack toward its gaping mouth.

"I got just what you're craving, bitch," Jack growled and threw a handful of murder marbles into its mouth.

He fought its heavy hinge-jaw and kicked its pointy teeth, trying to keep it from biting him in two until the murder marbles went off.

It seemed like forever until the explosion went off almost in his face. Blinded by the blast as it threw him backward, he frantically beat his wings. It slowed his fall but didn't stop it. He hit the ground hard and crumpled.

In moments, chaos erupted around him, his eyes burning until the afterimages from the explosion faded. When his vision cleared, Talia was standing over him. Murderous.

He covered his head with both arms and slammed his eyes shut.

"Jack Casey..." Her voice was like silent thunder. "I'm going to murder you."

He peered at her through his fingers, hands covering his face. The whole squad was behind her. Laughing at him.

"What happened to protect the vanguard?" he demanded.

Kesien shrugged and motioned at Talia. "Talk to the squad captain. If you live that long."

"Good luck, Jack," said Muriel with a smirk. "I picked you in the pool. I figure you'll last at least the first round before she smites you into next week. Anahera bet everything on Talia though."

Azrael walked up behind Talia and patted her on the shoulder. "Let me know when it's my turn to yell at him."

And just like that, the archangel walked away.

"Aby, help me out here!" he shouted.

"Of course, Jack," said Abaddon somewhere behind Talia. "I'll make sure you get a proper burial."

Talia smacked his breastplate and grabbed him by the shoulders, shaking him hard.

"You make me crazy!" she shouted. "You know that, don't you?"

"I knew that the first day we met," he said, smiling.

His smile went right through her and she kept glaring at him. "You ignored a direct order from your squad captain, Jack Casey."

"Which one? The one where you sang a bunch of high notes that I couldn't understand. Or the one where you just opened your mouth and I couldn't even hear the notes?"

He had no idea what orders she'd given the squad because he never heard any orders.

For a moment, she stared at him. She started to shout at him again, but it died on her lips as the realization hit her.

"By the Maker! Jack…" Her hand flew to her mouth. "I didn't say them out loud, did I?"

He shook his head, but the pain on her face cut right through him. "Even if I'd heard you tell me no, I'd have probably leaped down here anyway." He bowed his head. "So, go ahead and yell at me. I deserve it."

She slid to the ground and enfolded him in her arms, wings curving around him as she held him tight until he winced.

"You're hurt!" she cried.

"Just a little sore from that last fall," he said. "Damned Devourer had to spew me all over the cavern instead of dropping me like the others."

Her hands slid underneath his breastplate and he felt the heat of her hands as the glow of her healing light lit him up.

"Aw, man," Muriel cried, "No fireworks."

Kesien sighed. "Not even a little drama. Or Holy fire."

Talia glanced up at Kesien and Muriel. "How about some sparks?"

Jack cringed, setting himself for another reprimand as Talia turned back toward him. And smashed her mouth against his in a blistering kiss at least ten degrees hotter than this Hell chasm. Jack kissed her back until she was smeared in as much demon goo as he wore.

"Next time, you'll hear those commands, Jack Casey," she said and kissed him softly. "I'm sorry."

He shook his head. "No, babe, it was my fault. You were right every time. I'm not being careful and I threw myself down the same well that got the archangels. No wonder you guys are babysitting me. 'Cause I'm an idiot with seraphim powers."

She engulfed him with more healing light, drying up the demon goo covering him, and healing the bruises he'd gathered from this fight.

"You're not an idiot, Jack," she said. "You're young and headstrong. So focused on protecting others that you don't think you're vulnerable. You've got too much heart, lover." She kissed him again. "It's one of your best qualities. I just want to keep you safe, that's all. And with me forever."

He held her for a moment and then let her go.

"All I want is you, Tal. Somehow, despite me, you married me and you still love me. I have no clue why, but I'm so grateful. I've never loved anyone like I love you, Tal." His voice broke. "And I'll never love anyone else but you."

He was surprised to see the tears fill her eyes. The last remnants of her anger dissipated and she melted into his arms. When she'd regained her composure, she got him on his feet and made sure he wasn't hurt.

Then she turned to Azrael. "All right, sir," she said, chuckling as she stepped backward. "He's all yours."

Jack grimaced, bracing for the archangel's fiery reprimand.

After Azrael gave him Hell for trying to rescue the others, the archangel gave him Hell for taking on three greater demons alone. Then thanked him.

Talia healed the archangels' wings and they all flew out of the chasm, back to the tunnel. Jack followed Talia and the squad up and out. They landed behind the archangels and continued their push toward the Gates of Hell.

Jack knew that the closer they got to those gates, the more likely they'd run into hellhounds. And the gate guardians: Cerberus and Orthrus. He knew how to handle them, but not a legion pack of hellhounds. He'd never seen that many before. They were fast and relentless. In a legion pack, they'd be fatal.

"We're getting close to the Gates, aren't we?" Muriel asked, wiping her forehead with the back of her sleeve as the tunnel curved noticeably downward again.

"How can you tell?" Kesien asked.

"I heard a howl," she said.

"Let's pick up the pace," said Abaddon. "Before they pick up Jack's scent."

Jack groaned. Damn. Abaddon was right. His presence was like dropping a Big Mac in this tunnel.

"Squads, you heard Abaddon," Azrael called out. "We need to move faster."

Jack felt Talia and the rest of the squad close ranks around him as they matched the archangels' increased pace. He did his best to keep up.

If they survived the hellhounds—and the gate guardians—the next stop was the Gates of Hell. And Lucifer.

"Tal, have you been able to use omnificence to locate Berith?"

Talia shook her head as the walls of the tunnel slid past and the lava's glow grew brighter. Redder. "No, the terrain is interfering with it. Or maybe it's Lucifer, I don't know. I'll try again after we get past the gate guardians."

"Our only option is to fight through the hellhounds," said Abaddon. "And the guardians. Lucifer trained them to fight from pups. The fiercest of all his hellhounds. And the rarest. The two- and three-headed hellhounds."

"Luci has no compassion for anything but his revenge," said Jack. "Bet he's never played ball with them. Or fed them treats—well, besides humans."

"Jack, they're Hell creatures," said Kesien. "They're not like Earth's dogs which are about as angelic as a physical creature can get. Hellhounds are born with Hell instincts."

A mournful howl echoed somewhere ahead. The sound made Jack's skin crawl.

"What about cats?" Jack asked.

"There must be a little Hell creature mixed in with all that purring," said Kesien. "But their souls are pure light."

Another howl echoed through the tunnel.

The squads and the archangels picked up the pace again, moving faster. Stalagmites and stalactites rushed past on both sides, the heat roiling as lava rivers appeared on both sides of the passage as it got wider.

"We're almost at the junction," said Abaddon. "That's where the two lava rivers run side-by-side and then separate, creating the peninsula where the Gates of Hell stand. Cerberus and Orthrus reside on a steep, narrow path that runs between the two lava rivers and connects the tunnel to the towering peninsula. Where the pillar for the seventh seal stands. So be careful."

Falling off that dizzying narrow path on either side would be instant death in those lava rivers. He was glad he had wings for this fight.

He glanced over at the immense pillar that stood along the pathway. It looked like a stalagmite that had formed from dripping water and mineral deposits over millennia. It was as smooth, ringed with sediment layers, tall as the Gates of Hell, and about three feet wide. He vowed to steer clear of anything connected to seals and revelations.

"When we engage the guardians," Abaddon continued, "they will try to destroy all intruders. If they can't, they will howl for help. And believe me when I say that the hellhound guardians will summon a legion pack."

Azrael raised his hand into the air, halting the party about a hundred feet away from the pathway that wound up a steep hill toward the tall, forbidding black gates of Hell. He sang out a long series of notes, instructing the squads. Or the entire column. Or hell, maybe he just wanted to belt out that new Adele song? Jack had no clue because he didn't understand a single note that the archangel uttered.

When Azrael was finished, he turned around and motioned to Jack.

Jack blinked out of the squad formation and stood in front of the archangel.

"Jack, I gave all the squads behind us instructions to be ready to battle a legion pack of hellhounds. I told them that we needed them to engage the massive presence of hellhounds while Abaddon, the archangels, my best squad, and I engage the gate guardians. Hopefully, the rest of the assault force will keep the other hellhounds busy, giving us time and space to engage Orthrus and Cerberus."

A distant rumble shook the cavern, setting Jack on edge.

"Thanks for the explanation," he said, glancing behind him at the squads of death angels following one after another as the assault force's center and flanks caught up with the angels on point.

"My apologies for leaving you out," said Azrael, frowning as another howl pealed through the passageway.

Sounding closer.

"Thought I was going to have to make up my own orders again," Jack said with a laugh.

"Just listen to Talia and engage on my or Abaddon's order," Azrael replied, his gaze in motion. "Now that Abaddon's transformed, the guardians won't recognize him. They'll see him and us as a threat and will try to destroy us. So, stay in formation until we—"

Jack never heard the rest of the archangel's words because the entire passageway flooded with hellhounds.

Again, Azrael sang out angel notes.

In an instant, Talia and the squad blinked through the pack of hellhounds and crouched beside Azrael, shields and swords raised.

"Squad, form on the vanguard," she ordered. "Tight formation as we fight our way behind Abaddon and the archangels to the guardians. Wait for Azrael's signal to move."

Jack could barely make out the angels engaging the hellhounds below them as the legion pack descended like storm clouds. Red eyes burned against the orange glow of lava, sounds of snarling and tearing making him wince.

A storm of arrows erupted, Holy fire burning through the darkness toward the endless rush of hellhounds.

"Shields to the sun!" Talia shouted.

Deemah bashed a hellhound that leaped at them and then pointed her shield straight up toward the cavern's ceiling.

Kesien and Muriel pressed their shields together with Deemah's. Anahera and Talia quickly added theirs.

Jack called up his shield and closed the circle.

"All right, squad, move!" Azrael shouted.

Jack moved as one with Talia and her squad, keeping his shield against theirs as they closed the distance to the sheer, winding path that led up to Hell's Gates. One wrong move and they'd fall hundreds of feet through the blistering heat into one of the two lava rivers that ran on either side of the peninsula, surrounding the Gates to Hell on all sides. Another failsafe.

Jack remembered this landscape, but not from this side. Only from the peninsula that was cut off from these caverns by lava rivers. And the massive, forbidding black gates. There were only two ways out of Hell: burning up in the lava rivers or walking out those gates.

He glanced toward the assault force overrun with hellhounds and he wanted to go and help them. They were losing ground fast.

"Azrael..." said Sidriel, a pained look on her ebony face. Turiel looked stricken. "My squad's overwhelmed down there," she said. "I—"

"Go," Azrael replied. "Both of you."

"My Watchers, Azrael...they aren't—" Ramiel's gold eyes were glassy.

"You, too, Ramiel," said the archangel. "Abaddon, my squad, and I will take down the guardians."

"Let me clear you a path," said Jack.

He summoned a handful of murder marbles and threw them at the tangle of hellhounds rushing toward the path.

Explosions flung hellhounds in all directions as the archangels blinked through the smoke to help the struggling squads below.

"All right, squad," said Azrael, a steely look of calm settling on his face. "Let's hit those guardians with everything we've got."

Jack caught Talia's gaze and held it, wanting to tell her everything he felt in dozens of words, but all he could do was lay his hand against his heart and then hold it out to her. Her luminous grey eyes turned glassy as she reached out and cupped a handful of air. She pressed her closed hand to her heart and nodded at him as the squad moved as one beside Azrael.

Behind Abaddon, they all moved up the sharp rise toward the huge two- and three-headed hellhound guardians silhouetted in the glow of lava. Abaddon stretched his wings wide and slammed a large shield of light into the rocky soil behind them, blocking the packs of hellhounds from moving up the pathway toward the Gates.

Jack gripped the green strap that was taut across his breastplate, the duffle bag hanging at his left side, and summoned a sword of Holy fire as they moved up the path. Until the red glint of hellhound eyes was visible.

Cerberus barked out a vicious warning growl, his three snouts snapping as Orthrus shifted toward the path. Growling and snarling. Mouths foaming.

Shit, these things could tear them to pieces. They looked much more formidable and dangerous framed by the Gates of Hell than they had in his apartment or in that Seattle bridal suite. Or when he was power drunk.

"We move as one," Azrael repeated. "No one engages them alone unless it's Abaddon who knows these beasts better than any of us." He glared at Jack. "That includes you, Jack."

"Acknowledge your orders, vanguard," Talia shot back at him.

"Of course, I heard Azrael," he replied. "Dude's like four inches away from me."

Muriel and Kesien both snickered.

"Jack Casey," Talia snapped, pointing her shield of light at him. "I want to make sure that you know better than to approach those things by yourself." Talia's death angel glare could melt steel.

"Yes, Mrs. Casey," he answered. "And I also know not to touch a hot stove or go out without a coat in the cold. Hell, I even look both ways when crossing the street."

"Jack, you better look both ways right now," said Muriel, "Because Talia's about to run over you."

"Or make him sleep on the couch for the next millennium," said Talia, giving him her fiercest angel of death scowl. "Where's your coat, Jack? Don't you feel the cold?"

He tried not to laugh, but he couldn't help it. "Burnt to the ground," he said with a smile, shaking his head. "Sorry, babe, but huge multi-headed hellhounds really make me cranky."

"So, does watching them maul my husband," she replied.

"Orders acknowledged," he said finally with a chuckling. "Damn, when am I gonna learn not to argue with an angel of death?"

Talia smiled. "Maybe at our first anniversary? Either way, it'll be fun to find out."

"Let's see how they react," said Abaddon. "Maybe they will still recognize my scent?"

"Doubt it, dude," said Jack as Abaddon started up the path toward the gate guardians. "You don't smell like demon anymore."

As Abaddon got closer, Cerberus' growling intensified, his three sets of red eyes laser-focused on Abaddon. And not in a good way.

"Let's move, squad," said Azrael as he edged along behind Abaddon.

Talia motioned the squad behind Azrael and they all moved together with Jack in the center.

When Abaddon got within ten feet of Cerberus, the three-headed hellhound charged him, stopping about two inches from the archangel.

"Abaddon," said Azrael, "he's trying to warn you off with that charge. Maybe he does remember you? But be ready to blink just in case."

Abaddon nodded and turned his attention back to Cerberus. Orthrus hung back, deferring to his brother.

Jack felt bad, remembering the smaller two-headed hellhound eating steaks out of his hand in the bridal suite and wagging his little spiked tail. He even let Jack pet him.

"I'm just going to focus my gaze on the Gates and try to walk past him," said Abaddon in a slow, determined tone.

He pulled in a sharp breath and slowly started past Cerberus, keeping his wings still.

Cerberus whimpered for a moment, his three faces looking three shades of confused. But then the hulking, huge hellhound recovered quickly.

"Abaddon…" Azrael's voice was filled with all kinds of dread.

Hesitating only a moment, Cerberus turned and lunged at Abaddon, his three sets of teeth bared.

The archangel blinked ahead and leaped into the air, wings spread wide. He hovered above the snarling three-headed dog.

Jack frowned. "Hey! Why didn't we just fly over these mutts to the gates?"

The bars of the massive black gates stretched to the top of the cavern and embedded deep into the rock on all sides. There was no flying over or around those gates. But they could have just flown through the passageways and right up to the gates.

Azrael groaned, covering his eyes. "Because of that."

Cerberus leaped up from the pathway, stretching his long, delicate bat-like wings, and snatched Abaddon out of the air.

"How does the keeper of the key to the Gates of Hell forget that these bastards can fly?" Jack demanded.

Muriel's eyes filled with tears. "We have to help him!"

"Squad! Blink!" Azrael shouted.

Jack blinked with the squad, but with his seraphim powers, that trip was much farther ahead than even the archangel's blink. He found himself right behind Cerberus who was busy trying to tear off Abaddon's wings.

"Oh no—Jack!" Talia cried.

He had no control over the distance his blink covered. Even when it put him right in Cerberus' face. Er, faces.

Cerberus wheeled around, three heads baring sharp pointy teeth at him.

Jack froze as Cerberus advanced on him.

Then he remembered the duffle bag! He unzipped it and slowly reached inside, flinging a large cut of raw prime rib at Cerberus' nearest mouth.

Jack threw two more cuts at the hellhound guardian. Cerberus plopped onto the ground, each head joyfully chewing on prime rib.

But the fierce growl at his back startled him.

Orthrus. Running at him.

He threw his hands up as the two-headed hellhound guardian leaped on top of him, pinning him to the ground.

He held one of the heads back from his throat but felt the other head bite hard into the back of his thigh. He stifled a shout as he fumbled another cut of prime rib out of the duffle bag. One left. He dangled it over the mouth clamped onto his thigh and Orthrus released him, lunging for the prime rib. He tossed the last piece of prime rib at Orthrus' other head and Orthy caught it. He eased down on the ground beside Jack, spiked tail thumping the ground as he chewed on the raw meat.

"Good boy," said Jack and Orthrus' tail wagged harder.

"Jack, are you okay?" Talia's voice ached with worry.

"Fine," he said in a forced calm, his voice steady. "The rest of you get Abaddon and blink past to the gates. I'll be right behind you."

Azrael blinked past, followed by Talia, and her squad. They grabbed Abaddon and blinked along the pathway to the Gates of Hell.

Jack looked up to see both Cerberus and Orthrus inches away from his face. Staring, tails wagging.

"Okay, I was afraid of this moment," said Jack, moving his hand slowly into the duffle bag. "That you two would swallow those steaks whole and want more." He pulled out two massive rawhide bones. "Says they're for Great Danes and Newfies, but maybe you'll like 'em, huh?"

He tossed each hellhound brother a massive rawhide bone. Tails wagged harder as both Cerby and Orthy caught a rawhide bone in one of their mouths. They plopped down on the ground again, calmly chewing on the bones. He pulled out two shiny red balls and set one beside each hellhound and slowly, deliberately got to his feet. With both gate guardians distracted, he carefully pointed toward the Gates to Hell and blinked.

Talia and Kesien caught him as he stumbled.

The look on her face spoke volumes. She was gearing up for another lecture.

"Tal, I have a seraphim's blink, remember?" he replied, the back of his right thigh throbbing from the hellhound bite. "I didn't plan that."

"Nice work subduing them," she said finally and put her arm around his waist as she reached down to the tear in his Levi's. "Is it bad?"

"Hurts worse than the bite I took in my apartment, but I'm okay."

Both Azrael and Talia plied him with healing light until the bleeding stopped.

Something bounced behind Jack. Shit.

Slowly, he turned around. With one snout, Cerberus nudged the red rubber ball and it rolled against Jack's right sabaton. He picked it up as Orthrus bounded toward him. Orthy whined and dropped another red ball from one of his mouths.

"You just wanna play, don't you?" Jack asked with a smile.

He picked up both red balls and tossed them down the pathway. Toward the tall pillar that stretched from floor to ceiling in the cavern. But not close enough to hit it. He didn't want Heaven blaming him for toppling the pillar and breaking a seal. He wasn't going to let Pravuil write in his Book of Life of Death that he started the apocalypse either.

With excited barks, Orthrus and Cerberus both bounded after the rubber balls.

"What have you done to my hellhounds! My guardians!"

At the sound of that voice, Jack whirled around.

Lucifer. Scowling at him from behind the Gates of Hell. Holding Berith hostage beside him.

25

Talia fought the urge to shrink back from Lucifer as he stood at the Gates of Hell, talking to Jack like he was chatting with a neighbor. Which frightened her even more.

Lucifer's sunlit golden curls were bright against the lava's gleam, his piercing blue eyes sparkling with mirth, but Talia felt the rage simmering beneath his fake calm as his satin-black wings unfolded to their full wingspan and twitched against his shoulders. He wore a red suit with a red tie and black shirt, black dress shoes reflecting like a mirror.

"What did I do to them?" Jack repeated, pointing at the gate guardians as they romped together down the pathway, chasing those two red balls. "I fed them. And played with them. You never give them attention, dude. They probably try to bite you when you pass by. Oh, wait— So, how's the playpen treating you, Luci? Wish I'd thought to bring you a new squeaky toy."

Lucifer's eyes narrowed.

Berith looked terrified, unable to move in his grasp. Her wings were pinned against her back, her grey eyes filled with fear and trepidation.

By the Maker, she wanted to muzzle Jack. All that bravado was building to a fever pitch inside Lucifer. And she had no idea what he wanted with Jack. She feared that Lucifer would use transference like he'd used Vassago's rare power. And try to take control of Jack. Maybe Jack was right about it transferring will?

Talia grabbed hold of Jack's arm and pulled him back from the Gates.

"You monster!" Azrael shouted through gritted teeth and lunged at Lucifer who deftly stepped out of his reach, pulling Berith away from Azrael.

Lucifer laughed. "Such bad manners, Azrael. You'll have to wait your turn."

Muriel and Abaddon grabbed hold of Azrael, holding him back from Lucifer.

"Azrael!" Berith shouted, looking distraught, waving him away from the gate. "Get Jack out of here! Now!"

Lucifer was quiet for a moment. Then he snapped his fingers and behind him, Archangel Samael appeared with his hard grey eyes and long, windblown white hair. Carrying the Book of Secrets. And then Procel the Fallen appeared beside Samael, a tall, scarecrowish fallen angel with scraggly wheaten hair and dull blue eyes. Samael still had his soot-grey wings and Talia wanted to tear them off his back. But his halo had gone dark. Procel had no wings or halo. Lost during the fall from Heaven.

Kesien bared his teeth and launched himself at the Gates, trying to grab hold of Samael, that traitorous archangel, but Deemah and Anahera kept him back.

Lucifer's gaze flicked to Kesien then Abaddon and finally, it returned to Azrael. And Jack.

"Well," he said, chuckling, that energetic tone returning to his British accent. "Isn't this a traitor's reunion? Hello, Abaddon. Kesien, Deemah, say hello to your former boss. And meet Berith, a loyal follower who gleefully stabbed me in the back." His gaze settled on Jack. "And Jack Casey. Who made a deal and reneged on it to stab me in the back. After he lied to me, double-crossed me, and locked me in the Garden. Welcome home, traitors."

Talia felt the fear churn cold through her. She wrapped her hands around Jack's arm and held on for all she was worth. She wouldn't let him get another inch closer to Lucifer.

"Lucifer," said Abaddon in a dry tone.

"I'm going to destroy you, Samael!" Kesien shouted, white fire blazing in his eyes.

Samael looked unaffected, a jeering smile curving onto his face. Talia wanted to rip out his wing feathers, one at a time.

"We'll get back to you later, Kesien, but right now, we have matters to discuss." Lucifer's voice turned dark as he thrust Berith against the Gates' bars. "Now then, let's discuss, Jack, how you think you're going to rescue Berith through this gate. I'd snap her neck before you ever got inside." He shook his head. "How foolish and arrogant you are, Jack, to think yourself an equal to celestial beings that can crush you. Humans make me vomit." He nodded at the space in front of him. At the Gates. "Face me. Now."

Jack laughed and shook his head. "Forget it. I'm not willingly walking into any of your traps, Luci."

"Jack, run!" Berith begged, tears running down her face. "Now!"

"Procel, handle this," said Lucifer, rolling his eyes, boredom in his tone.

Procel's dull blue eyes closed to slits and he bowed his head.

Jack gasped as something grabbed hold of him and pulled him forward. One step closer to the Gates.

Tears ran in rivulets down Berith's face. "Oh, Jack, I told you not to come here. I begged you not to try and rescue me."

"Jack, your block!" Talia cried, holding onto him, trying to pull him back.

"Procel!" Lucifer snapped.

The fallen angel winced, groaning, his face scrunching as sweat beaded across his forehead.

Jack's body went board stiff, his expression intense, hands clenching into fists. Like he was fighting something. But suddenly, his face blanked of all emotion.

Procel held up his hand. He reached out, like he was grabbing hold of something, and yanked it toward him.

Dragging Jack out of Talia's hold and face-first into the Gates. Facing Berith on the other side.

"Sorry, Jack," said Lucifer, about six inches from Jack's face. "Please forgive Procel. He's still learning his craft."

"Let him go!" Talia demanded. "Let him go now."

"Such drama!" Lucifer cried, grinning. "It's the little things that make life worth living, isn't it?"

Lucifer snapped his fingers again. "Samael."

The disgraced Archangel of Death moved to Berith's right side, standing between her and Jack. Samael still had the Book of Secrets clutched in his arms.

The Book of Secrets shuddered a moment and then spewed a hail of Enochian symbols into the air. Glowing red, they hung above the Book for a moment and then exploded in a shower of sparks. Cascading down on top of Berith and then Jack.

"What's happening?" Talia cried.

A wash of blue light engulfed Jack. Followed by a harsh blood-red swath of light. When it faded, a yellow glow enveloped him, followed by a heavy flood of green light that began to turn frosty white across his face and arms.

"By the Maker!"

Talia watched, powerless, as the five elements of Creation surged over Jack.

The resurrect power! But Jack hadn't cast it. Had Procel cast it on Jack? Talia shook her head in confusion. But Procel didn't have access to the elements of Creation. He couldn't have awakened it. Samael didn't have it either. He couldn't awaken rare angel powers. And neither could Lucifer. Berith was pinned in Lucifer's grasp, so she didn't cast it. And wouldn't either.

That left only Talia and she knew that she hadn't cast it. So, who cast it? And how?

In moments, a terrible cracking sound emanated through the caverns.

Followed by Lucifer's giddy laughter.

Then the horrible revelation hit Talia like a bolt of Holy fire. Lucifer's tether! Casting resurrect had broken Lucifer's soul tether!

But the Gates of Hell were shut. He couldn't open them.

In the distance, a trumpet blew and everyone but Lucifer froze at the horrific sound.

A trumpet!

Wide-eyed, Talia jerked her head toward the sound. No, it couldn't be. A trumpet only sounded from Heaven when the first seal was broken. Had the Maker broken it?

Lucifer flung Berith into Procel and lunged at the Gates. Grabbing Jack by the throat as a second trumpet sounded, the sound chilling. Terrifying.

Another dire warning. Another seal!

Talia grabbed hold of Lucifer's arm, pounding it with her shield, but couldn't break his powerful grasp.

Choking the life out of Jack.

Jack couldn't even fight, weakened by transference and someone triggering the resurrect power on him. He gasped and wheezed, flailing, clawing at Lucifer's hand, but Lucifer's grip tightened.

The cavern began to tremble at the sound of the third and then the fourth trumpet!

"What's happening?" Muriel shouted.

Azrael's face was bone-white as he stared at Abaddon in horror.

"No!" Azrael shouted. "It's not possible. It's not possible! The seals!"

When the fifth trumpet sounded, the sixth echoed its mournful herald through Hell's caverns.

The ground began to quake, caverns tilting, Gates of Hell shaking.

Lucifer shoved Jack backward and he collapsed as a thunderous crash tore through the cavern.

"That's the sixth trumpet!" Azrael's voice had an edge of panic that terrified Talia.

Lucifer laughed and pointed toward the pillar below, on the path leading up to the Gates of Hell. He pointed at it with his thumb and forefinger, like a gun.

The cavern shook again, the massive pillar swaying.

Squinting, Lucifer pretended to sight his target and then pulled the trigger with the flick of his thumb.

The pillar shattered, exploding into a million little pieces that scattered like razor blades. Shards rained down on top of them.

"Shields to the sun!" Talia ordered, throwing her shield above her head and covering Jack with her body and shield.

Grinning, Lucifer pointed upward as the dust settled. As if on cue, the seventh trumpet sounded, heralding the last damning note across Hell, the Heavens, and the Earth.

"And seven!" Lucifer cried, holding out his arms and taking a deep bow. "Don't you just love a good jazz solo? With trumpets!" He laughed maniacally. "Not as much as I do."

"The seventh trumpet," Azrael lamented. "No…Abaddon—the Gates!"

Like the shriek of a thousand rusty hinges and the wail of a million damned souls, the Gates of Hell began to open.

Kesien, Muriel, and Abaddon tried to hold them closed, but the massive gates slammed open.

"No," Azrael said with a gasp. "The seals—by the Maker! All the seals have been broken. How? How!"

Lucifer blinked through the Gates and paused a moment, leaning against the opening to glare back at Azrael. Samael blinked past Lucifer and leaped into the air, wings outstretched. Book of Secrets in his arms. Procel ran through the Gates and down the pathway, disappearing into the tangle of hellhounds and angels below.

"I discovered that I needed three things to break your pathetic soul tether," Lucifer began, still looking bored. "I needed the Book of Secrets, Gadreel the Fallen's story which I got in Purgatory of all places, and Procel to awaken transference."

Azrael looked as confused as Talia felt. She kept her hand against Jack's neck, flooding him with healing light as she felt for a pulse while Lucifer was distracted. It was faint, but it was there.

She moved slowly, deliberately, trying her best not to draw his attention. Attention that would cost Jack his life.

"But the seals," Azrael cried, shaking his head. "Only the Maker can break the first seal."

"Wrong again, Azrael!" Lucifer's angry voice echoed through the ruined cavern. "How do you keep your job when you know nothing about anything? With my powers back, I have all of them. Yes, Azrael, that includes destroying the Book of Creation. The first seal."

"But you were tethered down here," Azrael fired back. "How could you—"

"Transference, old man! Keep up. I've been forcing my will on that injured cherub, Oseira." He let out a peal of laughter that reverberated through the cavern in layers. "Through Samael's rituals that erased angels of death and captured their Holy fire, I amassed enough Holy fire in Heaven to explode High House. So, I used Oseira to carry it into the Cloud Chamber."

"The Cloud Chamber," Kesien said with a gasp.

"Yes, that's right, Kesien," Lucifer said in a gloating tone. "The Cloud Chamber. Or former Cloud Chamber would be a better word choice. No matter." He motioned toward the ceiling. "Then I just transferred my will into Oseira, sent her to the Cloud Chamber, and... boom. No more Book of Creation." He made an explosion gesture with his hands. "No more High House, for that matter. I used the rest of the Holy fire cache on the other seals. And because of transference, it was just like being there myself."

"But the tether! You don't have resurrect!" Azrael shouted.

When Azrael saw Berith stirring behind the Gates, he rushed over and helped her to her feet. She looked dazed. Distraught.

Lucifer shook his head. "I did not, but Berith did. So, all I needed to complete my escape was Jack Casey. And the Book of Secrets. As a human, he's part of the Creation, so all of those elements remained within him after I forced you to cast resurrect on him. Yes, Azrael, Jack's tether was a misdirect. Both of them. Keep up. Then all I had to do was to get him and Berith together with the Book of Secrets and... no more tether!"

Jack shuddered and gasped, snapping up from the ground. He pulled in gulping breaths, his gaze wild as it flicked around the cavern. Talia held onto him with both hands, trying to ease his panic.

Lucifer stretched his great black wings and rose a foot off the ground. "All right, everyone, Happy Apocalypse!" he announced, filling Talia with a terror she'd never expected to feel. "But, before I go, a few things."

He turned toward Jack.

"Jack, now that the trumpets have heralded the end of your pathetic little world, take heart. Because I'll be back to kill you last. For now, I want you to see everything end up close and personal. Oh, so personal. And know that all of it was your fault."

"You vicious, cruel monster," Jack said with a snarl.

"Cruelty is relative, Jack," he said in a deadly serious tone. "Well, I'm off to do a little sightseeing. And by sightseeing, I mean destruction."

Azrael punched the wall, furious. "He used us to initiate the apocalypse!"

"Yes, Azrael," Lucifer said with a laugh. "Now that the trumpets have sounded, seven of my Hell princes—well, make that six. I'll need to promote someone to that seventh open position. Best start the interviews now. Anyway, they will become the seven travelers that will usher in plagues and death and pain upon the Earth. It will be like binge-watching the first season of A Game of Thrones all over again. I can't wait."

Lucifer lifted into the air, wings fluttering, but turned back to Azrael. "Oh, Azrael, after I've killed Jack Casey, I'm coming for Heaven. And the Maker. Ta-Ta. Must dash. Places to destroy and humans to murder."

Lucifer spun around and blinked across the cavern, shooting through the passageway and disappearing in a puff of smoke.

Jack coughed and stared at Talia in shock as Abaddon struggled to close the Gates of Hell with his great key.

"Azrael," said Abaddon. "I'll stay at Hell's Gates and close them.

Return to Heaven and find out if Lucifer was lying about the Cloud Chamber."

"All those angels," Berith said with a gasp, tears threading down her face. "And the seraphim. Azrael, the seraphim!"

Azrael held her close, his arms tightening around her like he'd never let her go again. He looked shell-shocked, but Jack looked sick. Devastated.

"Talia…" His voice was tight and broken. "This is all my fault. There are billions of people on Earth. And I've just unleashed Lucifer and seven of his Hell princes on my home." His face was ghostly pale as he stared past her at the open gates to Hell. "He'll kill millions."

She shook him and made him look at her, not through her. "Jack, listen to me. We'll find a way to stop this massacre. All of it."

His eyes were watery and he bit his lip, to hold it all inside. "We have to stop him. And the Apocalypse."

Together, maybe they had the power. After all, the Maker hadn't begun this war of light and dark. Lucifer did. Again—like the Rebellion.

Talia huddled beside Jack, holding him close. Regardless of how it began, she felt the weight of this daunting task.

Halt the Apocalypse…it sounded impossible, but somehow, they had to try.

The End of **THE CELESTIAL COUPLES SHOW:** *A Game of Lost Souls, Book Ten*

The story continues in…

THE ENOCHIAN APOCALYPSE SHOW: *A Game of Lost Souls, Book 11*

Read Chapter 1 Now!

AWARD-WINNING BESTSELLING AUTHOR
LISA SILVERTHORNE
THE ENOCHIAN APOCALYPSE SHOW
A GAME OF 11 LOST SOULS

NOVELS BY LISA SILVERTHORNE

Standalones:

ISABEL'S TEARS

LANDFALL

PACIFIC BLUE TATTOO

A Game of Lost Souls series:

THE CINDERELLA HOUR

THE PRINCE CHARMING HOUR

THE EVER AFTER HOUR

THE FALLEN HEARTS SEASON

THE RISING SPIRITS SEASON

THE ETERNAL SOULS SEASON

THE ROYAL WEDDING HOUR

THE HEAVENLY HONEYMOON HOUR

THE DIVINE NEWLYWEDS SHOW

THE CELESTIAL COUPLES SHOW

THE ENOCHIAN APOCALYPSE SHOW

Curse and Crown series:

THORN & BLADE

The Spiral series:

BETWEEN

REPRISE

AVENGE

The Resurrectionist Papers

GRAVE RECKONING

Short Story Collections

THE SOUND OF ANGELS

THE MAGIC OF ORDINARY THINGS

TIMELESS

Science Fiction Writing as L.S. Silverthorne

Standalones:

REDISCOVERY

Experiencing True Purple series:

RECOMBINANT, Book 1

HELIX, Book 2

SPLICE, Book 3

FORTHCOMING!

A Game of Lost Souls series:

The Angelic Anniversary Hour, Book Twelve

The Perdition Picture Show, Book Thirteen

Curse and Crown series:

Storm & Steel, Book Two

Dagger & Flame, Book Three

The Spiral series:

Ruin, Book 4

Descent, Book 5

The Resurrectionist Papers:

Corpses Delicti

Stiffed Again

Cease and Deceased

SCIENCE FICTION WRITING AS L.S. SILVERTHORNE

Experiencing True Purple series:

Cipher, Book 4

Renascence, Book 5

SNEAK PEEK: THE ENOCHIAN APOCALYPSE SHOW

CHAPTER 1

1

The tallest spire in Heaven was gone. Destroyed when Lucifer's Holy Firebomb blew up in the Cloud Chamber. Disintegrating most of the spire and decimating the smaller spires around it. Damaging the Archive's nearby shorter tower, the last remaining spire in the center of lower Heaven.

Talia stared in horror as she circled the smoky air where High House had once stood. Where the Archive teetered in the air currents, blackened, and covered in ash. The last remaining spire aloft.

All of the others had crumbled.

Tears turned to crystal and slid down her cheeks. Where were all those angels? She shuddered as the realization began to burn through her numbness.

Where were the seraphim? The cherubim? All the Watchers!

She held in a sob. And Poor Oseira. Who'd been injured, weakened by Lucifer's earlier assault on Heaven. Only to become prey for Procel's transference attack that had come from Hell.

Smoke drifted like spirits across Heaven's lower spires, skies dark and acrid with the smell of ozone, charred grass and stone still smoldering as Talia flew low over Eolowen, the grand hall undamaged by Holy Fire. And she was grateful for that bit of good news which was in short supply right now.

The eerie silence made her uneasy. Made the feathers ruffle across her wings. A cold chill quivered through her chest.

No songs carried along the breeze. No soft serene melodies lilted across Parrish blue skies that had turned a dirty grey now. Not a single note hung in the air to comfort them in this dark hour.

Azrael and three archangels flew beside her, the returning assault force still behind them, shocked silent at the devastation that Lucifer had wrought through Oseira using transference.

Before Lucifer escaped Hell and set the apocalypse into motion.

Like Talia's guard, the other archangels of death and their squads were ready to rescue any survivors and gather anything left of value within High House. And prepare to save what little they could of the Creation—now that Lucifer was free.

It was Earth's darkest hour.

Talia still felt terrible for poor Oseira. She hadn't asked for what happened to her. Had she known that she'd been carrying stores of Holy Fire into the Cloud Chamber? Ever since Samael's escape?

Oseira had been the closest angel to the blast. There would be no resurrecting her from the spire. So many other angels inside High House and the Cloud Chamber had met that same fate.

Tension and sorrow hung thick throughout the Heavens, the tinny resonance of the seven trumpets still sharp on the wind as Heaven prepared to send the first flight of angels.

To pour the first bowl of pain onto the Earth: Sickness.

And the billions of humans below had no idea what would soon befall them. And she felt powerless to stop it.

Especially with Lucifer's Hell princes about to walk the Earth and deliver seven payloads, one after each flight of angels touched the Earth.

Seven Travelers. About to unleash seven deadly anguishes on the Creation while Light and Dark battled for ultimate control of what remained. The Maker had not started this war with the Dark yet, but now, all of Heaven and Hell would be forced to fight it, with Lucifer leading the Dark in an assault that would dwarf his previous march on the Heavens.

Why hadn't the Maker intervened? Stopped Lucifer from unleashing the end of the world? Harming all of His Chosen in such a sudden and painful manner?

This time, Lucifer had a huge army, the entirety of dark forces at his command. And he had all his powers back. Heaven now knew that meant everything. Including those powers once given to the Maker's most powerful angel. Were they the powers of the Light Bringer? About to be used in Earth's darkest moment? Leading the darkest forces of vengeance and retribution—reserved only for the Maker?

With Heaven's forces scattered, destroyed, and in disarray, they had to regroup quickly while all of Heaven prepared for the seven flights. Talia's guard had to prepare for the sixth flight: the Enochian apocalypse. Where more angels would be lost than had fallen during the Rebellion. And somehow, with everything stacked against them, the angels had to defeat this overwhelming Dark and save the Creation at the same time.

It was an impossible task.

Where was the Maker? Why hadn't He contacted the lower reaches of Heaven? Sent them orders? Directed them?

Her anger spiked. Why did the lower Heavens have to flail in the stark cold of His silence when the end of the world was at hand?

For Heaven and the Creation? She didn't know anymore.

As she gaped at the destruction blanketing Heaven, she realized that all the upper-ranking angels had been aloft in High House. She winced. In the Cloud Chamber. Heaven's upper reaches must be in as much turmoil as they were down here. And probably protecting the soul portal and the Maker's Thrones.

Those were Lucifer's ultimate targets.

She bit her lip. Maybe the silence meant there was no one left to answer the calls for help?

And that terrified her.

Nevertheless, she sent up an urgent prayer, to send help and leadership downward. To help them fight through Armageddon when they hadn't even been trained to handle it yet.

Leaving the entirety of Heaven's death angel guard alone to flounder and fight an overwhelming force of evil would topple the lower Heavens.

And bring Lucifer to the edge of the Maker's Thrones.

Jack landed below her at Eolowen with Berith, but the rest of the assault force pressed onward to rescue angels and save what could be salvaged from the spires.

And learn how much of Lucifer's claims had been true.

Jack was distraught over Lucifer using him to escape Hell and start the apocalypse. And he was worried sick about what that meant for his world. Berith promised to watch over him until Talia returned.

But the Heaven that Talia knew had changed forever.

Tall, black thunderheads hung above once pristine, sparkling white buildings and the memory of tall, delicate spires, much of the grounds and the square coated in ash. Around the spire's rubble, once-white buildings and towers still burned, angels of death and Watchers struggling to smother roiling Holy Flames that required angel light to extinguish. Thick coils of black smoke merged with fleecy alabaster clouds floating above the smoldering crater that had once been the highest spire in Heaven—High House. And turned them grey and foreboding.

Heavy black clouds gathered all across Heaven, thunder and lightning filling the hefty, ominous silence. Accentuating the palpable absence.

Tears trickled from Talia's eyes and turned into crystals that rolled down her cheeks as she and Azrael circled the smoking crater where High House had been.

High House was gone, its spire reduced almost entirely to rubble, the Cloud Chamber a memory. She couldn't process it yet. And there had been no sighting of seraphim in the skies...or most of the cherubim once present in the spires. They were silent. Absent. Along with dozens and dozens of archangels, hundreds of angels, and hundreds of Watchers that had been in High House.

"Azrael," she said with a hiss, gripping his arm as she hovered above the blackened hollow below. "Where are the seraphim?" she asked in a broken voice. "And the cherubim?"

He shook his head, pain sharp in his charcoal grey eyes. "I don't know, Talia," he said in a quiet voice. "I don't feel their presence any longer. The Book of Creation was in the Cloud Chamber. I fear they were all destroyed in the blast."

Unlike Eolowen's terrace where she'd brought back several angels from oblivion, not even a glimmer of light reflected from the ash and destruction below. There was no way to bring these spire angels back, not even with her resurrect power. She felt miserable. Sick. As soon as casualties were healed, she and Berith would search for any traces of angel light, no matter how slight, and attempt to resurrect them.

Azrael sang a clear, aching requiem that floated above the smoke and ash and devastation. Somber tenor notes in a minor key that carried on the air currents across Heaven, delivering the horrible news about how Lucifer had used transference and poor Oseira to destroy the spire. Start the apocalypse.

As his dark Enochian melody drifted across Heaven, she heard the wave of grief met with whispers of retribution that quickly became a determined harmony beneath Azrael's dirge. An unstoppable rhythm that echoed across the Heavens.

Filling the horrible silence.

He also sent up a prayer to the Maker, asking for guidance and wisdom in this bleak time for Heaven and the Creation. And finally, in a commanding melody, he instructed all able angels to regroup at Eolowen, where the entirety of the death angel guard would assemble for further orders. If there were any cherubim or seraphim left.

But the silence that greeted them was painful. Alarming. The intense but comforting presence of the seraphim was strangely absent, the supporting harmonies of the cherubim extinguished. And still, not a sound from the Maker's Thrones.

Or the Maker.

Across from where the spire stood, the blackened Archive spire was badly damaged and teetering. Talia had no idea how it had remained standing so close to High House. The buildings and smaller spires surrounding High House had been obliterated, but somehow, the Archive survived.

"Death angels!" Azrael shouted. "We need to shore up the Archive spire before it topples. Get everyone out."

Daidrean and Laialus blinked toward the unsteady, soot-covered white spire, using their angelic powers alongside three squads of death angels. Rebenya took dozens of Watchers and flew inside the damaged spire to search for survivors. And lead them to safety.

Talia gripped Azrael's sleeve, her wings beating hard against the smoke and grit clogging the air currents, making flight difficult as thunder rolled across the Heavens in menacing waves.

"Do you want my squad at the Archive spire, too?"

He shook his head. "No, we may need your rare angel powers for survivors."

"Azrael, where is the Maker?" she cried. "If ever there was a time to address His angels in the lower Heavens, this is it. The apocalypse is in motion, all seven seals broken, and we know the Maker didn't set it into motion. High House is gone and the Archive is badly damaged—"

She gasped, thrusting her hand over her mouth. The Scribe! Pravuil had gone to High House to escort Oseira back there. Her eyes flooded with tears. Had he been in High House when the Holy Firebomb exploded?

"What's wrong, Talia?" Azrael asked as he took hold of her hands.

"The Scribe," she said in a thin, broken voice. "Azrael, he escorted Oseira back to High House when we left to rescue Berith."

The archangel's face turned pale and he let go of her hands, lifting another painful song across the lower Heavens. Begging Pravuil to check in with Eolowen. Or him.

Azrael called for the archangels and they blinked through the ranks to float in front of him. Sidriel looked shaken, her grey eyes glassy, long white hair blowing in the wind as she glanced at Turiel with his lion's mane of white hair, and then Ramiel who looked terrified, his gold eyes filling with tears, spiky white hair disheveled.

The archangels looked at a loss, confused as they looked to Azrael for guidance. They handled human deaths, not this.

Soon they'd have their hands full with the apocalypse. But this? Assuming command of the lower Heavens against the entirety of the Dark? Without the guidance of the seraphim and cherubim? They were lost.

But Azrael had stepped up—like he always did.

"There were so many Watchers in the spire, Azrael," Ramiel lamented, his voice filling with despair. "So many!"

The Heavens looked dim and foreboding, so much of its light extinguished by Lucifer's Holy Firebomb.

"What do we do now?" Turiel cried, glancing at the halted column of death angels fanning out across the dark skies. "With no seraphim and precious few cherubim, who will lead the coming war?"

Azrael held up his hands. "Everyone, regain your composure. I called for all survivors to regroup at Eolowen. As soon as we've assessed how many archangels, cherubim, and seraphim remain, we'll figure out our next course of action."

"Azrael," said Sidriel, her voice steadier, charcoal grey eyes bright against her ebony skin. "What happens with the flights of angels that must answer those trumpets? When each flight visits the Earth, one of the Seven Travelers will begin their terrible journey. And there aren't enough of us to stop them."

Talia's gaze returned to Azrael. The archangel of death looked focused, his charcoal gaze steely, silver black hair fluttering against the tops of his soot-grey wings. They were all looking to him for leadership and he was answering that call. None of them knew how to handle the breaking of the seals and the trumpet blasts, much less calling together the seven flights of angels. Or how they would engage Lucifer's forces in the skies above the Earth. But she knew that it would take Lucifer time to gather his Dark army.

The most immediate threats were the Seven Plagues and the Seven Travelers. Abaddon couldn't stop the Hell princes from leaving Hell, if he even knew who they were, and he couldn't keep those gates closed now that all seven seals had been broken. At least not to the Seven Travelers.

The only way to close those gates was to stop the Seven Travelers from delivering seven payloads to Earth and defeat Lucifer and his army. Unless the Maker intervened. They needed to talk to the Scribe—but she feared him lost now, along with so many other angels.

To save the Creation, they had to stop the Seven Travelers. To save Heaven, they had to defeat Lucifer's Dark army before the seventh flight of angels poured out its final bowl of destruction on Earth. The seventh flight was death for humanity.

The sixth flight was the Enochian apocalypse for angels. And it was the last point that they could save Jack and humanity.

Jack. Her heart fluttered against her chest. He may be the last source of seraphim power left in Heaven. Without seraphim, Heaven couldn't hope to defeat Lucifer's Dark army.

She looked upward, past the thunderheads and the smoke. Toward the upper Heavens, her heart heavy. Why hadn't the Maker responded? Sent His Throne angels through the portal to help His angels down here? Or at least give them some guidance.

Those questions haunted her.

Were all of them surrounding the portal as the last protection for the risen souls? Leaving everything below that portal as a sacrifice to save them? That thought terrified her.

"Thank you for your leadership, Azrael," said Sidriel as she turned toward the death angel forces surrounding them.

Azrael sang out an intense baritone melody.

"Everyone, search for survivors. Bring them to Eolowen where we have healers. We'll regroup there and assess what's left of our forces. Figure out how to stop the Seven Travelers and defeat Lucifer's Dark army."

Over four hundred angels of death and their accompanying Watchers dispersed over the smoking devastation to search for survivors.

"Sir," said Talia, "It's a good thing we took three guards of death angels and a massive complement of Watchers to assault the Gates of Hell."

Azrael frowned, glancing at her and then the other archangels. "Why do you say that, Talia?"

"Who knows how many we would have lost here—when Lucifer's Holy Firebomb ignited."

"That's a good point, Talia," said Sidriel with a nod toward the hundreds of angels of death that had descended through the smoke and ash toward the ruined spire and surrounding rubble that used to be buildings. "Thankfully, we still have an army left to answer Lucifer's forces now."

Azrael shook his head. "It's not enough, Sidriel. Lucifer has thousands and thousands of demons. Legions. Not to mention all the damned souls in Hell and the fallen angels at his side. A third of Heaven's angels fell with Lucifer and are still loyal to him."

"Regardless, it's a start," said Sidriel. "And it's better than what we might have had if we hadn't helped you rescue Berith."

A brief smile touched Azrael's dark expression.

"It is a start," said Azrael, charcoal grey eyes narrowing. "But we have to build a much bigger army to defeat Lucifer. "If he unleashes hordes of greater demons, we have to have cherubim to defeat them. And without seraphim support...I fear the outcome of this battle."

Talia patted his sleeve. "We still have Jack and his seraphim powers, sir."

A grin lit the archangel's face.

"Jack!" he cried. "His seraphim powers may be all that stands between us and Lucifer, Talia. I want a squad guarding him at all times. We can't lose those seraphim powers."

"Or Jack," Talia added.

Jack Casey meant everything to her. Besides, his seraphim powers were fragile. They had to protect him if they wanted access to those powers. He didn't have an unlimited reserve of Holy Fire like the seraphim, but he did carry their powers. She had seen him lay waste to half of Lucifer's previous army, take down Devourers, and match Lucifer blow for blow.

A pained expression pinched Azrael's face.

"Yes, of course, Talia," he said. "Forgive me. Jack isn't a weapon to use and discard. He's a human being and one of the Maker's cherished souls. But those seraphim powers of his might stop Lucifer in his tracks."

"He's a devastated human being right now, sir," she said with a sigh and motioned toward Eolowen. "He's blaming himself for starting the apocalypse and for letting Lucifer trick him into releasing that monster from Hell."

Azrael looked sad now.

"There is no way that Jack could have known. None of us knew. Now that Lucifer is free, Jack is in grave danger. I don't want either of you going anywhere without a squad at your back. Is that clear, Talia?"

She nodded. For Jack, she wouldn't argue that protection.

"And thank you for bringing Berith home to me," he said in a soft voice, his charcoal grey eyes turning glassy. "You and Jack gave her back to me and I'll always be grateful for that."

"You fought for Jack and me, sir," she said in a quiet tone. "Over and over. It was our turn to fight for you."

He blushed and cleared his throat as he returned his attention to the archangels.

"Sidriel, I want to know where Samael and his remaining guard are," the archangel ordered. "Ramiel, put your Watchers on Samael's trail and sing out if you locate them. I want to know if he's fighting beside Lucifer or sitting out of the fight." He turned toward Turiel. "Turiel, I want that Book of Secrets located. And all of you, be on the lookout for Pravuil, the Maker's Scribe. Everyone else, help locate survivors. Dismissed."

Sidriel and her guard blinked toward the ruins of the spire alongside Turiel and his guard. Ramiel and his Watchers moved toward the Archive.

"All right, Talia, send the guard down to the spire ruins and we'll start searching for any angel light still shining. Only after survivors have been found can we turn this into a resurrect search."

She nodded, the thought of that work grim. It meant looking for any splash or smear of light and then trying to resurrect the angel attached to it. But she'd examine every single stone remnant if it meant the chance of resurrecting a lost angel. If Jack had been lost out there, she'd turn over every stone and scour every bit of ash to bring him back.

"All right, guard," Talia sang out in crystalline soprano notes. "We're charged with searching the spire." She winced at the massive piles of once shiny white stones, shattered, blackened, and smoking across the crater below. "Look for survivors and remnants of light. Turn over every stone when it is removed. And don't forget the lower levels."

"Talia, have you seen how high the debris stands?" Muriel asked. "It may have filled up every part of those lower levels.

"If we have to dig out every single stone of that rubble, we'll clear it all. We have to know if anyone escaped into the lowest hollows of the spire." Talia pointed and blinked. "Break into your squads, tight formations, and let's move! Before the first flight of angels takes off for Earth."

Muriel, Anahera, Kesien, and Deemah gathered around her, wings nearly touching. Talia sang out a command to blink and together, they shot downward onto the blackened ground and crumbled white stones.

"How could any angel survive a blast of Holy Fire this massive?" Muriel lamented, brushing sable hair off her shoulder as she engulfed the stones in Holy light.

Talia summoned transference and lifted the first layer of stone out of the pit. She placed it on the ground beside the crater. Revealing more hard-packed stone and rubble. She winced. And handfuls of burnt wing feathers. They littered the stones.

Using resurrect, Talia searched the wing feathers and layers of stone for any flickers of light. Finding two.

Focusing on the light, Talia cast resurrect, cycling through blue light, red, yellow, green, and then frosty white until she brought back a Watcher. The young coppery-haired angel was overcome with emotion. She gripped Talia's hands, tears running down her face, and chirped a quick thanks before taking to the air to find the other Watchers.

"Azrael, I've brought back a survivor," Talia announced.

Ramiel blinked toward the terrified young Watcher and wrapped her in his wings, leading her away from the devastation.

"Thank you, Talia," said Ramiel.

Talia nodded and returned her concentration to the debris and the faint impression of light.

The other wisp of light was much more difficult. She fought shadows and uneven glimmers of light until a burst of gold light shot up from the crater and a cherubim stepped out of it. He was as tall as Kesien and had short, spiky white hair, gold hawk-like eyes, and a commanding presence. But his wings shuddered and he collapsed.

"Easy, cherub, you need healing," said Talia, lifting him out of the crater onto ash-covered grass.

"Thank you," he muttered. "I'm Cabriawn. My squad and I were just leaving the spire," he said in a tired voice as he rubbed his forehead, his halo beginning to pulse with gold light. "I was on flank, headed toward the main portal in the center of the spire when everything exploded and collapsed around me." His brow furrowed, gold eyes filling with sadness. "My squad. The spire...and all those angels." His eyes turned watery and his wings began to shake. "The seraphim..."

Talia sang a calming, healing melody and Cabriawn settled back into the grass, folding his wings protectively around his shoulders as he stared at the rubble and ruined buildings where the square used to be. His white robes were ashen and torn in several places, his white armor dented and covered in ash.

"We are still searching the debris for survivors," said Talia, motioning toward the crater. "I wish I had news about the seraphim, but it doesn't look hopeful."

"What happened in there?"

Cabriawn was a cherub. He might be one of the highest-ranking angels left in Heaven's lower reaches. He needed to know what happened.

"Lucifer used a rare angel power on a cherub."

Cabriawn's eyes widened and he sat up straight, staring at her, wings shifting nervously around his shoulders.

"What? Lucifer? On a cherub?"

Talia nodded. "Yes. He forced his will on the cherub and made her carry a massive cache of Holy Fire into the Cloud Chamber. Then he used the rare angel power of transference through a fallen angel to make her set it off."

Cabriawn gaped at her, his face shadowing with fear. "No...is—this true? He controlled a cherub? From Hell?"

"Unfortunately, yes, it's true." She bowed her head. "When Lucifer was ready, he sent Oseira into the Cloud Chamber to ignite the cache. It destroyed the spire almost completely."

"But why?" Cabriawn demanded. "Why?"

Talia pulled in a heavy breath. "To destroy the Book of Creation—and the first seal. Cabriawn, he set off the apocalypse."

For several moments, the cherub couldn't speak, couldn't react. He stared at her, unblinking, trying to process everything she'd told him, but it was all so overwhelming.

"But only the Maker can break the first seal!" His face was pinched, a mixture of dread and grief spreading across his long, angular face.

She had to tell him how it was possible, to make him understand the dire situation Heaven was facing right now.

"A while back, Lucifer engineered a Phoenix Shift and got his powers back. Everything, Cabriawn. Including his power as the Maker's most powerful angel. His left hand. The angel that the Maker had trusted to break the first seal in the event that He could not."

Cabriawn looked panicked now, his gaze flicking around him at the ruins and the devastation.

"This is the worst news you could have given me," said the cherub, glancing up at the dark sky as thunderheads rumbled across the Heavens. "We've even lost the quiet peace of blue skies and white clouds."

"There's more," she said and he stiffened. "The seven trumpets have blown and the Gates of Hell have opened. Lucifer is now free with all his powers and we're facing his overwhelming Dark army when the sixth flight of angels descends on the skies above Earth."

He looked ill now. "The Enochian apocalypse," he mumbled. "Much more than a third of Heaven's angels are foretold to fall in this battle of light and dark. Much more than during the Rebellion."

She nodded. What else could she tell him?

"And the Seven Travelers will soon set out from the Gates of Hell for Earth, each with a deadly payload to unleash on the Creation after each flight of angels. If they aren't stopped, they will destroy everything the Maker created. And Lucifer's Dark army will destroy the lower Heavens after Lucifer eliminated the seraphim and most of the cherubim here."

"What?" Cabriawn shouted. "All the seraphim? Are you certain?"

"We're combing the rubble for them or enough light to use resurrect on them," Talia explained above the shifting of heavy blackened stones and debris as angels of death lifted them out of the crater. "We're down to angels of death, Watchers, and a handful of archangels. As far as I know, you're the only cherub we've found so far —unless your squad is still on patrol."

Cabriawn hurriedly closed his eyes. "Let me search for their brands."

He was silent for several moments until a smile lit his face. "My squad—they're still out there! Patrolling the Gates of Heaven! They're safe."

There were five angels to a squad, so Heaven had five cherubim including Cabriawn left. That would make a big difference.

"What a relief!" Talia cried and relaxed her wings against her back. "They'll be needed in the fight with Lucifer, Cabriawn. Everyone's been instructed to regroup at Eolowen, so we'll know how many angels are left and we'll try to form an army without seraphim. A cherubim patrol will be invaluable."

He nodded and reached out to grip her hand a moment.

"Thank you, Talia," he said with a brief smile. "I'll join up with my squad and we will fly to Eolowen and start organizing a defensive force from the survivors."

"Be safe, Cabriawn," she said as he struggled to his feet and spread his wings.

"You, too," he replied and took to the air, soaring toward the Corridor of Pervasive Light.

When he disappeared behind a tall thunderhead, dark skies swallowing up his sparkling white wings, Talia blinked back into the crater and began poring over more stones and rubble for smears of light.

It seemed like forever before the guard had removed enough debris to locate the lowest chambers of the spire. Or more hard-packed rubble. In that lowest chamber, Archangel Raziel had used some dark power to chain the seraphim and cherubim down there with a Devourer of Angels. Where Jack had blocked Azrael and her squad with a ward, preventing them from entering the cavernous area while he fought the Devourer. Azrael and the squad had been furious at him, but Jack managed to defeat the Devourer and save the cherubim and seraphim in the process.

There was a slim chance that some angels had fallen from the spire and landed below, in the lower level blocked by enormous piles of debris. Only through transference could she clear all of this stone. If angels had to carry it out of here, it could take weeks. With transference, it might take hours.

Azrael was at her shoulder as Muriel and Kesien hovered above a small, spiraling hole that dropped deep into darkness.

"You think anyone's really down there?" Muriel asked, glancing up at Azrael.

"Let's find out," said Azrael.

He sang out a call into the opening as Deemah and Kesien removed more debris to widen the hole, but it was still only inches. Seeing darkness beneath those stones—and not more stone—gave her a little hope though.

They waited for a chorus, a song, or even a single note in response. One that would let them know that someone had survived Lucifer's Holy Firebomb.

But all that floated back was silence. Pure. Total.

Until an alto melody floated through the air, startling them. Survivors!

But then she realized that song had come from Eolowen. It was Berith.

Talia frowned as Azrael's expression darkened.

"She's saying that something's wrong with Jack," said Azrael.

Her heart began to race and for a moment she couldn't breathe.

"Is he hurt? Or sick?" Talia demanded, singing back her response.

It seemed like forever until Berith's warm and familiar alto notes hung in the wind again.

"Talia, he's…struggling," Berith intoned, the notes sounding urgent. "Please come back to Eolowen. I don't know how to help him. And Azrael, there are dozens and dozens of distraught angels here looking for leadership. Please come back, too."

Talia didn't know what Berith meant about Jack, but it frightened her. Besides, the redeemed angel of death wouldn't have called them back to Eolowen if the situation hadn't been urgent. Berith didn't panic. She'd spent enough time in Hell to know when something was dire and when the situation was just difficult. Especially with the seraphim in danger and critical rescue efforts underway.

Jack was the love of her life, but his seraphim powers were necessary to rescue angels. His pain made her chest ache.

She had to go back.

Talia turned to Azrael.

"Sir, it's Jack—I need to go to him."

"Of course, Talia," said Azrael. "But I want your squad beside you. Take them and return. I'll have Daidrean oversee the rest of the guard and focus their efforts here at High House. As soon as they're back removing rubble, I'll be right behind you. To direct the surviving angels and check on Jack. We need his help, too."

She nodded and called formation.

In moments, Muriel and Anahera blinked beside her. Kesien and Deemah were at her back in another moment.

"Talia, what's wrong with Jack?" Muriel asked.

She shook her head. "Berith didn't say. Just that I needed to return to Eolowen. With Azrael."

"Hope the kid's okay," said Kesien as he brushed a tangle of black curls out of his eyes. "He went through a lot at Lucifer's hands this time."

Talia was afraid that Lucifer had done something else horrible to Jack down in Hell and they were just now discovering it. Like a soul tether or something worse than marking him for every Hell creature to locate across Heaven and Earth. Maybe he'd been injured in the confrontation with Lucifer and had just told someone? She winced. Or collapsed.

Either way, she had to get back to her husband. Fast.

ABOUT THE AUTHOR

LISA SILVERTHORNE, an award-winning bestselling author, has published 25 novels and 150 short stories and novelettes in many genres. She is the author of *A Game of Lost Souls* series, *Experiencing True Purple* series, *The Spiral*, *The Resurrectionist Papers,* and a new series, *Curse and Crown*. She lives in Las Vegas, Nevada.

Before you go, you are invited to please leave a **review of this book**!

Reviews are a wonderful way to help an author. They are also an exciting opportunity to share your honest thoughts with other readers, so **please post yours,** in as many places as possible!

Thanks for reading! We appreciate your support!

facebook.com/lisa.silverthorne.writer
bookbub.com/profile/lisa-silverthorne
amazon.com/author/lisasilverthorne
tiktok.com/@lisasilverthorne